BEST-LOVED
DOG
STORIES

BEST-LOVED DOG STORIES

Edited by

VANESSA MITCHELL

Color Plates by

DAVID THOMPSON

Reader's Digest

The Reader's Digest Association, Inc.
Pleasantville, N. Y. • Montreal

A Reader's Digest Book
Edited and Designed by
Michael O'Mara Books Limited

The credits and acknowledgments that appear on pages 284–5
are hereby made a part of this copyright page

Copyright © 1998 by Michael O'Mara Books Limited

The color pictures in this volume
are by David Thompson (Beehive Illustration)

Library of Congress Cataloging-in-Publication Data
has been applied for.

ISBN 0-7621-0089-3

Printed in England

CONTENTS

Contents

JOCK:
TOP DOG

James Herriot
(British) 1916–95

I HAD only to sit up in bed to look right across Darrowby to the hills beyond.

I got up and walked to the window. It was going to be a fine morning and the early sun glanced over the weathered reds and greys of the jumbled roofs, some of them sagging under their burden of ancient tiles, and brightened the tufts of green where trees pushed upwards from the gardens among the bristle of chimney pots. And behind everything the calm bulk of the fells.

It was my good fortune that this was the first thing I saw every morning; after Helen, of course, which was better still.

Following our honeymoon we had set up our first home on the top of Skeldale House. Siegfried, my boss up to my wedding and now my partner, had offered us free use of these empty rooms on the third storey and we had gratefully accepted; and though it was a makeshift arrangement there was an airy charm, an exhilaration in our high perch that many would have envied.

Helen soon had the kettle boiling and we drank our first cup of tea by the window looking down on the long garden. From up here we had an aerial view of the unkempt lawns, the fruit trees, the wisteria climbing the weathered brick towards our window, and the high walls with their old stone copings stretching away to the cobbled yard under the elms. Every day I went up and down that path to the garage in the yard but it looked so different from above.

After breakfast I went downstairs, collected my gear, including suture material for a foal which had cut its leg, and went out the side door into the garden. Just about opposite the rockery I turned and looked up at our window. It was open at the bottom and an arm emerged holding a dishcloth. I waved and the dishcloth waved back furiously. It was the start to every day.

And, driving from the yard, it seemed a good start. In fact everything was good. The raucous cawing of the rooks in the trees above, the clean fragrance of the air which greeted me every morning, and the challenge and interest of my job.

This was the real Yorkshire with the clean limestone wall riding the hill's edge and the path cutting brilliant green through the crowding heather. And, walking face on to the scented breeze, I felt the old tingle of wonder at being alone on the wide moorland where nothing stirred and the spreading miles of purple blossom and green turf reached away until it met the hazy blue of the sky.

But I wasn't really alone. There was Sam, and he made all the difference. Helen had brought a lot of things into my life and Sam was one of the most precious; he was a beagle and her own personal pet. He would have been about two years old when I first saw him and I had no way of knowing that he was to be my faithful companion, my car dog, my friend who sat by my side through the lonely hours of driving until his life ended at the age of fourteen. He was the first of a series of cherished dogs whose comradeship has warmed and lightened my working life.

Sam adopted me on sight. It was as though he had read the *Faithful Hound Manual* because he was always near me; paws on the dashboard, as he gazed eagerly through the windscreen on my rounds, head resting on my foot in our bed-sitting room, trotting just behind me wherever I moved. If I had a beer in a pub he would be under my chair and even when I was having a haircut you only had to lift the white sheet to see Sam crouching beneath my legs. The only place I didn't dare take him was to the cinema and on these occasions he crawled under the bed and sulked.

Most dogs love car riding but to Sam it was a passion which never waned – even in the night hours; he would gladly leave his basket when the world was asleep, stretch a couple of times and follow me out into the cold. He would be on to the seat before I got the car door fully open and this action became so much a part of my life that for a long time after his death I still held the door open unthinkingly, waiting for him. And I still remember the pain I felt when he did not bound inside.

And having him with me added so much to the intermissions I granted myself on my daily rounds. Whereas in offices and factories they had tea breaks I just stopped the car and stepped out into the splendour which was always at hand and walked for a spell down hidden lanes, through woods, or as today, along one of the grassy tracks which ran over the high tops. I like my fellow men but there are times when it is wonderful to be utterly alone in a wide landscape. Here I can find peace and tranquillity.

This thing which I had always done had a new meaning now. Anybody who has ever walked a dog knows the abiding satisfaction which comes from giving pleasure to a loved animal, and the sight of the little form trotting ahead of me lent a depth which had been missing before.

The dry stone walls climbed up the bare hillsides on the far side of the valley. Those wonderful walls, often the only sign of the hand of man, symbolise the very soul of the high Pennines, the endlessly varying pattern of grey against green, carving out ragged squares and oblongs, pushing long antennae to impossible heights until they disappear into the lapping moorland on the summits.

Round the curve of the path I came to where the tide of heather lapped thickly down the hillside on a little slope facing invitingly into the sun. It was a call I could never resist. I looked at my watch; oh, I had a few minutes to spare before my appointment with Robert Corner. In a moment I was stretched out on the springy stems, the most wonderful natural mattress in the world.

Lying there, eyes half closed against the sun's glare, the heavy heather fragrance around me, I could see the cloud shadows racing across the flanks of the fells, throwing the gulleys and crevices into momentary gloom but trailing a fresh flaring green in their wake.

Those were the days when I was most grateful I was in country practice; the shirtsleeve days when the bleak menace of the bald heights melted into friendliness, when I felt at one with all the airy life and growth about me and was glad that I had become what I never thought I would be, a doctor of farm animals.

A long-eared head blotted out the sunshine as Sam came and sat on my chest. He looked at me questioningly. He didn't hold with this laziness but I knew if I didn't move after a few minutes he would curl up philosophically on my ribs and have a sleep until I was ready to go. But this time I answered the unspoken appeal by sitting up and he leaped around me in delight as I rose and began to make my way back to the car.

The injured foal was at Robert Corner's farm and I hadn't been there long before I spotted Jock, his sheepdog. And I began to watch the dog because behind a vet's daily chore of treating his patients there is always the fascinating kaleidoscope of animal personality and Jock was an interesting case.

A lot of farm dogs are partial to a little light relief from their work. They like to play and one of their favourite games is chasing cars off the premises. Often I drove off with a hairy form galloping alongside and the dog would usually give a final defiant bark after a few hundred yards to speed me on my way. But Jock was different.

He was really dedicated. Car chasing to him was a deadly serious art which he practised daily without a trace of levity. Corner's farm was at the end of a long track, twisting for nearly a mile between its stone walls down through the gently sloping fields to the road below and Jock didn't consider he had done his job properly until he had escorted his chosen vehicle right to the very foot. So his hobby was an exacting one.

I watched him now as I finished stitching the foal's leg and began to tie on a bandage. He was slinking about the buildings, a skinny little creature who, without his mass of black and white hair would have been an almost invisible mite, and he was playing out a transparent charade of pretending he was taking no notice of me – wasn't the least bit interested in my presence, in fact. But his furtive glances in the direction of the stable, his repeated criss-crossing of my line of vision gave him away. He was waiting for his big moment.

When I was putting on my shoes and throwing my wellingtons into the boot I saw him again. Or rather part of him; just a long nose and one eye protruding from beneath a broken door. It wasn't until I had started the engine and begun to move off that he finally declared himself, stealing out from his hiding place, body low, tail trailing, eyes fixed intently on the car's front wheels, and as I gathered speed and headed down the track he broke into an effortless lope.

I had been through this before and was always afraid he might run in front of me so I put my foot down and began to hurtle downhill. This was where Jock came into his own. I often wondered how he'd fare against a racing greyhound because by golly he could run. That sparse frame housed a perfect physical machine and the slender limbs reached and flew again and again, devouring the stony ground beneath, keeping up with the speeding car with joyful ease.

There was a sharp bend about half way down and here Jock invariably sailed over the wall and streaked across the turf, a little dark blur against the green, and having craftily cut off the corner he reappeared like a missile zooming over the grey stones lower down. This put him into a nice position for the run to the road and when he finally saw me on to the tarmac my last view of him was of a happy panting face looking after me. Clearly he considered it was a job well done and he would wander quite contentedly back up to the farm to await the next exciting session, perhaps with the postman or the baker's van.

And there was another side to Jock. He was an outstanding performer at the sheepdog trials and Mr. Corner had won many trophies with him. In fact the farmer could have sold the little animal for a lot of money but couldn't be persuaded to part with him. Instead he purchased a bitch, a scrawny little female counterpart of Jock and a trial winner in her own right. With this combination Mr. Corner thought he could breed some world-beating types for sale. On my visits to the farm the bitch joined in the car-chasing but it seemed as though she was doing it more or less to humour her new mate and she always gave up at the first bend leaving Jock in command. You could see her heart wasn't in it.

Then the pups arrived, seven fluffy black-and-white balls tumbling about the yard and getting under everybody's feet. Jock watched indulgently as they tried to follow him in his pursuit of my vehicle and you could almost see him laughing as they fell over their feet and were left trailing far behind.

It happened that I didn't have to go there for about ten months but I saw Robert Corner in the market occasionally and he told me he was training the pups and they were shaping well. Not that they needed much training; it was in their blood and he said they had tried to round up the cattle and sheep nearly as soon as they could walk. When I finally saw them they were like seven Jocks – meagre, darting little creatures flitting noiselessly about the buildings – and it didn't take me long to find out that they had learned more than sheep herding from their father. There was something very evocative about the way they began to prowl around in the background as I prepared to get into my car, peeping furtively from behind straw bales, slinking with elaborate nonchalance into favourable positions for a quick getaway. And as I settled in my seat I could sense they were all crouched in readiness for the off.

I revved my engine, let in the clutch with a bump and shot across the yard and in a second the immediate vicinity erupted in a mass of hairy forms. I roared on to the track and put my foot down and on either side of me the little animals pelted along shoulder to shoulder, their faces all wearing the intent fanatical expression I knew so well. When Jock cleared the wall the seven pups went with him and when they reappeared and entered the home straight I noticed something different. On past occasions Jock had always had one eye on the car – this was what he considered his opponent; but now on that last quarter mile as he hurtled along at the head of a shaggy phalanx he was glancing at the pups on either side as though they were the main opposition.

And there was no doubt he was in trouble. Superbly fit though he was, these stringy bundles of bone and sinew which he had fathered had all his speed plus the newly minted energy of youth and it was taking every shred of his power to keep up with them. Indeed there was one terrible moment when he stumbled and was engulfed by the bounding creatures around him; it seemed that all was lost but there was a core of steel in Jock. Eyes popping, nostrils dilated, he fought his way through the pack until by the time we reached the road he was once more in the lead.

But it had taken its toll. I slowed down before driving away and looked down at the little animal standing with lolling tongue and heaving flanks on the grass verge. It must have been like this with all the other vehicles and it wasn't a merry game any more. I suppose it sounds silly to say you could read a dog's thoughts but everything in his posture betrayed the mounting apprehension that his days of supremacy were numbered. Just round the corner lay the unthinkable ignominy of being left trailing in the rear of that litter of young upstarts and as I drew away Jock looked after me and his expression was eloquent.

'How long can I keep this up?'

I felt for the little dog and on my next visit to the farm about two months later I wasn't looking forward to witnessing the final degradation which I felt was inevitable. But when I drove into the yard I found the place strangely unpopulated.

Robert Corner was forking hay into the cows' racks in the byre. He turned as I came in.

'Where are all your dogs?' I asked.

He put down his fork. 'All gone. By gaw, there's a market for good workin' sheepdogs. I've done right well out of t'job.'

'But you've still got Jock?'

'Oh aye, ah couldn't part with t'awd lad. He's over there.'

And so he was, creeping around as of old, pretending he wasn't watching me. And when the happy time finally arrived and I drove away it was like it used to be with the lean little animal haring along by the side of the car, but relaxed, enjoying the game, winging effortlessly over the wall and beating the car down to the tarmac with no trouble at all.

I think I was as relieved as he was that he was left alone with his supremacy unchallenged; that he was still top dog.

REX

D. H. Lawrence
(British) 1885–1930

SINCE every family has its black sheep, it almost follows that every man must have a sooty uncle. Lucky if he hasn't two. However, it is only with my mother's brother that we are concerned. She had loved him dearly when he was a little blond boy. When he grew up black, she was always vowing she would never speak to him again. Yet when he put in an appearance, after years of absence, she invariably received him in a festive mood, and was even flirty with him.

He rolled up one day in a dogcart, when I was a small boy. He was large and bullet-headed and blustering, and this time, sporty. Sometimes he was rather literary, sometimes colored with business. But this time he was in checks, and was sporty. We viewed him from a distance.

The upshot was, would we rear a pup for him. Now, my mother detested animals about the house. She could not bear the mix-up of human with animal life. Yet she consented to bring up the pup.

My uncle had taken a large, vulgar public house in a large and vulgar town. It came to pass that I must fetch the pup. Strange for me, a member of the Band of Hope, to enter the big, noisy, smelly plate-glass-and-mahogany public house. It was called The Good Omen. Strange to have my uncle towering over me in the passage, shouting, 'Hello, Johnny, what d'yer want?' He didn't know me. Strange to think he was my mother's brother, and that he had his bouts when he read Browning aloud with emotion and éclat.

Rex

I was given tea in a narrow, uncomfortable sort of living-room, half kitchen. Curious that such a palatial pub should show such miserable private accommodations, but so it was. There was I, unhappy, and glad to escape with the soft fat pup. It was wintertime, and I wore a big-flapped black overcoat, half cloak. Under the cloak sleeves I hid the puppy, who trembled. It was Saturday, and the train was crowded, and he whimpered under my coat. I sat in mortal fear of being hauled out for traveling without a dog ticket. However, we arrived, and my torments were for nothing.

The others were wildly excited over the puppy. He was small and fat and white, with a brown-and-black head: a fox terrier. My father said he had a lemon head – some such mysterious technical phraseology. It wasn't lemon at all, but colored like a field bee. And he had a black spot at the root of his spine.

It was Saturday night – bath night. He crawled on the hearthrug like a fat white teacup, and licked the bare toes that had just been bathed.

'He ought to be called Spot,' said one. But that was too ordinary. It was a great question, what to call him.

'Call him Rex – the King,' said my mother, looking down on the fat, animated little teacup, who was chewing my sister's little toe and making her squeal with joy and tickles. We took the name in all seriousness.

'Rex – the King!' We thought it was just right. Not for years did I realize that it was a sarcasm on my mother's part. She must have wasted some twenty years or more of irony on our incurable naïveté.

It wasn't a successful name, really. Because my father, and all the people in the street, failed completely to pronounce the monosyllable Rex. They all said Rax. And it always distressed me. It always suggested to me seaweed, and rack-and-ruin. Poor Rex!

We loved him dearly. The first night we woke to hear him weeping and whinnying in loneliness at the foot of the stairs. When it could be borne no more, I slipped down for him, and he slept under the sheets.

'I won't have that little beast in the beds. Beds are not for dogs,' declared my mother callously.

'He's as good as we are!' we cried, injured.

'Whether he is or not, he's not going in the beds.'

I think now my mother scorned us for our lack of pride. We were a little infra dig, we children.

The second night, however, Rex wept the same and in the same way was comforted. The third night we heard our father plod downstairs, heard several slaps administered to the yelping, dismayed puppy, and heard the amiable, but to us heartless, voice saying, 'Shut it then! Shut thy noise, 'st hear? Stop in thy basket, stop there!'

'It's a shame!' we shouted in muffled rebellion, from the sheets.

'I'll give you shame if you don't hold your noise and go to sleep,' called our mother from her room. Whereupon we shed angry tears and went to sleep. But there was a tension.

'Such a houseful of idiots would make me detest the little beast, even if he was better than he is,' said my mother.

But as a matter of fact, she did not detest Rexie at all. She only had to pretend to do so, to balance our adoration. And in truth, she did not care for close contact with animals. She was too fastidious. My father, however, would take on a real dog's voice, talking to the puppy: a funny, high, singsong falsetto which he seemed to produce at the top of his head. ''S a pretty little dog! 'S a pretty little doggy! Ay! Yes! He is, yes! Wag thy strunt, then! Wag thy strunt, Raxie! Ha-ha! Nay, tha munna –' This last as the puppy, wild with excitement at the strange falsetto voice, licked my father's nostrils and bit my father's nose with his sharp little teeth.

''E makes blood come,' said my father.

'Serves you right for being so silly with him,' said my mother. It was odd to see her as she watched the man, my father, crouching and talking to the little dog and laughing strangely when the little creature bit his nose and tousled his beard. What does a woman think of her husband at such a moment?

My mother amused herself over the names we called:

'He's an angel – he's a little butterfly – Rexie, my sweet!'

'Sweet! A dirty little object!' interpolated my mother. She and he had a feud from the first. Of course he chewed boots and worried our stockings and swallowed our garters. The moment we took off our stockings he would dart away with one, we after him. Then as he hung, growling vociferously, at one end of the stocking, we at the other, we would cry:

'Look at him, Mother! He'll make holes in it again.' Whereupon my mother darted at him and spanked him sharply.

'Let go, sir, you destructive little fiend.'

But he didn't let go. He began to growl with real rage, and hung on viciously. Mite as he was, he defied her with a manly fury. He did not hate her, nor she him. But they had one long battle with one another.

'I'll teach you, my jockey! Do you think I'm going to spend my life darning after your destructive little teeth! I'll show you if I will!'

But Rexie only growled more viciously. They both became really angry, whilst we children expostulated earnestly with both. He would not let her take the stocking from him.

'You should tell him properly, Mother. He won't be driven,' we said.

'I'll drive him further than he bargains for. I'll drive him out of my sight for ever, that I will,' declared my mother, truly angry. He would put her into a real temper, with his tiny, growling defiance.

'He's sweet! A Rexie, a little Rexie!'

'A filthy little nuisance! Don't think I'll put up with him.'

And to tell the truth, he was dirty at first. How could he be otherwise, so young! But my mother hated him for it. And perhaps this was the real start of their hostility. For he lived in the house with us. He would wrinkle his nose and show his tiny dagger teeth in fury when he was thwarted, and his growls of real battle-rage against my mother rejoiced us as much as they angered her. But at last she caught him in flagrante. She pounced on him, rubbed his nose in the mess, and flung him out into the yard. He yelped with shame and disgust and indignation. I shall never forget the sight of him as he rolled over, then tried to turn his head away from the disgust of his own muzzle, shaking his little snout with a sort of horror, and trying to sneeze it off. My sister gave a yell of despair, and dashed out with a rag and a pan of water, weeping wildly. She sat in the middle of the yard with the befouled puppy, and shedding bitter tears, she wiped him and washed him clean. Loudly she reproached my mother. 'Look how much bigger you are than he is. It's a shame, it's a shame!'

'You ridiculous little lunatic, you've undone all the good it would do him, with your soft ways. Why is my life made a curse with animals! Haven't I enough as it is –'

There was a subdued tension afterward. Rex was a little white chasm between us and our parent.

He became clean. But then another tragedy loomed. He must be docked. His floating puppy tail must be docked short. This time my father was the enemy. My mother agreed with us that it was an unnecessary cruelty. But my father was adamant. 'The dog'll look a fool all his life, if he's not docked.' And there was no getting away from it. To add to the horror, poor Rex's tail must be *bitten* off. Why bitten? we asked, aghast. We were assured that biting was the only way. A man would take the little tail and just nip it through with his teeth, at a certain joint. My father lifted his lips and bared his incisors, to suit the description. We shuddered. But we were in the hands of fate.

Rex was carried away, and a man called Rowbotham bit off the superfluity of his tail in the Nags Head, for a quart of best and bitter. We lamented our poor diminished puppy, but agreed to find him more manly and *comme il faut*. We should always have been ashamed of his little whip of a tail if it had not been shortened. My father said it had made a man of him.

Perhaps it had. For now his true nature came out. And his true nature, like so much else, was dual. First he was a fierce, canine little beast, a beast of rapine and blood. He longed to hunt, savage-ly. He lusted to set his teeth in his prey. It was no joke with him. The old canine Adam stood first in him, the dog with fangs and glaring eyes. He flew at us when we annoyed him. He flew at all intruders, particularly the postman. He was almost a peril to the neighborhood. But not quite. Because close second in his nature stood that fatal need to love, the *besoin d'aimer* which at last makes an end of liberty. He had a terrible, terrible necessity to love, and this trammeled the native, savage hunting beast which he was. He was torn between two great impulses: the native impulse to hunt and kill, and the strange, secondary, supervening impulse to love and obey. If he had been left to my father and mother, he would have run wild and got himself shot. As it was, he loved us children with a fierce, joyous love. And we loved him.

When we came home from school we would see him standing at the end of the entry, cocking his head wistfully at the open country in front of him, and meditating whether to be off or not: a white, inquiring little figure, with green savage freedom in front of him. A cry from a far distance from one of us, and like a bullet he hurled himself down the road, in a mad game. Seeing him coming, my sister invariably turned and fled, shrieking with delighted terror. And he would leap straight up her back, and bite her and tear her clothes. But it was only an ecstasy of savage love, and she knew it. She didn't care if he tore her pinafores. But my mother did.

My mother was maddened by him. He was a little demon. At the least provocation, he flew. You had only to sweep the floor, and he bristled and sprang at the broom. Nor would he let go. With his scruff erect and his nostrils snorting rage, he would turn up the whites of his eyes at my mother as she wrestled at the other end of the broom. 'Leave go, sir, leave go!' She wrestled and stamped her foot, and he answered with horrid growls. In the end it was she who had to let go. Then she flew at him, and he flew at her. All the time we had him he was within a hairsbreadth of savagely biting her. And she knew it. Yet he always kept sufficient self-control.

We children loved his temper. We would drag the bones from his mouth, and put him into such paroxysms of rage that he would twist his head right over and lay it on the ground upside down, because he didn't know what to do with himself, the savage was so strong in him and he must fly at us. 'He'll fly at your throat one of these days,' said my father. Neither he nor my mother dared have touched Rex's bone. It was enough to see him bristle and roll the whites of his eyes when they came near. How near he must have been to driving his teeth right into us cannot be told. He was a horrid sight snarling and crouching at us. But we only laughed and rebuked him. And he would whimper in the sheer torment of his need to attack us.

He never did hurt us. He never hurt anybody, though the neighborhood was terrified of him. But he took to hunting. To my mother's disgust, he would bring large dead bleeding rats and lay them on the hearthrug, and she had to take them up on a shovel. For he would not remove them. Occasionally he brought a mangled rabbit, and sometimes, alas, fragmentary poultry. We were in terror of prosecution. Once he came home bloody and feathery and rather sheepish-looking. We cleaned him and questioned him and abused him. Next day we heard of six dead ducks. Thank heaven no one had seen him.

But he was disobedient. If he saw a hen he was off, and calling would not bring him back. He was worst of all with my father, who would take him for walks on Sunday morning. My mother would not walk a yard with him. Once, walking with my father, he rushed off at some sheep in a field. My father yelled in vain. The dog was at the sheep, and meant business. My father crawled through the hedge, and was upon him in time. And now the man was in a paroxysm of rage. He dragged the little beast into the road and thrashed him with a walking stick.

'Do you know you're thrashing that dog unmercifully?' said a passerby.

'Ay, an' mean to,' shouted my father.

The curious thing was that Rex did not respect my father any the more for the beatings he had from him. He took much more heed of us children, always.

But he let us down also. One fatal Saturday he disappeared. We hunted and called, but no Rex. We were bathed, and it was bedtime, but we would not go to bed. Instead we sat in a row in our nightdresses on the sofa, and wept without stopping. This drove our mother mad.

'Am I going to put up with it? Am I? And all for that hateful little beast of a dog! He shall go! If he's not gone now, he shall go.'

Our father came in late, looking rather queer, with his hat over his eye. But in his staccato tippled fashion he tried to be consoling.

'Never mind, my duckie, I s'll look for him in the morning.'

Sunday came – oh, such a Sunday. We cried, and didn't eat. We scoured the land, and for the first time realized how empty and wide the earth is when you're looking for something. My father walked for many miles – all in vain. Sunday dinner, with rhubarb pudding, I remember, and an atmosphere of abject misery that was unbearable.

'Never,' said my mother, 'never shall an animal set foot in this house again, while I live. I knew what it would be! I knew.'

The day wore on, and it was the black gloom of bedtime, when we heard a scratch and an impudent little whine at the door. In trotted Rex, mud-black, disreputable, and impudent. His air of off-hand 'How d'ye do!' was indescribable. He trotted round with *suffisance*, wagging his tail as if to say, 'Yes, I've come back. But I didn't need to. I can carry on remarkably well by myself.' Then he walked to his water, and drank noisily and ostentatiously. It was rather a slap in the eye for us.

He disappeared once or twice in this fashion. We never knew where he went. And we began to feel that his heart was not so golden as we had imagined.

But one fatal day reappeared my uncle and the dogcart. He whistled to Rex, and Rex trotted up. But when he wanted to examine the lusty, sturdy dog, Rex became suddenly still, then sprang free. Quite jauntily he trotted round – but out of reach of my uncle. He leaped up, licking our faces, and trying to make us play.

'Why, what ha' you done wi' the dog – you've made a fool of him. He's softer than grease. You've ruined him. You've made a damned fool of him,' shouted my uncle.

Rex was captured and hauled off to the dogcart and tied to the seat. He was in a frenzy. He yelped and shrieked and struggled, and was hit on the head, hard, with the butt end of my uncle's whip, which only made him struggle more frantically. So we saw him driven away, our beloved Rex, frantically, madly fighting to get to us from the high dogcart, and being knocked down, whilst we stood in the street in mute despair.

After which, black tears, and a little wound which is still alive in our hearts.

I saw Rex only once again, when I had to call just once at The Good Omen. He must have heard my voice, for he was upon me in the passage before I knew where I was. And in the instant I knew how he loved us. He really loved us. And in the same instant there was my uncle with a whip, beating and kicking him back, and Rex cowering, bristling, snarling.

My uncle swore many oaths, how we had ruined the dog forever, made him vicious, spoiled him for showing purposes, and been altogether a pack of mard-soft fools not fit to be trusted with any dog but a gutter mongrel.

Poor Rex! We heard his temper was incurably vicious, and he had to be shot.

And it was our fault. We had loved him too much, and he had loved us too much. We never had another pet.

It is a strange thing, love. Nothing but love has made the dog lose his wild freedom, to become the servant of man. And this very servility or completeness of love makes him a term of deepest contempt – 'You dog!'

We should not have loved Rex so much, and he should not have loved us. There should have been a measure. We tended, all of us, to overstep the limits of our own natures. He should have stayed outside human limits, we should have stayed outside canine limits. Nothing is more fatal than the disaster of too much love. My uncle was right, we had ruined the dog.

My uncle was a fool, for all that.

GARM –
A HOSTAGE

Rudyard Kipling
(British) 1865–1936

ONE night, a very long time ago, I drove to an Indian military encampment called Mian Mir to see amateur theatricals. At the back of the Infantry barracks a soldier, his cap over one eye, rushed in front of the horses and shouted that he was a dangerous highway robber. As a matter of fact, he was a friend of mine, so I told him to go home before anyone caught him; but he fell under the pole, and I heard voices of a military guard in search of someone.

The driver and I coaxed him into the carriage, drove home swiftly, undressed him and put him to bed, where he waked next morning with a sore headache, very much ashamed. When his uniform was cleaned and dried, and he had been shaved and washed and made neat, I drove him back to barracks with his arm in a fine white sling, and reported that I had accidentally run over him. I did not tell this story to my friend's sergeant, who was a hostile and unbelieving person, but to his lieutenant, who did not know us quite so well.

Three days later my friend came to call, and at his heels slobbered and fawned one of the finest bull-terriers – of the old-fashioned breed, two parts bull and one terrier – that I had ever set eyes on. He was pure white, with a fawn-coloured saddle just behind his neck, and a fawn diamond at the root of his thin whippy tail. I had admired him distantly for more than a year; and Vixen, my own fox-terrier, knew him too, but did not approve.

'E's for you,' said my friend; but he did not look as though he liked parting with him.

'Nonsense! That dog's worth more than most men, Stanley,' I said.
"'E's that and more. 'Tention!'"

The dog rose on his hind legs, and stood upright for a full minute.
'Eyes right!'

He sat on his haunches and turned his head sharp to the right.
At a sign he rose and barked twice. Then he shook hands with his
right paw and bounded lightly to my shoulder. Here he made himself into a necktie, limp and lifeless, hanging down on either side of my
neck. I was told to pick him up and throw him in the air. He fell
with a howl and held up one leg.

'Part o' the trick,' said his owner. 'You're going to die now. Dig
yourself your little grave an' shut your little eye.'

Still limping, the dog hobbled to the garden edge, dug a hole and lay
down in it. When told that he was cured, he jumped out, wagging
his tail, and whining for applause. He was put through half a dozen
other tricks, such as showing how he would hold a man safe (I was
that man, and he sat down before me, his teeth bared, ready to
spring), and how he would stop eating at the word of command. I
had no more than finished praising him when my friend made a
gesture that stopped the dog as though he had been shot, took a
piece of blue-ruled canteen-paper from his helmet, handed it to me
and ran away, while the dog looked after him and howled. I read:

*Sir – I give you the dog because of what you got me out of. He is the best I
know, for I made him myself, and he is as good as a man. Please do not
give him too much to eat, and please do not give him back to me, for I'm
not going to take him, if you will keep him. So please do not try to give
him back any more. I have kept his name back, so you can call him anything and he will answer, but please do not give him back. He can kill a
man as easy as anything, but please do not give him too much meat. He
knows more than a man.*

Vixen sympathetically joined her shrill little yap to the bull-
terrier's despairing cry, and I was annoyed, for I knew that a man
who cares for dogs is one thing, but a man who loves one dog is
quite another. Dogs are at the best no more than verminous
vagrants, self-scratchers, foul feeders, and unclean by the law of

Moses and Mohammed; but a dog with whom one lives alone for at least six months in the year; a free thing, tied to you so strictly by love that without you he will not stir or exercise; a patient, temperate, humorous, wise soul, who knows your moods before you know them yourself, is not a dog under any ruling.

I had Vixen, who was all my dog to me; and I felt what my friend must have felt, at tearing out his heart in this style and leaving it in my garden.

However, the dog understood clearly enough that I was his master, and did not follow the soldier. As soon as he drew breath I made much of him, and Vixen, yelling with jealousy, flew at him. Had she been of his own sex, he might have cheered himself with a fight but he only looked worriedly when she nipped his deep iron sides, laid his heavy head on my knee, and howled anew. I meant to dine at the Club that night, but as darkness drew in, and the dog snuffed through the empty house like a child trying to recover from a fit of sobbing, I felt that I could not leave him to suffer his first evening alone. So we fed at home, Vixen on one side, and the stranger-dog on the other; she watching his every mouthful, and saying explicitly what she thought of his table manners, which were much better than hers.

It was Vixen's custom, till the weather grew hot, to sleep in my bed, her head on the pillow like a Christian; and when morning came I would always find that the little thing had braced her feet against the wall and pushed me to the very edge of the cot. This night she hurried to bed purposefully, every hair up, one eye on the stranger, who had dropped on a mat in a helpless, hopeless sort of way, all four feet spread out, sighing heavily. She settled her head on the pillow several times, to show her little airs and graces, and struck up her usual whiney sing-song before slumber. The stranger-dog softly edged towards me. I put out my hand and he licked it. Instantly my wrist was between Vixen's teeth, and her warning *aaarh!* said as plainly as speech, that if I took any further notice of the stranger she would bite.

I caught her behind her fat neck with my left hand, shook her severely, and said:

'Vixen, if you do that again you'll be put into the veranda. Now, remember!'

She understood perfectly, but the minute I released her she mouthed my right wrist once more, and waited with her ears back and all her body flattened, ready to bite. The big dog's tail thumped the floor in a humble and peace-making way.

I grabbed Vixen a second time, lifted her out of bed like a rabbit (she hated that and yelled), and, as I had promised, set her out in the veranda with the bats and the moonlight. At this she howled. Then she used coarse language – not to me, but to the bull-terrier – till she coughed with exhaustion. Then she ran around the house try-ing every door. Then she went off to the stables and barked as though someone were stealing the horses, which was an old trick of hers. Last she returned, and her snuffing yelp said, 'I'll be good! Let me in and I'll be good!'

She was admitted and flew to her pillow. When she was quieted I whispered to the other dog, 'You can lie on the foot of the bed.' The bull jumped up at once, and though I felt Vixen quiver with rage, she knew better than to protest. So we slept till the morning, and they had early breakfast with me, bite for bite, till the horse came round and we went for a ride. I don't think the bull had ever followed a horse before. He was wild with excitement, and Vixen, as usual, squealed and scuttered and scooted, and took charge of the procession.

There was one corner of a village near by, which we generally passed with caution, because all the yellow pariah-dogs of the place gathered about it. They were half-wild, starving beasts, and though utter cowards, yet where nine or ten of them get together they will mob and kill and eat an English dog. I kept a whip with a long lash for them. That morning they attacked Vixen, who, perhaps of design, had moved from beyond my horse's shadow.

The bull was ploughing along in the dust, fifty yards behind, rolling in his run, and smiling as bull-terriers will. I heard Vixen squeal; half a dozen of the curs closed in on her; a white streak came up behind me; a cloud of dust rose near Vixen, and, when it cleared, I saw one tall pariah with his back broken, and the bull wrenching another to earth. Vixen retreated to the protection of my whip, and the bull padded back smiling more than ever, covered with the blood of his enemies. That decided me to call him 'Garm of the Bloody Breast', who was a great person in his time, or 'Garm' for short; so, leaning forward, I told him what his temporary name would be. He looked up while I repeated it, and then raced away. I shouted 'Garm!' He stopped, raced back, and came up to ask my will.

Then I saw that my soldier friend was right, and that that dog knew and was worth more than a man. At the end of the ride I gave an order which Vixen knew and hated. 'Go away and get washed!' I said. Garm understood some part of it, and Vixen interpreted the rest, and the two trotted off together soberly. When I went to the back veranda Vixen had been washed snowy-white, and was very proud of herself, but the dog-boy would not touch Garm on any account unless I stood by. So I waited while he was being scrubbed, and Garm, with the soap creaming on the top of his broad head, looked at me to make sure that this was what I expected him to endure. He knew perfectly that the dog-boy was only obeying orders.

'Another time,' I said to the dog-boy, 'you will wash the great dog with Vixen when I send them home.'

'Does *he* know?' said the dog-boy, who understood the ways of dogs.

'Garm,' I said, 'another time you will be washed with Vixen.'

I knew that Garm understood. Indeed, next washing-day, when Vixen as usual fled under my bed, Garm stared at the doubtful dog-boy in the veranda, stalked to the place where he had been washed last time, and stood rigid in the tub.

But the long days in my office tried him sorely. We three would drive off in the morning at half-past eight and come home at six or later. Vixen, knowing the routine of it, went to sleep under my table; but the confinement ate into Garm's soul. He generally sat on the veranda looking out on the Mall; and well I knew what he expected.

Sometimes a company of soldiers would move along on their way to the Fort, and Garm rolled forth to inspect them; or an officer in uniform entered into the office, and it was pitiful to see poor Garm's welcome to the cloth – not the man. He would leap at him, and sniff and bark joyously, then run to the door and back again. One afternoon I heard him bay with a full throat – a thing I had never heard before – and he disappeared. When I drove into my garden at the end of the day a soldier in white uniform scrambled over the wall at the far end, and the Garm that met me was a joyous dog. This happened twice or thrice a week for a month.

I pretended not to notice, but Garm knew and Vixen knew. He would glide homewards from the office about four o'clock, as though he were only going to look at the scenery, and this he did so quietly that but for Vixen I should not have noticed him. The jealous little dog under the table would give a sniff and a snort, just loud enough to call my attention to the flight. Garm might go out forty times in the day and Vixen would never stir, but when he slunk off to see his true master in my garden she told me in her own tongue. That was the one sign she made to prove that Garm did not altogether belong to the family. They were the best of friends at all times, *but*, Vixen explained that I was never to forget Garm did not love me as she loved me.

I never expected it. The dog was not my dog – could never be my dog – and I knew he was as miserable as his master who tramped eight miles a day to see him. So it seemed to me that the sooner the two were reunited the better for all. One afternoon I sent Vixen home alone in the dog-cart (Garm had gone before), and rode over to cantonments to find another friend of mine, who was an Irish soldier and a great friend of the dog's master.

I explained the whole case, and wound up with:

'And now Stanley's in my garden crying over his dog. Why doesn't he take him back? They're both unhappy.'

'Unhappy! There's no sense in the little man any more. But 'tis his fit.'

'What *is* his fit? He travels fifty miles a week to see the brute, and he pretends not to notice me when he sees me on the road; and I'm as unhappy as he is. Make him take the dog back.'

'It's his penance he's set himself. I told him by way of a joke, after you'd run over him so convenient that night, when he was drunk – I said if he was a Catholic he'd do penance. Off he went wid that fit in his little head *an'* a dose of fever, an' nothin' would suit but givin' you the dog as a hostage.'

'Hostage for what? I don't want hostages from Stanley.'

'For his good behaviour. He's keepin' straight now, the way it's no pleasure to associate wid him.'

'Has he taken the pledge?'

'If 'twas only that I need not care. Ye can take the pledge for three months on an' off. He sez he'll never see the dog again, an' *so* mark you, he'll keep straight for evermore. Ye know his fits? Well, this is wan of them. How's the dog takin' it?'

'Like a man. He's the best dog in India. Can't you make Stanley take him back?'

'I can do no more than I have done. But ye know his fits. He's just doin' his penance. What will he do when he goes to the Hills? The docthor's put him on the list.'

It is the custom in India to send a certain number of invalids from each regiment up to stations in the Himalayas for the hot weather; and though the men ought to enjoy the cool and the comfort, they miss the society of the barracks down below, and do their best to come back or to avoid going. I felt that this move would bring matters to a head, so I left Terrence hopefully, though he called after me:

'He won't take the dog, sorr. You can lay your month's pay on that. Ye know his fits.'

I never pretended to understand Private Ortheris; and so I did the next best thing – I left him alone.

That summer the invalids of the regiment to which my friend belonged were ordered off to the Hills early, because the doctors thought marching in the cool of the day would do them good. Their route lay south to a place called Umballa, a hundred and twenty miles or more. Then they would turn east and march up into the Hills to Kasauli or Dugshai or Subathoo. I dined with the officers the night before they left – they were marching at five in the morning. It was midnight when I drove into my garden, and surprised a white figure flying over the wall.

'That man,' said my butler, 'has been here since nine, making talk to that dog. He is quite mad. I did not tell him to go away because he has been here many times before, and because the dog-boy told me that if I told him to go away, that great dog would immediately slay me. He did not wish to speak to the Protector of the Poor, and he did not ask for anything to eat or drink.'

'Kadir Buksh,' said I, 'that was well done, for the dog would surely have killed thee. But I do not think the white soldier will come any more.'

Garm slept ill that night and whimpered in his dreams. Once he sprang up with a clear, ringing bark, and I heard him wag his tail till it waked him and the bark died out in a howl. He had dreamed he was with his master again, and I nearly cried. It was all Stanley's silly fault.

The first halt which the detachment of invalids made was some miles from their barracks, on the Amritsar road, and ten miles distant from my house. By a mere chance one of the officers drove back for another good dinner at the Club (cooking on the line of march is always bad), and there we met. He was a particular friend of mine, and I knew that he knew how to love a dog properly. His pet was a big retriever who was going up to the Hills for his health, and, though it was still April, the round, brown brute puffed and panted in the Club veranda as though he would burst.

'It's amazing,' said the officer, 'what excuses these invalids of mine make to get back to barracks. There's a man in my company now asked me for leave to go back to cantonments to pay a debt he'd forgotten. I was so taken by the idea I let him go, and he jingled off in an *ekka* as pleased as Punch. Ten miles to pay a debt! Wonder what it was really,'

'If you'll drive me home I think I can show you,' I said.

So he went over to my house in his dog-cart with the retriever; and on the way I told him the story of Garm.

'I was wondering where that brute had gone to. He's the best dog in the regiment,' said my friend. 'I offered the little fellow twenty rupees for him a month ago. But he's a hostage, you say, for Stanley's good conduct. Stanley's one of the best men I have – when he chooses.'

'That's the reason why,' I said. 'A second-rate man wouldn't have taken things to heart as he has done.'

We drove in quietly at the far end of the garden, and crept round the house. There was a place close to the wall all grown about with tamarisk trees, where I knew Garm kept his bones. Even Vixen was not allowed to sit near it. In the full Indian moonlight I could see a white uniform bending over the dog.

'Good-bye, old man,' we could not help hearing Stanley's voice. 'For 'Eving's sake don't get bit and go mad by any measley pi-dog. But you can look after yourself, old man. *You* don't get drunk an' run about 'ittin' your friends. You takes your bones an' eats your biscuit, an' kills your enemy like a gentleman. I'm goin' away – don't 'owl – I'm goin' off to Kasauli, where I won't see you no more.'

I could hear him holding Garm's nose as the dog drew it up to the stars.

'You'll stay here an' be'ave, an' – an' I'll go away an' try to be'ave, an' I don't know 'ow to leave you. I don't think—'

'I think this is damn silly,' said the officer, patting his foolish, fubsy old retriever. He called to the private who leaped to his feet, marched forward, and saluted.

'You here?' said the officer, turning away his head.

'Yes, sir, but I'm just goin' back.'

'I shall be leaving here at eleven in my cart. You come with me. I can't have sick men running about all over the place. Report yourself at eleven, *here*.'

We did not say much when we went indoors, but the officer muttered and pulled his retriever's ears.

He was a disgraceful, overfed doormat of a dog; and when he waddled off to my cookhouse to be fed, I had a brilliant idea.

At eleven o'clock that officer's dog was nowhere to be found, and you never heard such a fuss as his owner made. He called and shouted and grew angry, and hunted through my garden for half an hour.

Then I said:

'He's sure to turn up in the morning. Send a man in by rail, and I'll find the beast and return him.'

'Beast?' said the officer. 'I value that dog considerably more than I value any man I know. It's all very fine for you to talk – your dog's here.'

So she was – under my feet – and, had she been missing, food and wages would have stopped in my house till her return. But some people grow fond of dogs not worth a cut of the whip. My friend had to drive away at last with Stanley in the back seat; and then the dog-boy said to me:

'What kind of animal is Bullen Sahib's dog? Look at him!'

I went to the boy's hut, and the fat old reprobate was lying on a mat carefully chained up. He must have heard his master calling for twenty minutes, but had not even attempted to join him.

'He has no face,' said the dog-boy scornfully. 'He is a *punniar-kooter* [a spaniel]. He never tried to get that cloth off his jaws when his master called. Now Vixen-baba would have jumped through the window, and that Great Dog would have slain me with his muzzled mouth. It is true that there are many kinds of dogs.'

Next evening who should turn up but Stanley. The officer had sent him back fourteen miles by rail with a note begging me to return the retriever if I had found him, and, if I had not, to offer huge rewards. The last train to camp left at half-past ten, and Stanley stayed till ten talking to Garm. I argued and entreated, and even threatened to shoot the bull-terrier, but the little man was firm as a rock, though I gave him a good dinner and talked to him most severely. Garm knew as well as I that this was the last time he could hope to see his man, and followed Stanley like a shadow. The retriever said nothing, but licked his lips after his meal and waddled off without so much as saying 'Thank you' to the disgusted dog-boy.

So that last meeting was over, and I felt as wretched as Garm, who moaned in his sleep all night. When we went to the office he found a place under the table close to Vixen, and dropped flat till it was time to go home. There was no more running out into the verandas, no slinking away for stolen talks with Stanley. As the weather

'Outside, a white pomeranian with black ears sniffed
disgustedly at a banana skin in the gutter.'
MAKING MONEY OUT OF DOGS

'He was small and fat and white, with a brown-and-black head:
He crawled . . . and licked the bare toes that had just been bathed.'
REX

'Willie crawled out from under the bedclothes,
blinking and looking somewhat rumpled.'
LOST DOG

'They would bump into him when he was stooping over the dish
of milk and porridge, and his head was so big and his legs so weak
that he would tip up and go heels over head into the dish.'
THE PICK OF THE PUPPIES

grew warmer the dogs were forbidden to run beside the cart, but sat at my side on the seat. Vixen with her head under the crook of my left elbow, and Garm hugging the left handrail.

Here Vixen was ever in great form. She had to attend to all the moving traffic, such as bullock-carts that blocked the way, and camels, and led ponies; as well as to keep up her dignity when she passed low friends running in the dust. She never yapped for yapping's sake, but her shrill, high bark was known all along the Mall, and other men's terriers ki-yied in reply, and bullock-drivers looked over their shoulders and gave us the road with a grin.

But Garm cared for none of these things. His big eyes were on the horizon and his terrible mouth was shut. There was another dog in the office who belonged to my chief. We called him 'Bob the Librarian,' because he always imagined vain rats behind the bookshelves, and in hunting for them would drag out half the old newspaper-files. Bob was a well-meaning idiot, but Garm did not encourage him. He would slide his head round the door panting, 'Rats! Come along, Garm!' and Garm would shift one forepaw over the other, and curl himself round, leaving Bob to whine at a most uninterested back. The office was nearly as cheerful as a tomb in those days.

Once, and only once, did I see Garm at all contented with his surroundings. He had gone for an unauthorized walk with Vixen early one Sunday morning, and a very young and foolish artillery-man (his battery had just moved to that part of the world) tried to steal both. Vixen, of course, knew better than to take food from soldiers, and, besides, she had just finished her breakfast. So she trotted back with a large piece of the mutton that they issue to our troops, laid it down on my veranda, and looked up to see what I thought. I asked her where Garm was, and she ran in front of the house to show me the way.

About a mile up the road we came across our artilleryman sitting very stiffly on the edge of a culvert with a greasy handkerchief on his knees. Garm was in front of him, looking rather pleased. When the man moved leg or hand, Garm bared his teeth in silence. A broken string hung from his collar, and the other half of it lay, all warm, in the artilleryman's still hand. He explained to me, keeping his eye straight in front of him, that he had met this dog (he called him awful names) walking alone, and was going to take him to the Fort to be killed for a masterless pariah.

I said that Garm did not seem to me much of a pariah, but that he had better take him to the Fort if he thought best. He said he did not care to do so. I told him to go to the Fort alone. He said he did not want to go at that hour, but would follow my advice as soon as I had called off the dog. I instructed Garm to take him to the Fort, and Garm marched him solemnly up to the gate, one mile and a half under a hot sun, and I told the quarter-guard what had happened; but the young artilleryman was more angry than was at all necessary when they began to laugh. Several regiments, he was told, had tried to steal Garm in their time.

That month the hot weather shut down in earnest, and the dogs slept in the bathroom on the cool wet bricks where the bath is placed. Every morning, as soon as the man filled my bath, the two jumped in, and every morning the man filled the bath a second time. I said to him that he might as well fill a small tub especially for the dogs. 'Nay,' said he smiling, 'it is not their custom. They would not understand. Besides, the big bath gives them more space.'

The punkah-coolies who pull the punkahs day and night came to know Garm intimately. He noticed that when the swaying fan stopped I would call out to the coolie and bid him pull with a long stroke. If the man still slept I would wake him up. He discovered, too, that it was a good thing to lie in the wave of air under the punkah. Maybe Stanley had taught him all about this in barracks. At any rate, when the punkah stopped, Garm would first growl and cock his eye at the rope, and if that did not wake the man – it nearly always did – he would tiptoe forth and talk in the sleeper's ear. Vixen was a clever little dog, but she could never connect the punkah and the coolie; so Garm gave me grateful hours of cool sleep. But he was utterly wretched – as miserable as a human being; and in his misery he clung so close to me that other men noticed it, and were envious. If I moved from one room to another Garm followed; if my pen stopped scratching, Garm's head was thrust into my hand; if I turned, half-awake, on the pillow, Garm was up at my side, for he knew that I was his only link with his master, and day and night, and night and day, his eyes asked one question – 'When is this going to end?'

Living with the dog as I did, I never noticed that he was more than ordinarily upset by the hot weather, till one day at the Club a man said: 'That dog of yours will die in a week or two. He's a shadow.' Then I dosed Garm with iron and quinine, which he hated; and I felt very anxious. He lost his appetite, and Vixen was allowed to eat his dinner under his eyes. Even that did not make him swallow, and we held a consultation on him, of the best man-doctor in the place; a lady-doctor, who had cured the sick wives of kings; and the Deputy Inspector-General of the veterinary service of all India. They pronounced upon his symptoms, and I told them his story, and Garm lay on a sofa licking my hand.

'He's dying of a broken heart,' said the lady-doctor suddenly.

"Pon my word,' said the Deputy Inspector-General, 'I believe Mrs. Macrae is perfectly right – as usual.'

The best man-doctor in the place wrote a prescription, and the veterinary Deputy Inspector-General went over it afterwards to be sure that the drugs were in the proper dog-proportions; and that was the first time in his life that our doctor ever allowed his pre-scriptions to be edited. It was a strong tonic, and it put the dear boy on his feet for a week or two; then he lost flesh again. I asked a man I knew to take him up to the Hills with him when he went, and the man came to the door with his kit packed on the top of the car-riage. Garm took in the situation at one red glance. The hair rose along his back; he sat down in front of me, and delivered the most awful growl I have ever heard in the jaws of a dog. I shouted to my friend to get away at once, and as soon as the carriage was out of the garden Garm laid his head on my knee and whined. So I knew his answer, and devoted myself to getting Stanley's address in the Hills.

My turn to go to the cool came late in August. We were allowed thirty days' holiday in a year, if no one fell sick, and we took it as we could be spared. My chief and Bob the Librarian had their holiday first, and when they were gone I made a calendar, as I always did, and hung it up at the head of my cot, tearing off one day at a time till they returned. Vixen had gone up to the Hills with me five times before; and she appreciated the cold and the damp and the beautiful wood fires there as much as I did.

'Garm,' I said, 'we are going back to Stanley at Kasauli. Kasauli – Stanley; Stanley – Kasauli.' And I repeated it twenty times. It was not Kasauli really, but another place. Still I remembered what Stanley had said in my garden on the last night, and I dared not change the name. Then Garm began to tremble; then he barked; and then he leaped up at me, frisking and wagging his tail.

'Not now,' I said, holding up my hand. 'When I say "Go," we'll go, Garm.' I pulled out the little blanket coat and spiked collar that Vixen always wore up in the Hills to protect her against sudden chills and thieving leopards, and I let the two smell them and talk it over. What they said of course I do not know, but it made a new dog of Garm. His eyes were bright; and he barked joyfully when I spoke to him. He ate his food, and he killed his rats for the next three weeks, and when he began to whine I had only to say 'Stanley – Kasauli; Kasauli – Stanley,' to wake him up. I wish I had thought of it before.

My chief came back, all brown with living in the open air, and very angry at finding it so hot in the Plains. That same afternoon we three and Kadir Buksh began to pack for our month's holiday, Vixen rolling in and out of the bullock-trunk twenty times a minute, and Garm grinning all over and thumping on the floor with his tail. Vixen knew the routine of travelling as well as she knew my office-work. She went to the station, singing songs, on the front seat of the carriage, while Garm sat with me. She hurried into the railway carriage, saw Kadir Buksh make up my bed for the night, got her drink of water, and curled up with her black-patch eye on the tumult of the platform. Garm followed her (the crowd gave him a lane all to himself) and sat down on the pillows with his eyes blazing, and his tail a haze behind him.

We came to Umballa in the hot misty dawn, four or five men, who had been working hard for eleven months, shouting for our dâks – the two-horse travelling carriages that were to take us up to

Kalka at the foot of the Hills. It was all new to Garm. He did not understand carriages where you lay at full length on your bedding, but Vixen knew and hopped into her place at once; Garm following. The Kalka road, before the railway was built, was about forty-seven miles long, and the horses were changed every eight miles. Most of them jibbed, and kicked, and plunged, but they had to go, and they went rather better than usual for Garm's deep bay in their rear.

There was a river to be forded, and four bullocks pulled the carriage, and Vixen stuck her head out of the sliding-door and nearly fell into the water while she gave directions. Garm was silent and curious, and rather needed reassuring about Stanley and Kasauli. So we rolled, barking and yelping, into Kalka for lunch, and Garm ate enough for two.

After Kalka the road wound among the Hills, and we took a curricle with half-broken ponies, which were changed every six miles. No one dreamed of a railroad to Simla in those days, for it was seven thousand feet up in the air. The road was more than fifty miles long, and the regulation pace was just as fast as the ponies could go. Here, again, Vixen led Garm from one carriage to the other; jumped into the back seat and shouted. A cool breath from the snows met us about five miles out of Kalka, and she whined for her coat, wisely fearing a chill on the liver. I had had one made for Garm too, and, as we climbed to the fresh breezes, I put it on, and Garm chewed it uncomprehendingly, but I think he was grateful.

'Hi-yi-yi-yi!' sang Vixen as we shot around the curves; 'Toot-toot-toot!' went the driver's bugle at the dangerous places, and 'Yow! Yow! Yow! Yow!' bayed Garm. Kadir Buksh sat on the front seat and smiled. Even he was glad to get away from the heat of the Plains that stewed in the haze behind us. Now and then we would meet a man we knew going down to his work again, and he would say: 'What's it like below?' and I would shout: 'Hotter than cinders. What's it like above?' and he would shout back: 'Just perfect!' and away we would go.

Suddenly Kadir Buksh said, over his shoulder: 'Here is Solon'; and Garm snored where he lay with his head on my knee. Solon is an unpleasant little cantonment, but it has the advantage of being cool and healthy. It is all bare and windy, and one generally stops at a rest-house near by for something to eat. I got out and took both dogs with me, while Kadir Buksh made tea. A soldier told us we should find Stanley 'out there,' nodding his head towards a bare, bleak hill.

When we climbed to the top we spied that very Stanley, who had given me all this trouble, sitting on a rock with his face in his hands, and his overcoat hanging loose about him. I never saw anything so lonely and dejected in my life as this one little man, crumpled up and thinking, on the great grey hill-side.

Here Garm left me.

He departed without a word, and, so far as I could see, without moving his legs. He flew through the air bodily, and I heard the whack of him as he flung himself at Stanley, knocking the little man clean over. They rolled on the ground together, shouting, and yelping, and hugging. I could not see which was dog and which was man, till Stanley got up and whimpered.

He told me that he had been suffering from fever at intervals, and was very weak. He looked all he said, but even while I watched, both man and dog plumped out to their natural sizes, precisely as dried apples swell in water. Garm was on his shoulder, and his breast and feet all at the same time, so that Stanley spoke all through a cloud of Garm – gulping, sobbing, slavering Garm. He did not say anything that I could understand, except that he had fancied he was going to die, but that now he was quite well, and that he was not going to give up Garm any more to anybody under the rank of Beelzebub.

Then he said he felt hungry, and thirsty, and happy.

We went down to tea at the rest-house, where Stanley stuffed himself with sardines and raspberry jam, and beer, and cold mutton and pickles, when Garm wasn't climbing over him; and then Vixen and I went on.

Garm saw how it was at once. He said good-bye to me three times, giving me both paws one after another, and leaping on to my shoulder. He further escorted us, singing Hosannas at the top of his voice, a mile down the road. Then he raced back to his own master.

Vixen never opened her mouth, but when the cold twilight came, and we could see the lights of Simla across the hills, she snuffled with her nose at the breast of my ulster. I unbuttoned it, and tucked her inside. Then she gave a contented little sniff, and fell fast asleep, her head on my breast, till we bundled out of Simla, two of the four happiest people in all the world that night.

SUKI,
THE REJECT

Diana Pullein-Thompson
(British) 1925–

I T was a cold February day when I stared into a run full of miserable female dogs, all under one year old. These were society's young rejects with not a pedigree among them, animals picked up in the streets or found abandoned in house or shed and brought to a Midland city kennels. Now several had curled into tight, shivering balls of fur on the wet concrete floor. One opened an eye, looked at me as though to say, 'No, you don't want me,' and closed it again. I longed to take them all, but I had come to choose a calm, small one as a companion for our tall, thoroughbred, rough-coated collie, Angus, who was highly strung and hated being left alone.

'Surely these dogs are very ill?' I hazarded.

'It's grief,' replied the kennel maid.

At the back, totally composed, stood Suki, a mixture, I suspect, of King Charles spaniel, working collie and, perhaps, long-haired dachshund. She was mainly black with beautiful reddish tan markings, which included a tan waistcoat, tan hoops above her appealing eyes, a tan muzzle, tan paws and undercarriage and lighter brown fluffier hair above her hocks which we later called her 'plus fours'. She met my eyes with an unwavering stare. And it was love at first sight. I paid four pounds fifty pence for Suki. She had only been in six, not the seven regulatory, days, but the official who gave me a receipt agreed to overlook the discrepancy.

I bought Suki a lead, clipped it on her mean collar which had Tipsy scratched on it, and we stepped out into the street without a backward glance. She walked to the station with utter composure, as though she had expected me to come to rescue her; she happily stepped into the train and halfway home decided to sit on my lap.

She entered our house with equal aplomb, and although mortified when I told her off for peeing on the breakfast-room carpet (from then on she was house-trained) she greeted Angus with controlled enthusiasm. I fed them in separate dishes. Suki gobbled her dinner and then approached Angus who, chivalrous to females but aggressive to his own sex, stepped back so she could gobble up his too. 'No,' I said. 'No, no!' and Suki's intense desire to please ensured she never took her companion's food again.

Two days later Suki came on heat, which meant she must be about six months old. The vet said I should give her more time to settle down, before bringing her in for her routine vaccinations, but within twenty-four hours he saw her anyway, because she developed a runny nose, a distressing cough and a temperature of 105 degrees Fahrenheit. She had caught distemper, a would-be killer, which might leave her with St. Vitus's dance or epilepsy. Was it worth going on? the vet asked. His bills would be far higher than the four pounds fifty I had paid for this bedraggled little stray. Then my thoughts went back to Barney, whom my mother had nursed through distemper, a lovable black spaniel, who suffered occasionally from fits, but lived a long and happy life and enriched my childhood.

Never mind the expense, we would fight to the last to save Suki, I said, and remembered with anguish those shivering balls of fur. Something must be done, I declared, and my vet said he would speak to the kennels' vet. Back home, I telephoned a town councillor who was, I knew, on the kennels' committee and asked her to visit the place and look into the matter. Suki's illness was disgusting and debilitating. The discharge from her nose was so copious I wore an old boiler suit when I handled her. If she tried to walk she fell over, so we carried her in and out of the garden to perform her natural duties. Angus, who liked his own way, was upset at being kept apart. His last year's distemper vaccination protected him from Suki's disease, but we were afraid he might try mating her. Then, as Suki fought for her life, her season ended abruptly and that worry was over.

Suki survived without any of the side-effects the vet had feared and by the time she was on the mend we had bonded closely. Henceforth she would not go out for walks with any other member of the family if I was around. She was a quick and instinctive learner. If I patted my leg and said 'Heel' she obeyed at once, but, wanting to feel owned, she preferred to be on the lead in the street.

She adored Angus; every evening after their main meal the two of them went up to our bedroom to play, wrestling and growling, so ferociously that we called them the Dinosaurs.

In quieter moments Suki groomed Angus, licking the inside of his ears and combing his thick hair with her fine teeth. She copied his manners, never rushing to gobble up her dinner or stealing food at home, however hungry she might be. She learned not to take tit-bits from strangers and to walk like him with an aristocratic air, so that when people asked what her breed was we invented one: 'A tasselled Afghan hunting dog,' we said.

But Angus had a naughty streak, too, which divided Suki's loyalties between him and us. She fetched him one day at our request when he had obstinately gone the wrong way down a track, proudly leading him back by a short piece of rope dangling from his collar. But he must have indicated his annoyance for she would never repeat this useful exercise. The crunch came when we left them alone in the house for three hours one evening and Angus decided to take his revenge with Suki's help. We returned home to find the hall carpet rolled up against the front door. When we eventually got inside the house the dogs slunk away guiltily, tails down, while we looked on the havoc they had wrought: torn tea towels, rugs rolled up; our daughter's slippers brought downstairs and chewed. Later Angus threw us a sideways glance which clearly said 'serves you right', but Suki was so mortified by our anger that her confidence in him was dented and he was never able to enlist her help again.

Perhaps it was Suki's basic composure which made her so different from other dogs, a calmness which allowed her to sum up situations and listen carefully when she was addressed. The number of human words she understood quickly multiplied. And she had a remarkable capacity to make the most of every expedition, loving both the town, where she quickly acquired many canine friends, and the country, where Angus taught her how to handle cattle. Unlike him, she loved swimming and chasing rabbits and looking out of the car window as we drove around. Unlike him, too, she did not unpack shopping in the back of the car in the hope of finding ham, the only food Angus ever stole.

When Angus grew old Suki looked after him even more assiduously, acting as his eyes and ears, but she accepted his gradual muscle wastage, senility and eventual death with equanimity. Soon afterwards we moved to Chiswick, four miles from central London, where she immediately collected a circle of friends on the local Greens.

By now Suki was so civilised I could take her anywhere and she became my constant companion when I travelled across the country researching a book on prime ministers' consorts. She stayed with me in hotels. She visited stately homes and met Lord Home and his much loved Labrador at The Hirsel. She sat by my chair when I lunched in pubs. She accompanied me to Chiswick dress shops and lay contentedly outside changing cubicles while I tried on dresses. Like most dogs she was interested in clothes because they signalled what I was about to do. Dog-walking clothes were always welcomed, but high heels and evening dresses lowered her tail. The in-betweens were, like suitcases, a source for watchfulness and uncertainty, until I told her whether or not she was 'coming'.

One example of how Suki always got the best out of everything was her love for our children's pets, which she would watch for hours, and wash if she had the opportunity. She found guinea pigs so adorable that when she discovered that a neighbour down the road had a pen full of them, she would refuse to pass the gate until she had been allowed in to sit among them. When our son brought back a white-hooded Norwegian rat which he had saved from the ferrets at a nature centre where he worked as a volunteer, Suki could not have been happier. Ratty became a friend and perhaps as far as possible, a surrogate puppy.

Another human occupation Suki adored was house-hunting. Before we moved from the Midlands to London, she accompanied us round countless houses with excited interest. Whenever possible she liked to examine views from the windows. Bathrooms were also especially important to her – she would run back to take a quick recce if she thought we had missed one out. Sometimes we had to control her nosiness to avoid causing offence. Occasionally it was clear she hated a particular house, perhaps sensing some past tragedy or distrusting the owners.

'Suki hated the vibes in that one,' we would say afterwards.

The place we bought had a small, almost bare, paved garden with one border where Suki quickly made herself a small bower. We were afraid she might be depressed by the lack of space, but there was a bonus – a black Pekinese, Tato, who lived next door, a dog of impeccable pedigree and minute appetite. Tato's Greek owner fed him on a menu fit for a king and there were always leftovers, which in time, became Suki's. We met Tato on our morning walks, but I suspect it was the smell of Mediterranean cooking which tempted Suki to slip through the fence and make cautious overtures to his owner, which led to little dishes of leftovers being put before her. And so, although she had moved to London, Suki's life soon became full with weekends in the country and trips to Richmond Park with the canine friends she had made.

And then there was Christmas, that annual event which Suki looked forward to with increasing anticipation as soon as she saw presents being wrapped in fancy paper. The arrival and decoration of the tree increased her happy excitement. On the day she shared the children's Christmas stockings before running downstairs to look for her own bag of goodies.

Lunch with my sister, Josephine, meant more presents for Suki and a dinner party in the evening at our house provided her with guests to welcome, for Angus, who had perfected the art of canine host, had taught her how to greet visitors and, if they were staying, escort them to their rooms.

Josephine was a special friend because she looked after Suki when we went abroad and knew how to lighten her depression when we left. Then, encouraged, Suki would shake herself several times before settling down to enjoy her stay. Three days a week she went with Josephine to the Pen Club and became accustomed to office life. She sat in on committee meetings, elegantly draping herself across a chair, and grew used to different walks, for, above all, she was adaptable.

By now Suki had perfected her stares, those vital expressions dogs use to manipulate human beings. There was the astonished stare, eyes large, ears up, to express amazed disappointment when an expected morsel has not been offered; the reproachful stare, eyes mournful, ears down when a dog is about to be left at home; the hopeful stare (so hard to refuse) when Suki made it clear she expected your generosity. All these stares were guaranteed to make all but the most hard-hearted feel bad if they did not comply with the dog's wishes. And Suki was now following the usual progress of a well-treated domestic dog: four years servant, four years equal, four years tyrant; only she was the most charming tyrant, no barking, no bullying, just persuasive pleading and stares.

As Suki grew older her pleasures changed. She stopped chasing rabbits but adored visiting friends. If there was tea she gently indicated that she should have some in a saucer, and, this lapped-up carefully, she would nudge me until I asked whether she might go upstairs to explore. Then, admission granted, we would hear her hurrying from room to room, stopping to look out of windows; sometimes, halfway down, she would realise she had once again forgotten to examine the bathroom, and then she would go back and look in the bath. At some point, if the weather was fine, she asked to walk in the garden. Finally, after an hour, she would nudge me again, suggesting it was time we left.

Was Suki, I wondered, ever fantasising about another move? She liked our London house, but found it cold, which prompted reproachful stares and the pathetic sight of a small spaniel-like figure sitting very close to an unswitched-on electric fire. If she was, her wish came true, for now that our children were nearly grown-up, we decided to sell our country cottage and buy a larger London house. And to Suki's joy another search began.

We chose a house in the same area with a larger garden. It had very efficient central heating and was carpeted throughout, and

Suki could see a resident squirrel from some of the windows. We left her with Josephine for a couple of days while the move took place, and when Josephine brought her back she knew exactly where we were. For, although she had visited the house only twice and Josephine had to park the car some distance away, Suki dragged her at the gallop to our new address. Had she heard us say this was the house we wanted? By now she certainly understood more of our conversation than we would once have believed possible.

Installed in the new house, Suki missed Tato, but loved the carpets and the heating, and never again asked that an electric fire be switched on. It was a good place in which to grow old, nearer to the Greens where she loved to meet her friends, and with a wide gentle staircase. And there was a bonus when our son rescued a white mouse wandering in the road. He made it an adventure playground in a large fish tank, and Suki, whom we always felt wanted a pet of her own, spent many hours watching it jumping from branch to branch and running in and out of toilet-roll tunnels. So the years passed and by now this dog who had come to us an ill, forsaken crossbreed of doubtful parentage, from horrible kennels, had won our hearts with a mixture of sensitive perception, lasting gratitude, an understanding that touched on telepathy and an abiding wish to please. In some ways, I suspect, she knew us better than we knew ourselves.

There came a time when I wanted to describe her success on paper, which I did in the form of a letter written by an old dog, Suki, to a puppy on how to manipulate human beings and thus achieve complete canine contentment. It was published as a book and Suki posed for publicity photographs, sitting in a chair gazing thoughtfully at a typewriter, turning a typewritten page with her nose and visiting a post-box. The publishers gave a launch party for the book on one of the Greens. Forty-one dogs came, all her friends, but one – the local vet's liver-coloured labrador who could open a tin of dog meat with his teeth. It was too much. Suki, overwhelmed but still composed, moved away from everyone until her paw was needed to guide the knife that cut the celebratory cake.

She lived another two years, growing rather deaf and blind, but enjoying walks on a lead and still able to manage her life well in her own house. We never knew her birth date but when she died she must have been only a few weeks from her sixteenth birthday. She had watched our children grow up and to me her death seemed to herald the end of an era in our lives.

APRIL
DAY

Mazo de la Roche
(Canadian) 1885–1961

A Sketch in Temperaments

IT was seven in the morning and the Scottie and the Cairn knew that soon it would be time to get up. They heard stirrings in the house below. They slept on the top floor in a dressing-room between the bedrooms of their mistresses, Zia and Cara. The two round dog baskets, with the cretonne cushions exactly alike, stood side by side. Dan, the Scottie, was able to look straight into Robbie's face.

Out of his almond-shaped eyes that were set high in his hard brindle head, Dan gazed lovingly into Robbie's face, veiled in fine grey hair which stood in tremulous half-curls on his brow, curved into a tiny moustache on his lip, and turned velvet and close on his ears.

Robbie knew that Dan was staring at him and the love did not matter, for, at this moment, he wanted nothing but to be let alone. He was savouring the last delicious doze before the moment when he would spring out of his basket. He kept his eyes shut tight. His head rested against the side of the basket, helpless-looking, like a little child's.

Dan stared and stared. A quiver ran down his spine, making the tip of his tail vibrate. He was sixteen months old and Robbie had had his first birthday last week. Dan seemed much the older, for he often had a dour look. He poured out his soul in love to Robbie all day long.

48

Now a felt-slippered step shuffled outside the door and it opened a little way. The cook put in her head. 'Come, boys, come now, time to get up,' she said and held the door open wide enough for them to pass through.

Dan jumped from his basket and reared himself on his hind legs. He waved his fore-paws at the cook, but she had barely a word for him. Robbie was her charmer.

Now, as he coyly descended the stairs behind her, she encouraged him with endearments. At each landing he lay on his back and rolled, talking to himself in a low pleasant growl.

'Come along, darling, do,' urged the cook, halfway down the stairs, but she had to plod back to the landing to persuade him.

Dan had gone down the two flights of stairs like a bullet. Now he stood waiting by the open front door, looking back over his shoulder. When Robbie reached the bottom step, Dan ran out and Robbie after him.

They went to their usual place under the weeping rose tree that was newly in leaf. The sun had just risen above the great shoulder of the nearest hill. The spring morning lay spread before them, to the distant mountains of Wales.

Shoulder to shoulder they trotted round the house and up the slope, pushing aside the faces of daffodils and narcissus, hastening a little as they neared the denseness of trees. Among the trees there was a moist mossy twilight and across it flitted the brown hump of a young rabbit. Dan saw it first. He gave a cry, as of agony, and hurled himself into the wood. With a little moan of bewilderment Robbie flew after him, not yet knowing what he chased.

Head to tail, they dived into the green twilight. The rabbit whirled beneath the prickly fortress of a holly bush. Out at the other side it flew, skimming the wet grass, its ears flat in stark terror. Dan circled the holly bush, screaming.

Now Robbie was sure that what they were pursuing had escaped, though he had never known what it was. He stood pensive a moment, listening to Dan's screams, then drifted back toward the house. He found the front door shut, as the cook did against their return, so he went to the green knoll outside the kitchen window and sat there under the green-and-white spread of the sycamore tree. He looked imploringly, from under his fine fringe, into the window at the cook bending over the range, at the maid putting on her cap, tucking her curls beneath it.

He heard the clump of a step on the cobbled path and saw the milkman coming with his carrier of milk. It was a shock to find that he had drawn so near without molestation. Robbie hurled himself down the knoll, screaming and champing at the milkman's legs. The cook came out of the kitchen calling:

'Robbie! Robbie! He won't hurt you! He's as gentle as a lamb!'

She said this every morning to the milkman who never believed her but came on grumbling. The cook picked Robbie up and he let his head rest against her bosom. She still held him a moment after the milkman had gone. He was patient but he wanted to go upstairs.

As soon as she put him down he glided along the hall and up the two flights of stairs. He scratched on the door of the dressing-room. Zia opened it and she and Cara told him how good and beautiful he was. He lay on his back looking up at them gently but haughtily, savouring their homage. His pointed grey paws hung quiet.

He saw the gas fire burning and stretched himself before it.

At first Dan did not miss Robbie, then suddenly realised that he had gone back to the house. What might not Robbie be doing without him? He tore across the grass, found the front door shut and barked insistently till it was opened by the maid.

On his short legs he pulled himself up the stairs and scratched peremptorily on the door of the dressing-room. Inside he reared and walked on his hind legs for a few steps with the sturdy grace of a pony stallion. He rolled his eyes toward the cupboard where the big glass marble lived. Zia went to the cupboard.

'Oh, must he have that?' said Cara. 'It makes such a noise!'

'He says he must,' said Zia. She laid the glass marble, with the silver bear in its middle, on the floor.

With a growl of joy, Dan pounced on it. He struck it with his paw, then bounded after it. Up and down the room he chased it, pushing it swiftly with his nose then panting after it, banging it against the wall and, at last, between Robbie's paws.

Robbie hated the marble with a bitter hatred. The rolling and the noise of it made him feel sick. Now he lay, with half-closed eyes, guarding it between his paws. Dan looked up into Zia's face.

'Robbie's got my ball,' his look said.

'Get it, then,' said Zia.

Dan approached Robbie tremblingly, pretending he was afraid or really being afraid.

Zia gave him back the marble. He struck it with his muzzle, then flew after it growling. After a little he began to gnaw it.

'Enough!' said Zia, taking it from him. 'You'll ruin your teeth.'

The four went down to breakfast. The dogs' plates stood waiting, filled with bits of hard-toasted brown bread. They crunched in delight, Dan's tail waving, Robbie's laid close. The moment they had finished they ran to the table to beg. Dan sat staring up out of glowing eyes. Cara dropped bits of bacon to him which he caught with a snap. Robbie mounted the arm of the settee behind Zia's chair. He put his paws on her shoulder and his cheek close to hers, so that she gave him bits of roll and honey.

At the first whiff of cigarette smoke Dan clambered into his basket and Robbie established himself on the fender stool, with his back turned to the table. He wore a look of disdain.

The children came in on their way to school. The dogs suffered themselves to be caressed but they wanted to doze.

As the sun shone warmer they went to the drive and stretched themselves at ease, ready for what might happen. Each time an errand boy came through the gate they went after him, exploding in barks as they ran. Cara or Zia or the gardener called to them, apologised for them, petted them for coming when they were called. They felt fearless and proud and obedient, wagging their tails after each sortie.

After a while the cook brought bones to them. She chose the biggest, hardest bone for Dan and the one with the most juicy meat on it for Robbie. But it was Dan who looked up at her in an ecstasy of gratitude; Robbie who took his haughtily, as though it were no more than he had expected. They settled down with the bones, eyeing each other distrustfully before they began to gnaw.

51

Dan gnawed his bone in long steady grinds, wearing it down with his strong teeth, exposing its granular interior, arching his muscular neck above it. Robbie ripped the red meat from his, gnawed at the end where the marrow was, grew tired and rose with the bone in his mouth, looking about for a place to bury it.

Dan saw this with dismay. To bury so soon! It could not be done! He darted at Robbie and tried to take the bone from him. Robbie lifted his lip in a defensive sneer. He growled in his throat. Dan returned to his own bone.

After a little while Robbie glided into the shrubbery and began to dig in the moist mossy earth. He buried the bone well, drawing the earth over it with paws and delicate nose. He came out of the shrubbery just as Cara came out of the house.

'Too much bone,' she said, 'you're having too much bone.' She went toward Dan.

He wagged his tail at her to take the sting from his ferocious growl. 'Don't touch my bone!' he shouted. 'Don't touch my bone!'

'You'd growl at me!' cried Cara, and she made a dart for the bone.

He caught it up and romped away from her.

Zia came out of the house with collars and leads in one hand and a dog brush in the other.

'Walkee, walkee,' she said as she came. 'Walkee, walkee!'

Dan dropped his bone and ran to her. Robbie danced toward her. Jealously Dan shouldered him away, pulling him gently by the ear. He loved him but he did not want him making up to Zia.

She took Dan in her hands and laid him flat. She began vigorously to brush him. He stretched himself at full length, giving himself to the brush in delight, kicking joyfully when it touched a sensitive spot. He showed his teeth in a grin of love and beamed up at Zia.

When Dan was brushed Zia stretched out her hand for Robbie, but he slid from under it like water. He looked at her coyly from over his shoulder. He kept always just out of reach, as she followed him on her knees across the grass.

'Walkee, walkee,' she cooed. 'Brushee, brushee!'

He bowed politely and touched her hand with his nose but was gone before she could catch him.

'Very well,' said Zia, 'we'll go without you.'

She and Cara went into the house, ignoring Robbie. When they came down with their coats and hats on he was sitting on the pink best chair. Zia caught him up, sat down with him on her lap and began to brush him. He could tolerate this. He sat resigned as she brushed his long delicate hair first up, then down, then in a swirl to follow the streamline of his spine. But when she put the harness and lead on him he stiffened himself and an icy aloofness came into his eyes. He looked as aloof as a carved unicorn on the top of a stone gateway. He was not Robbie at all.

But he was himself again as he and Dan trotted down the drive and through the gate shoulder to shoulder, their mistresses on the other end of the leads. They turned from the main road into a country road past the fields where the new lambs were being suckled and the glossy hunters were nibbling the grass, past the duck-pond. Robbie averted his eyes from the ducks with a bleak look as though he could not bear the sight of them but Dan, now off the lead, looked at them with beaming interest. He beamed up at Zia. 'What about it?' his eyes asked.

'Don't dare!' said Zia.

On and on they walked, the great hills always rising before them, the primrose wreaths palely blooming on the banks. But hills and flowers meant nothing to the dogs. The thousand scents of road and ditch meant much. A rabbit had passed this way. A weasel had passed that. Only an hour ago the Hunt had crossed the road.

Dan never wearied of the pleasures of the road. He jogged jauntily on and on as though he would go for ever. From a front view, one saw first his pricked ears, with the tail appearing exactly between them, then the strong shoulders, the bent elbows and the round paws that padded one over the other as though he were climbing a ladder.

Now Robbie was bored. He wanted to go home. He drifted along the road like a resigned little old lady with her grey shawl draped about her. He looked neither to right nor left.

They took the short cut home through the lane where the holly berries still shone bright among the prickly leaves. They found the break in the hedge. Zia lifted Dan over first, then followed him. Cara handed Robbie over and came last. She took off his harness and lead.

He stood crouching while it was undone, then sped forward like a slim grey arrow, past the house, past the stables, into the wild-wood. Each breath was a protest against restraint. He felt free and cruel as a fox.

Now he was chasing a rabbit, all his boredom gone. Through the green twilight of the wood they sped, terror in one, joy in the other. Under the thick clammy leaves of rhododendrons, under the prickling boughs of holly, through thorny undergrowth that tore out locks of Robbie's hair and scratched his face. Neither he nor the rabbit uttered a sound. They flew silently, as though in a dream.

Then suddenly the rabbit was gone, swallowed up in a burrow. Robbie lay panting, his heart throbbing. He pulled some of the burrs from his paws and his tail. After a while he remembered his dinner, his home. He trotted along a path and was passing the orchard when he saw that the hens had been let out of their run and were strutting about among the daffodils.

He hesitated by a hole in the hedge and peered through at them. His eyes were bleak, as when he had turned his gaze away from the ducks. But now he did not turn away. He stared and stared. He was alone. There was no one to stop him.

He glided through the hedge and sprang fiercely on the nearest hen. She flapped her big red wings and ran squawking, with him on her back. She fell and still holding her by the neck, he threw her from side to side till she stopped struggling. All the other hens and the cock were in a panic, running here and there among the trees, each thinking it was its turn next. Robbie, with the face of a little gar-goyle, ran after them. He whimpered in his delight.

The red feathers were scattered over the grass. Five bundles of them lay still and two more huddled in weakness and fear. The rest of the flock were safe in their run. Robbie stood looking in at them. They were all right there. That was where they belonged. In the orchard they were wild things to be pursued.

The front door stood open. He glided into the sitting-room. Dan was curled up in his basket, asleep after a good dinner, but he jumped out and came to meet Robbie. He sniffed Robbie's mouth and his tail quivered in recognition of the scent there. He grinned joyfully at Robbie.

But Robbie wanted his dinner. He went to the kitchen and found the maid. He danced about her, gently nipped her ankles in their black cotton stockings. She snatched him up and rocked him in her arms.

'Oh, baby, baby, little baby!'

His beautiful eyes pleaded but she could not bear to put him down. She snuggled her rosy cheek against him, then held him at arms' length in her hands, adoring him. He looked at her, docile yet roguish. When she put her face near enough he gave her nose a swift nip. She hugged him close.

At last his plate was set in front of him, boiled cod mixed with vegetables. He ate less daintily than usual, for he was very hungry. Dan stood watching him and, when he had finished, came to his plate and licked it thoroughly. Robbie took a big drink out of the brown earthen dish, then went back to the sitting-room and stretched himself at length on the settee. Dan returned to his basket.

For some reason the settee did not satisfy Robbie, though generally it was his favourite spot. He jumped down and came to the basket and gazed in at Dan. Dan turned up his belly and rolled his eyes at Robbie but, after a little, he scrambled out of the basket and on to the settee. Robbie drifted into the basket.

While they were still drowsy Zia came with brush and comb and began to groom them. They were to go to the photographer's and already they were late for the appointment but they must look their best. The car was at the door and now Zia slid under the wheel and Cara sat in the seat behind with a little dog on either side of her. They were as pretty as pictures, she told them.

They sat looking noble, till the car went into low gear on the steep hill and they felt the threat of the engine's vibration. They yawned and drooped, then hid their faces in Cara's lap and gave themselves up to misery. But on the level their spirits returned and they began to romp in exhilaration, growl at each other, stand upright on the seat, breast to breast.

What grand puppies, the photographer said, and placed them side by side on a settee and hid his head in the camera. That was only the beginning.

Dan jumped to the floor and, when he was lifted to the settee, Robbie jumped down. They did this till they were excited and panting and spoken to severely. Then they cowered on the settee, looking like curs. The photographer barked loudly and they had hysterics. Robbie suffered the photographer to put him on the settee and admonish him but Dan raised his voice and barked: 'Don't touch me, man!' He showed his teeth in a threatening grin. Then suddenly he was well behaved and posed nobly, sometimes in profile, sometimes full-face but always fine, like the prize-winner at a dog show.

Now there was only Robbie to cope with, but Robbie had become all wriggles and gaiety. Being photographed was funnier than he could bear. He lay on his back and kicked his joy in it.

Then, at last, he sat still. But now Dan was tired. He curled himself into a tight ball and fell asleep. When he was raised he had no backbone but lolled and looked imbecile. Zia produced toffee and fed them. The trick was done! The camera clicked.

Now there was shopping and they sat alone in the car while Zia and Cara went into the shops. It was lonely in the car. Dan attended to his paws, licking them till his nails shone like ebony. Sometimes, by mistake, licking the cushion of the car. Robbie never licked his paws. He ignored sore spots which Dan would have licked incessantly. So, to pass the time, Robbie gnawed the polished wood of the window frame. It was awkward to get at but he managed it. They were nearly home when Cara discovered the tooth-marks. 'Which of you did this?' she demanded sternly.

Dan looked guilty, contrite, but Robbie knew nothing about it. His eyes spoke innocence from under his silken fringe. Cara smacked the top of Dan's lean flat skull. He burrowed into a corner, ashamed.

Presently Robbie's thoughts returned to the window frame and he gave it a last gnaw as they passed through the gate.

'So – it was you, Robbie!' cried Cara. 'Oh, poor Dan, why were you so silly?' She pulled Dan from his corner and patted him. Robbie leaped lightly from the car when it stopped and, pursued by Dan, sped into the wilderness. Soon they were chasing a rabbit and Dan's screams echoed among the trees.

They came back in time for tea. They stood shoulder to shoulder, yearning toward the teapot. They had their saucers of weak tea, then got into the basket together and slept.

The gardener stood, strong and bent, in the corner of the room, the loam scraped from his boots, his hands washed clean.

'Thur's been fowls killed,' he said, 'seven on 'em. Some time this marnin', it were. I think one o' our little fellers done it.'

Cara turned pale. 'How awful! Are you sure it was one of ours?'

'Thur's been no other on t' place, ma'am. T' gates is all shut fast.'

He bent over the basket and with his gentle thick hand lifted Dan's lip and looked at the double row of white teeth laid evenly together, a little underhung but not much.

'Nubbut thure.'

As gently but less cautiously he looked in Robbie's mouth. Quickly he folded down the soft lip. ''Tis him, for sartin,' he said quietly. 'Thures a bit o' feather between his teeth. I'm not surprised, ma'am. He killed one once afore. I caught him at it. He thinks they didn't orter be runnin' in t' orchard. But 'tis only a puppy. Don't you fret. He'll not do it again.'

Robbie looked coyly up at them. He laid a pointed paw on each side of his face and looked up lovingly into Cara's eyes.

'He'll never do it again,' comforted the gardener.

As the sun slanted in at the west window and the children were getting ready for bed, Dan and Robbie went to the nursery for their evening play. Dan romped with the children. He was rough with them, but they must not pull him about. 'Have a care how you handle me!' his warning growl came.

Robbie drifted about, always just outside the game. But, when the children caught him, he surrendered himself to be held uncomfortably in small arms, to be dandled on small hard knees.

Toward evening the air had become warmer. Without question

the birds and flowers opened their hearts to summer. Starlings walked about the lawn, staring into daisy faces. Dan and Robbie lay before the door serenely facing the great spread of hills unrolled before them. Their sensitive nostrils put aside the smell of the wall-flower and drank in what rich animal scents came their way.

They lay as still as carven dogs except for the faint fluttering of the hair on Robbie's crown. Dan faced the breeze with head stark, neck arched and thick like a little stallion.

When two gipsy women clumped up the drive selling mimosa the dogs did not bark but watched their coming and their going tranquilly. They were steeped in the new sweet warmth of the evening.

But when they were turned out for a last run before bedtime, it was different. The air came sharply from the highest hill. The earth sent its quickness up into them. Robbie ran into the wildwood but Dan found a hedgehog and worked himself into a rage before its prickles. Cara and Zia found him in the blackness beneath a yew tree and turned the beam of an electric torch on him. On the bright green of grass the hedgehog sat like a bundle of autumn leaves, impervious.

'Open up! Open up!' shouted Dan, his teeth wet and gleaming.

Robbie came drifting out of the shrubbery and sat down watch-ing the pair, knowing the hopelessness of the onslaught. Dan put his nose against the prickles and started back, shouting still louder: 'Open up! Open up!'

But the hedgehog held itself close, impervious as a burr.

'Enough!' said Zia and tucked Dan under her arm.

Cara pounced on Robbie. The hedgehog was left to his dreams.

Snug in their baskets they lay in the dressing-room, the velvet darkness pressing closer and closer. Dan lay stretched as though running but Robbie's four feet lay bunched close together. His head was thrown back, his ears tilted alert for the whispering of dreams. What did he hear? The cry of a rabbit in a trap? Or some ghostly cackle from the poultry-yard?

He woke. He sat up in his basket and uttered a loud accusing bark at what had disturbed him. His own voice was comforting. He had never before barked so sonorously, so much like Dan. The comfort of the barking gave him deep peace. He kept on and on. Cara came in at the door. She turned on the light.

Robbie looked at her wonderingly, his little head pillowed on his pointed paw. Dan gave a sheepish grin and hung his head. He had got out of his basket to meet her.

'Naughty, naughty, naughty!' said Cara. 'Back to your bed, Dan! Not another bark out of you!'

Dan slunk back to his basket, curled himself close. . . .

The shadows would not let Robbie be. Out of them came mysterious things to disturb him. He went to the open window and sat on the ledge, framed in ivy. He barked steadily on an even more sonorous note. He had lovely sensations. He felt that he could go on till dawn.

But he heard the door of Cara's room open and, in one graceful leap, he was back in his basket. Small and stern, Cara entered the room. In her room Zia was lying with the blankets over her head. In shame Dan went to meet Cara.

'It is the end, Dan,' she said mournfully. 'You must go into the box-room by yourself.'

She took his basket and he humbly followed her, stopping only to nozzle Robbie as he passed. She put him in the furthest, darkest corner of the box-room where, if he did bark, he would scarcely be heard. She went back to bed. There was beautiful quiet. Zia uncovered her head.

Robbie was alone now and he gave full vent to the trouble that was in him. He forgot all but the mournful majesty of his barking as he sat on the window ledge.

When Cara came into the room he disregarded her till she took him into her arms. Then he laid his head confidingly on her shoulder and gave himself up to what might befall. It befell that he was laid on the foot of her bed. It seemed almost too good to be true. Everywhere there was peace and slumber.

At half-past seven the cook heavily mounted the stairs. She opened the door of the dressing-room and saw the one empty basket. She knocked on Cara's door and opened it.

'Half-past seven, madam,' she said, 'and I can't find the puppies at all!'

'Dan is in the box-room. Robbie is here.'

Dan and Robbie met in the passage. They kissed, then pranced about each other joyfully. They nipped the cook's ankles as they descended the stairs. Another April day had begun!

COMET

Samuel A. Derieux
(American) 1891–1922

No puppy ever came into the world under more favourable conditions than Comet. He was descended from a famous family of pointers. Both his mother and father were champions. Before he opened his eyes, while he was still crawling about over his brothers and sisters, blind as puppies are at birth, Jim Thompson, Mr. Devant's kennel master, picked him out.

'That's the best un in the bunch.'

When he was only three weeks old he pointed a butterfly that lit in the yard in front of his nose.

'Come here, Molly,' yelled Jim to his wife. 'Pointed – the little cuss!'

When Thompson started taking the growing pups out of the yard, into the fields to the side of the Devants' great southern winter home, Oak Knob, it was Comet who strayed farthest from the man's protecting care. And when Jim taught them all to follow when he said 'Heel,' to drop when he said 'Drop,' and to stand stock-still when he said 'Ho,' he learned far more quickly than the others.

At six months he set his first covey of quail, and remained perfectly staunch. 'He's goin' to make a great dog,' said Thompson. Everything – size, muscle, nose, intelligence, earnestness – pointed to the same conclusion. Comet was one of the favoured of the gods.

One day, after the leaves had turned red and brown and the mornings grown chilly, a crowd of people, strangers to him, arrived at Oak Knob. Then out of the house with Thompson came a big man in tweed clothes, and the two walked straight to the curious young dogs, who were watching them with shining eyes and wagging tails.

'Well, Thompson,' said the big man, 'which is the future champion you've been writing me about?'

'Pick him out for yourself, sir,' said Thompson confidently.

After that they talked a long time planning for the future of Comet. His yard training was now over (Thompson was only yard trainer), and he must be sent to a man experienced in training and handling for field trials.

'Larsen's the man to bring him out,' said the big man in tweeds, who was George Devant himself. 'I saw his dogs work in the Canadian Derby.'

Thompson spoke hesitatingly, apologetically, as if he hated to bring the matter up. 'Mr. Devant . . . you remember, sir, a long time ago Larsen sued us for old Ben.'

'Yes, Thompson; I remember, now that you speak of it.'

'Well, you remember the court decided against him, which was the only thing it could do, for Larsen didn't have any more right to that dog than the Sultan of Turkey. But, Mr. Devant, I was there, and I saw Larsen's face when the case went against him.'

Devant looked keenly at Thompson.

'Another thing, Mr. Devant,' Thompson went on, still hesitatingly; 'Larsen had a chance to get hold of this breed of pointers and lost out, because he dickered too long, and acted cheesy. Now they've turned out to be famous. Some men never forget a thing like that. Larsen's been talkin' these pointers down ever since, sir.'

'Go on,' said Devant.

'I know Larsen's a good trainer. But it'll mean a long trip for the young dog to where he lives. Now, there's an old trainer lives near here, Wade Swygert. There never was a straighter man than him. He used to train dogs in England.'

Devant smiled. 'Thompson, I admire your loyalty to your friends; but I don't think much of your business sense. We'll turn over some of the others to Swygert, if he wants 'em. Comet must have the best. I'll write Larsen to-night, Thompson. Tomorrow, crate Comet and send him off.'

Just as no dog ever came into the world under more favourable auspices, so no dog ever had a bigger 'send-off' than Comet. Even the ladies of the house came out to exclaim over him, and Marian Devant, pretty, eighteen, and a sportswoman, stooped down, caught his head between her hands, looked into his fine eyes, and wished him 'Good luck, old man'. In the living-room the men laughingly drank toasts to his future, and from the high-columned portico Marian Devant waved him good-bye, as in his clean padded crate he was driven off, a bewildered youngster, to the station.

Two days and two nights he travelled, and at noon of the third day, at a lonely railroad station in a prairie country that rolled like a heavy sea, he was lifted, crate and all, off the train. A lean, pale-eyed, sanctimonious-looking man came toward him.

'Some beauty that, Mr. Larsen,' said the agent as he helped Larsen's man lift the crate on to a small truck.

'Yes,' drawled Larsen in a meditative voice, 'pretty enough to look at – but he looks scared – er – timid.'

'Of course he's scared,' said the agent; 'so would you be if they was to put you in some kind of a whale of a balloon an' ship you in a crate to Mars.'

The station agent poked his hands through the slats and patted the head. Comet was grateful for that, because everything was strange. He had not whined nor complained on the trip, but his heart had pounded fast, and he had been homesick.

And everything continued to be strange: the treeless country through which he was driven, the bald house and huge barns where he was lifted out, the dogs that crowded about him when he was turned into the kennel yard. These eyed him with enmity and walked round and round him. But he stood his ground staunchly for a youngster, returning fierce look for fierce look, growl for growl, until the man called him away and chained him to a kennel.

For days Comet remained chained, a stranger in a strange land. Each time at the click of the gate announcing Larsen's entrance he sprang to his feet from force of habit, and stared hungrily at the man for the light he was accustomed to see in human eyes. But with just a glance at him the man would turn one or more of the other dogs loose and ride off to train them.

But he was not without friends of his own kind. Now and then another young dog (he alone was chained up) would stroll his way with wagging tail, or lie down near by, in that strange bond of sympathy that is not confined to man. Then Comet would feel better and would want to play, for he was still half puppy. Sometimes he would pick up a stick and shake it, and his partner would catch the other end. They would tug and growl with mock ferocity, and then lie down and look at each other curiously.

If any attention had been paid him by Larsen, Comet would have quickly overcome his feeling of strangeness. He was no milksop. He was like an overgrown boy, off at college or in some foreign city. He was sensitive, and not sure of himself. Had Larsen gained his confidence, it would all have been different. And as for Larsen – he knew that perfectly well.

One fine sunny afternoon Larsen entered the yard, came straight to him, and turned him loose. In the exuberance of his spirits he ran round and round the yard, barking in the faces of his friends. Larsen let him out, mounted a horse, and commanded him to heel. He obeyed with wagging tail.

A mile or more down the road Larsen turned off into the fields. Across his saddle was something the young pointer had had no experience with – a gun. That part of his education Thompson had neglected, at least put off, for he had not expected that Comet would be sent away so soon. That was where Thompson had made a mistake.

At the command 'Hi on' the young pointer ran eagerly around the horse, and looked up into the man's face to be sure he had heard aright. At something he saw there the tail and ears drooped momentarily, and there came over him again a feeling of strangeness, almost of dismay. Larsen's eyes were mere slits of blue glass, and his mouth was set in a thin line.

At a second command, though, he galloped off swiftly, boldly. Round and round an extensive field of straw he circled, forgetting any feeling of strangeness now, every fibre of his being intent on the hunt, while Larsen, sitting on his horse, watched him with appraising eyes.

Suddenly there came to Comet's nose the smell of game birds, strong, pungent, compelling. He stiffened into an earnest, beautiful point. Heretofore in the little training he had had Thompson had come up behind him, flushed the birds, and made him drop. And now Larsen, having quickly dismounted and tied his horse, came up behind him, just as Thompson had done, except that in Larsen's hand was the gun.

The old-fashioned black powder of a generation ago makes a loud explosion. It sounds like a cannon compared with the modern smokeless powder now used by all hunters. Perhaps it was only an accident that had caused Larsen before he left the house to load his pump gun with black powder shells.

As for Comet he only knew that the birds rose; then above his head burst an awful roar, almost splitting his tender eardrums, shocking every sensitive nerve, filling him with terror such as he had never felt before. Even then, in the confusion and horror of the surprise, he turned to the man, head ringing, eyes dilated. A single reassuring word, and he would have steadied. As for Larsen, though, he declared afterward (to others and to himself even) that he noticed no nervousness in the dog; that he was only intent on getting several birds for breakfast.

Twice, three times, four times, the pump gun bellowed in its cannon-like roar, piercing the eardrums, shattering the nerves. Comet turned; one more glance backward at a face, strange, exultant – and then the puppy in him conquered. Tail tucked, he ran away from that shattering noise.

Miles he ran. Now and then, stumbling over briars, he yelped. Not once did he look back. His tail was tucked, his eyes crazy with fear. Seeing a house, he made for that. It was the noon hour, and a group of farm hands was gathered in the yard. One of them, with a cry 'Mad dog!' ran into the house after a gun. When he came out, they told him the dog was under the porch. And so he was. Pressed against the wall, in the darkness, the magnificent young pointer with the quivering soul waited, panting, eyes gleaming, the horror still ringing in his ears.

Here Larsen found him that afternoon. A boy crawled underneath the porch and dragged him out. He, who had started life favoured of the gods, who that morning even had been full of high spirits, who had circled a field like a champion, was now a cringing, shaking creature, like a homeless cur.

And thus it happened that Comet came home, in disgrace – a gun-shy dog, a coward, expelled from college, not for some youthful prank, but because he was – yellow. And he knew he was disgraced. He saw it in the face of the big man, Devant, who looked at him in the yard where he had spent his happy puppyhood, then turned away. He knew it because of what he saw in the face of Jim Thompson.

In the house was a long and plausible letter, explaining how it happened:

I did everything I could. I never was as surprised in my life. The dog's hopeless.

As for the other inhabitants of the big house, their minds were full of the events of the season: de luxe hunting parties, more society events than hunts; lunches in the woods served by uniformed butlers; launch rides up the river; arriving and departing guests. Only one of them, except Devant himself, gave the gun-shy dog a thought. Marian Devant came out to visit him in his disgrace. She stooped before him as she had done on that other and happier day, and again caught his head between her hands. But his eyes did not meet hers, for in his dim way he knew he was not now what he had been.

'I don't believe he's yellow – inside!' she declared, looking up at Thompson, her cheeks flushed.

Thompson shook his head.

'I tried him with a gun, Miss Marian,' he declared. 'I just showed it to him, and he ran into his kennel.'

'I'll go get mine. He won't run from me.'

But at sight of her small gun it all came back. Again he seemed to hear the explosion that had shattered his nerves. The Terror had entered his very soul. In spite of her pleading, he made for his kennel. Even the girl turned away from him now. And as he lay panting in the shelter of his kennel he knew that never again would men look at him as they had looked, or life be sweet to him as it had been.

Then there came to Oak Knob an old man to see Thompson. He had been on many seas, he had fought in a dozen wars, and had settled at last on a little truck farm near by. Somewhere, in his life full of adventure and odd jobs, he had trained dogs and horses. His face was lined and seamed, his hair was white, his eyes piercing, blue and kind. Wade Swygert was his name.

'There's been dirty work,' he said, when he looked at the dog. 'I'll take him if you're goin' to give him away.'

Give him away – who had been Championship hope!

Marian Devant came out and looked into the face of the old man, shrewdly, understandingly.

'Can you cure him?' she demanded.

'I doubt it, miss,' was the sturdy answer.

'You will try?'

The blue eyes lighted up. 'Yes, I'll try.'

'Then you can have him. And – if there's any expense—'

'Come, Comet,' said the old man.

That night, in a neat, humble house, Comet ate supper, placed before him by a stout old woman, who had followed this old man to the ends of the world. That night he slept before their fire. Next day he followed the old man all about the place. Several days and nights passed this way, then, while he lay before the fire, old Swygert came in with a gun. At sight of it Comet sprang to his feet. He tried to rush out of the room, but the doors were closed. Finally, he crawled under the bed.

Every night after that Swygert got out the gun, until he crawled under the bed no more. Finally, one day the man fastened the dog to a tree in the yard, then came out with a gun. A sparrow lit in a tree, and he shot it. Comet tried to break the rope. All his panic had returned; but the report had not shattered him as that other did, for the gun was loaded light.

After that, frequently the old man shot a bird in his sight, loading the gun more and more heavily, and each time after the shot coming to him, showing him the bird, and speaking to him kindly, gently. But for all that the Terror remained in his heart.

One afternoon the girl, accompanied by a young man, rode over on horseback, dismounted, and came in. She always stopped when she was riding by.

'It's mighty slow business,' old Swygert reported; 'I don't know whether I'm makin' any headway or not.'

That night old Mrs. Swygert told him she thought he had better give it up. It wasn't worth the time and worry. The dog was just yellow.

Swygert pondered a long time. 'When I was a kid,' he said at last, 'there came up a terrible thunderstorm. It was in South America. I was water boy for a railroad gang, and the storm drove us in a shack. While lightnin' was hittin' all around, one of the grown men told me it always picked out boys with red hair. My hair was red, an' I was little and ignorant. For years I was skeered of lightnin'. I never have quite got over it. But no man ever said I was yellow.'

Again he was silent for a while. Then he went on: 'I don't seem to be makin' much headway, I admit that. I'm lettin' him run away as far as he can. Now I've got to shoot an' make him come toward the gun himself, right while I'm shootin' it.'

Next day Comet was tied up and fasted, and next, until he was gaunt and famished. Then, on the afternoon of the third day, Mrs. Swygert, at her husband's direction, placed before him, within reach of his chain, some raw beefsteak. As he started for it, Swygert shot. He drew back, panting, then, hunger getting the better of him, started again. Again Swygert shot.

After that for days Comet 'Ate to music,' as Swygert expressed it. 'Now,' he said, 'he's got to come toward the gun when he's not even tied up.'

Not far from Swygert's house is a small pond and on one side the banks are perpendicular. Toward this pond the old man, with the gun under his arm, and the dog following, went. Here in the silence of the woods, with just the two of them together, was to be a final test.

On the shelving bank Swygert picked up a stick and tossed it into the middle of the pond with the command to 'fetch'. Comet sprang eagerly in and retrieved it. Twice this was repeated. But the third time, as the dog approached the shore, Swygert picked up the gun and fired.

Quickly the dog dropped the stick, then turned and swam toward the other shore. Here, so precipitous were the banks, he could not get a foothold. He turned once more and struck out diagonally across the pond. Swygert met him and fired.

Over and over it happened. Each time, after he fired, the old man stooped down with extended hand and begged him to come on. His face was grim now, and, though the day was cool, sweat stood out on his brow. 'You'll face the music,' he said, 'or you'll drown. Better be dead than called yellow.'

The dog was growing weary now. His head was barely above water. His efforts to clamber up the opposite bank were feeble, frantic. Yet, each time as he drew near the shore Swygert fired.

He was not using light loads now. He was using the regular load of the bird hunter. Time had passed for temporizing. The sweat was standing out all over his face. The sternness in his eyes was terrible to see, for it was the sternness of a man who is suffering.

A dog can swim a long time. The sun dropped over the trees. Still the firing went on, regularly, like a minute gun.

Just before the sun set an exhausted dog staggered toward an old man almost as exhausted as he. The dog had been too near death and was too faint to care now for the gun that was being fired over his head. On and on he came, toward the man, disregarding the noise of the gun. It would not hurt him, that he knew at last. He might have many enemies, but the gun, in the hands of this man, was not one of them. Suddenly old Swygert sank down and took the dripping dog in his arms.

'Old boy,' he said, 'old boy.'

That night Comet lay before the fire, and looked straight into the eyes of a man, as he used to look in the old days.

Next season Larsen, glancing over his sporting papers, was astonished to see that among promising Derbys the fall trials had called forth was a pointer named Comet. He would have thought it some other dog than the one who had disappointed him so by turning out gun-shy, in spite of all his efforts to prevent, had it not been for

69

the fact that the entry was booked as: 'Comet; owner, Miss Marian Devant; handler, Wade Swygert.'

Next year he was still more astonished to see in the same paper that Comet, handled by Swygert, had won first place in a Western trial, and was prominently spoken of as a National Championship possibility. As for him, he had no young entries to offer, but was staking everything on the National Championship, where he was to enter Larsen's Peerless II.

It was strange how things fell out – but things have a habit of turning out strangely in field trials, as well as elsewhere. When Larsen reached the town where the National Championship was to be run, there on the street, straining at the leash held by old Swygert, whom he used to know, was a seasoned young pointer, with a white body, a brown head, and a brown saddle spot – the same pointer he had seen two years before turn tail and run in that terror a dog never quite overcomes.

But the strangest thing of all happened that night at the drawing, when, according to the slips taken at random from a hat, it was declared that on the following Wednesday Comet, the pointer, was to run with Peerless II.

It gave Larsen a strange thrill, this announcement. He left the meeting and went straightway to his room. There for a long time he sat pondering. Next day at a hardware store he bought some black powder and some shells.

The race was to be run next day, and that night in his room he loaded half-a-dozen shells. It would have been a study in faces to watch him as he bent over his work, on his lips a smile. Into the shells he packed all the powder they could stand, all the powder his trusted gun could stand, without bursting. It was a load big enough to kill a bear, to bring down a buffalo. It was a load that would echo and re-echo in the hills.

On the morning that Larsen walked out in front of the judges and the field, Peerless II at the leash, old Swygert, with Comet at his side, he glanced around at the 'field,' or spectators. Among them was a handsome young woman, and with her, to his amazement, George Devant. He could not help chuckling inside himself as he thought of what would happen that day, for once a gun-shy dog, always a gun-shy dog – that was *his* experience.

As for Comet, he faced the straw fields eagerly, confidently, already a veteran. Long ago fear of the gun had left him, for the most part. There were times when at a report above his head he still trembled, and the shocked nerves in his ear gave a twinge like that of a bad tooth. But always at the quiet voice of the old man, his god, he grew steady, and remained staunch.

Some disturbing memory did start within him to-day as he glanced at the man with the other dog. It seemed to him as if in another and an evil world he had seen that face. His heart began to pound fast, and his tail drooped for a moment. Within an hour it was all to come back to him – the terror, the panic, the agony of that far-away time.

He looked up at old Swygert, who was his god, and to whom his soul belonged, though he was booked as the property of Miss Marian Devant. Of the arrangements he could know nothing, being a dog. Old Swygert, having cured him, could not meet the expenses of taking him to field trials. The girl had come to the old man's assistance, an assistance which he had accepted only under condition that the dog should be entered as hers, with himself as handler.

'Are you ready, gentlemen?' the judges asked.

'Ready,' said Larsen and old Swygert.

And Comet and Peerless II were speeding away across that field, and behind them came handlers, and judges and spectators, all mounted.

It was a race people still talk about, and for a reason, for strange things happened that day. At first there was nothing unusual. It was like any other field trial. Comet found birds, and Swygert, his handler, flushed them and shot. Comet remained steady. Then Peerless II found a covey, and Larsen flushed them and shot. And so for an hour it went.

Then Comet disappeared, and old Swygert, riding hard and looking for him, went out of sight over a hill. But Comet had not gone far. As a matter of fact, he was near by, hidden in some high straw, pointing a covey of birds. One of the spectators spied him, and called the judges' attention to him. Everybody, including Larsen, rode up to him, but still Swygert had not come back.

They called him, but the old man was a little deaf. Some of the men rode to the top of the hill but could not see him. In his zeal he had got a considerable distance away. Meanwhile, here was his dog, pointed.

If any one had looked at Larsen's face he would have seen the exultation there, for now his chance had come – the very chance he had been looking for. It's a courtesy one handler sometimes extends another who is absent from the spot, to go in and flush his dog's birds.

'I'll handle this covey for Mr. Swygert,' said Larsen to the judges, his voice smooth and plausible, on his face a smile.

And thus it happened that Comet faced his supreme ordeal without the steadying voice of his god.

He only knew that ahead of him were birds, and that behind him a man was coming through the straw, and that behind the man a crowd of people on horseback were watching him. He had become used to that, but when, out of the corner of his eye, he saw the face of the advancing man, his soul began to tremble.

'Call your dog in, Mr. Larsen,' directed the judge. 'Make him backstand.'

Only a moment was lost, while Peerless, a young dog himself, came running in and at a command from Larsen stopped in his tracks behind Comet, and pointed. Larsen's dogs always obeyed, quickly, mechanically. Without ever gaining their confidence, Larsen had a way of turning them into finished field-trial dogs. They obeyed, because they were afraid not to.

According to the rules the man handling the dog has to shoot as the birds rise. This is done in order to test the dog's steadiness when a gun is fired over him. No specification is made as to the size of the shotgun to be used. Usually, however, small-gauge guns are carried. The one in Larsen's hands was a twelve gauge, and consequently large.

All morning he had been using it over his own dog. Nobody had paid any attention to it, because he shot smokeless powder. But now, as he advanced, he reached into the left-hand pocket of his hunting coat, where six shells rattled as he hurried along. Two of these he took out and rammed into the barrels.

As for Comet, still standing rigid, statuesque, he heard, as has been said, the brush of steps through the straw, glimpsed a face, and trembled. But only for a moment. Then he steadied, head high, tail straight out. The birds rose with a whir – and then was repeated that horror of his youth. Above his ears, ears that would always be tender, broke a great roar. Either because of his excitement, or because of a sudden wave of revenge, or of a determination to make sure of the dog's flight, Larsen had pulled both triggers at once. The combined report shattered through the dog's eardrums, it shivered through his nerves, he sank in agony into the straw.

Then the old impulse to flee was upon him, and he sprang to his feet, and looked about wildly. But from somewhere in that crowd behind him came to his tingling ears a voice – clear, ringing, deep, the voice of a woman – a woman he knew – pleading as his master used to plead, calling on him not to run, but to stand.

'Steady,' it said. 'Steady, Comet!'

It called him to himself, it soothed him, it calmed him, and he turned and looked toward the crowd. With the roar of the shotgun the usual order observed in field trials was broken up. All rules seemed to have been suspended. Ordinarily, no one belonging to 'the field' is allowed to speak to a dog. Yet the girl had spoken to him. Ordinarily, the spectators must remain in the rear of the judges. Yet one of the judges had himself wheeled his horse about and was galloping off, and Marian Devant had pushed through the crowd and was riding toward the bewildered dog.

He stood staunch where he was, though in his ears was still a throbbing pain, and though all about him was this growing confusion he could not understand. The man he feared was running across the field yonder, in the direction taken by the judge. He was blowing his whistle as he ran. Through the crowd, his face terrible to see, his own master was coming. Both the old man and the girl had dismounted now, and were running toward him.

'I heard,' old Swygert was saying to her. 'I heard it! I might 'a' known! I might 'a' known!'

'He stood,' she panted, 'like a rock – oh, the brave, beautiful thing!'

'Where is that—' Swygert suddenly checked himself and looked around.

A man in the crowd (they had all gathered about now), laughed.

'He's gone after his dog,' he said. 'Peerless has run away!'

LOST DOG

Penelope Lively
(British) 1933–

Dogs are odd. They are animals, no doubt about that; but to other animals they often seem like offshoots of human beings. This was certainly true of the dog at Fifty-four Pavilion Road, a rough-haired white terrier called Willie. The other creatures in the house thought Willie a helpless fellow because he depended on the Dixon family for food and a roof over his head. Mind, in the case of the mice this could have been said of them also, but I suppose they would have retorted that at least they risked life and limb to get their meals whereas Willie had his handed to him in a bowl. But the real difference is one of outlook rather than the getting of food and shelter. Dogs tend to take a human point of view; they even behave, up to a point, like people.

Willie loved Mrs. Dixon. In fact, he didn't just love Mrs. Dixon – he adored and worshipped her. He was polite to the rest of the family, but it was Mrs. Dixon who was the centre of his world. He had a healthy respect for Mr. Dixon, and he put up with the children – Julie who was nine and Andy who was seven. He had rather mixed feelings about the baby, since he was jealous of him and suspected (rightly, I'm afraid) that Mrs. Dixon loved the baby more than she loved him. But most of Willie's time was spent trailing around after Mrs. Dixon, moping if she wasn't there, and admiring her when she was. He would sit in the kitchen, or the sitting room or wherever she happened to be and croon to her in dog language which of course Mrs. Dixon neither heard nor understood.

'Oh, you are so beautiful,' he would sing, 'you are so beautiful and so wise and so clever. There is no one like you. I will do anything for you. You are the sun and the moon and I want to live all by myself with you for ever and ever . . .'

It was just as well that Mrs. Dixon, who was a down-to-earth, no nonsense sort of person, was deaf to all this. She was fond of Willie, very fond, though she told him off for being greedy and lazy and always getting underfoot so that she was constantly falling over him.

'It's not me that's underfoot,' Willie would grumble, 'It's you who are overdog. But I forgive you because you are so wonderful and I admire you and adore you and if you want to step on me just go right ahead and do so.'

The Dixons had got Willie when he was young from the RSPCA as an unwanted dog. Perhaps this was why Willie was so devoted to Mrs. Dixon; she had thought he looked pathetic and said, 'Let's have that one.' And so it had all begun. And now Willie was, in dog terms, middle-aged, but he still thought Mrs. Dixon was his mother and his rescuer and his benefactor and sang to her daily of his feelings and howled every time she went out. 'Alo-o-o-ne,' he would wail. 'She has left me alone again and I am wretched and she is cruel and she doesn't love me and I am all al-o-o-o-one.' After about five minutes he would get tired of this, find himself a nice warm comfortable place and sleep soundly till she came back again.

One Sunday the Dixons all went out to a wild-life park. Since wild-life parks do not welcome dogs Willie had to be left behind. Mrs. Dixon put out a very large meal for him so that there would be no question of him getting hungry if they were late back. Willie watched her do this with an expression of abject misery that said, quite distinctly, that he thought her unfeeling and insensitive to imagine for a moment that he would be able to eat a thing, deserted and abandoned and unloved. Mrs. Dixon told him briskly that he'd be fine. The Dixons left the house, locked the door, got into the car and drove off. Willie howled for exactly five minutes, then stopped, found that he was actually feeling a little peckish after all, went to his bowl and wolfed down half a tin of dog food and a handful of biscuits in thirty seconds flat.

'Creep!' said Sam, the father of the mouse family whose home was at the bottom of a box of old newspapers under the stairs. He had come out for a quick day-time forage around the kitchen.

'Mind your own business!' snarled Willie. He felt comfortably sleepy now, after that extra large meal, and was wondering where to curl up and have a good long snooze. The door to the sitting room was shut, which was a nuisance – he was specially fond of the sofa.

Sam whisked up onto the dresser, discovered that Mrs. Dixon had left out the packet of dog biscuits, nipped inside and helped himself to one. 'Your trouble,' he continued, with his mouth full of biscuit, 'is that you've no sense of get up and go. No push. No oomph and zoom. You just hang about – wait for it to happen . . .'

'Leave those biscuits alone,' spluttered Willie.

'No way,' said Sam. 'Proves my point. All things come to them as helps themselves. Now me, I go out and look for it.'

Willie glared. 'Belt up, can't you.'

Sam shrugged. 'Now if you spoke nicely to me I might see my way to chucking you down an extra biscuit.'

But Willie was no longer hungry. He was extremely full and very sleepy. He couldn't be bothered to quarrel with Sam any more. He pottered out of the kitchen and up the stairs, in search of a good sleeping place. He looked in the children's room, which was a muddle of toys and did not interest him. The bathroom was boring also. But then he discovered to his joy the Dixons' bedroom door had been left not properly closed. He gave it a good shove with his nose and went in. Oh, wonderful! If there was one place in the house that Willie preferred above all it was Mr. and Mrs. Dixon's bed; it was the one place, also, that was absolutely forbidden. But here he was, all alone, no one would discover him – as soon as he heard them coming back he could dash down the stairs and go through the welcome home routine as hard as he could. No one would know where he had been.

He jumped up on the bed and shuffled around a bit to make himself a nice nest. Then it occurred to him that he could do better than that. He scrabbled at the cover, got his nose underneath, heaved up the sheet and blankets and wriggled right down to the bottom of the bed. It was dark, private, and smelled gloriously of Mrs. Dixon. It was paradise. Dogs, long ago and far back in their ancestries, were den animals, which is why they still like creeping under the furniture and into cosy, hidden places.

Willie had found the perfect den. He gave a great sigh of contentment and sank into a deep, deep sleep.

Towards the end of the afternoon the Dixons returned. Willie, buried in the bottom of the bed, heard nothing. He was still sleeping off that extra large meal. He slept and slept.

The Dixons searched for Willie. They searched the whole house. Mrs. Dixon popped her head round the bedroom door, saw that the bed was a little untidy but thought that the children had been jumping on it. She came downstairs again and an almighty argument broke out between Mr. and Mrs. Dixon as to whether or not Mr. Dixon had seen to it that Willie was back inside the house before they left.

'You knew I was busy getting the picnic ready,' scolded Mrs. Dixon. 'I told you to put him out in the garden for five minutes and then see he was safe in the kitchen. You must have left him outside.'

'And he's gone off and got run over,' wailed Julie Dixon.

'Or been stolen,' cried Andy Dixon.

'I tell you he was in the kitchen,' shouted their father.

'He can't have been,' snapped Mrs. Dixon.

'And I tell you he was,' bawled her husband.

The argument died down, as family arguments will. Whoever had done what, Willie was no longer there, which was the important thing. The children were sent to ask all the neighbours if anyone had seen anything of him. Mr. Dixon drove around in the car, looking for him. There was nothing to be seen or heard of a squarish, rather overweight rough-haired white terrier.

Mrs. Dixon rang up the police, who were polite and took down details but made it clear that they could not, as she suggested, put several men on the job immediately. They did, they gently pointed out, have other things to do apart from looking for people's lost dogs. Mrs. Dixon, by now, was quite distraught; she put the phone down and turned on Mr. Dixon again.

The entire Dixon family were by now squabbling. Mr. Dixon –

poor fellow – was blamed for having left Willie outside, however much he went on insisting that he hadn't. The children kept bursting into tears as they imagined the dreadful things that must have happened. Mrs. Dixon, who just felt guilty in general, was snapping at everyone. Eventually she said that they had had a long day and everyone was overtired and had better go to bed. She drove the children into the bath, scurried them through their supper and tucked them up. Then she and her husband watched the news – there were no headlines, as she felt there ought to be, about 'All police leave was cancelled in the Birmingham area this evening as the search intensified for a small white terrier named Willie . . .' At last they locked the front door, turned out the lights and went upstairs.

They undressed. Mrs. Dixon used the bathroom. She came back to the bedroom and took off the bedcover. She said, 'The children have been messing about in here again – just look at the state this is in.' Mrs. Dixon folded the cover, put it on the chair, kicked off her slippers and slid down into the bed.

Her feet landed on something warm and hairy. She shot backwards with a yell.

Willie crawled out from under the bedclothes, blinking and looking somewhat rumpled. He saw Mrs. Dixon standing beside the bed in her nightdress, began to fling himself joyfully at her, remembered with horror that he had no business to be where he was, panicked and tried to dive under the bed, where he stuck fast.

Mr. Dixon hauled him out by the back legs. The children, woken by the commotion, came rushing in. Willie rolled over on his back and cringed at everyone, rolling his eyes till the whites showed. 'Don't beat me,' he begged. 'Don't murder me. It was all a ghastly mistake. I didn't mean to. I swear I never will again. If you weren't so cruel and horrible, leaving me all on my own without a bite to eat and those blessed mice making fun of me, it would never have happened.'

Willie wasn't beaten. Some stern words were said, especially by Mr. Dixon. Willie was marched smartly downstairs and put to bed in the kitchen. He never got into the Dixons' bed again; not, I'm afraid, because he had learned a lesson but because Mrs. Dixon took special care not to leave the door of the bedroom open.

MAKING MONEY
OUT OF DOGS
A tale of the great depression

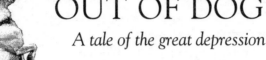

Len Lower
(Australian) 1903–47

'I've been readin' the paper, Bill, and I've got an idea.'
'You don't say! Well, them newspapers must be improvin'
outer sight. 'Ang out the flag – little Jimmy's got an idear.'

'Listen to me. Work is as scarce in Sydney as the butter in a
hot-dog.'

'Too right, James. Too blooming true.'

'Don't interrupt me, you igerant cow, or I'll take my singlet off
you! As I was sayin' about this idea – you know the "Lost and
Found" column?'

'Yeah.'

'Well, look at the hundreds of things that are lost every day and
found by people who ain't lookin' for 'em. And the rewards! There's
money just for the picking up!'

'Yes! I know – "Lost, small leather bag, containing slate and
pencil, between Manly and Petersham. Finder keep slate, return
bag" – and rolls of notes. Now, I ask you, Jimmie, did you ever 'ear of
anyone finding a roll of notes? No! of course you didn't. It's a
damn lie!'

'There's jewellery,' suggested Jimmy.

'Huh! 'Angin' round waitin' for someone to drop their diamond
tiara outer the tram.'

'Well, what about lost cats and dogs?'

'Look 'ere! If you think I'm going to spend me time crawlin' over roofs collecting cats, in the 'opes that one of 'em's lost – you're mistaken. My ruddy oath, you are!'

'Dogs,' remarked Jimmy. 'Now here's one: 'Lost, white pomeranium, black ears, answers to name of "Oozles".' You'd sight that dog out of a million. A white pom with black ears!'

Bill walked to the window and draped himself over the sill.

'A fine chance,' he remarked to the street, 'a man's got "Oozlin" every dog 'e sees with – Hoi! Blime!'

With a rush that knocked his friend off the chair, Bill had left the window, and was now clattering down the stairs to the front door.

Jimmy picked himself up, and gazed out the window.

'Struth!' he yelled, and dived for the door.

Outside, a white pomeranian with black ears sniffed disgustedly at a banana skin in the gutter.

''Ead 'im orf!' gasped Bill.

Jimmy spat disgustedly over his shoulder:

'Nobody mistook me for Nurmi before,' he panted. ''Ead 'im orf yourself.'

The dog, not having the incentive of an urgent need of cash, gave in; and Bill, first on the scene, gathered him up.

'That your dog?'

'Eh?' said Bill, turning to the constable who had apparently manifested himself from a hole in the road.

'Course he's my dorg! I wouldn't be bustin' meself chasin' someone else's dorg. S'matter of fact, me and my mate (pointing to Jimmy who had just lumbered up) were trainin' 'im. I tell y'constable (he dropped his voice to a whisper), first time we gives 'im a run at the tin 'are – be on 'im.'

He moved off.

'Walk quick, you mug,' said Jimmy fearfully. 'They don't race pomeraniums after hares! You nearly cruelled it.'

It was a long walk back.

'Well,' said Bill, in the safety of their lodgings, 'there 'e is.'

'Yes,' said Jimmy, gazing down at the dog.

'Poor liddle Oozles. Here, Oozles, Oozles!'

'Oh, Blime! Oozles!' said Bill, 'what a name to give the poor little cow. No wonder 'e's got black ears. 'Ere, Stinker!'

The dog wearily wagged his busy tail.

'There, y'are!' said Bill, triumphantly. ''E knows a proper dorg's name when 'e 'ears it.'

Jimmy was studying the paper again.

'He belongs to "Dilhurst," Darlinghurst Road. We'll give him that frankfurt you was keeping for your tea, and then I'll take him along.'

'Orright,' said Bill, 'I'll starve.'

Man and dog were gone an hour, when Bill, from his eyrie in the window, sighted them coming back.

'Aw, strike me pink!' he muttered, withdrawing himself from the window, 'I knew 'e'd muck it up.'

He sat on the bed, turning over in his mind a few pithy remarks to be delivered to James.

The door opened.

''Ullo, brains! What the 'ell did you bring the dorg back for? No wonder you can't get a job. You got about as much gumption as a politician—'

'Shut up, Sunshine! Gaze on this, an' apologize.'

Two pound notes were waving before his eyes. His mouth opened.

'Now shut up!' said Jimmy. 'I'll do all the talkin', same as I do all the thinkin'.'

He seated himself on the bed and commenced.

'I goes up to the house, a big flash joint it is, knocks at the door, and a tony old tart comes as soon as she hears I've got the dog. "My little Oozlums", she says. "Diddums got losty wosty?" Fair make you vomit.'

'She asks me a lot of questions, and I tells her 'ow I threw meself in front of a 'bus just in time to save him, and she comes to light with a quid.'

'Well, I'm going out the gate, and there's a bloke waiting for me.'

'"Did you bring that damn dog back?" he says, real fierce.'

'"Yes," I says, "an' I had a hard job to fetch him."'

'"Lord!" he says, "and I had a hell of a job losing him."'

'He does his block.'

'"I don't want the rotten thing in the house," he yaps. "How much did my wife give you?"'

'I tells him a quid.'

'"Well, look here," he says, "here's another quid. You hang about, and I'll push him out the door when she's not looking, and you lose him! See! Lose him!"'

'Yes,' said Bill. 'Go on.'

'Well, I waits, and sure enough out comes Oozles—'

'Stinker,' amended Bill.

'And I pounces on him, and here we are.'

With a flourish, Jimmy pocketed a pound and handed Bill the other.

'Well, what'll we do with the dorg?' said Bill.

'I got another idea,' said James. 'I'm goin' out now to buy him a chop and drink your health, William.'

'I can't let you do everythink without 'elping you sometimes,' said Bill. 'I'll go with you.'

Next morning, an excited Bill was reading to his mate: 'Lorst, a valuable white pomer-what's-its-name, with black ears. Strayed from "Dilhurst," Darlinghurst Road. Answers to name of Oozles. Reward £3. Detainer persecuted.'

Jimmy smiled indulgently at his friend. 'That was my other idea,' he said calmly. 'That's why I brought him back. It's your turn to find him now.'

Bill gazed at him.

'Well, I won't say you're brainy; but for low cunning you'd beat a sackful of monkeys, Jimmy. I'm erstounded at you. I'll take Stinker up this afternoon.'

'And after that we'll have to find another dog,' said Jimmy. 'This one'll be played out.'

'You know, James, we could make a business of this dorg-findin'. "Lorst dorgs recovered – findings executed with utmost dispatch" – an' all that. Work it up into a big business, an' sell out.'

'I'll think it over,' said Jimmy loftily.

Late that afternoon, Bill stood at the door of 'Dilhurst.'

'Yairs,' Bill was saying, 'the young 'ooligans had 'im tied on the tram line, an' I was just in time to stop the tram.'

'Did you give them in charge?' asked the lady indignantly.

'Every bloomin' one of 'em, missus. Eleven there was – an' I 'ope for Stink – for Oozles' sake, they get six months each.'

'Henry,' she said, turning to a man who had appeared in the hallway, 'this man has just brought my little Oozles back.'

'Oh! Has he?'

He came to the door.

'Just wait a moment and I'll bring you your reward,' said the lady to Bill, and disappeared.

'Where did you find that rotten pampered mongrel?' whispered the man. 'You ought to have more sense than to bring the thing back here.'

'But you lorst it!' said Bill, agape.

'Take it away! You curse – yes, and I am very pleased indeed to see that there are still men kind enough to take care of a defence-less doggie-woggie.'

'Give this to the man and thank him nicely, Henry,' said the lady from behind his back.

Three pounds changed hands, and disappeared into Bill's pocket.

'Well, I'll be goin',' said Bill.

'Stop!' hissed the man, gazing after his wife's retreating form. 'Here!' – A fiver!

'Here!' – the dog!

Bill took both.

'Take it to b—!'

'Bankstown?' suggested Bill.

'Bourke!' blurted the man. 'Get!'

Bill got.

Contentedly Oozles trotted alongside him back to the lodging house.

Jim was there.

'Mug! Mug! Oh what a large, empty blooming mug! What did you bring him back for?'

'Gaze on this bunch,' said Bill, flourishing the notes, 'an' go down on yore bended knees an' weep tears of blood!'

'Willie,' said James earnestly, 'if that dog is seen with us, we'll get years in the cooler.'

'Why?' said Bill, in amazement.

'You know that cop what saw us pick him up? Well, I seen him today and he buttons me. That old tart must have notified all the police stations about that dog. He's worth pounds and pounds! I didn't know how to get out of it, and I finishes up telling him the truth about us wanting to get the reward, and how we took him back, and it ain't our fault if he's lost again. We're alright now, because he was a decent John; but if we're seen with that dog again – we'll finish up eatin' with a wooden spoon!'

'Gaw!' exclaimed Bill.

'Did the bloke tell you to take him away?'

'Yeah. To Bankstown.'

'That's the ticket! You take him to Bankstown, and leave him. Go now – better wrap him up in a parcel so no one'll see him.'

The wrapping of a live dog in a newspaper is no easy job, nor is it any easier keeping him in the parcel whilst going past policemen. Bill drew a huge sigh of relief as the train bore him back from Bankstown – dogless – and the two men spent a happy evening over several bottles and a bed-full of fish and chips.

It was therefore with feelings of intense horror that Bill viewed the spectacle of a dilapidated pomeranian dog wagging his tail on the mat next morning.

He called Jim, and pointed.

They looked at each other, and a telepathic vision of prison cells communicated itself to their minds.

'Wrap 'im again,' said Bill tersely. 'It's your turn to lose 'im this time.'

In silence they wrapped him. Jim took him away, and some considerable time elapsed before he returned.

'Took him to Manly,' he said, throwing his hat on the bed. 'Put yer 'at on again,' said Bill.

'Why?'

'We're movin'.'

'Why? What did she say?'

''Oo?'

'The landlady?'

'Nothink. She don't know we're goin'.'

'Well, what—?'

'Do y'think,' said Bill, getting annoyed, 'we want to be 'ere when that damn dorg comes back?'

'Strike me! No. Got all my things?'

'I got your singlet an' the shavin' soap.'

'That's right, come on. Walk soft.'

SNAPSHOT
OF A DOG

James Thurber
(American) 1894–1961

I ran across a dim photograph of him the other day. He's been dead 25 years. His name was Rex (my two brothers and I named him) and he was a bull terrier. 'An American bull terrier,' we used to say, proudly; none of your English bulls. He had one brindle eye that sometimes made him look like a clown and sometimes reminded you of a politician with derby hat and cigar. The rest of him was white except for a brindle saddle and a brindle stocking on a hind leg. Nevertheless, there was a nobility about him. He was big and muscular and beautifully made. He never lost his dignity even when trying to accomplish the extravagant tasks my brother and I used to set for him.

One of these was the bringing of a ten-foot wooden rail into the yard through the back gate. We would throw it out into the alley and tell him to get it. Rex was as powerful as a wrestler, and he would catch the rail at the balance, lift it clear of the ground, and trot with great confidence toward the gate. Of course, the gate being only four feet wide, he couldn't bring the rail in broadside. He found that out when he got a few terrific jolts, but he wouldn't give up. He finally figured out how to do it, by dragging the rail, holding onto one end, growling. He got a great, wagging satisfaction out of his work.

He was a tremendous fighter, but he never started fights. He never went for a dog's throat but for one of its ears (that teaches a dog a lesson), and he would get his grip, close his eyes, and hold on. He could hold on for hours. His longest fight lasted from dusk to

87

almost pitch-dark, one Sunday. It was fought with a large, snarly nondescript belonging to a large colored man. When Rex finally got his ear grip, the brief whirlwind of snarling turned to screeching. It was frightening to listen to and to watch. The Negro boldly picked the dogs up, swung them around his head, and finally let them fly like a hammer in a hammer throw, but although they landed ten feet away, with a great plump, Rex still held on. Working their way to the middle of the car tracks, two or three streetcars were held up by the fight. A motorman tried to pry Rex's jaws open with a switch rod; somebody lighted a stick and held it to Rex's tail but he paid no attention. Rex's joy of battle, when battle was joined, was almost tranquil. He had a kind of pleasant expression during fights, his eyes closed in what would have seemed to be sleep had it not been for the turmoil of the struggle. The Fire Department finally had to be sent for and a powerful stream of water turned on the dogs for several moments before Rex finally let go.

The story of that Homeric fight got all around town, and some of our relatives considered it a blot on the family name. They insisted that we get rid of Rex, but nobody could have made us give him up. We would have left town with him first. It would have been different, perhaps, if he had ever looked for trouble. But he had a gentle disposition. He never bit a person in the ten strenuous years that he lived, nor ever growled at anyone except prowlers.

Swimming was his favorite recreation. The first time he ever saw a body of water, he trotted nervously along the steep bank for a while, fell to barking wildly, and finally plunged in from a height of eight feet or more. I shall always remember that shining, virgin dive. Then he swam upstream and back just for the pleasure of it, like a man. It was fun to see him battle upstream against a stiff current, growling every foot of the way. He had as much fun in the water as any person I have ever known. You didn't have to throw a stick into the water to get him to go in. Of course, he would bring back a stick if you did throw one in. He would have brought back a piano if you had thrown one in.

That reminds me of the night he went a-roving in the light of the moon and brought back a small chest of drawers he had found somewhere – how far from the house nobody ever knew. There were no drawers in the chest when he got it home, and it wasn't a good one – just an old cheap piece abandoned on a trash heap. Still it was something he wanted, probably because it presented a nice problem in transportation. We first knew about his achievement when, deep in the night, we heard sounds as if two or three people were trying to tear the house down. We came downstairs and turned on the porch light. Rex was on the top step, trying to pull the thing up, but it had caught and he was just holding his own. I suppose he would have held his own until dawn if we hadn't helped him. Next day we carted the chest miles away and threw it out. If we had thrown it out nearby, he would have brought it home again, as a small token of his integrity in such matters.

There was in his world no such thing as the impossible. Even death couldn't beat him down. He died, it is true, but only, as one of his admirers said, after 'straight-arming the death angel' for more than an hour. Late one afternoon he wandered home, too slowly and uncertainly to be the Rex that had trotted briskly homeward up our avenue for ten years. I think we all knew when he came through the gate that he was dying. He had apparently taken a terrible beating, probably from the owner of some dog he had got into a fight with. His head and body were scarred, and some of the brass studs of his heavy collar were sprung loose. He licked at our hands and, staggering, fell, but got up again. We could see that he was looking for someone. One of his three masters was not home. He did not get home for an hour. During that hour the bull terrier fought against death as he had fought against the cold, strong current of the creek. When the person he was waiting for did come through the gate, whistling, ceasing to whistle, Rex walked a few wobbly paces toward him, touched his hand with his muzzle, and fell down again. This time he didn't get up.

HERMANN
– A HAPPY
ENDING

James Herriot
(British) 1916–95

W AS there no peace in a vet's life? I wondered fretfully as I
hurried my car along the road to Gilthorpe village. Eight
o'clock on a Sunday evening and here I was trailing off to visit a
dog ten miles away which, according to Helen who had taken the
message, had been ailing for more than a week.

After a long and busy day, I had hoped for a quiet evening, yet
here I was back on the treadmill, staring through the windscreen at
the roads and the walls which I saw day in, day out. When I left
Darrowby the streets of the little town were empty in the gathering
dusk and the houses had that tight-shut, comfortable look which
raised images of armchairs and pipes and firesides, and now as I saw
the lights of the farms winking on the fellsides I could picture the
stocksmen dozing contentedly with their feet up.

I had not passed a single car on the darkening road. There was
nobody out but Herriot.

I was really sloshing around in my trough of self-pity when I drew up
outside a row of greystone cottages at the far end of Gilthorpe. Mrs.
Cundall, Number 4, Chestnut Row, Helen had written on the slip
of paper and as I opened the gate and stepped through the tiny strip of
garden my mind was busy with half-formed ideas of what I was
going to say.

My few years' experience in practice had taught me that it did
no good at all to remonstrate with people for calling me out at

unreasonable times. I knew perfectly well that my words never seemed to get through to them and that they would continue to do so exactly as they had done before, but for all that I had to say something if only to make me feel better.

No need to be rude or ill-mannered, just a firm statement of the position; that vets liked to relax on Sunday evenings just like other people; that we did not mind at all coming out for emergencies but that we did object to having to visit animals which had been ill for a week.

I had my speech fairly well prepared when a little middle-aged woman opened the door.

'Good evening, Mrs. Cundall,' I said, slightly tight-lipped.

'Oh, it's Mr. Herriot.' She smiled shyly. 'We've never met but I've seen you walkin' round Darrowby on market days. Come inside.'

The door opened straight into the little low-beamed living-room and my first glance took in the shabby furniture and some pictures framed in tarnished gilt when I noticed that the end of the room was partly curtained off.

Mrs. Cundall pulled the curtain aside. In a narrow bed a man was lying, a skeleton-thin man whose eyes looked up at me from hollows in a yellowed face.

'This is my husband, Ron,' she said cheerfully, and the man smiled and raised a bony arm from the quilt in greeting.

'And here is your patient – Hermann,' she went on, pointing to a little dachshund who sat by the side of the bed.

'Hermann?'

'Yes, we thought it was a good name for a German sausage dog.' They both laughed.

'An excellent name. He looks just like a Hermann.'

The little animal gazed up at me, bright-eyed and welcoming. I bent down and stroked his head and the pink tongue flickered over my fingers.

I ran my hand over the glossy skin. 'He looks very healthy. What's the trouble?'

'Oh, he's fine in himself,' Mrs. Cundall replied. 'Eats well and everything, but over the last week he's been goin' funny on 'is legs.

We weren't all that worried but tonight he sort of flopped down and couldn't get up again.'

'I see. I noticed he didn't seem keen to rise when I patted his head.' I put my hand under the little dog's body and gently lifted him on to his feet. 'Come on, lad,' I said. 'Come on, Hermann, let's see you walk.'

As I encouraged him he took a few hesitant steps but his hind end swayed progressively and he soon dropped into the sitting position again.

'It's his back, isn't it?' Mrs. Cundall said. 'He's strong enough on 'is forelegs.'

'That's ma trouble, too,' Ron murmured in a soft husky voice, but he was smiling and his wife laughed and patted the arm on the quilt.

I lifted the dog on to my knee. 'Yes, the weakness is certainly in the back.' I began to palpate the lumbar vertebrae, feeling my way along, watching for any sign of pain.

'Has he hurt 'imself?' Mrs. Cundall asked. 'Has somebody hit 'im? We don't usually let him out alone but sometimes he sneaks through the garden gate.'

'There's always the possibility of an injury,' I said. 'But there are other causes.' There were indeed – a host of unpleasant possibilities. I did not like the look of this little dog at all. This syndrome was one of the things I hated to encounter in canine practice.

'Can you tell me what you really think?' she said. 'I'd like to know.'

'Well, an injury could cause haemorrhage or concussion or oedema – that's fluid – all affecting his spinal cord. He could even have a fractured vertebra but I don't think so.'

'And how about the other causes.'

'There's quite a lot. Tumours, bony growths, abscesses or discs can press on the cord.'

'Discs?'

'Yes, little pads of cartilage and fibrous tissue between the vertebrae. In long-bodied dogs like Hermann they sometimes protrude into the spinal canal. In fact I think that is what is causing his symptoms.'

Ron's husky voice came again from the bed. 'And what's 'is prospects, Mr. Herriot?'

Oh, that was the question. Complete recovery or incurable paralysis. It could be anything. 'Very difficult to say at this moment,' I replied. 'I'll give him an injection and some tablets and we'll see how he goes over the next few days.'

I injected an analgesic and some antibiotic and counted out some salicylate tablets into a box. We had no steroids at that time. It was the best I could do.

'Now then, Mr. Herriot.' Mrs. Cundall smiled at me eagerly. 'Ron has a bottle o' beer every night about this time. Would you like to join 'im?'

'Well . . . it's very kind of you but I don't want to intrude . . .'

'Oh, you're not doing that. We're glad to see you.'

She poured two glasses of brown ale, propped her husband up with pillows and sat down by the bed.

'We're from South Yorkshire, Mr. Herriot,' she said.

I nodded. I had noticed the difference from the local accent.

'Aye, we came up here after Ron's accident, eight years ago.'

'What was that?'

'I were a miner,' Ron said. 'Roof fell in on me. I got a broken back, crushed liver and a lot o' other internal injuries, but two of me mates were killed in the same fall so ah'm lucky to be 'ere.' He sipped his beer. 'I've survived, but doctor says I'll never walk no more.'

'I'm terribly sorry.'

'Nay, nay,' the husky voice went on. 'I count me blessings and I've got a lot to be thankful for. Ah suffer very little and I've got t'best wife in the world.'

Mrs. Cundall laughed. 'Oh, listen to 'im. But I'm right glad we came to Gilthorpe. We used to spend all our holidays in the Dales. We were great walkers and it was lovely to get away from the smoke and the chimneys. The bedroom in our old house just looked out on a lot o' brick walls but Ron has this big window right by 'im and he can see for miles.'

'Yes, of course,' I said. 'This is a lovely situation.' The village was perched on a high ridge on the fellside and that window would command a wide view of the green slopes running down to the river and climbing high to the wildness of the moor on the other side. This sight had beguiled me so often on my rounds and the grassy paths climbing among the airy tops seemed to beckon to me. But they would beckon in vain to Ron Cundall.

'Gettin' Hermann was a good idea, too,' he said. 'Ah used to feel a bit lonely when t'missus went into Darrowby for shoppin' but the little feller's made all the difference. You're never alone when you've got a dog.'

I smiled. 'How right you are. What is his age now, by the way?'

'He's six,' Ron replied. 'Right in the prime o' life, aren't you, old lad.' He let his arm fall by the bedside and his hand fondled the sleek ears.

'That seems to be his favourite place.'

'Aye, it's a funny thing, but 'e allus sits there. T'missus is the one who has to take 'im walks and feeds 'im but he's very faithful to me. He has a basket over there but this is 'is place. I only have to reach down and he's there.'

This was something that I had seen on many occasions with disabled people; that their pets stayed close by them as if conscious of their role of comforter and friend.

I finished my beer and got to my feet. Ron looked up at me. 'Reckon I'll spin mine out a bit longer.' He glanced at his half-full glass. 'Ah used to shift about six pints some nights when I went out wi' the lads but you know, I enjoy this one bottle just as much. Strange how things turn out.'

His wife bent over him, mock-scolding. 'Yes, you've had to right your ways. You're a reformed character, aren't you?'

They both laughed as though it were a stock joke between them.

'Well, thank you for the drink, Mrs. Cundall. I'll look in to see Hermann on Tuesday.' I moved towards the door.

As I left I waved to the man in the bed and his wife put her hand on my arm. 'We're very grateful to you for comin' out at this time on a Sunday night, Mr. Herriot. We felt awful about callin' you, but you understand it was only today that the little chap started going off his legs like that.'

'Oh, of course, of course, please don't worry. I didn't mind in the least.'

And as I drove through the darkness I knew that I didn't mind – now. My petty irritation had evaporated within two minutes of my entering that house and I was left only with a feeling of humility. If that man back there had a lot to be thankful for, how about me? I had everything. I only wished I could dispel the foreboding I felt about his dog. There was a hint of doom about those symptoms of Hermann and yet I knew I just had to get him right . . .

The following Tuesday he looked much the same, possibly a little worse.

'I think I'd better take him back to the surgery for X-ray,' I said to Mrs. Cundall. 'He doesn't seem to be improving with the treatment.'

In the car Hermann curled up happily on the passenger seat.

I had no need to anaesthetise him or sedate him when I placed him on our newly acquired X-ray machine. Those hind quarters stayed still all by themselves. A lot too still for my liking.

I was no expert at interpreting X-ray pictures but at least I could be sure there was no fracture of the vertebrae. Also, there was no sign of bony extoses, but I thought I could detect a narrowing of the space between a couple of the vertebrae which would confirm my suspicions of a protrusion of a disc. I could do nothing more than continue with my treatment and hope.

By the end of the week hope had grown very dim. I had supplemented the salycilates with long-standing remedies like tincture of nux vomica and other ancient stimulant drugs, but when I saw Hermann on the Saturday he was unable to rise. I tweaked the toes of his hind limbs and was rewarded by a faint reflex movement, but with a sick certainty I knew that complete posterior paralysis was not far away.

A week later I had the unhappy experience of seeing my prognosis confirmed in the most classical way. When I entered the door of the Cundall's cottage Hermann came to meet me, happy and welcoming in his front end but dragging his hind limbs helplessly behind him.

'Hello, Mr. Herriot.' Mrs. Cundall gave me a wan smile and looked down at the little creature stretched frog-like on the carpet. 'What d'you think of him now?'

I bent and tried the reflexes. Nothing. I shrugged my shoulders, unable to think of anything to say. I looked at the gaunt figure in the bed, the arm outstretched as always on the quilt. 'Good morning, Ron,' I said as cheerfully as I could, but there was no reply. The face was averted, looking out of the window. I walked over to the bed. Ron's eyes were staring fixedly at the glorious panorama of the moor and fell, at the pebbles of the river, white in the early sunshine, at the crisscross of the grey walls against the green. His face was expressionless. It was as though he did not know I was there.

I went back to his wife. I don't think I have ever felt more miserable.

'Is he annoyed with me?' I whispered.

'No, no, no, it's this.' She held out a newspaper. 'It's upset him something awful.'

I looked at the printed page. There was a large picture at the top, a picture of a dachshund exactly like Hermann. This dog, too, was paralysed but its hind end was supported by a little four-wheeled bogie. In the picture it appeared to be sporting with its mistress. In fact it looked quite happy and normal except for those wheels.

Ron seemed to hear the rustle of the paper because his head came round quickly. 'What d'ye think of that, Mr. Herriot? D'ye agree with it?'

'Well . . . I don't really know, Ron. I don't like the look of it, but I suppose the lady in the picture thought it was the only thing to do.'

'Aye, maybe.' The husky voice trembled. 'But ah don't want Hermann to finish up like that.' The arm dropped by the side of the bed and his fingers felt around on the carpet, but the little dog was still splayed out near the door. 'It's 'opeless now, Mr. Herriot, isn't it?'

'Well, it was a black look-out from the beginning,' I said. 'These cases are so difficult. I'm very sorry.'

'Nay, I'm not blamin' you,' he said. 'You've done what ye could, same as vet for that dog in the picture did what 'e could. But it was no good, was it? What do we do now – put 'im down?'

'Rex was as powerful as a wrestler, and he would catch
the rail at the balance, lift it clear of the ground,
and trot with great confidence toward the gate.'
SNAPSHOT OF A DOG

'. . . his servant entered, carrying in front of her, opossum-like,
a tiny creature whose black head peeped out from the folds of
her apron, which she had turned up to form a pocket.'
THE COMING OF RIQUET

'When he was only three weeks old he pointed a butterfly
that lit in the yard in front of his nose.'

COMET

'He was of that particular shade of dark brown which in sunshine
flashes "all over into gold". His eyes were "startled eyes of hazel bland".
His ears were "tasselled"; his "slender feet" were "canopied
in fringes" and his tail was broad.'

FLUSH: A BIOGRAPHY

'No, Ron, forget about that just now. Sometimes paralysis cases just recover on their own after many weeks. We must carry on. At this moment I honestly cannot say there is no hope.'

I paused for a moment, then turned to Mrs. Cundall. 'One of the problems is the dog's natural functions. You'll have to carry him out into the garden for that. I'm sure you'll soon learn how to cope.'

'Oh, of course, of course,' she replied. 'I'll do anything. As long as there's some hope.'

'There is, I assure you, there is.'

But on the way back to the surgery the thought hammered in my brain. That hope was very slight. Spontaneous recovery did some-times occur but Hermann's condition was extreme. I repressed a groan as I thought of the nightmarish atmosphere which had begun to surround my dealings with the Cundalls. The paralysed man and the paralysed dog. And why did that picture have to appear in the paper just at this very time? Every veterinary surgeon knows the feeling that fate has loaded the scales against him and it weighed on me despite the bright sunshine spreading into the car.

However, I kept going back every few days. Sometimes I took a couple of bottles of brown ale along in the evening and drank them with Ron. He and his wife were always cheerful but the little dog never showed the slightest sign of improvement. He still had to pull his useless hind limbs after him when he came to greet me, and though he always returned to his station by his master's bed, nuzzling up into Ron's hand, I was beginning to resign myself to the certainty that one day that arm would come down from the quilt and Hermann would not be there.

It was on one of these visits that I noticed an unpleasant smell as I entered the house. There was something familiar about it.

I sniffed and the Cundalls looked at each other guiltily. There was a silence and then Ron spoke.

'It's some medicine ah've been givin' Hermann. Stinks like 'ell but it's supposed to be good for dogs.'

'Oh yes?'

'Aye, well . . .' His fingers twitched uncomfortably on the bedclothes. 'It was Bill Noakes put me on to it. He's an old mate o' mine – we used to work down t'pit together – and he came to visit me last weekend. Keeps a few whippets, does Bill. Knows a lot about dogs and 'e sent me this stuff along for Hermann.'

Mrs. Cundall went to the cupboard and sheepishly presented me with a plain bottle. I removed the cork and as the horrid stench rose up to me my memory became suddenly clear. Asafoetida, a common constituent of quack medicines before the war and still lingering on the shelves of occasional chemist shops and in the medicine chests of people who liked to doctor their own animals.

I had never prescribed the stuff myself but it was supposed to be beneficial in horses with colic and dogs with digestive troubles. My own feeling had always been that its popularity had been due solely to the assumption that anything which stank as badly as that must have some magical properties, but one thing I knew for sure was that it could not possibly do anything for Hermann.

I replaced the cork. 'So you're giving him this, eh?'

Ron nodded. 'Aye, three times a day. He doesn't like it much, but Bill Noakes has great faith in it. Cured hundreds o' dogs with it, 'e says.' The deep-sunk eyes looked at me with a silent appeal.

'Well, fine, Ron,' I said. 'You carry on. Let's hope it does the trick.'

I knew the asafoetida couldn't do any harm and since my treatment had proved useless I was in no position to turn haughty. But my main concern was that these two nice people had been given a glimmer of hope, and I wasn't going to blot it out.

Mrs. Cundall smiled and Ron's expression relaxed. 'That's grand, Mr. Herriot,' he said. 'Ah'm glad ye don't mind. I can dose the little feller myself. It's summat for me to do.'

It was about a week after the commencement of the new treatment that I called in at the Cundalls as I was passing through Gilthorpe.

'How are you today, Ron?' I asked.

'Champion, Mr. Herriot, champion.' He always said that, but today there was a new eagerness in his face. He reached down and lifted his dog on to the bed. 'Look 'ere.'

He pinched the little paw between his fingers and there was a faint but definite retraction of the leg. I almost fell over in my haste to grab at the other foot. The result was the same.

'My God, Ron,' I gasped, 'the reflexes are coming back.'

He laughed his soft husky laugh. 'Bill Noakes' stuff's working, isn't it?'

A gush of emotions, mainly professional shame and wounded pride, welled in me, but it was only for a moment. 'Yes, Ron,' I replied, 'it's working. No doubt about it.'

He stared up at me. 'Then Hermann's going to be all right?'

'Well, it's early days yet, but that's the way it looks to me.'

It was several weeks more before the little dachshund was back to normal and of course it was a fairly typical case of spontaneous recovery with nothing whatever to do with the asafoetida or indeed with my own efforts. Even now, thirty years later, when I treat these puzzling back conditions with steroids, I wonder how many of them would have recovered without my aid. Quite a number, I imagine.

Sadly, despite the modern drugs, we still have our failures and I always regard a successful termination with profound relief.

But that feeling of relief has never been stronger than it was with Hermann and I can recall vividly my final call at the cottage in Gilthorpe. As it happened it was around the same time as my first visit – eight o'clock in the evening, and when Mrs. Cundall ushered me in, the little dog bounded joyously up to me before returning to his post by the bed.

'Well, that's a lovely sight,' I said. 'He can gallop like a racehorse now.'

Ron dropped his hand down and stroked the sleek head. 'Aye, isn't it grand. By heck, it's been a worryin' time.'

'Well, I'll be going.' I gave Hermann a farewell pat. 'I just looked in on my way home to make sure all was well. I don't need to come any more now.'

'Nay, nay,' Ron said. 'Don't rush off. You've time to have a bottle o' beer with me before ye go.'

I sat down by the bed and Mrs. Cundall gave us our glasses before pulling up a chair for herself. It was exactly like that first night.

I poured my beer and looked at the two of them. Their faces glowed with friendliness and I marvelled because my part in Hermann's salvation had been anything but heroic.

In their eyes everything I have done must have seemed bumbling and ineffectual and in fact they must be convinced that all would have been lost if Ron's old chum from the coal-face had not stepped in and effortlessly put things right.

At best they could only regard me as an amiable fathead and all the explanations and protestations in the world would not alter that. But though my ego had been bruised I did not really care. I was witnessing a happy ending instead of a tragedy and that was more important than petty self-justification. I made a mental resolve never to say anything which might spoil their picture of this triumph.

I was about to take my first sip when Mrs. Cundall spoke up. 'This is your last visit, Mr. Herriot, and all's ended well. I think we ought to drink some sort o' toast.'

'I agree,' I said. 'Let's see, what shall it be? Ah yes, I've got it.' I raised my glass. 'Here's to Bill Noakes.'

VERDUN
BELLE

Alexander Woollcott
(American) 1887–1943

I first heard the saga of Verdun Belle's adventure as it was being told one June afternoon under a drowsy apple-tree in the troubled valley of the Marne.

The story began in a chill, grimy Lorraine village, where, in hovels and haymows, a disconsolate detachment of United States marines lay waiting the order to go up into that maze of trenches of which the crumbling traces still weave a haunted web around the citadel bearing the immortal name of Verdun.

Into this village at dusk one day in the early spring of 1918 there came out of space a shabby, lonesome dog – a squat setter of indiscreet, complex and unguessable ancestry.

One watching her as she trotted intently along the aromatic village street would have sworn that she had an important engagement with the mayor and was, regretfully, a little late.

At the end of the street she came to where a young buck private lounged glumly on a doorstep. Halting in her tracks, she sat down to contemplate him. Then, satisfied seemingly by what she sensed and saw, she came over and flopped down beside him in a most companionable manner, settling herself comfortably as if she had come at last to her long journey's end. His pleased hand reached over and played with one silken chocolate-coloured ear.

Somehow that gesture sealed a compact between those two. There was thereafter no doubt in either's mind that they belonged to each other for better or for worse, in sickness and in health, through weal and woe, world without end.

She ate when and what he ate. She slept beside him in the day, her muzzle resting on his leg so that he could not get up in the night and go forgetfully back to America without her noticing it.

To the uninitiated onlookers her enthusiasm may not have been immediately explicable. In the eyes of his top sergeant and his company clerk he may well have seemed an undistinguished warrior, freckle-faced and immensely indifferent to the business of making the world safe for democracy.

Verdun Belle thought him the most charming person in all the world. There was a loose popular notion that she had joined up with the company as mascot and belonged to them all. She affably let them think so, but she had her own ideas on the subject.

When they moved up into the line she went along and was so obviously trench-broken that they guessed she had already served a hitch with some French regiment in that once desperate region.

They even built up the not implausible theory that she had come to them lonely from the grave of some little soldier in faded horizon blue.

Certainly she knew trench ways, knew in the narrowest of passages how to keep out from underfoot and was so well aware of the dangers of the parapet that a plate of chicken bones up there would not have interested her. She even knew what gas was, and after a reminding whiff of it became more than reconciled to the regulation gas mask, which they patiently wrecked for all subsequent human use because an unimaginative War Department had not foreseen the peculiar anatomical specifications of Verdun Belle.

In May, when the outfit was engaged in the exhausting activities which the High Command was pleased to describe as 'resting,' Belle thought it a convenient time to present an interested but amply forewarned regiment with seven wriggling casuals, some black and white and mottled as a mackerel sky, some splotched with the same brown as her own.

These newcomers complicated the domestic economy of the leathernecks' haymow, but they did not become an acute problem until that memorable night late in the month when breathless word bade these troops be up and away.

The Second Division of the A.E.F. was always being thus picked up by the scruff of the neck and flung across France. This time the enemy had snapped up Soissons and Rheims and were pushing with dreadful ease and speed towards the remembering Marne.

Foch had called upon the Americans to help stem the tide. Ahead of the marines, as they scrambled across the monotonous plain of the Champagne, there lay amid the ripening wheat fields a mean and hilly patch of timber called Belleau Wood. Verdun Belle went along.

The leatherneck had solved the problem of the puppies by drowning four and placing the other three in a basket he had begged from a village woman.

His notion that he could carry the basket would have come as a shock to whatever functionary back in Washington designed the marine pack, which, with its neat assortment of food supplies, extra clothing, emergency restoratives, and gruesome implements for destruction, had been so painstakingly calculated to exhaust the capacity of the human back. But in his need the young marine somehow contrived to add an item not in the regulations – namely, one basket containing three unweaned and faintly resentful puppies.

By night and by day the troop movement was made, now in little wheezing trains, now in swarming lorries, now afoot.

Sometimes Belle's crony rode. Sometimes (under pressure of popular clamour against the room he was taking up) he would yield up his place to the basket and jog along with his hand on the tail-board, with Belle trotting behind him.

All the soldiers in Christendom seemed to be moving across France to some nameless crossroads over the hill. Obviously this was no mere shift from one quiet sector to another. They were going to war.

Everyone had assured the stubborn youngster that he would not be able to manage, and now misgivings settled on him like crows.

He guessed that Verdun Belle must be wondering too. He turned to assure her that everything would be all right. She was not there. Ahead of him, behind him, there was no sign of her. No one within call had seen her quit the line. He kept telling himself she would show up. But the day went and the night came without her.

He jettisoned the basket and pouched the pups in his forest-green shirt in the manner of kangaroos. In the morning one of the three was dead. And the problem of transporting the other two was now tangled by the circumstance that he had to feed them.

An immensely interested old woman in the village where they halted at dawn, vastly amused by this spectacle of a soldier trying to carry two nursing puppies to war, volunteered some milk for the cup of his mess kit, and with much jeering advice from all sides, and, by dint of the eye-dropper from his pack, he tried sheepishly to be a mother to the two waifs. The attempt was not shiningly successful.

He itched to pitch them over the fence. But if Verdun Belle had not been run over by some thundering camion, if she lived she would find him, and then what would he say when her eyes asked what he had done with the pups?

So, as the order was shouted to fall in, he hitched his pack to his back and stuffed his charges back into his shirt.

Now, in the morning light, the highway was choked. Down from the lines in agonized, grotesque rout came the stream of French life from the threatened countryside, jumbled fragments of fleeing French regiments. But America was coming up the road.

It was a week in which the world held its breath.

The battle was close at hand now. Field hospitals, jostling in the river of traffic, sought space to pitch their tents. The top sergeant of one such outfit was riding on the driver's seat of an ambulance. Marines in endless number were moving up fast.

It was one of these who, in a moment's halt, fell out of line, leaped to the step of the blockaded ambulance, and looked eagerly into the medico top sergeant's eyes.

'Say, buddy,' whispered the youngster, 'take care of these for me. I lost their mother in the jam.'

The Top found his hands closing on two drowsy pups.

All that day the field-hospital personnel was harried by the task of providing nourishment for the two casuals who had been thus unexpectedly attached to them for rations. Once established in a farmhouse (from which they were promptly shelled out), the Top went over the possible provender and found that the pups were not yet equal to a diet of bread, corn syrup and corned willy. A stray cow, loosed from her moorings in the great fight, was browsing tentatively in the next field, and two orderlies who had carelessly reminisced of life on their farms back home were detailed to induce her co-operation.

But the bombardment had brought out a certain moody goatishness in this cow, and she would not let them come near her. After a hot and maddening chase that lasted two hours, the two milkmen reported a complete failure to their disgusted chief.

The problem was still unsolved at sundown, and the pups lay faint in their bed of absorbent cotton out in the garden, when, bringing up the rear of a detachment of marines that straggled past, there trotted a brown-and-white setter.

'It would be swell if she had milk in her,' the top sergeant said reflectively, wondering how he could salvage the mascot of an outfit on the march.

But his larcenous thoughts were waste. At the gate she halted dead in her tracks, flung her head high to sniff the air, wheeled sharp to the left and became just a streak of brown and white against the ground. The entire staff came out and formed a jostling circle to watch the family reunion.

After that it was tacitly assumed that these casuals belonged. When the hospital was ordered to strife farther back beyond the reach of the whining shells, Verdun Belle and the pups were entrusted to an ambulance driver and went along in style. They all moved – bag, baggage and livestock – into the deserted little Château of the Guardian Angel, of which the front windows were curtained against the eyes and dust of the road, but of which the rear windows looked out across drooping fruit trees upon a sleepy, murmurous, multi-coloured valley, fair as the Garden of the Lord.

The operating tables, with acetylene torches to light them, were set up in what had been a tool shed. Cots were strewn in the orchard alongside. Thereafter for a month there was never rest in that hospital.

The surgeons and orderlies took spells, snatching morsels of sleep and returning a few hours later to relieve the others. But Verdun Belle took no time off. Between cat naps in the corner, due attentions to her restive brood and an occasional snack for herself, she managed somehow to be on hand for every ambulance, cursorily examining each casualty as he was lifted to the ground.

Then, in the four o'clock dark of one morning, the orderly bending over a stretcher that had just been rested on the ground was hit by something that half-bowled him over.

The projectile was Verdun Belle. Every quivering inch of her proclaimed to all concerned that here was a case she was personally in charge of. From nose to tail tip she was taut with excitement, and a kind of eager whimpering bubbled up out of her as if she ached to sit back on her haunches and roar to the star-spangled sky but was really too busy at the moment to indulge herself in any release so satisfying to her soul. For here was this mess of a leatherneck of hers to be washed up first. So like him to get all dirty the moment her back was turned! The first thing he knew as he came to was the feel of a rough pink tongue cleaning his ears.

I saw them all next day. An ambling passer-by, I came upon two cots shoved together under an apple-tree. Belle and her ravenous pups occupied one of these. On the other the young marine – a gas case, I think, but maybe his stupor was shell-shock and perhaps he had merely had a crack on the head – was deep in a dreamless sleep. Before drifting off he had taken the comforting precaution to reach out one hand and close it tight on a silken ear.

Later that day he told me all about his dog. I doubt if I ever knew his name, but some quirk of memory makes me think his home was in West Philadelphia and that he had joined up with the marines when he came out of school.

I went my way before dark and never saw them again, nor ever heard tell what became of the boy and his dog. I never knew when, if ever, he was shipped back into the fight, nor where, if ever, those two met again. It is, you see, a story without an end, though there must be those here and there in this country who witnessed and could set down for us the chapter that has never been written.

I hope there was something prophetic in the closing paragraph of the anonymous account of Verdun Belle which appeared the next week in the A.E.F. newspaper, *The Stars and Stripes*. That paragraph was a benison which ran in this wise:

> Before long they would have to ship him on to the evacuation hospital, on from there to the base hospital, on and on and on. It was not very clear to anyone how another separation could be prevented. It was a perplexing question, but they knew in their hearts they could safely leave the answer to someone else. They could leave it to Verdun Belle.

AN ADVENTURE WITH A DOG

John Muir

(Scots-American) 1838–1914

IN the summer of 1880 I set out from Fort Wrangel in a canoe, with the Reverend S. H. Young, my former companion, and a crew of Indians, to continue the exploration of the icy region of southeastern Alaska, begun in the fall of 1879. After the necessary provisions, blankets, etc., had been collected and stowed away, and the Indians were in their places ready to dip their paddles, while a crowd of their friends were looking down from the wharf to bid them good-bye and good luck, Mr. Young, for whom we were waiting, at length came aboard, followed by a little black dog that immediately made himself at home by curling up in a hollow among the baggage. I like dogs, but this one seemed so small, dull, and worthless that I objected to his going, and asked the missionary why he was taking him. 'Such a helpless wisp of hair will only be in the way,' I said; 'you had better pass him up to one of the Indian boys on the wharf, to be taken home to play with the children. This trip is not likely to be a good one for toy dogs. He will be rained on and snowed on for weeks, and will require care like a baby.' But the missionary assured me that he would be no trouble at all; that he was a perfect wonder of a dog – could endure cold and hunger like a polar bear, could swim like a seal, and was wondrous wise, etc., making out a list of virtues likely to make him the most interesting of the company.

Nobody could hope to unravel the lines of his ancestry. He was short-legged, bunchy-bodied, and almost featureless – something like a muskrat. Though smooth, his hair was long and silky, so that when the wind was at his back it ruffled, making him look shaggy. At first sight his only noticeable feature was his showy tail, which was about as shady and airy as a squirrel's, and was carried curling forward nearly to his ears. On closer inspection you might see his thin, sensitive ears and his keen dark eyes with cunning tan spots. Mr. Young told me that when the dog was about the size of a wood rat he was presented to his wife by an Irish prospector at Sitka, and that when he arrived at Fort Wrangel he was adopted by the Stickeen Indians as a sort of new good-luck totem, and named 'Stickeen' for the tribe, with whom he became a favorite. On our trip he soon proved himself a queer character – odd, concealed, independent, keeping invincibly quiet, and doing many inexplicable things that piqued my curiosity. Sailing week after week through the long, intricate channels and inlets among the innumerable islands and mountains of the coast, he spent the dull days in sluggish ease, motionless, and apparently as unobserving as a hibernating marmot. But I discovered that somehow he always knew what was going forward. When the Indians were about to shoot at ducks or seals, or when anything interesting was to be seen along the shore, he would rest his chin on the edge of the canoe and calmly look out. When he heard us talking about making a landing, he roused himself to see what sort of place we were coming to, and made ready to jump overboard and swim ashore as soon as the canoe neared the beach. Then, with a vigorous shake to get rid of the brine in his hair, he went into the woods to hunt small game. But though always the first out of the canoe, he was always the last to get into it. When we were ready to start he could never be found, and refused to come to our call. We soon found out, however, that though we could not see him at such times, he saw us, and from the cover of the briers and huckleberry bushes in the fringe of the woods was watching the canoe with wary eye. For as soon as we were fairly off, he came trotting down the beach, plunged into the surf, and swam after us, knowing well that we would cease rowing and take him in. When the contrary little vagabond came alongside, he was lifted by the neck, held at arm's length a moment to drip, and dropped aboard. We tried to cure him of this trick by compelling him to swim farther before stopping for him; but this did no good: the longer the swim, the better he seemed to like it.

Though capable of most spacious idleness, he was always ready for excursions or adventures of any sort. When the Indians went into the woods for a deer, Stickeen was sure to be at their heels, provided I had not yet left camp. For though I never carried a gun, he always followed me, forsaking the hunting Indians, and even his master, to share my wanderings. The days that were too stormy for sailing I spent in the woods, or on the mountains or glaciers, wherever I chanced to be; and Stickeen always insisted on follow-ing me, gliding through the dripping huckleberry bushes and prickly *Panax* and *Rubus* tangles like a fox, scarce stirring their close-set branches, wading and wallowing through snow, swimming ice-cold streams, jumping logs and rocks and the crusty hummocks and crevasses of glaciers with the patience and endurance of a determined mountaineer, never tiring or getting discouraged. Once he followed me over a glacier the surface of which was so rough that it cut his feet until every step was marked with blood; but he trotted on with Indian fortitude until I noticed his pain and, taking pity on him, made him a set of moccasins out of a handkerchief. But he never asked help or made any complaint, as if, like a philosopher, he had learned that without hard work and suffering there could be no pleasure worth having.

Yet nobody knew what Stickeen was good for. He seemed to meet danger and hardships without reason, insisted on having his own way, never obeyed an order, and the hunters could never set him on anything against his will, or make him fetch anything that was shot. I tried hard to make his acquaintance, guessing there must be something in him; but he was as cold as a glacier, and about as invulnerable to fun, though his master assured me that he played at home, and in some measure conformed to the usages of civilization. His equanimity was so immovable it seemed due to unfeeling igno-rance. Let the weather blow and roar, he was as tranquil as a stone; and no matter what advances you made, scarce a glance or a tail wag would you get for your pains. No superannuated mastiff or bulldog grown old in office surpassed this soft midget in stoic dignity. He sometimes reminded me of those plump, squat, unshakeable cacti of the Arizona deserts that give no sign of feeling. A true child of the wilderness, holding the even tenor of his hidden life with the silence and serenity of nature, he never displayed a trace of the elfish vivacity and fun of the terriers and collies that we all know, nor of their touching affection and devotion. Like children, most small dogs beg to be loved and allowed to love, but Stickeen seemed a very Diogenes, asking only to be let alone. He seemed neither old nor young. His strength lay in his eyes. They looked as old as the hills, and as young and as wild. I never tired looking into them. It was like looking into a landscape; but they were small and rather deep-set, and had no explaining puckers around them to give out particulars. I was accustomed to look into the faces of plants and animals, and I watched the little sphinx more and more keenly as an interesting study. But there is no estimating the wit and wisdom concealed and latent in our lower fellow-mortals until made manifest by profound experiences; for it is by suffering that dogs as well as saints are developed and made perfect.

After we had explored the glaciers of the Sumdum and Tahkoo inlets, we sailed through Stephen's Passage into Lynn Canal, and thence through Icy Strait into Cross Sound, looking for unexplored inlets leading toward the ice fountains of the Fairweather Range. While the tide was in our favor in Cross Sound we were accompanied by a fleet of icebergs drifting out to the ocean from Glacier Bay. Slowly we crawled around Vancouver's Point, Wimbleton, our frail canoe tossed like a feather on the massive swells coming in past Cape Spenser. For miles the Sound is bounded by precipitous cliffs which looked terribly stern in gloomy weather. Had our canoe been crushed or upset, we could have gained no landing here; for the cliffs, as high as those of Yosemite, sink perfectly sheer into deep water. Eagerly we scanned the immense wall on the north side for the first sign of an opening, all of us anxious except Stickeen, who dozed in peace or gazed dreamily at the tremendous precipices when he heard us talking about them. At length we discovered the entrance of what is now called Taylor Bay, and about five o'clock reached the head of it, and encamped near the front of a large glacier which extends as an abrupt barrier all the way across from wall to wall of the inlet, a distance of three or four miles.

On first observation the glacier presented some unusual features, and that night I planned a grand excursion for the morrow. I awoke early, called not only by the glacier, but also by a storm. Rain, mixed with trailing films of scud and the ragged, drawn-out nether surfaces of gray clouds, filled the inlet, and was sweeping forward in a thick, passionate, horizontal flood, as if it were all passing over the country instead of falling on it. Everything was streaming with life and motion – woods, rocks, waters, and the sky. The main perennial streams were booming, and hundreds of new ones, born of the rain, were descending in gray and white cascades on each side of the inlet, fairly streaking their rocky slopes, and roaring like the sea. I had intended making a cup of coffee before starting, but when I heard the storm I made haste to join it; for in storms nature has always something extra fine to show us, and if we have wit to keep in right relations with them the danger is no more than in home-keeping, and we can go with them rejoicing, sharing their enthusiasm, and chanting with the old Norsemen, 'The blast of the tempest aids our oars; the hurricane is our servant, and drives us whither we wish to go.' So I took my ice ax, buttoned my coat, put a piece of bread in my pocket, and set out. Mr. Young and the Indians were asleep, and so, I hoped, was Stickeen; but I had not gone a dozen rods before he left his warm bed in the tent, and came boring through the blast after me. That a man should welcome storms for their exhilarating music and motion, and go forth to see God making landscapes, is reasonable enough but what fascination could there be in dismal weather for this poor, feeble wisp of a dog, so pathetically small? Anyhow, on he came, breakfastless, through the choking blast. I stopped, turned my back to the wind, and gave him a good, dissuasive talk. 'Now don't,' I said, shouting to make myself heard in the storm – 'now don't, Stickeen. What has got into your queer noddle now? You must be daft. This wild day has nothing for you. Go back to camp and keep warm. There is no game abroad – nothing but weather. Not a foot or wing is stirring. Wait and get a good breakfast with your master, and be sensible for once. I can't feed you or carry you, and this storm will kill you.' But nature, it seems, was at the bottom of the affair; and she gains her ends with dogs as well as with men, making us do as she likes, driving us on her ways, however rough. So after ordering him back again and again to ease my conscience, I saw that he was not to be shaken off; as well might the earth try to shake off the moon. I had once led his master into trouble, when he fell on one of the topmost jags of a mountain, and dislocated his arms. Now the turn of his humble companion was coming. The dog just stood there in the wind, drenched and blinking, saying doggedly, 'Where thou goest I will go.' So I told him to come on, if he must, and gave him a piece of the bread I had put in my pocket for breakfast. Then we pushed on in company, and thus began the most memorable of all my wild days.

The level flood, driving straight in our faces, thrashed and washed us wildly until we got into the shelter of the trees and ice cliffs on the east side of the glacier, where we rested and listened and looked on in comfort. The exploration of the glacier was my main object, but the wind was too high to allow excursions over its open surface, where one might be dangerously shoved while balancing for a jump on the brink of a crevasse. In the meantime the storm was a fine study. Here the end of the glacier, descending over an abrupt swell of resisting rock about five hundred feet high, leans forward and falls in majestic ice cascades. And as the storm came down the glacier from the north, Stickeen and I were beneath the main current of the blast, while favorably located to see and hear it. A broad torrent, draining the side of the glacier, now swollen by scores of new streams from the mountains, was rolling boulders along its rocky channel between the glacier and the woods with thudding, bumping, muffled sounds, rushing toward the bay with tremendous energy, as if in haste to get out of the mountains, the waters above and beneath calling to each other, and all to the ocean, their home. Looking southward from our shelter, we had this great torrent on our left, with mossy woods on the mountain slope above it, the glacier on our right, the wild, cascading portion of it forming a multitude of towers, spires, and flat-topped battlements seen through the trees, and smooth gray gloom ahead. I tried to draw the marvelous scene in my notebook, but the rain fell on my page in spite of all that I could do to shelter it, and the sketch seemed miserably defective.

When the wind began to abate I traced the east side of the glacier. All the trees standing on the edge of the woods were barked and bruised, showing high ice-mark in a very telling way, while tens of thousands of those that had stood for centuries on the bank of the glacier farther out lay crushed and being crushed. In many places I could see, down fifty feet or so beneath, the margin of the glacier mill, where trunks from one to two feet in diameter were being ground to pulp against outstanding rock ribs and bosses of the bank. About three miles above the front of the glacier, I climbed to the surface of it by means of ax steps, made easy for Stickeen; and as far as the eye could reach, the level, or nearly level, glacier stretched away indefinitely beneath the gray sky, a seemingly boundless prairie of ice. The rain continued, which I did not mind; but a tendency to fogginess in the drooping clouds made me hesitate about venturing far from land. No trace of the west shore was visible, and in case the misty clouds should settle, or the wind again become violent, I feared getting caught in a tangle of crevasses. Lingering undecided, watching the weather, I sauntered about on the crystal sea. For a mile or two out I found the ice remarkably safe. The marginal crevasses were mostly narrow, while the few wider ones were easily avoided by passing around them, and the clouds began to open here and there. Thus encouraged, I at last pushed out for the other side; for nature can make us do anything she likes, luring us along appointed ways for the fulfillment of her plans. At first we made rapid progress, and the sky was not very threatening, while I took bearings occasionally with a pocket compass, to enable me to retrace my way more surely in case the storm should become blinding; but the structure lines of the ice were my main guide. Toward the west side we came to a closely crevassed section, in which we had to make long, narrow tacks and doublings, tracing the edges of tremendous longitudinal crevasses, many of which were from twenty to thirty feet wide, and perhaps a thousand feet deep, beautiful and awful. In working a way through them I was severely cautious, but Stickeen came on as unhesitatingly as the flying clouds. Any crevasse that I could jump he would leap without so much as halting to examine it. The weather was bright and dark, with quick flashes of summer and winter close together. When the clouds opened and the sun shone, the glacier was seen from shore to shore, with a bright array of encompassing mountains partly revealed, wearing the clouds as garments, black in the middle, burning on the edges, and the whole icy prairie seemed to burst into a bloom of iris colors from myriads of crystals. Then suddenly all the glorious show would be again smothered in gloom. But Stickeen seemed to care for none of these things, bright or dark, nor for the beautiful wells filled to the brim with water so pure that it was nearly invisible, the rumbling, grinding moulins, or the quick-flashing, glinting, swirling streams in frictionless channels of living ice. Nothing seemed novel to him. He showed neither caution nor curiosity. His courage was so unwavering that it seemed due to dullness of perception, as if he were only blindly bold; and I warned him that he might slip or fall short. His bunchy body seemed all one skipping muscle, and his peg legs appeared to be jointed only at the top.

We gained the west shore in about three hours, the width of the glacier here being about seven miles. Then I pushed northward, in order to see as far back as possible into the fountains of the Fairweather Mountains, in case the clouds should rise. The walking was easy along the margin of the forest, which, of course, like that on the other side, had been invaded and crushed by the swollen glacier. In an hour we rounded a massive headland and came suddenly on another outlet of the glacier, which, in the form of a wild ice cascade, was pouring over the rim of the main basin toward the ocean with the volume of a thousand Niagaras. The surface was broken into a multitude of sharp blades and pinnacles leaning forward, something like the updashing waves of a flood of water descending a rugged channel. But these ice waves were many times higher than those of river cataracts, and to all appearance motionless. It was a dazzling white torrent two miles wide, flowing between high banks black with trees. Tracing its left bank three or four miles, I found that it discharged into a freshwater lake, filling it with icebergs.

I would gladly have followed the outlet, but the day was waning, and we had to make haste on the return trip to get off the ice before dark. When we were about two miles from the west shore the clouds dropped misty fringes, and snow soon began to fly. Then I began to feel anxiety as to finding a way in the storm through the intricate network of crevasses which we had entered. Stickeen showed no fear. He was still the same silent, sufficient, uncomplaining Indian philosopher. When the storm darkness fell he kept close behind me. The snow warned us to make haste, but at the same time hid our way. At rare intervals the clouds thinned, and mountains looming in the gloom, frowned and quickly vanished. I pushed on as best I could, jumping innumerable crevasses, and for every hundred rods or so of direct advance traveling a mile in doubling up and down in the turmoil of chasms and dislocated masses of ice. After an hour or two of this work we came to a series of longitudinal crevasses of appalling width, like immense furrows. These I traced with firm nerve, excited and strengthened by the danger, making wide jumps, poising cautiously on the dizzy edges after cutting hollows for my feet before making the spring, to avoid slipping or any uncertainty on the farther sides, where only one trial is granted – exercise at once frightful and inspiring. Stickeen flirted across every gap I jumped, seemingly without effort. Many a mile we thus traveled, mostly up and down, making but little real headway in crossing, most of the time running instead of walking, as the danger of spending the night on the glacier became threatening. No doubt we could have weathered the storm for one night, and I faced the chance of being compelled to do so; but we were hungry and wet, and the north wind was thick with snow and bitterly cold, and of course that night would have seemed a long one. Stickeen gave me no concern. He was still the wonderful, inscrutable philosopher, ready for anything. I could not see far enough to judge in which direction the best route lay, and had simply to grope my way in the snow-choked air and ice. Again and again I was put to my mettle, but Stickeen followed easily, his nerves growing more unflinching as the dangers thickened; so it always is with mountaineers.

At length our way was barred by a very wide and straight crevasse, which I traced rapidly northward a mile or so without finding a crossing or hope of one, then southward down the glacier about as far, to where it united with another crevasse. In all this distance of perhaps two miles there was only one place where I could possibly jump it; but the width of this jump was nearly the utmost I dared attempt, while the danger of slipping on the farther side was so great that I was loath to try it. Furthermore, the side I was on was about a foot higher than the other, and even with this advantage it seemed dangerously wide. One is liable to underestimate the width of crevasses where the magnitudes in general are great. I therefore measured this one again and again, until satisfied that I could jump it if necessary, but that in case I should be compelled to jump back to the higher side, I might fail. Now a cautious mountaineer seldom takes a step on unknown ground which seems at all dangerous, that he cannot retrace in case he should be stopped by unseen obstacles ahead. This is the rule of mountaineers who live long; and though in haste, I compelled myself to sit down and deliberate before I broke it. Retracing my devious path in imagination, as if it were drawn on a chart, I saw that I was recrossing the glacier a mile or two farther upstream, and was entangled in a section I had not before seen. Should I risk this dangerous jump, or try to regain the woods on the west shore, make a fire, and have only hunger to endure while waiting for a new day? I had already crossed so broad a tangle of dangerous ice that I saw it would be difficult to get back to the woods through the storm; while the ice just beyond the present barrier seemed more promising, and the east shore was now perhaps about as near as the west. I was therefore eager to go on; but this wide jump was a tremendous obstacle. At length, because of the dangers already behind me, I determined to venture against those that might be ahead, jumped, and landed well, but with so little to spare that I more than ever dreaded being compelled to take that jump back from the lower side. Stickeen followed, making nothing of it.

But within a distance of a few hundred yards we were stopped again by the widest crevasse yet encountered. Of course I made haste to explore it, hoping all might yet be well. About three-fourths of a mile upstream it united with the one we had just crossed, as I feared it would. Then, tracing it down, I found it joined the other great crevasse at the lower end, maintaining a width of forty to fifty feet. We were on an island about two miles long and from one hundred to three hundred yards wide, with two barely possible ways of escape – one by the way we came, the other by an almost inaccessible sliver-bridge that crossed the larger crevasse from near the middle of the island. After tracing the brink, I ran back to the sliver-bridge and cautiously studied it. Crevasses caused by strains from variations of the rate of motion of different parts of the glacier and by convexities in the channel are mere cracks when they first open – so narrow as hardly to admit the blade of a pocketknife – and widen gradually, according to the extent of the strain. Now some of these cracks are interrupted like the cracks in wood, and, in opening, the strip of ice between overlapping ends is dragged out; and if the flow of the glacier there is such that no strain is made on the sliver, it maintains a continuous connection between the sides, just as the two sides of a slivered crack in wood that is being split are con-nected. Some crevasses remain open for years, and by the melting of their sides continue to increase in width long after the opening strain has ceased, while the sliver-bridges, level on top at first, and perfectly safe, are at length melted to thin, knife-edged blades, the upper portion being most exposed to the weather; and since the exposure is greatest in the middle, they at length curve downward like the cables of suspension bridges. This one was evidently very old, for it had been wasted until it was the worst bridge I ever saw. The width of the crevasse was here about fifty feet, and the sliver, crossing diagonally, was about seventy feet long, was depressed twenty-five or thirty feet in the middle, and the upcurving ends were attached to the sides eight or ten feet below the surface of the glacier. Getting down the nearly vertical wall to the end of it and up the other side were the main difficulties, and they seemed all but insurmountable. Of the many perils encountered in my years of wandering in mountain altitudes, none seemed so plain and stern and merciless as this. And it was presented when we were wet to the skin and hungry, the sky was dark with snow, and the night near, and we had to fear the snow in our eyes and the disturbing action of the wind in any movement we might make. But we were forced to face it. It was a tremendous necessity.

Beginning not immediately above the sunken end of the bridge, but a little to one side, I cut nice hollows on the brink for my knees to rest in; then, leaning over, with my short-handled ax cut a step sixteen or eighteen inches below, which, on account of the sheerness of the wall, was shallow. That step, however, was well made; its floor sloped slightly inward, and formed a good hold for my heels. Then, slipping cautiously upon it, and crouching as low as possible, with my left side twisted toward the wall, I steadied myself with my left hand in a slight notch, while with the right I cut other steps and notches in succession, guarding against glinting of the ax, for life or death was in every stroke, and in the niceness of finish of every foothold. After the end of the bridge was reached, it was a delicate thing to poise on a little platform which I had chipped on its upcurving end, and, bending over the slippery surface, get astride of it. Crossing was easy, cutting off the sharp edge with careful strokes, and hitching forward a few inches at a time, keeping my balance with my knees pressed against its sides. The tremendous abyss on each side I studiously ignored. The surface of that blue sliver was then all the world. But the most trying part of the adventure was, after working my way across inch by inch, to rise from the safe position astride that slippery strip of ice, and to cut a ladder in the face of the wall – chipping, climbing, holding on with feet and fingers in mere notches. At such times one's whole body is eye, and common skill and fortitude are replaced by power beyond our call or knowledge. Never before had I been so long under deadly strain. How I got up the cliff at the end of the bridge I never could tell. The thing seemed to have been done by somebody else. I never have had contempt of death, though in the course of my explorations I oftentimes felt that to meet one's fate on a mountain, in a grand canyon, or in the heart of a crystal glacier would be blessed as compared with death from disease, a mean accident in a street, or from a sniff of sewer gas. But the sweetest, cleanest death, set thus calmly and glaringly clear before us, is hard enough to face, even though we feel gratefully sure that we have already had happiness enough for a dozen lives.

But poor Stickeen, the wee, silky, sleekit beastie – think of him! When I had decided to try the bridge, and while I was on my knees cutting away the rounded brow, he came behind me, pushed his head past my shoulder, looked down and across, scanned the sliver and its approaches with his queer eyes, then looked me in the face with a startled air of surprise and concern, and began to mutter and whine, saying as plainly as if speaking with words, 'Surely you are not going to try that awful place?' This was the first time I had seen him gaze deliberately into a crevasse or into my face with a speaking look. That he should have recognized and appreciated the danger at the first glance showed wonderful sagacity. Never before had the quick, daring midget seemed to know that ice was slippery, or that there was such a thing as danger anywhere. His looks and the tones of his voice when he began to complain and speak his fears were so human that I unconsciously talked to him as I would to a boy, and in trying to calm his fears perhaps in some measure moderated my own. 'Hush your fears, my boy,' I said. 'We will get across safe, though it is not going to be easy. No right way is easy in this rough world. We must risk our lives to save them. At the worst we can only slip; and then how grand a grave we shall have! And by and by our nice bones will do good in the terminal moraine.' But my sermon was far from reassuring him; he began to cry, and after taking another piercing look at the tremendous gulf, ran away in desperate excitement, seeking some other crossing. By the time he got back, baffled, of course, I had made a step or two. I dared not look back, but he made himself heard; and when he saw that I was certainly crossing, he cried aloud in despair. The danger was enough to daunt anybody, but it seems wonderful that he should have been able to weigh and appreciate it so justly. No mountaineer could have seen it more quickly or judged it more wisely, discriminating between real and apparent peril.

After I had gained the other side he howled louder than ever, and after running back and forth in vain search for a way of escape, he would return to the brink of the crevasse above the bridge, moaning and groaning as if in the bitterness of death. Could this be the silent, philosophic Stickeen? I shouted encouragement, telling him the bridge was not so bad as it looked, that I had left it flat for his feet, and he could walk it easily. But he was afraid to try it. Strange that so small an animal should be capable of such big, wise fears! I called again and again in a reassuring tone to come on and fear nothing; that he could come if he would only try. Then he would hush for a moment, look again at the bridge, and shout his unshakeable conviction that he could never, never come that way; then lie back in despair, as if howling: 'Oh-o-o, what a place! No-o-o, I can never go-o-o down there!' His natural composure and courage had vanished utterly in a tumultuous storm of fear. Had the danger been less, his distress would have seemed ridiculous. But in this gulf – a huge, yawning sepulcher big enough to hold everybody in the territory – lay the shadow of death, and his heartrending cries might well have called Heaven to his help. Perhaps they did. So hidden before, he was transparent now, and one could see the workings of his mind like the movements of a clock out of its case. His voice and gestures were perfectly human, and his hopes and fears unmistakable, while he seemed to understand every word of mine. I was troubled at the thought of leaving him. It seemed impossible to get him to venture. To compel him to try by fear of being left, I started off as if leaving him to his fate, and disappeared back of a hummock; but this did no good, for he only lay down and cried. So after hiding a few minutes, I went back to the brink of the crevasse, and in a severe tone of voice shouted across to him that now I must certainly leave him – I could wait no longer; and that if he would not come, all I could promise was that I would return to seek him next day. I warned him that if he went back to the woods the wolves would kill him, and finished by urging him once more by words and gestures to come on. He knew very well what I meant, and at last, with the courage of despair, hushed and breathless, he lay down on the brink in the hollow I had made for my knees, pressed his body against the ice to get the advantage of the friction, gazed into the first step, put his little feet together, and slid them slowly down into it, bunching all four in it, and almost standing on his head. Then, without lifting them, as well as I could see through the snow, he slowly worked them over the edge of the step, and down into the next and the next in succession in the same way, and gained the bridge. Then lifting his feet with the regularity and slowness of the vibrations of a seconds' pendulum, as if counting and measuring one, two, three, holding himself in dainty poise, and giving separate attention to each little step, he gained the foot of the cliff, at the top of which I was kneeling to give him a lift should he get within reach. Here he halted in dead silence, and it was here I feared he might fail, for dogs are poor climbers. I had no cord. If I had had one, I would have dropped a noose over his head and hauled him up. But while I was thinking whether an available cord might be made out of clothing, he was looking keenly into the series of notched steps and fingerholds of the ice ladder I had made, as if counting them and fixing the position of each one in his mind. Then suddenly up he came, with a nervy, springy rush, hooking his paws into the notches and steps so quickly that I could not see how it was done, and whizzed past my head, safe at last!

And now came a scene! 'Well done, well done, little boy! Brave boy!' I cried, trying to catch and caress him; but he would not be caught. Never before or since have I seen anything like so passionate a revulsion from the depths of despair to uncontrollable, exultant, triumphant joy. He flashed and darted hither and thither as if fairly demented, screaming and shouting, swirling round and round in giddy loops and circles like a leaf in a whirlwind, lying down and rolling over and over, sidewise and heels over head, pouring forth a tumultuous flood of hysterical cries and sobs and gasping mutterings. And when I ran up to him to shake him, fearing he might die of joy, he flashed off two or three hundred yards, his feet in a mist of motion; then, turning suddenly, he came back in wild rushes, and launched himself at my face, almost knocking me down, all the time screeching and screaming and shouting as if saying, 'Saved! Saved! Saved!' Then away again, dropping suddenly at times with his feet in the air, trembling, and fairly sobbing. Such passionate emotion was enough to kill him. Moses' stately song of triumph after escaping the Egyptians and the Red Sea was nothing to it. Who could have guessed the capacity of the dull, enduring little fellow for all that most stirs this mortal frame? Nobody could have helped crying with him.

But there is nothing like work for toning down either excessive fear or joy. So I ran ahead, calling him, in as gruff a voice as I could command, to come on and stop his nonsense, for we had far to go, and it would soon be dark. Neither of us feared another trial like this. Heaven would surely count one enough for a lifetime. The ice ahead was gashed by thousands of crevasses, but they were common ones. The joy of deliverance burned in us like fire, and we ran without fatigue, every muscle, with immense rebound, glorying in its strength. Stickeen flew across everything in his way, and not till dark did he settle into his normal foxlike, gliding trot. At last the mountains crowned with spruce came in sight, looming faintly in the gloaming, and we soon felt the solid rock beneath our feet, and were safe. Then came weariness. We stumbled down along the lateral moraine in the dark, over rocks and tree trunks, through the bushes and devil-club thickets and mossy logs and boulders of the woods where we had sheltered ourselves in the morning. Then out on the level mud slope of the terminal moraine. Danger had vanished, and so had our strength. We reached camp about ten o'clock, and found a big fire and a big supper. A party of Hoona Indians had visited Mr. Young, bringing a gift of porpoise meat and wild strawberries, and hunter Joe had brought in a wild goat. But we lay down, too tired to eat much, and soon fell into a troubled sleep. The man who said, 'The harder the toil the sweeter the rest,' never was profoundly tired. Stickeen kept springing up and muttering in his sleep, no doubt dreaming that he was still on the brink of the crevasse; and so did I – that night and many others, long afterward, when I was nervous and overtired.

Thereafter Stickeen was a changed dog. During the rest of the trip, instead of holding aloof, he would come to me at night, when all was quiet about the campfire, and rest his head on my knee, with a look of devotion, as if I were his god. And often, as he caught my eye, he seemed to be trying to say, 'Wasn't that an awful time we had together on the glacier?'

None of his old friends know what finally became of him. When my work for the season was done I departed for California, and never saw the dear little fellow again. Mr. Young wrote me that in the summer of 1883 he was stolen by a tourist at Fort Wrangel, and taken away on a steamer. His fate is wrapped in mystery. If alive he is very old. Most likely he has left this world – crossed the last crevasse – and gone to another. But he will not be forgotten. Come what may, to me Stickeen is immortal.

BLOOD
WILL TELL

Don Marquis
(American) 1878–1937

I am a middle-size dog, with spots on me here and there, and several different colors of hair mixed in even where there aren't any spots, and my ears are frazzled a little on the ends where they have been chewed in fights.

At first glance you might not pick me for an aristocrat. But I am one. I was considerably surprised when I discovered it, as nothing in my inmost feelings up to that time, nor in the treatment which I had received from dogs, humans, or boys, had led me to suspect it.

I can well remember the afternoon on which the discovery was made. A lot of us dogs were lying in the grass, up by the swimming hole, just lazing around, and the boys were doing the same. All the boys were naked and comfortable, and no humans were about, the only thing near being a cow or two and some horses, and although large they are scarcely more human than boys. Everybody had got tired of swimming, and it was too hot to drown out gophers or fight bumblebees, and the boys were smoking grapevine cigarettes and talking.

Us dogs was listening to the boys talk. A Stray Boy, by which I mean one not claimed or looked out for or owned by any dog, says to Freckles Watson, who is my boy:

'What breed would you call that dog of yours, Freck?'

I pricked up my ears at that. I cannot say that I had ever set great store by breeds up to the time that I found out I was an aristocrat myself, believing, as Bill Patterson, a human and the town drunkard, used to say when intoxicated, that often an honest heart beats beneath the outcast's ragged coat.

125

'Spot ain't any *one* particular breed,' says Freckles. 'He's considerably mixed.'

'He's a mongrel,' says Squint Thompson, who is Jack Thompson's boy.

'He ain't,' says Freckles, so huffy that I saw a mongrel must be some sort of a disgrace. 'You're a link, link liar, and so's your Aunt Mariar, and you're another.'

'A dog,' chips in the Stray Boy, 'has either got to be a thoroughbred or a mongrel. He's either an aristocrat or else he's a common dog.'

'Spot ain't any common dog,' says Freckles, sticking up for me. 'He can lick any dog in town within five pounds of his weight.'

'He's got some spaniel in him,' says the Stray Boy.

'His nose is pointed like a hound's nose,' says Squint Thompson.

'Well,' says Freckles, 'neither one of them kind of dogs is a common dog.'

'Spot has got some bulldog blood in him, too,' says Tom Mulligan, an Irish boy owned by a dog by the name of Mutt Mulligan. 'Did you ever notice how Spot will hang on so you can't pry him loose, when he gets into a fight?'

'That proves he is an aristocratic kind of dog,' says Freckles.

'There's some bird-dog blood in Spot,' says the Stray Boy, sizing me up careful.

'He's got some collie in him, too,' says Squint Thompson. 'His voice sounds just like a collie's when he barks.'

'But his tail is more like a coach dog's tail,' says Tom Mulligan.

'His hair ain't, though,' says the Stray Boy. 'Some of his hair is like a setter's.'

'His teeth are like a mastiff's,' says Mutt Mulligan's boy Tom. And they went on like that; I never knew before there were so many different kinds of thoroughbred dog. Finally Freckles says:

'Yes, he's got all them different kinds of thoroughbred blood in him, and he's got other kinds you ain't mentioned and that you ain't slick enough to see. You may think you're running him down, but what you say just *proves* he ain't a common dog.'

I was glad to hear that. It was beginning to look to me that they had a pretty good case for me being a mongrel.

'How does it prove it?' asked the Stray Boy.

'Well,' says Freckles, 'you know who the king of Germany is, don't you?'

They said they'd heard of him from time to time.

'Well,' says Freckles, 'if you were a relation of the king of Germany you'd be a member of the German royal family. You fellows may not know that, but you would. You'd be a swell, a regular high-mucky-muck.'

They said they guessed they would.

'Now, then,' says Freckles, 'if you were a relation to the king of Switzerland, too, you'd be just *twice* as swell, wouldn't you, as if you were only related to one royal family? Plenty of people are related to just *one* royal family.'

Tom Mulligan butts in and says that way back, in the early days, his folks was the kings of Ireland; but no one pays any attention.

'Suppose, then, you're a cousin of the queen of England into the bargain and your granddad was king of Scotland, and the prince of Wales and the emperor of France and the sultan of Russia and the rest of those royalties were relations of yours, wouldn't all that royal blood make you *twenty times* as much of a high-mucky-muck as if you had just *one* measly little old king for a relation?'

The boys had to admit that it would.

'You wouldn't call a fellow with all that royal blood in him a *mongrel*, would you?' says Freckles. 'You bet your sweet life you wouldn't! A fellow like that is darned near on the level with a congressman or a vice-president. Whenever he travels around in the old country they turn out the brass band; and the firemen and the Knights of Pythias and the Modern Woodmen parade, and the mayor makes a speech, and there's a picnic and firecrackers, and he gets blamed near anything he wants. People kowtow to him, just like they do to a swell left-handed pitcher or a champion prize fighter. If you went over to the old country and called a fellow like that a mongrel, and it got out on you, you would be sent to jail for it.'

Tom Mulligan says yes, that is so; his granddad came to this country through getting into some kind of trouble about the king of England, and the king of England ain't anywhere near as swell as the fellow Freckles described, nor near so royal, neither.

'Well, then,' says Freckles, 'it's the same way with my dog Spot here. *Any* dog can be full of just *one* kind of thoroughbred blood. That's nothing! But Spot here has got more different kinds of thoroughbred blood in him than any dog you ever saw. By your own say-so he has. He's got *all* kinds of thoroughbred blood in him. If there's any kind he ain't got, you just name it, will you?'

'He ain't got any Great Dane in him,' yells the Stray Boy, hating to knuckle under.

'You're a liar – he has, too,' says Freckles.

The Stray Boy backed it, and there was a fight. All us dogs and boys gathered around in a ring to watch it, and I was more anxious than anybody else. For the way that fight went, it was easy to see, would decide what I was.

Well, Freckles licked that Stray Boy, and rubbed his nose in the mud, and that's how I come to be an aristocrat.

Being an aristocrat may sound easy. And it may look easy to outsiders. And it may really be easy for them that are used to it. But it wasn't easy for *me*. It came on me suddenly, the knowledge that I was one, and without warning. I didn't have any time to practice up being one. One minute I wasn't one, and the next minute I was; and while, of course, I felt important over it, there were spells when I would get kind of discouraged, too, and wish I could go back to being a common dog again. I kept expecting my tastes and habits to change. I watched and waited for them to. But they didn't. No change at all set in on me. But I had to pretend I was changed. Then I would get tired of pretending, and be downhearted about the whole thing, and say to myself: 'There has been a mistake. I am *not* an aristocrat after all.'

I might have gone along like that for a long time, partly in joy over my noble birth, and partly in doubt, without ever being certain, if it had not been for a happening which showed, as Freckles said, that blood will tell.

It happened the day Wilson's World's Greatest One-Ring Circus and Menagerie came to our town. Freckles and me, and the other dogs and boys, and a good many humans, too, followed the street parade around through town and back to the circus lot. Many went in, and the ones that didn't have any money hung around outside a while and explained to each other they were going at night, because a circus is more fun at night anyhow. Freckles didn't have any money, but his dad was going to take him that night, so when the parade was over him and me went back to his dad's drugstore on Main Street, and I crawled under the soda-water counter to take a nap.

Freckles' dad, that everyone calls Doc Watson, is a pretty good fellow for a human, and he doesn't mind you hanging around the store if you don't drag bones in or scratch too many fleas off. So I'm there considerable in right hot weather. Under the soda-water counter is the coolest place for a dog in the whole town. There's a zinc tub under there always full of water, where Doc washes the soda-water glasses, and there's always considerable water slopped onto the floor. It's damp and dark there always. Outdoors it may be so hot in the sun that your tongue hangs out of you so far you tangle your feet in it, but in under there you can lie comfortable and snooze, and when you wake up and want a drink there's the tub with the glasses in it. And flies don't bother you because they stay on top of the counter where soda water has been spilled.

Circus day was a hot one, and I must have drowsed off pretty quick after lying down. I don't know how long I slept, but when I waked up it was with a start, for something important was going on outside in Main Street. I could hear people screaming and swearing and running along the wooden sidewalk, and horses whinnying, and dogs barking, and old Tom Cramp, the city marshal, was yelling out that he was an officer of the law, and the steam whistle on the flour mill was blowing. And it all seemed to be right in front of our store. I was thinking I'd better go out and see about it, when the screen doors crashed like a runaway horse had come through them, and the next minute a big yellow dog was back of the counter, trying to scrooch down and scrouge under it like he was scared and was

hiding. He backed me into the corner without seeing me or knowing I was there, and like to have squashed me.

No dog – and it never struck me that maybe this wasn't a dog –
no dog can just calmly sit down on me like that when I'm waking
up from a nap, and get away with it, no matter *how* big he is, and in
spite of the darkness under there I could see and feel that this was
the biggest dog in the world. I had been dreaming I was in a fight,
anyhow, when he crowded in there with his hindquarters on top of
me, and I bit him on the hind leg.

When I bit him he let out a noise like a thrashing machine starting
up. It wasn't a bark. Nothing but the end of the world coming could
bark like that. It was a noise more like I heard one time when the
boys dared Freckles to lie down between the cattle guards on the
railroad track and let a train run over him about a foot above his
head, and I laid down there with him and it nearly deefened both of us.
When he let out that noise I says to myself, 'Great guns! What kind of
a dog have I bit?'

And as he made that noise he jumped, and over went the
counter, marble top and all, with a smash, and jam into the show
window he went, with his tail swinging, and me right after him,
practically on top of him. It wasn't that I exactly intended to chase
him, you understand, but I was rattled on account of that awful
noise he had let out, and I wanted to get away from there, and I
went the same way he did. So when he bulged through the window
glass onto the street I bulged right after him, and as he hit the sidewalk I bit him again. The first time I bit him because I was sore, but the
second time I bit him because I was so nervous I didn't know what I
was doing, hardly. And at the second bite, without even looking
behind him, he jumped clean over the hitch rack and a team of
horses in front of the store and landed right in the middle of the
road with his tail between his legs.

And then I realized for the first time he wasn't a dog at all. He
was the circus lion.

Mind you, I'm not saying that I would have bit him at all if I'd
a-known at the start he was a lion.

And I ain't saying I *wouldn't* 'a' bit him, either.

But actions speak louder than words, and records are records, and you can't go back on them, and the fact is I *did* bite him. I bit him twice.

And that second bite, when we came bulging through the window together, the whole town saw. It was getting up telephone poles, and looking out of second-story windows, and crawling under sidewalks and into cellars, and trying to hide behind the town pump; but no matter where it was trying to get to, it had one eye on that lion, and it saw me chasing him out of that store. I don't say I would have chased him if he hadn't been just ahead of me, anyhow, and I don't say I wouldn't have chased him, but the facts are I *did* chase him.

The lion was just as scared as the town – and the town was so scared it didn't know the lion was scared at all – and when his trainer got hold of him in the road he was tickled to death to be led back to his cage, and he lay down in the far corner of it, away from the people, and trembled till he shook the wagon it was on.

But if there was any further doubts in any quarter about me being an aristocrat, the way I bit and chased that lion settled 'em forever. That night Freckles and Doc went to the circus, and I marched in along with them. And every kid in town, as they saw Freckles and me marching in, says:

'There goes the dog that licked the lion!'

And Freckles, every time anyone congratulated him on being the boy that belonged to that kind of a dog, would say:

'Blood will tell! Spot's an aristocrat, he is.'

And him and me and Doc Watson, his dad, stopped in front of the lion's cage that night and took a good long look at him. He was a kind of an old moth-eaten lion, but he was a lion all right, and he looked mighty big in there. He looked so big that all my doubts come back on me, and I says to myself: 'Honest, now, if I'd a-known he was a lion, and that *big* a lion, when I bit him, *would* I have bit him, or would I not?'

But just then Freckles reached down and patted me on the head and said: 'You wasn't afraid of him, was you, old Spot! Yes, sir, blood will tell!'

TURI – SON
OF REPO

Lady Kitty Ritson
(British) 1887–1969

Dick Preston got out of the car and stretched himself. He was stiff and he wanted a cigarette badly. He puffed at it happily for a few minutes, then he thought of the puppy in the basket and determined to give it a run.

He opened the lid, peered within and swore firmly. The basket was empty and there was a small hole in the side.

He shook his head trying to think where the puppy could have escaped. Then he remembered. He had stopped twenty miles back to look inside the bonnet, but it had never struck him that the pup would have enough initiative to gnaw through a basket and then to creep out of the car.

But Dick had reckoned without knowing the breed of dog with which he was dealing.

At that moment Turi was sitting in a meadow, surveying the landscape. He was four months old and a Finnish Spitz, pricked of ear, curled of tail and the colour of a fox. His dark eyes regarded the surrounding country with curiosity, but he kept very still.

Most puppies would have been terrified at finding themselves alone, but the Finnish Spitz does not know the meaning of the word panic. He is always cautious, but he is immensely self-reliant. Only that morning he had been taken away from his breeder, having been bought by Dick Preston as a present for his fiancée. He had found the basket an unpleasant place and he had promptly gnawed a hole. To jump out of the car while the man's head was buried under the bonnet presented no difficulties, and he saw no possible reason for remaining with him.

At the end of a quarter of an hour Turi trotted across to the shelter of a wood. A Finnish Spitz does not like remaining exposed to view for long, for he is too close to the wild to think it is prudent. Arrived in the copse, he spent several minutes cleaning his paws and arranging his coat. Then he caught a mouse, which he ate and finally, curling up in a ball, he went to sleep.

He was awakened from his slumbers by hearing the voice of Dick Preston.

'Come along, good little man, come along,' it said wheedlingly. Turi peered at him with very black eyes, but remained absolutely still and inaudible. He saw no possible reason for obeying the voice, which meant nothing to him. He knew quite well where home lay, although it was a matter of eighty miles or more away. A Finnish Spitz takes no account of distance, and will travel four hundred miles or more to return home. Later on, he would turn his black, quivering nose in that direction, but for the moment he was perfectly happy.

Dick called and called, then he swore and paced up and down. The puppy watched him with unblinking eyes – eyes which were rather reminiscent of his Lappish cousins the reindeer-dogs. Even his nose remained quiet.

After a time the man went away. He was angry, for he had paid a large sum for the puppy, the breed being as yet scarce in England, but there was nothing more he could do. Turi lay there a while longer. Utter peace brooded over the country. A million stars hung in the sky and the Milky Way – the 'Wolf-Trail' of the Indians – was like a strip of pale silver.

The foxes were moving now and a vixen trotted down a glade, two cubs running at her heels. She saw the puppy, but she paid no heed.

Turi unwound himself. Away in the distance he smelt fire, and to him a camp fire meant the awakening of atavistic memories, which pricked his instincts to action.

He moved lightly on his small, creamy paws through the wood until he caught the gleam of a fire. There was also the smell of food.

The tug of home was fretting him a little, but he wished to investigate before he turned in that direction.

Arrived at the edge of the wood he sniffed delicately and then moved forward. There were human beings, he realised, inside the caravan, but they would not interfere. The warmth of the embers drew him; but, clever though he was, he was only a puppy and he had failed to locate the gipsy lurcher dog. The latter leapt on him and shook him silently, and only Turi's luck prevented the lurcher from breaking his neck.

The puppy screamed piercingly, and the gipsy tumbled out of the caravan and in two seconds had rescued Turi.

He was not a Romany, merely an out-of-work individual who preferred strolling along the roads to living on charity. He soothed the bundle of red fur, and in less than a minute the puppy was quiet. A Finnish Spitz never loses his philosophical attitude for long.

'Look like a fox, you do,' the man said, but he did not make the common mistake of thinking that it was a fox. He knew too much about wild life for that. He gave him a piece of meat, which Turi bolted, and took him into the caravan. It was gloriously stuffy and the puppy snuggled down on a piece of sacking, his nose under his tail. No genuine dweller in the wild cares for night air, whether he be man or beast. That fad is left to the dwellers in cities.

Next morning was a perfect June day and the man looked at the puppy with interest.

'You're a rum 'un,' he said, but he realised that here was a pedigree dog. He liked the little beast, but no good ever came to people of his description if they held on to something valuable, however honestly come by. It would be wiser to lose him again, he thought. So he gave him nothing to eat, but he prevented the lurcher from worrying him, by tying his dog underneath the caravan.

Although he did not know it, his direction was the same as that which the puppy's instinct told him he must take for home, so Turi trotted along contentedly enough. He disappeared for a few minutes and returned dragging a half-grown pullet after him. It was not dead, but the man, looking round swiftly, soon despatched it and his lips relaxed into a grin.

'You need training, son,' he commented, 'killing's all right, but you must kill and retrieve secretly, not murder in broad daylight. You'll be getting me into trouble. I'll have to lose you.'

They were passing a big stone gateway at the moment and Turi trotted inside to have a look. The man improved the occasion by shying a stone after the puppy. That did the trick. A Finnish Spitz never forgives a blow. He gave the stone-thrower a glance out of his dark eyes, which became suddenly oblique, and his tail slackened its proud curl for a moment. Then he trotted on.

The drive turned a sharp corner and Turi arrived at another gateway just as a string of race-horses came out. The trainer was sitting on his hack watching them go by, the older, steadier horses in front and the youngsters behind, with lads at their heads. They went quietly and kindly enough, except one chestnut two-year-old, big and well made, with a hint of white showing behind the eye, which was as dark as Turi's own. He threw his head about, shied at nothing and suddenly broke into a sweat.

Bill Turner, the trainer, sighed. The best of the lot by a long way, that colt, but scary like his dam and unreasonably highly strung. It was always the way. Let them be promising, faultless in breeding, and they developed temperaments that spoiled everything.

The lad hung on to the colt's head and then, as the latter reared, he turned and looked at him.

'Don't look at him!' Bill Turner shouted irritably, 'Don't you know better than that?'

The colt backed, snorting and sweating, and Bill Turner swore under his breath.

Turi had remained unnoticed. He liked the smell of horses, and he crossed the road unconcernedly and sat on his haunches in a particularly typical attitude, an attitude which all Finnish Spitzs adopt when they are considering life. His dark eyes were unblinking, but his black nose quivered.

The colt caught sight of him and stopped to stare. Turi remained motionless till the string moved on, then he trotted after the chestnut colt, while the latter, seeming to have forgotten his misgivings, strode out quietly.

'What *is* that?' Bill Turner asked dazedly, 'a fox?'

'Don't know, sir; looks like a kind of a dog to me.' 'Well, go on. The colt seems to have taken a fancy to it, whatever it is.'

The string moved on to the training ground and Bill Turner spoke to the three leading boys.

'Now, no racing, mind, d'ye hear me? Canter them up slowly.'

'Yes, sir.'

He watched the youngsters following the old horse, which was to lead them, then he swore again to himself as he saw Turi trotting far ahead. He heaved a sigh of relief as the puppy disappeared into the hedgerow. He didn't want a dog getting in the way, making the youngsters swerve and bolt.

He watched them pass him. Jove! the chestnut colt was going well. He was striding out, yet going kindly, with pricked ears and quiet eye. Well named, Sunbright, by Golden Sun out of Pleiades. He was 'sun-bright' indeed, with that coat. There was something there, way out of the ruck, if only Fate would be kind for a bit.

He trotted across to where the boys had stopped, and at that moment he noticed Turi sitting like a small Billikin in the shadow of the hedgerow. The pup trotted across the turf, and the colt reached out his head and nickered.

'Take 'em home,' he directed, 'and if that object wants to come, he can. Give him something to eat. The colt seems to have taken a fancy to him.'

The string turned for home, and Turi kept a few yards from Sunbright's side. There was just the least hint of weariness in the proudly carried tail, which was as yet far from its adult plumy beauty. He was only a pup and he was living life to the full. He remained in the middle of the yard while the lads did their work, then he walked over to the colt's box and lay down in the corner, snuggling into the golden wheaten straw, which was so nearly the colour of his coat. He soon fell asleep and the colt smelt him, turned away and began eating.

By the time his lad came back the feed was gone and the colt was resting quietly.

'Well, I never!' the lad said. 'Wot's up with him?'

As a rule Sunbright was a pernickety 'doer', snuffling over his feed in that manner which breaks the heart of lads and trainer.

He told the head lad the glad news, and the latter came to look for himself. Turi stirred, woke up and sat upon his haunches, looking up into Sunbright's face. The colt bent his head and blew over him, and the puppy sneezed, but did not move.

'Well—' said old Bob, voicing his feelings in terse but unprintable manner. 'I've 'eard of horses getting balmy over goats and all manner of things, but who'd 'ave thought it of this colt? 'Ere, give that objec' somethin' to eat. If 'e's to be a – mascot, 'e must be fed. 'Alf a fox 'e is, I tell you.'

Whatever the stable thought of Turi's origin, they blessed him, from Bill Turner downwards. They provided him with the best of food, of which he occasionally ate sparingly and disdainfully. A Finnish Spitz thrives best when he lives 'off the land'. Uncounted mice, an occasional mole (the summer was dry and the moles were hard put to it), young birds, and quantities of cabbage stalks and other trifles formed his diet. His coat grew redder and denser and his tail was a thing of beauty, sweeping forward in a curve and pressed against his tawny flank, its creamy underside like a signal in the distance.

He had not quite reached his full height, eighteen inches at the shoulder, but he was growing daily. His 'Mongol' eyes were as beautiful as ever, and he was brimful of that elusive thing, quality. Why not? Was he not 'Turi Repospoika,' meaning 'Turi, son of Repo,' and behind him stretched a long line of ancestors, as proud and as beautiful as Sunbright's own?

Had not his ancestors hunted game for their masters in the dense Finnish forests, yes, even dared death at the paws of the mighty bear? Had they not shared their camp fires and gazed unblinkingly at the dance of the Northern Lights? Did they not understand the magic of the Lapps and the tunes which they chanted?

He was 'Turi, the Beautiful,' although the stable called him 'Foxie'.

Perhaps one man alone dimly understood his worth, and that man was Bill Turner. About a week after the pup's arrival, he had read an advertisement in two dog papers and one daily paper, from which he gathered that a certain gentleman named Dick Preston was extraordinarily anxious to find the whereabouts of a lost Finnish Spitz. A large reward was mentioned, but Bill Turner had dreams of a much larger reward.

Ever since the arrival of Turi, Sunbright had become a different creature. He no longer blew over his food, but ate it up. So long as the dog accompanied him at exercise he was tractable and sensible, but let the pup absent himself for a day, as once happened when important hunting was afoot, and he became distraught, refusing his food, seeing shadows where none existed, and throwing the stable into a state of irritable despair.

Bill Turner knew that in the colt he had something outstanding if his temperament could be kept from asserting itself. He saw bright visions of winning big money at Doncaster with him in the autumn, and at the bare idea of losing Turi, his blood ran cold. He burned the papers in which the advertisement appeared, and promised himself that if Sunbright fulfilled expectations he would offer Dick Preston such a price for the dog that he would forgive the fact that he, Bill, was practically a thief.

As the weeks passed, he hoped that Preston had given up all hope of finding the dog, and daily Turi paced by Sunbright's side, or flashed along the downs, a few yards away, tail outstretched, when the colt was doing his gallops. He never got in the way, but he was never far off. A Finnish Spitz has an uncanny habit of disappearing and then apparently materialising out of thin air. But except on two occasions, he never missed a night in the colt's box, and he sat like a small nurse while Sunbright ate his food.

He dropped in to tea one afternoon at Bill Turner's cottage. He settled himself on the rug and went to sleep. Bill offered him a piece of cake, which Turi inspected, but refused until he had sniffed it carefully.

Then he played 'mouse' with it, and having 'killed' it, he took some more, but he disdained to ask for it.

Thereafter, he made a point of coming in to see Bill at tea-time, while the stables were sunk in their afternoon rest and Sunbright was dozing in his box. When feeding time was due he knew by instinct and, stretching himself, he would clean his paws and his face, arrange his coat and stroll in as the lads arrived. He was there when Bill came to make his evening visit, but he stayed with the chestnut colt and did not make a round of the stables.

One evening, about ten o'clock, the trainer looked in quietly and found the colt lying down and Turi, a golden blur against the brighter chestnut, in his corner.

'And I thought I knew about horses,' he said to himself, smiling, as he withdrew quietly.

The weeks sped on and his hopes rose higher. Sunbright had filled out, partly, no doubt, because he was maturing, but largely because he had ceased fretting himself into fiddle-strings over everything and nothing.

If only he could win the Champagne Stakes with him at Doncaster.

If it is true, in a general way, that nothing succeeds like success, it is doubly so with a trainer. One run of success seems to bring another in its train, and Luck, that sweet and fickle lady, plays a leading part. Up to date she had not smiled on Bill Turner. He had had good horses, but just not good enough, or else something totally unforeseen and unpreventable had happened at the last minute. He had staked everything he had, and while Bill was not a man to go down without a struggle, there is a limit beyond which the stoutest spirit cannot hope to win through.

Sunbright was right, just right, and few people know how difficult it is to reach that point at the psychological moment. There was an air of tense expectancy over the whole stable.

'I suppose the dog'll go with the colt, sir?' old Bob asked.

'Lord, yes!' the trainer said. 'We might as well not go if the dog stayed behind.'

Turi was in the full glory of his coat. It stood out in a magnificent ruff round his neck, rich as the colour of falling beech leaves, shading to a creamy white on his paws, but dazzlingly white on the under-part of his plume.

Bill looked at him as he stood, a little more than a week before the race, in the middle of the yard.

He jumped as Bob said meditatively: 'Who'd 'ave thought that little objec' would 'ave turned into a dog like 'im? Looks as though he must 'ave something good be'ind 'im. 'E's never a come-by-chance. I shouldn't wonder whether 'e's not as well bred as the colt, in 'is way.'

'Oh, I don't know,' Bill answered non-committally. 'Looks like an over-size Pom. to me,' and he changed the subject quickly.

That afternoon the trainer went up to London and did not get home till late. The next morning was as glorious as only a bright September day can be, and he whistled as he threw a leg over his hack. He cantered up to the training ground a little late, and saw Sunbright with four others flash past him. Instantly his eye detected something amiss.

He hurried up to Bob.

'What's the matter with the colt?' he asked, hoping, against the dictates of his own common sense, that the answer would be ''E's all right, sir.'

'Dog never come back last night,' the head lad answered gloomily. 'The colt didn't touch his food, and 'e broke out last thing when I went to look at 'im. This morning 'e's all over the place.'

'It *would* happen,' Bill Turner said drearily, 'it would happen! Well, we might just as well keep Sunbright at home, and that's all there is to it.'

Bob nodded his head. There was nothing more to say, in his opinion.

'Can't think why somebody couldn't have kept an eye on the dog,' Bill broke out irritably and, as he knew, quite unjustly, but he was too sore to count his words. 'Seems as if I can't go away for an afternoon but something goes wrong.'

He rode over to the colt and looked at him. He was sweating, and the white of his eye was all too prominent. As a twig covered with a few rustling leaves blew by, he shied violently.

'Take 'em all in,' Bill ordered, 'and go and look for that dog. I'll give five pounds to the man who finds him. Hang it all, he's never run away before, why should he choose this of all days to do it?'

But 'Turi, son of Repo,' had not run away. Once an adult Finnish

Spitz has settled on his home, it is for life. Puppy recollections may be blurred, but never later ones. Sell him, and he promptly breaks his heart, or dies in the attempt to return.

Turi had looked for Bill at tea-time and, finding him absent, had gone for a stroll. There were one or two squirrels which he desired to harry, and one of the squirrels flashed across the road and Turi went in pursuit.

It was not entirely the fault of the driver of the fast little sports car, but he might have stopped, for he knew well enough what he had done. The wheel caught the dog a glancing blow and simply hurled him through the hedgerow, where he lay completely stunned.

Presently he recovered consciousness, his body one dreadful, large pain. He tried to crawl in the direction of home, but it was useless and, obeying his most primitive instinct, he just managed to drag himself into the dense undergrowth of the copse, where his enemies the squirrels looked down at him and chattered.

He was three miles from home and he fell again into a state of stupor, a state induced by merciful Nature, who knows when quiet is more essential than medicine. He did not hear the voices of the searchers in the distance; his dull eyes were closed and his bedraggled coat was thick with clotted dust and traces of oil. He lay and suffered with that complete acquiescence which we have forgotten how to practise. No sooner do we have a pain than we seek to find alleviation for it.

In the stables despair reigned. Sunbright lost ground in a couple of days.

'We'll ease him up,' Bill Turner said; 'that'll do less harm than pressing him while he's in this state. If the dog turns up within the next twenty-four hours, we've a chance. But he won't. I know my Luck.'

But he was wrong, and Luck, who loves a bit of gallantry, took a hand.

At midday on the fourth day a little draggled 'object' crawled into the yard. His tongue was parched from thirst. His hind leg dragged and his eyes were filmy, but – he had reached home. His indomitable spirit had triumphed over his battered, weary body.

Bob saw him first and rushed forward. He lifted him in an infinitely gentle manner.

'Tell the Governor,' he ordered, and three minutes later Bill was in the yard.

'Run over by a car,' he said, 'and then left to die.'

There was a sort of subdued growl from the assembled lads, and could the guilty driver have found himself there, he would have known what lynching meant.

'Ask Mr. Stainton to come at once,' Bill ordered, and laid Turi gently down at his feet. The filmy eyes opened and the dog made a little effort to crawl in the direction of Sunbright's box. Bill picked him up and took him into a shady corner where the golden sun motes did not fall. He lay there outstretched, hardly breathing, but the colt turned instantly and gave a low nicker.

'Gently with him, boy,' Bill warned needlessly.

Sunbright walked across with velvet-like movement, and for a brief instant there shot out a little swollen tongue from Turi's mouth. The trainer took a saucer of milk from a lad and held it close to the hot muzzle. It was lapped, with intakes of breath between each sip; but it was lapped.

Bill thought no more about the race, he merely gazed in that admiration which all decent men feel for a gallant spirit.

'You little sportsman,' he muttered almost tenderly, and he tilted the saucer, so that the last creamy drop went down. Then Turi stretched himself out again with a sigh and the smallest whimper of pain and slept.

Half an hour later the vet looked at him doubtfully.

'He's too bruised for me to be able to say whether there's any internal injury or not,' he said. 'I'm inclined to think not. These dogs are extraordinary; they'll recover through sheer force of will-power. You can do nothing but let him rest and eat what he can.'

'Brand's Essence, milk,' suggested Bill, and the vet nodded.

'I should move him from here,' the latter said, 'the colt might step on him.'

The trainer shook his head.

'I believe it was the colt that brought him home,' and he told Stainton the story.

'I've come across such instances once or twice,' he said. 'It makes one think. I can't afford to be sentimental,' he added, 'but this sort of thing leaves one wondering.'

He answered the unspoken question in Bill's eyes. 'See how he is when the day comes for the colt to go to Doncaster, and be guided by what the dog wants to do.'

There was no question about what Turi wanted to do when the time came. From the moment he came home, their positions seemed to have been reversed, and it was Sunbright who had watched over the dog. He had eaten up at once, and become quiet and collected again. The moment the colt returned to his box, Turi raised his head, quivered his black nose, and sank once more into slumber. He lapped up milk and Brand's Essence, and the day before Sunbright was due to entrain he walked out into the yard, weakly, it is true, but still using all his legs.

It was sunny outside, and slowly the plumy tail rose from its drooping position and curled slowly along his golden back.

He made the journey in the colt's box in the lad's arms, and that night dog and horse slept calmly and quietly in their new quarters.

'Come on, hasn't he?' Lord Kinmartin, the colt's owner, said to Bill Turner as he ran his eyes over Sunbright in the paddock where the autumn sunshine made the colt's quarters gleam like the sheen on a bronze medal.

'I'd never have believed he'd have filled out so well. What's this story about him and a dog?'

'It's true enough,' the trainer said, 'there's the dog.' He pointed to Turi, who, still bandaged on his hind leg, was tucked under a lad's arm.

He told Sunbright's owner the tale and the latter grunted.

'It's all over the course,' he said. 'At any rate, it's good publicity.'

As Lord Kinmartin's considerable fortune had been largely made by the help of publicity, he was an authority on the subject. Certainly the Press had got hold of the story, and already a dozen reporters had besieged Bill Turner with requests for the full tale, and several photos had been taken of Turi. But Bill had only told them a little and they were still eager for more.

Turi was the last thing the colt saw as he left the paddock. He cantered down the straight towards the starting-gate, in company with the favourite, Grey Cloud, Hurry Up, the second favourite, Gay Girl, Bright Boy, All Alone, and six others.

Ted Norton was up on Sunbright. He was not one of the fashionable jockeys, but Bill Turner liked him. He was always in sympathy with his mount, although there might be cleverer jockeys at riding a hard finish.

He brought Sunbright up alert and fairly calm, a contrast to his former behaviour when, sweating and fretting, there had been great difficulty in bringing him up to the tapes. Something down the line wheeled, and was brought into line again.

'Are you all ready?'

'No, sir. Wait, sir. Yes. . . .'

The tapes sprang up.

'Go!'

Sunbright leapt forward. Ted Norton felt the power of the colt beneath him with a faint surprise, but with a growing sense of satisfaction. He steadied slightly, not daring to do more, for Bill Turner had warned him.

'You can't be certain of him. He thinks, and he thinks quicker than one does oneself.'

Three furlongs to go. Three of them were beaten and the colt was not fully stretched and lying fifth. Ted let him go and he swept past Gay Girl and Bright Boy.

Two furlongs. Dared he risk it now? He called on Sunbright and he saw Hurry Up's quarters come back. He was level with his girth, with his shoulder – he was past him.

There was only Grey Cloud now and at the distance post he drew level with him. Then the grey colt forged ahead again, but Sunbright hung on.

Could he do it? He asked the chestnut and he responded magnificently. Every stride nearer.

There was a wild roaring from the crowd. 'Who is it?' 'The colt with the dog!'

'Sunbright wins, he doesn't – Grey Cloud has it. No. Sunbright! Sunbright!'

The chestnut head with the white blaze was in front as the judge's box flashed past.

Pandemonium broke forth. There was noisy cheering. The sentimental English crowd loves a good story, and by now everybody knew about Turi. A few women had backed the colt out of sentiment, but he carried little money and the bookmakers were content.

Sunbright was led in, Lord Kinmartin at his head, but nobody heeded him. A little prick-eared face with black unwinking eyes peered over the rails. Turi sat enthroned in a lad's arms. Sunbright stared across, then nickered gaily. The crowd went mad and pressed round the lad to pat the dog. The reporters nearly choked with excitement.

Turi looked at them and gave the Finnish Spitz's typical little caterwaul.

'*Ou-ah-h-h!*' said Turi, son of Repo.

THE COMING OF RIQUET

Anatole France
(French) 1844–1922

SEATED at his table one morning in front of the window, against which the leaves of the plane-tree quivered, M. Bergeret, who was trying to discover how the ships of Aeneas had been changed into nymphs, heard a tap at the door, and forthwith his servant entered, carrying in front of her, opossum-like, a tiny creature whose black head peeped out from the folds of her apron, which she had turned up to form a pocket. With a look of anxiety and hope upon her face, she remained motionless for a moment, then she placed the little thing upon the carpet at her master's feet.

'What's that?' asked M. Bergeret.

It was a little dog of doubtful breed, having something of the terrier in him, and a well-set head, a short, smooth coat of a dark tan colour, and a tiny little stump of a tail. His body retained its puppy-like softness, and he went sniffing at the carpet.

'Angélique,' said M. Bergeret, 'take this animal back to its owner.'

'It has no owner, Monsieur.'

M. Bergeret looked silently at the little creature, who had come to examine his slippers, and was giving little sniffs of approval. M. Bergeret was a philologist, which perhaps explains why at this juncture he asked a vain question.

'What is he called?'

'Monsieur,' replied Angélique, 'he has no name.'

M. Bergeret seemed put out at this answer: he looked at the dog sadly, with a disheartened air.

Then the little animal placed its two front paws on M. Bergeret's

146

slipper, and, holding it thus, began innocently to nibble at it. With a sudden access of compassion M. Bergeret took the tiny nameless creature upon his knee. The dog looked at him intently, and M. Bergeret was pleased at his confiding expression.

'What beautiful eyes!' he cried.

The dog's eyes were indeed beautiful, the pupils of a golden-flecked chestnut set in warm white. And his gaze spoke of simple, mysterious thoughts, common alike to the thoughtful beasts and simple men of the earth.

Tired, perhaps, with the intellectual effort he had made for the purpose of entering into communication with a human being, he closed his beautiful eyes, and, yawning widely, revealed his pink mouth, his curled-up tongue, and his array of dazzling teeth.

M. Bergeret put his hand into the dog's mouth, and allowed him to lick it, at which old Angélique gave a smile of relief.

'A more affectionate little creature doesn't breathe,' she said.

'The dog,' said M. Bergeret, 'is a religious animal. In his savage state he worships the moon and the lights that float upon the waters. These are his gods, to whom he appeals at night with long-drawn howls. In the domesticated state he seeks by his caresses to conciliate those powerful genii who dispense the good things of this world – to wit, men. He worships and honours men by the accomplishment of the rites passed down to him by his ancestors: he licks their hands, jumps against their legs, and when they show signs of anger towards him he approaches them crawling on his belly as a sign of humility, to appease their wrath.'

'All dogs are not the friends of man,' remarked Angélique. 'Some of them bite the hand that feeds them.'

'Those are the ungodly, blasphemous dogs,' returned M. Bergeret, 'insensate creatures like Ajax, the son of Telamon, who wounded the hand of the golden Aphrodite. These sacrilegious creatures die a dreadful death, or lead wandering and miserable lives. They are not to be confounded with those dogs who, espousing the quarrel of their own particular god, wage war upon his enemy, the neighbouring god. They are heroes. Such, for example, is the dog of Lafolie, the butcher, who fixed his sharp teeth into the leg of the tramp

Pied-d'Alouette. For it is a fact that dogs fight among themselves like men, and Turk, with his snub nose, serves his god Lafolie against the robber gods, in the same way that Israel helped Jehovah to destroy Chamos and Moloch.'

The puppy, however, having decided that M. Bergeret's remarks were the reverse of interesting, curled up his feet and stretched out his head, ready to go to sleep upon the knees that harboured him.

'Where did you find him?' asked M. Bergeret.

'Well, Monsieur, it was M. Dellion's *chef* gave him to me.'

'With the result,' continued M. Bergeret, 'that we now have this soul to care for.'

'What soul?' asked Angélique.

'This canine soul. An animal is, properly speaking, a soul; I do not say an immortal soul. And yet, when I come to consider the positions this poor little beast and I myself occupy in the scheme of things, I recognize in both exactly the same right to immortality.'

After considerable hesitation, old Angélique, with a painful effort that made her upper lip curl up and reveal her two remaining teeth, said:

'If Monsieur does not want a dog, I will return him to M. Dellion's *chef*; but you may safely keep him, I assure you. You won't see or hear him.'

She had hardly finished her sentence when the puppy, hearing a heavy van rolling down the street, sat bolt upright on M. Bergeret's knees, and began to bark both loud and long, so that the window-panes resounded with the noise.

M. Bergeret smiled.

'He's a watch-dog,' said Angélique, by way of excuse. 'They are by far the most faithful.'

'Have you given him anything to eat?' asked M. Bergeret.

'Of course,' returned Angélique.

'What does he eat?'

'Monsieur must be aware that dogs eat bread and meat.'

Somewhat piqued, M. Bergeret retorted that in her eagerness she might very likely have taken him away from his mother before he was old enough to leave her, upon which he was lifted up again and re-examined, only to make sure of the fact that he was at least six months old.

M. Bergeret put him down on the carpet, and regarded him with interest.

'Isn't he pretty?' said the servant.

'No, he is not pretty,' replied M. Bergeret. 'But he is engaging, and has beautiful eyes. That is what people used to say about me,' added the professor. 'when I was three times as old, and not half as intelligent. Since then I have no doubt acquired an outlook upon the universe which he will never attain. But, in comparison with the Absolute, I may say that my knowledge equals his in the smallness of its extent. Like his, it is a geometrical point in the infinite.' Then, addressing the little creature who was sniffing the waste-paper basket, he went on: 'Smell it out, sniff it well, take from the outside world all the knowledge that can reach your simple brain through the medium of that black truffle-like nose of yours. And what though I at the same time observe, and compare, and study? We shall never know, neither the one nor the other of us, why we have been put into this world, and what we are doing in it. What are we here for, eh?'

As he had spoken rather loudly, the puppy looked at him anxiously, and M. Bergeret, returning to the thought which had first filled his mind, said to the servant:

'We must give him a name.'

With her hands folded in front of her she replied laughingly that that would not be a difficult matter.

Upon which M. Bergeret made the private reflection that to the simple all things are simple, but that clear-sighted souls, who look upon things from many and divers aspects, invisible to the vulgar mind, experience the greatest difficulty in coming to a decision about even the most trivial matters. And he cudgelled his brains, trying to hit upon a name for the little living thing that was busily engaged in nibbling the fringe of the carpet.

'All the names of dogs,' thought he, 'preserved in the ancient treatises of the huntsmen of old, such as Fouilloux, and in the verses of our sylvan poets such as La Fontaine – Finaud, Miraut,

Briffaut, Ravaud, and such-like names, are given to sporting dogs, who are the aristocracy of the kennel, the chivalry of the canine race. The dog of Ulysses was called Argos, and he was a hunter too, so Homer tells us. "In his youth he hunted the little hares of Ithaca, but now he was old and hunted no more." What we require is something quite different. The names given by old maids to their lap-dogs would be more suitable, were they not usually pretentious and absurd. Azor, for instance, is ridiculous!'

So M. Bergeret ruminated, calling to memory many a dog name, without being able to decide, however, on one that pleased him. He would have liked to invent a name, but lacked the imagination.

'What day is it?' he asked at last.

'The ninth,' replied Angélique. 'Thursday, the ninth.'

'Well, then!' said M. Bergeret, 'can't we call the dog Thursday, like Robinson Crusoe who called his man Friday, for the same reason?'

'As Monsieur pleases,' said Angélique. 'But it isn't very pretty.'

'Very well,' said M. Bergeret, 'find a name for the creature yourself, for, after all, you brought him here.'

'Oh, no,' said the servant. 'I couldn't find a name for him; I'm not clever enough. When I saw him lying on the straw in the kitchen, I called him Riquet, and he came up and played about under my skirts.'

'You called him Riquet, did you?' cried M. Bergeret. 'Why didn't you say so before? Riquet he is and Riquet he shall remain; that's settled. Now be off with you, and take Riquet with you. I want to work.'

'Monsieur,' returned Angélique, 'I am going to leave the puppy with you; I will come for him when I get back from market.'

'You could quite well take him to market with you,' retorted M. Bergeret.

'Monsieur, I am going to church as well.'

It was quite true that she really was going to church at Saint-Exupère, to ask for a Mass to be said for the repose of her husband's soul. She did that regularly once a year, not that she had even been informed of the decease of Borniche, who had never communicated with her since his desertion, but it was a settled thing in the good woman's mind that Borniche was dead. She had therefore no fear of his coming to rob her of the little she had, and did her best to fix things up to his advantage in the other world, so long as he left her in peace in this one.

'Eh!' ejaculated M. Bergeret. 'Shut him up in the kitchen or some other convenient place, and do not wor—'

He did not finish his sentence, for Angélique had vanished, purposely pretending not to hear, that she might leave Riquet with his master. She wanted them to grow used to one another, and she also wanted to give poor, friendless M. Bergeret a companion. Having closed the door behind her, she went along the corridor and down the steps.

M. Bergeret set to work again and plunged head foremost into his *Virgilius nauticus*. He loved the work; it rested his thoughts, and became a kind of game that suited him, for he played it all by himself. On the table beside him were several boxes filled with pegs, which he fixed into little squares of cardboard to represent the fleet of Aeneas. Now while he was thus occupied he felt something like tiny fists tapping at his legs. Riquet, whom he had quite forgotten, was standing on his hind legs patting his master's knees, and wagging his little stump of a tail. When he tired of this, he let his paws slide down the trouser leg, then got up and began his coaxing over again. And M. Bergeret, turning away from the printed lore before him, saw two brown eyes gazing up at him lovingly.

'What gives a human beauty to the gaze of this dog,' he thought, 'is probably that it varies unceasingly, being by turns bright and vivacious, or serious and sorrowful; because through these eyes his little dumb soul finds expression for thought that lacks nothing in depth nor sequence. My father was very fond of cats, and, consequently, I liked them too. He used to declare that cats are the wise man's best companions, for they respect his studious hours. Bajazet, his Persian cat, would sit at night for hours at a stretch, motionless and majestic, perched on a corner of his table. I still remember the agate eyes of Bajazet, but those jewel-like orbs concealed all thought, that owl-like stare was cold, and hard, and wicked. How much do I prefer the melting gaze of the dog!'

Riquet, however, was agitating his paws in frantic fashion, and M. Bergeret, who was anxious to return to his philological amusements, said kindly, but shortly:

'Lie down, Riquet!'

Upon which Riquet went and thrust his nose against the door through which Angélique had passed out. And there he remained, uttering from time to time plaintive, meek little cries. After a while he began to scratch, making a gentle rasping noise on the polished floor with his nails. Then the whining began again followed by more scratching. Disturbed by these sounds, M. Bergeret sternly bade him keep still.

Riquet peered at him sorrowfully with his brown eyes, then, sitting down, he looked at M. Bergeret again, rose, returned to the door, sniffed underneath it, and wailed afresh.

'Do you want to go out?' asked M. Bergeret.

Putting down his pen, he went to the door, which he held a few inches open. After making sure that he was running no risk of hurting himself on the way out, Riquet slipped through the doorway and marched off with a composure that was scarcely polite. On returning to his table, M. Bergeret, sensitive man that he was, pondered over the dog's action. He said to himself:

'I was on the point of reproaching the animal for going without saying either good-bye or thank you, and expecting him to apologize for leaving me. It was the beautiful human expression of his eyes that made me so foolish. I was beginning to look upon him as one of my own kind.'

After making this reflection M. Bergeret applied himself anew to the metamorphosis of the ships of Aeneas, a legend both pretty and popular, but perhaps a trifle too simple in itself for expression in such noble language. M. Bergeret, however, saw nothing incongruous in it. He knew that the nursery tales have furnished material for nearly all epics, and that Virgil had carefully collected together in his poem the riddles, the puns, the uncouth stories, and the puerile imaginings of his forefathers; that Homer, his master and the master of all the bards, had done little more than tell over again what the good wives of Ionia and the fishermen of the islands had been narrating for more than a thousand years before him. Besides, for the time being, this was the least of his worries; he had another far more important preoccupation. An expression, met with in the course of the charming story of the metamorphosis, did not appear sufficiently plain to him. That was what was worrying him.

'Bergeret, my friend,' he said to himself, 'this is where you must open your eyes and show your sense. Remember that Virgil always expresses himself with extreme precision when writing on the technique of the arts; remember that he went yachting at Baiae, that he was an expert in naval construction, and that therefore his language, in this passage, must have a precise and definite signification.'

And M. Bergeret carefully consulted a great number of texts, in order to throw a light upon the word which he could not understand, and which he had to explain. He was almost on the point of grasping the solution, or, at any rate, he had caught a glimpse of it, when he heard a noise like the rattling of chains at his door, a noise which, although not alarming, struck him as curious. The disturbance was presently accompanied by a shrill whining, and M. Bergeret, interrupted in his philological investigations, immediately concluded that these importunate wails must emanate from Riquet.

As a matter of fact, after having looked vainly all over the house for Angélique, Riquet had been seized with a desire to see M. Bergeret again. Solitude was as painful to him as human society was dear. In order to put an end to the noise, and also because he had a secret desire to see Riquet again, M. Bergeret got up from his armchair and opened the door, and Riquet re-entered the study with the same coolness with which he had quitted it, but as soon as he saw the door close behind him he assumed a melancholy expression, and began to wander up and down the room like a soul in torment.

He had a sudden way of appearing to find something of interest beneath the chairs and tables, and would sniff long and noisily; then he would walk aimlessly about or sit down in a corner with an air of great humility, like the beggars who are to be seen in church porches. Finally he began to bark at a cast of Hermes which stood upon the mantelshelf, whereupon M. Bergeret addressed him in words full of just reproach.

'Riquet! Such vain agitation, such sniffing and barking were better suited to a stable than to the study of a professor, and they lead one to suppose that your ancestors lived with horses whose straw litters they shared. I do not reproach you with that. It is only natural you should have inherited their habits, manners, and tendencies as well as their close-cropped coat, their sausage-like body, and their long, thin nose. I do not speak of your beautiful eyes, for there are few men, few dogs even, who can open such beauties to the light of day. But, leaving all that aside, you are a mongrel, my friend, a mongrel from your short, bandy legs to your head. Again I am far from despising you for that. What I want you to understand is that if you desire to live with me, you will have to drop your mongrel manners and behave like a *scholar*, in other words, to remain silent and quiet, to respect work, after the manner of Bajazet, who of a night would sit for four hours without stirring, and watch my father's pen skimming over the paper. He was a silent and tactful creature. How different is your own character, my friend! Since you came into this chamber of study your hoarse voice, your unseemly snufflings and your whines, that sound like steam whistles, have constantly confused my thoughts and interrupted my reflections. And now you have made me lose the drift of an important passage in Servius, referring to the construction of one of the ships of Aeneas. Know then, Riquet, my friend, that this is the house of silence and the abode of meditation, and that if you are anxious to stay here you must become literary. Be quiet!'

Thus spoke M. Bergeret. Riquet, who had listened to him with mute astonishment, approached his master, and with suppliant gesture placed a timid paw upon the knee, which he seemed to revere in a fashion that savoured of long ago. Then a kind thought struck M. Bergeret. He picked him up by the scruff of his neck, and put him upon the cushions of the ample easy chair in which he was sitting. Turning himself round three times, Riquet lay down, and then remained perfectly still and silent. He was quite happy. M. Bergeret was grateful to him, and as he ran through Servius he occasionally stroked the close-cropped coat, which, without being soft, was smooth and very pleasant to the touch. Riquet fell into a gentle doze, and communicated to his master the generous warmth of his body, the subtle, gentle heat of a living, breathing thing. And from that moment M. Bergeret found more pleasure in his *Virgilius nauticus*.

From floor to ceiling his study was lined with deal shelves, bearing books arranged in methodical order. One glance, and all that remains to us of Latin thought was ready to his hand. The Greeks lay half-way up. In a quiet corner, easy to access, were Rabelais, the excellent story-tellers of the *Cent nouvelles nouvelles*, Bonaventure des Périers, Guillaume Bouchet, and all the old French 'conteurs,' whom M. Bergeret considered better adapted to humanity than writings in the more heroic style, and who were the favourite reading of his leisure. He possessed them in cheap modern editions only, but he had discovered a poor bookbinder in the town who covered his volumes with leaves from a book of anthems, and it gave M. Bergeret the keenest pleasure to see these free-spoken gentlemen thus clad in Requiems and Misereres. This was the sole luxury and the only peculiarity of his austere library. The other books were paper-backed or bound in poor and worn-out bindings. The gentle friendly manner in which they were handled by their owner gave them the look of tools set out in a busy man's workshop. The books of archaeology and art found a resting-place on the highest shelves, not by any means out of contempt, but because they were not so often used.

Now, while M. Bergeret worked at his *Virgilius nauticus* and shared his chair with Riquet, he found, as chance would have it, that it was necessary to consult Ottfried Müller's little *Manual*, which happened to be on one of the topmost shelves.

There was no need of one of those tall ladders on wheels topped by railings and a shelf, to enable him to reach the book; there were ladders of this description in the town library, and they had been used by all the great book-lovers of the eighteenth and nineteenth centuries; indeed, several of the latter had fallen from them, and thus died honourable deaths, in the manner spoken of in the pamphlet entitled: *Des bibliophiles qui moururent en tombant de leur échelle*. No, indeed! M. Bergeret had no need of anything of the sort. A small pair of folding steps would have served his purpose excellently well, and he had once seen some in the shop of Clérambaut, the cabinet-maker, in the Rue de Josde. They folded up, and looked just the thing, with their bevelled uprights each pierced with a trefoil as a grip for the hand. M. Bergeret would have given anything to possess them, but the state of his finances, which were somewhat involved, forced him to abandon the idea. No one knew better than he did that financial ills are not mortal, but, for all that, he had no steps in his study.

In place of such a pair of steps he used an old cane-bottomed chair, the back of which had been broken, leaving only two horns or antennae, which had shown themselves to be more dangerous than useful. So they had been cut to the level of the seat, and the chair had become a stool. There were two reasons why this stool was ill- fitted to the use to which M. Bergeret was wont to put it. In the first place the woven-cane seat had grown slack with long use, and now contained a large hollow, making one's foothold precarious. In the second place the stool was too low, and it was hardly possible when standing upon it to reach the books on the highest shelf, even with the finger-tips. What generally happened was that in the endeavour to grasp one book, several others fell out; and it depended upon their being bound or paper-covered whether they lay with broken corners, or sprawled with leaves spread like a fan or a concertina.

Now, with the intention of getting down the *Manual* of Ottfried Müller, M. Bergeret quitted the chair he was sharing with Riquet, who, rolled into a ball with his head tight pressed to his body, lay in warm comfort, opening one voluptuous eye, which he re-closed as quickly. Then M. Bergeret drew the stool from the dark corner where it was hidden and placed it where it was required, hoisted himself upon it, and managed, by making his arm as long as possible, and straining upon tiptoe, to touch, first with one, then with two fingers, the back of a book which he judged to be the one he was needing. As for the thumb, it remained below the shelf and rendered no assistance whatever. M. Bergeret, who found it therefore exceedingly difficult to draw out the book, made the reflection that the reason why the hand is a precious implement is on account of the position of the thumb, and that no being could rise to be an artist who had four feet and no hands.

'It is to the hand,' he reflected, 'that men owe their power of becoming engineers, painters, writers, and manipulators of all kinds of things. If they had not a thumb as well as their other fingers, they would be as incapable as I am at this moment, and they could never have changed the face of the earth as they have done. Beyond a doubt it is the shape of the hand that has assured to man the conquest of the world.'

Then, almost simultaneously, M. Bergeret remembered that monkeys, who possess four hands, have not, for all that, created the arts, nor disposed that earth to their use, and he erased from his mind the theory upon which he had just embarked. However, he did the best he could with his four fingers. It must be known that Ottfried Müller's *Manual* is composed of three volumes and an atlas. M. Bergeret wanted volume one. He pulled out first the second volume, then the atlas, then volume three, and finally the book that he required. At last he held it in his hands. All that now remained for him to do was to descend, and this he was about to do when the cane seat gave way beneath his foot, which passed through it. He lost his balance and fell to the ground, not as heavily as might have been feared, for he broke his fall by grasping at one of the uprights of the bookshelf.

He was on the ground, however, full of astonishment, and wearing on one leg the broken chair; his whole body was permeated and as though constricted by a pain that spread all over it, and that presently settled itself more particularly in the region of the left elbow and hip upon which he had fallen. But, as his anatomy was not seriously damaged, he gathered his wits together; he had got so far as to realize that he must draw his right leg out of the stool in which it had so unfortunately become entangled, and that he must be careful to raise himself up on his right side, which was unhurt. He was even trying to put this into execution when he felt a warm breath upon his cheek, and turning his eyes, which fright and pain had for the moment fixed, he saw close to his cheek Riquet's little face.

At the sound of the fall Riquet had jumped down from the chair and run to his unfortunate master; he was now standing near him in a state of great excitement; then he commenced to run round him. First he came near out of sympathy, then he retreated out of fear of some mysterious danger. He understood perfectly well that a misfortune had taken place, but he was neither thoughtful nor clever enough to discover what it was; hence his anxiety. His fidelity drew him to his suffering friend, and his prudence stopped him on the very brink of the fatal spot. Encouraged at length by the calm and silence which eventually reigned, he licked M. Bergeret's neck and looked at him with eyes of fear and of love. The fallen master smiled, and the dog licked the end of his nose. It was a great comfort to M. Bergeret, who freed his right leg, stood erect, and limped good-humouredly back to his chair.

Riquet was there before him. All that could be seen of his eyes was a gleam between the narrow slit of the half-closed lids. He seemed to have forgotten all about the adventure that a moment before had so stirred them both. The little creature lived in the present, with no thought of time that had run its course; not that he was wanting in memory, inasmuch as he could remember, not his own past alone, but the faraway past of his ancestors, and his little head was a rich store-house of useful knowledge; but he took no pleasure in remembrance, and memory was not for him, as it was for M. Bergeret, a divine muse.

Gently stroking the short, smooth coat of his companion, M. Bergeret addressed him in the following affectionate terms:

'Dog! at the price of the repose which is dear to your heart, you came to me when I was dismayed and brought low. You did not laugh, as any young person of my own species would have done. It is true that however joyous or terrible nature may appear to you at times, she never inspires you with a sense of the ridiculous. And it is for that very reason, because of your innocent gravity, that you are the surest friend a man can have. In the first instance I inspired confidence and admiration in you, and now you show me pity.

'Dog! when we first met on the highway of life, we came from the two poles of creation; we belong to different species. I refer to this with no desire to take advantage of it, but rather with a strong sense of universal brotherhood. We have hardly been acquainted two hours, and my hand has never yet fed you. What can be the meaning of the obscure love for me that has sprung up in your little heart? The sympathy you bestow on me is a charming mystery, and I accept it. Sleep, friend, in the place that you have chosen!'

Having thus spoken, M. Bergeret turned over the leaves of Ottfried Müller's *Manual*, which with marvellous instinct he had kept in his hand both during and after his fall. He turned over the pages, and could not find what he sought.

Every moment, however, seemed to increase the pain he was feeling.

'I believe,' he thought, 'that the whole of my left side is bruised and my hip swollen. I have a suspicion that my right leg is grazed all over and my left elbow aches and burns, but shall I cavil at pain that has led me to the discovery of a friend?'

His reflections were running thus when old Angélique, breathless and perspiring, entered the study. She first opened the door, and then she knocked, for she never permitted herself to enter without knocking. If she had not done so before she opened the door, she did it after, for she had good manners, and knew what was expected of her. She went in therefore, knocked, and said:

'Monsieur, I have come to relieve you of the dog.'

M. Bergeret heard these words with decided annoyance. He had not as yet inquired into his claims to Riquet, and now realized that he had none. The thought that Madame Borniche might take the animal away from him filled him with sadness, yet, after all, Riquet did belong to her. Affecting indifference, he replied:

'He's asleep; let him sleep!'

'Where is he, I don't see him,' remarked old Angélique.

'Here he is,' answered M. Bergeret. 'In my chair.'

With her two hands clasped over her portly figure, old Angélique smiled, and, in a tone of gentle mockery, ventured:

'I wonder what pleasure the creature can find in sleeping there behind Monsieur!'

'That,' retorted M. Bergeret, 'is his business.'

Then, as he was of inquiring mind, he immediately sought of Riquet his reasons for the selection of his resting-place, and lighting on them, replied with his accustomed candour:

'I keep him warm, and my presence affords a sense of security; my comrade is a chilly and homely little animal.' Then he added: 'Do you know, Angélique? I will go out presently and buy him a collar.'

BEING
A PUBLIC
CHARACTER

Don Marquis
(American) 1878–1937

E VER since I bit a circus lion, believing him to be another dog
like myself, only larger, I have been what Doc Watson calls a
Public Character in our town.

Freckles, my boy, was a kind of Public Character, too. He went
round bragging about my noble blood and bravery, and all the other
boys and dogs in town sort of looked up to him and thought how
lucky he was to belong to a dog like me. And he deserved whatever
glory he got out of it, Freckles did. For, if I do say it myself, there's
not a dog in town got a better boy than my boy Freckles, take him
all in all. I'll back him against any dog's boy that is anywhere near
his size, for fighting, swimming, climbing, foot-racing, or throwing
stones farthest and straightest. Or I'll back him against any stray
boy, either.

Well, some dogs may be born Public Characters, and like it. And
some may be brought up to like it. I've seen dogs in those travelling
Uncle Tom's Cabin shows that were so stuck on themselves they
wouldn't hardly notice us town dogs. But with me, becoming a Public
Character happened all in a flash, and it was sort of hard for me to
get used to it. One day I was just a private kind of a dog, as you
might say, eating my meals at the Watsons' back door, and pretending
to hunt rats when requested, and not scratching off too many fleas
in Doc Watson's drug store, and standing out from underfoot when
told, and other unremarkable things like that. And the next day I

had bit that lion and was a Public Character, and fame came so sudden I scarcely knew how to act.

Even drummers from big places like St. Louis and Chicago would come into the drug store and look at my teeth and toe-nails, as if they must be different from other dogs' teeth and toe-nails. And people would come tooting up to the store in their little cars, and get out and look me over and say:

'Well, Doc, what'll you take for him?' and Doc would wink, and say:

'He's Harold's dog. You ask Harold.'

Which Harold is Freckles's other name. But any boy that calls him Harold outside of the schoolhouse has got a fight on his hands, if that boy is anywhere near Freckles's size. Harry goes, or Hal goes, but Harold is a fighting word with Freckles. Except, of course, with grown people. I heard him say one day to Tom Mulligan, his parents thought Harold was a name, or he guessed they wouldn't have given it to him; but it wasn't a name, it was a handicap.

Freckles would always say, 'Spot ain't for sale.'

And even Heinie Hassenyager, the butcher, got stuck on me after I got to be a Public Character. Heinie would come two blocks up Main Street with lumps of Hamburg steak, which is the kind someone has already chewed for you, and give them to me. Steak, mind you, not old grisly scraps. And before I became a Public Character Heinie even begrudged me the bones I would drag out of the box under his counter when he wasn't looking.

My daily hope was that I could live up to it all. I had always tried, before I happened to bite that lion, to be a friendly kind of a dog towards boys and humans and dogs, all three. I'd always been expected to do a certain amount of tail-wagging and be friendly. But as soon as I got to be a Public Character, I saw right away that I wasn't expected to be *too* friendly any more. So, every now and then, I'd growl a little, for no reason at all. A dog that has bit a lion is naturally expected to have fierce thoughts inside of him; I could see that. And you have got to act the way humans expect you to act if you want to slide along through the world without too much trouble.

So when Heinie would bring me the ready-chewed steak I'd growl at him a little bit. And then I'd bolt and gobble the steak like I didn't think so darned much of it, after all, and was doing Heinie a big personal favour to eat it. And now and then I'd pretend I wasn't going to eat a piece of it unless it was chewed finer for me, and growl at him about that.

That way of acting made a big hit with Heinie, too. I could see that he was honoured and flattered because I didn't go any further than just a growl. It gave him a chance to say he knew how to manage animals. And the more I growled, the more steak he brought. Everybody in town fed me. I pretty near ate myself to death for a while there, besides all the meat I buried back of Doc Watson's store to dig up later.

But my natural disposition is to be friendly. I would rather be loved than feared, which is what Bill Petterson, the village drunkard, used to say. When they put him into the calaboose every Saturday afternoon he used to look out between the bars on the back window and talk to the boys and dogs that had gathered round and say that he thanked them one and all for coming to an outcast's dungeon as a testimonial of affection, and he would rather be loved than feared. And my natural feelings are the same. I had to growl and keep dignified and go on being a Public Character, and often I would say to myself that it was losing me all my real friends, too.

The worst of it was that people, after a week or so, began to expect me to pull something else remarkable. Freckles, he got up a circus, and charged pins and marbles, and cents, when he found anyone that had any, to get into it, and I was the principal part of that circus. I was in a cage, and the sign over me read:

SPOT, THE DOG THAT LICKED A LION
TEN PINS ADMITION

To feed the lion-eater, one cent or two white
    chiney marbles extry but bring your own meat.
Pat him once on the head twinty pins, kids under
    five not allowed to.

163

For shaking hands with Spot the lion-eater,
    girls not allowed, gents three white chinies,
    or one aggie marble.
Lead him two blocks down the street and back,
    one cent before starting, no marbles or pins
    taken for leading him.
For sicking him on the cats three cents or one
    red cornelian marble if you furnish the cat.
    Five cents to use Watson's cat. Watson's
    biggest Tom-cat six cents must be paid
    before sicking. Small kids and girls not
    allowed to sick him on cats.

Well, we didn't take in any cat-sicking money. And it was just as well. You never can tell what a cat will do. But Freckles put it in because it sounded sort of fierce. I didn't care for being caged and circused that way myself. And it was right at that circus that considerable trouble started.

Seeing me in a cage like that, all famoused-up, with more meat poked through the slats than two dogs could eat, made Mutt Mulligan and some of my old friends jealous.

Mutt, he nosed by the cage and sniffed. I nosed a piece of meat out of the cage to him. Mutt grabbed it and gobbled it down, but he didn't thank me any. Mutt, he says:

'There's a new dog down town that says he blew in from Chicago. He says he used to be a Blind Man's Dog on a street corner there. He's a pretty wise dog, and he's a right ornery-looking dog, too. He's peeled considerably where he has been bit in fights.'

'Well, Mutt,' says I, 'as far as that goes I'm peeled considerable myself where I've been in fights.'

'I know you are, Spot,' says Mutt. 'You don't need to tell me that. I've peeled you some myself from time to time.'

'Yes,' I says, 'you did peel me some, Mutt. And I've peeled you some, too. More'n that, I notice that right leg of yours is a little stiff yet where I got to it about three weeks ago.'

'Well, then, Spot,' says Mutt, 'maybe you want to come down here and see what you can do to my other three legs. I never saw the day I wouldn't give you a free bite at one leg and still be able to lick you on the other three.'

'You wouldn't talk that way if I was out of this cage,' I says, getting riled.

'What did you ever let yourself be put into that fool cage for?' says Mutt. 'You didn't have to. You got such a swell head on you the last week or so that you gotta be licked. You can fool boys and humans all you want to about that accidental old lion, but us dogs got your number, all right. What that Blind Man's Dog from Chicago would do to you would be a plenty!'

'Well, then,' I says, 'I'll be out of this cage along about supper, time. Suppose you bring that Blind Man's Dog round here. And if he ain't got a spiked collar on to him, I'll fight him. I won't fight a spike-collared dog to please anybody.'

And I wouldn't, neither, without I had one on myself. If you can't get a dog by the throat or the back of his neck, what's the use of fighting him? You might just as well try to eat a blacksmith shop as fight one of those spike-collared dogs.

'Hey, there!' Freckles yelled at Tom Mulligan, who is Mutt Mulligan's boy. 'You get your fool dog away from the lion-eater's cage!'

Tom, he hissed Mutt away. But he says to Freckles, being jealous himself. 'Don't be scared, Freck, I won't let my dog hurt yours any. Spot, he's safe. He's in a cage where Mutt can't get to him.'

Freckles got riled. He says, 'I ain't in any cage, Tom.'

Tom, he didn't want to fight very bad. But all the other boys and dogs was looking on. And he'd sort of started it. He didn't figure that he could shut up that easy. And there was some girls there, too.

'If I was to make a pass at you,' says Tom, 'you'd wish you was in a cage.'

Freckles, he didn't want to fight so bad, either. But he was run-ning this circus, and he didn't feel he could afford to pass by what Tom said too easy. So he says:

'Maybe you think you're big enough to put me into a cage.'

'If I was to make a pass at you,' says Tom, 'there wouldn't be enough left of you to put in a cage.'

'Well, then,' says Freckles, 'why don't you make a pass at me?'

'Maybe you figure I don't dast to,' says Tom.

'I didn't say you didn't dast to,' says Freckles; 'anyone that says I said you didn't dast to is a link, link, liar, and so's his Aunt Mariar.'

Tom, he says, 'I ain't got any Aunt Mariar. And you're another and dasn't back it!'

Then some of the other kids put chips on to their shoulders. And each dared the other to knock his chip off. And the other kids pushed, and jostled them into each other till both chips fell off, and they went at it then. Once they got started they got really mad and each did all he knew how.

And right in the midst of it Mutt run in and bit Freckles on the calf of his leg. Any dog will fight for his boy when his boy is getting the worst of it. But when Mutt did that I give a budge against the wooden slats on the cage and two of them came off, and I was on top of Mutt. The circus was in the barn, and the hens began to scream and the horses began to stomp, and all the boys yelled, 'Sick 'im!' and 'Go to it!' and danced around and hollered, and the little girls yelled, and all the other dogs began to bark, and it was a right lively and enjoyable time. But Mrs. Watson, Freckles's Mother, and the hired girl ran out from the house and broke the fight up.

Grown women are like that. They don't want to fight themselves, and they don't seem to want anyone else to have fun. You got to be a hypocrite around a grown woman to get along with her at all. And then she'll feed you and make a lot of fuss over you. But the minute you start anything with real enjoyment in it she's surprised to see you acting that way. Nobody was licked satisfactory in that fight, or licked anyone else satisfactory.

Well, that night after supper, along comes that Blind Man's Dog. Never did I see a Blind Man's Dog that was as tight-skinned. I ain't a dog that brags, myself, and I don't say I would have licked that heavy a dog right easy, even if he had been a loose-skinned dog. What I do say is that I had been used to fighting loose-skinned dogs that you can get some sort of a reasonable hold on to while you are working around for position. And running into a tight-skinned dog that way, all of a sudden and all unprepared for it, would make anybody nervous. How are you going to get a purchase on a tight-skinned dog when you've been fighting loose-skinned dogs for so long that your teeth and jaws just naturally set themselves for a loose-skinned dog without thinking of it?

Lots of dogs wouldn't have fought him at all when they realized how they had been fooled about him, and how tight-skinned he was. But I was a Public Character now, and I had to fight him. More than that, I ain't ready to say yet that that dog actually licked me. Freckles he hit him in the ribs with a lump of soft coal, and he got off of me and run away before I could get my second wind. There's no telling what I would have done to that Blind Man's Dog, tight-skinned as he was, if he hadn't run away before I got my second wind.

Well, there's some mighty peculiar dogs in this world, let alone boys and humans. The word got round town, in spite of his running away like that before I got my second wind, that that Blind Man's Dog, so called, had actually licked me! Many pretended to believe it. Every time Freckles and me went down the street someone would say:

'Well, the dog that licked the lion got licked himself, did he?'

And if it was a lady said it, Freckles would spit on the sidewalk through the place where his front teeth are out and pass on politely as if he hadn't heard, and say nothing. And if it was a man that said it Freckles would thumb his nose at him. And if it was a girl that said it he would rub a handful of sand into her hair. And if it was a boy anywhere near his size, there would be a fight. If it was too big a boy, Freckles would sling railroad iron at him.

For a week or so it looked like Freckles and I were fighting all the time. On the way to school, and all through recess-times, and after school, and every time we went on to the street. I got so chewed and he got so busted up that we didn't hardly enjoy life.

No matter how much you may like to fight, some of the time you would like to pick the fights yourself and not have other people picking them off of you. Kids began to fight Freckles that wouldn't have dast to stand up to him a month before. I was still a Public Character, but I was getting to be the kind you josh about instead of the kind you are proud to feed. I didn't care so awful much for myself, but I hated it for Freckles. For when they got us pretty well hacked, all the boys began to call him Harold again.

And after they had called him Harold for a week he must have begun to think of himself as Harold. For one Sunday afternoon when there wasn't any school, instead of going swimming with the other kids or playing baseball, or anything, he went and played with girls.

He must have been pretty well downhearted and felt himself pretty much of an outcast, or he wouldn't have done that. I am an honest dog, and the truth must be told, the disgrace along with everything else, and the truth is that he played with girls of his own accord that day – not because he was sent to their house on an errand, not because it was a game got up with boys and girls together, not because it was cousins and he couldn't dodge them, but because he was an outcast. Any boy will play with girls when all the boys and girls are playing together, and some girls are nearly as good as boys; but no boy is going off alone to look up a bunch of girls and play with them without being coaxed unless he has had considerable of a downfall.

Right next to the side of our yard was the Wilkins's. They had a bigger house and a bigger yard than ours. Freckles was sitting on the top of the fence looking into their orchard when the three Wilkins girls came out to play. There was only two boys in the Wilkins family, and they was twins; but they were only year-old babies and didn't amount to anything. The two oldest Wilkins girls, the taffy-coloured-haired one and the squint-eyed one, each had one of the twins, taking care of it. And the other Wilkins girl, the pretty one, she had one of those big dolls made as big as a baby. They were rolling those babies and the doll round the grass in a wheelbarrow, and the wheel came off, and that's how Freckles happened to go over.

'Up in the attic,' says the taffy-coloured-haired one, when he had fixed up the wheelbarrow, 'there's a little old express wagon with one wheel off that would be better'n this wheelbarrow. Maybe you could fix that wheel on, too, Harold.'

Freckles, he fell for it. After he got the wagon fixed, they got to playing charades and fool girl games like that. The hired girl was off for the afternoon, and pretty soon Mrs. Wilkins hollered up the stairs that she was going to be gone for an hour, and to take good care of the twins, and then we were alone in the place.

Well, it wasn't much fun for me. They played and they played, and I stuck to Freckles – though his name was called nothing but Harold all that afternoon, and for the first time I said to myself 'Harold' seemed to fit. I stuck to him because a dog should stick to his boy, and a boy should stick to his dog, no matter what the disgrace. But after a while I got pretty tired and lay down on a rug, and a new kind of flea struck me. After I had chased him down and cracked him with my teeth I went to sleep.

I must have slept pretty sound and pretty long. All of a sudden I waked up with a start, and almost choking, for the place was smoky. I barked and no one answered.

I ran out to the landing, and the whole house was full of smoke. The house was on fire, and it looked like I was alone in it. I went down the back stairway, which didn't seem so full of smoke, but the door that led out on to the first-floor landing was locked, and I had to go back up again.

By the time I got back up, the front stairway was a great deal fuller of smoke, and I could see glints of flame winking through it way down below. But it was my only way out of that place. On the top step I stumbled over a grey wool bunch of something or other, and I picked it up in my mouth. Think I, 'That is Freckles's grey sweater, that he is so stuck on. I might as well take it down to him.'

It wasn't so hard for a lively dog to get out of a place like that, I thought. But I got kind of confused and excited, too. And it struck me all of a sudden, by the time I was down to the second floor, that that sweater weighed an awful lot.

I dropped it on the second floor, and ran into one of the front bedrooms and looked out.

By Jings! The whole town was in the front yard and in the street.

And in the midst of the crowd was Mrs. Wilkins, carrying on like mad.

'My baby!' she yelled. 'Save my baby. Let me loose! I'm going after my baby!'

I stood up on my hind legs, with my head just out of that bedroom window, and the flame and smoke licking up all around me, and barked.

'My doggie! My doggie!' yells Freckles, who was in the crowd. 'I must save my doggie!' And he made a run for the house, but someone grabbed him and slung him back.

And Mrs. Wilkins made a run, but they held her, too. The front of the house was one sheet of flame. Old Pop Wilkins, Mrs. Wilkins's husband, was jumping up and down in front of Mrs. Wilkins yelling, here was her baby. He had a real baby in one arm and that big doll in the other, and was so excited he thought he had both babies. Later I heard what had happened. The kids had thought that they were getting out with both twins but one of them had saved the doll and left a twin behind. The squint-eyed girl and the taffy-coloured-haired girl and the pretty girl was howling as loud as their mother. And every now and then some man would make a rush for the front door, but the fire would drive him back. And everyone was yelling advice to everyone else, except one man who was calling on the whole town to get him an axe. The volunteer fire engine was there, but there wasn't any water to squirt through it, and it had been backed up too near the house and had caught fire and was burning up.

Well, I thinks that baby will likely turn up in the crowd somewhere, after all, and I'd better get out of here myself while the getting was good. I ran out of the bedroom, and run into that bunched-up grey bundle again.

I ain't saying that I knew it was the missing twin in a grey shawl when I picked it up the second time. And I ain't saying that I didn't know it. But the fact is that I did pick it up. I don't make any brag that I would have risked my life to save Freckles's sweater. It may be I was so rattled I just picked it up because I had had it in my mouth before and didn't quite know what I was doing.

But the *record* is something you can't go behind, and the record is that I got out the back way and into the back yard with that bundle swinging from my mouth, and walked round into the front yard and laid that bundle down – *and it was the twin!*

I don't make any claim that I *knew* it was the twin till I got into the front yard, mind you. But you can't prove I *didn't* know it was.

And nobody tried to prove it. The grey bundle let out a squall.

'My baby!' yells Mrs. Wilkins. And she kissed me. I rubbed it off with my paw. And then the taffy-coloured-haired one kissed me. But when I saw the squint-eyed one coming I got behind Freckles and barked.

'Three cheers for Spot!' yelled the whole town. And they give them.

And then I saw what the lay of the land was, so I wagged my tail and barked.

It called for that hero stuff, and I throwed my head up and looked noble – and pulled it.

An hour before Freckles and me had been outcasts. And now we was Public Characters again. We walked down Main Street and we owned it. And we hadn't any more than got to Doc Watson's drug store than in rushed Heinie Hassenyager with a lump of Hamburg steak, and with tears in his eyes.

'It's got chicken livers mixed in it, too!' says Heinie.

I ate it. But while I ate it, I growled at him.

171

THE DOG AT THE GERMAN INN

from *Three Men on the Bummel*

Jerome K. Jerome
(British) 1859–1927

I T was a comfortable little restaurant, where they cooked well. We
stopped there for a couple of hours, and dried ourselves and fed
ourselves, and talked about the view; and just before we left an
incident occurred that shows how much more stirring in this world
are the influences of evil compared with those of good.

A traveller entered. He seemed a careworn man. He carried a
brick in his hand, tied to a piece of rope. He entered nervously and
hurriedly, closed the door carefully behind him, saw to it that it was
fastened, peered out of the window long and earnestly, and then,
with a sigh of relief, laid his brick upon the bench beside him and
called for food and drink.

There was something mysterious about the whole affair. One
wondered what he was going to do with the brick, why he had
closed the door so carefully, why he had looked so anxiously from
the window; but his aspect was too wretched to invite conversation,
and we forebore, therefore, to ask him questions. As he ate and
drank he grew more cheerful, sighed less often. Later he stretched
his legs, lit an evil-smelling cigar, and puffed in calm contentment.

Then it happened. It happened too suddenly for any detailed
explanation of the thing to be possible. I recollect a Fräulein entering the room from the kitchen with a pan in her hand. I saw her
cross to the outer door. The next moment the whole room was in an
uproar. One was reminded of those pantomime transformation

scenes where, from among floating clouds, slow music, waving flowers, and reclining fairies, one is suddenly transported into the midst of shouting policemen tumbling over yelling babies, swells fighting pantaloons, sausages and harlequins, buttered slides and clowns. As the Fräulein of the pan touched the door it flew open, as though all the spirits of sin had been pressed against it, waiting. Two pigs and a chicken rushed into the room; a cat that had been sleeping on a beer barrel spluttered into fiery life. The Fräulein threw her pan into the air and lay down on the floor. The gentleman with the brick sprang to his feet, upsetting the table before him with everything upon it.

One looked to see the cause of the disaster; one discovered it at once in the person of a mongrel terrier with pointed ears and a squirrel's tail. The landlord rushed out from another door, and attempted to kick him out of the room. Instead, he kicked one of the pigs, the fatter of the two. It was a vigorous, well-planted kick, and the pig got the whole of it, none of it was wasted. One felt sorry for the poor animal; but no amount of sorrow anyone else might feel for him could compare with the sorrow he felt for himself. He stopped running about; he sat down in the middle of the room, and appealed to the solar system generally to observe the unjust thing that had come upon him. They must have heard this complaint in the valleys round about, and have wondered what upheaval of nature was taking place among the hills.

As for the hen it scuttled, screaming, every way at once. It was a marvellous bird; it seemed to be able to run up a straight wall quite easily; and it and the cat between them fetched down most everything that was not already on the floor. In less than forty seconds there were nine people in that room, all trying to kick one dog. Possibly, now and again, one or another may have succeeded, for occasionally the dog would stop barking in order to howl. But it did not discourage him. Everything has to be paid for, he evidently argued, even a pig and chicken hunt; and, on the whole, the game was worth it.

Besides, he had the satisfaction of observing that, for every kick he received, most other living things in the room got two. As for the unfortunate pig – the stationary one, the one that still sat lamenting in the centre of the room – he must have averaged a steady four. Trying to kick this dog was like playing football with a ball that was never there – not when you went to kick it, but after you had started to kick it, and had gone too far to stop yourself, so that the kick had to go on in any case, your only hope being that your foot would find something or another solid to stop it, and so save you from sitting down on the floor noisily and completely. When anybody did kick the dog it was by pure accident, when they were not expecting to kick him; and, generally speaking, this took them so unawares that, after kicking him, they fell over him. And everybody, every half-minute, would be certain to fall over the pig – the sitting pig, the one incapable of getting out of anybody's way.

How long the scrimmage might have lasted it is impossible to say. It was ended by the judgement of George. For a while he had been seeking to catch, not the dog but the remaining pig, the one still capable of activity. Cornering it at last, he persuaded it to cease running round and round the room, and instead to take a spin out-side. It shot through the door with one long wail.

We always desire the thing we have not. One pig, a chicken, nine people, and a cat, there was nothing in that dog's opinion compared with the quarry that was disappearing. Unwisely, he darted after it, and George closed the door on him and shot the bolt.

Then the landlord stood up and surveyed all the things that were lying on the floor.

'That's a playful dog of yours,' said he to the man who had come in with the brick.

'He's not my dog,' replied the man sullenly.

'Whose dog is it then?' said the landlord.

'I don't know whose dog it is,' answered the man.

'That won't do for me, you know,' said the landlord, picking up a picture of the German Emperor, and wiping beer from it with his sleeve.

'I know it won't,' replied the man. 'I never expected it would. I'm tired of telling people it isn't my dog. They none of them believe me.'

'What do you want to go about with him for, if he's not your dog?' said the landlord. 'What's the attraction about him?'

'I don't go about with him,' replied the man; 'he goes about with me. He picked me up this morning at ten o'clock, and he won't leave me. I thought I had got rid of him when I came in here. I left him busy killing a duck more than a quarter of an hour away. I'll have to pay for that, I expect, on my way back.'

'Have you tried throwing stones at him?' asked Harris.

'Have I tried throwing stones at him!' replied the man contemptuously. 'I've been throwing stones at him till my arm aches with throwing stones; and he thinks it's a game, and brings them back to me. I've been carrying this beastly brick about with me for over an hour, in the hope of being able to drown him, but he never comes near enough for me to get hold of him. He just sits six inches out of reach with his mouth open and looks at me.'

'It's the funniest story I've heard for a long while,' said the landlord.

'Glad it amuses somebody,' said the man.

We left him helping the landlord to pick up the broken things and went our way. A dozen yards outside the doorway the faithful animal was waiting for his friend. He looked tired but contented.

DOG AT TIMOTHY'S

John Galsworthy
(British) 1867–1933

M RS. Septimus Small, known in the Forsyte family as Aunt
Juley, returning from service at St. Barnabas', Bayswater, on
a Sunday morning in the Spring of 1878, took by force of habit the
path which led her into the then somewhat undeveloped gardens of
Kensington. The Reverend Thomas Scoles had been wittier than
usual, and she had the longing to stretch her legs, which was the
almost invariable effect of his 'nice' sermons. While she walked, in
violet silk under a black mantle, with very short steps – skirts being
extremely narrow in that year of grace – she was thinking of dear
Hester and what a pity it was that she always had such a headache
on Sunday mornings – the sermon would have done her so much
good! For now that dear Ann was unable to stand the fatigue of
service, she did feel that Hester ought to make a point of being well
enough to go to church. What dear Mr. Scoles had said had been so
helpful – about the lilies of the fields never attempting to improve
their figures, and yet, about ladies of fashion in all their glory never
being attired like one of them. He had undoubtedly meant 'bustles'
– so witty – and Hester would have enjoyed hearing it, because only
yesterday, when they had been talking about the Grecian bend,
Emily had come in with dear James and said that the revival of
crinolines was only a question of time and that she personally
intended to be in the fashion the moment there was any sign of it.
Dear Ann had been rather severe with her; and James had said he
didn't know what was the use of them. Of course, crinolines did
take up a great deal of room, and a 'bustle', though it was warmer,

did not. But Hester had said they were both such a bore, she didn't see why they were wanted; and now Mr. Scoles had said it too. She must really think about it, if Mr. Scoles thought they were bad for the soul; he always said something that one had to think about afterwards. He would be *so* good for Hester! And she stood a minute looking out over the grass.

Dear, dear! That little white dog was running about a great deal. Was it lost? Backwards and forwards, round and round! What they called – she believed – a Pomeranian, quite a new kind of dog. And, seeing a bench, Mrs. Septimus Small bent, with a little backward heave to save her 'bustle', and sat down to watch what was the matter with the white dog. The sun, flaring out between two Spring clouds, fell on her face, transfiguring the pouting puffs of flesh, which seemed trying to burst their way through the network of her veil. Her eyes, of a Forsyte grey, lingered on the dog with the greater pertinacity in that of late – owing to poor Tommy's (their cat's) disappearance, very mysterious – she suspected the sweep – there had been nothing but 'Polly' at Timothy's to lavish her affection on. This dog was draggled and dirty, as if it had been out all night, but it had a dear little pointed nose. She thought, too, that it seemed to be noticing her, and at once had a swelling-up sensation underneath her corsets. Almost as if aware of this, the dog came sidling, and sat down on its haunches in the grass, as though trying to make up its mind about her. Aunt Juley pursed her lips in the endeavour to emit a whistle. The veil prevented this, but she held out her gloved hand. 'Come, little dog – nice little dog!' It seemed to her dear heart that the little dog sighed as it sat there, as if relieved that at last someone had taken notice of it. But it did not approach. The tip of its bushy tail quivered, however, and Aunt Juley redoubled the suavity of her voice: 'Nice little fellow – come then!'

The little dog slithered forward, humbly wagging its entire body, just out of reach. Aunt Juley saw that it had no collar. Really, its nose and eyes were sweet!

'Pom!' she said. 'Dear little Pom!'

The dog looked as if it would let her love it, and sensation increased beneath her corsets.

'Come, pretty!'

Not, of course, that he was pretty, all dirty like that; but his ears were pricked, and his eyes looked at her, bright, and rather round their corners – most intelligent! Lost – and in London! It was like that sad little book of Mrs. – What *was* her name – not the authoress of *Jessica's First Prayer?* – dear, dear! Now, fancy forgetting that! The dog made a sudden advance, and curved like a C, all fluttering, was now almost within reach of her gloved fingers, at which it sniffed. Aunt Juley emitted a purring noise. Pride was filling her heart that out of all the people it *might* have taken notice of, she should be the only one. It had put out its tongue now, and was panting in the agony of indecision. Poor little thing! It clearly didn't know whether it dared try another master – not, of course, that she could possibly take it home, with all the carpets, and dear Ann so particular about everything being nice, and – Timothy! Timothy would be horrified! And yet —! Well, they couldn't prevent her stroking its little nose. And she too panted slightly behind her veil. It *was* agitating! And then, without either of them knowing how, her fingers and the nose were in contact. The dog's tail was now perfectly still; its body trembled. Aunt Juley had a sudden feeling of shame at being so formidable; and with instinct inherited rather than acquired, for she had no knowledge of dogs, she slid one finger round an ear and scratched. It *was* to be hoped he hadn't fleas! And then! The little dog leaped on her lap. It crouched there just as it had sprung, with its bright eyes upturned to her face. A strange dog – her dress – her Sunday best! It *was* an event! The little dog stretched up, and licked her chin. Almost mechanically Aunt Juley rose. And the little dog slipped off. Really she didn't know – it took such liberties! Oh! dear – it *was* thin, fluttering round her feet! What would Mr. Scoles say? Perhaps if she walked on! She turned towards home, and the dog followed her skirt at a distance of six inches. The thought that she was going to eat roast beef, Yorkshire pudding, and mince pies, was almost unbearable to Aunt Juley, seeing it gaze up as if saying: 'Some for me! Some for me!' Thoughts warred within her: must she 'shoo' and threaten it with her parasol? Or should she —? Oh! This would never do! Dogs could be *so* — she had heard? And then – the responsibility! And fleas! Timothy couldn't endure fleas! And it might not know how to behave in a house! Oh, no! She really couldn't! The little dog suddenly raised one paw. Tt, tt! Look at its little face! And a fearful boldness attacked Aunt Juley. Turning resolutely towards the gate of the Gardens, she said in a weak voice: 'Come along, then!' And the little dog came. It was dreadful!

While she was trying to cross the Bayswater Road, two or three of those dangerous hansom cabs came dashing past – so reckless! – and in the very middle of the street a 'growler' turned round, so that she had to stand quite still. And, of course, there was 'no policeman'. The traffic was really getting beyond bounds. If only she didn't meet Timothy coming in from his constitutional, and could get a word with Smither – a capable girl – and have the little dog fed and washed before anybody saw it. And then? Perhaps it could be kept in the basement till somebody came to claim it. But how could people come to claim it if they didn't know it was there? If only there were someone to consult! Perhaps Smither would know a policeman – only she hoped not – policemen were rather dangerous for a nice-looking girl like Smither, with her colour, and such a figure, for her age. Then, suddenly, realising that she had reached home, she was seized by panic from head to heel. There was the bell – it was not the epoch of latchkeys; and there the smell of dinner – yes, and the little dog had smelt it! It was now or never. Aunt Juley pointed her parasol at the dog and said very feebly: 'Shoo!' But it only crouched. She couldn't drive it away! And with an immense daring she rang the bell. While she stood waiting for the door to be opened, she almost enjoyed a sensation of defiance. She was doing a dreadful thing, but she didn't care! Then, the doorway yawned, and her heart sank slowly towards her high and buttoned boots.

'Oh, Smither! This poor little dog has followed me. Nothing has ever followed me before. It must be lost. And it looks so thin and dirty. What *shall* we do?'

The tail of the dog, edging into the home of that rich smell, fluttered.

'Aoh!' said Smither – she was young! 'Paw little thing! Shall I get Cook to give it some scraps, Ma'am!' At the word 'scraps' the dog's eyes seemed to glow.

'Well,' said Aunt Juley, 'you do it on your own responsibility, Smither. Take it downstairs quickly.'

She stood breathless while the dog, following Smither and its nose, glided through the little hall and down the kitchen stairs. The pit-pat of its feet roused in Aunt Juley the most mingled sensations she had experienced since the death of Septimus Small.

She went up to her room, and took off her veil and bonnet. What *was* she going to say? She went downstairs without knowing.

In the drawing-room, which had just had new pampas grass, Ann, sitting on the sofa, was putting down her prayer-book; she always read the Service to herself. Her mouth and chin looked very square, and there was an expression in her old grey eyes as if she were in pain. She wanted her lunch, of course – they were trying hard to call it lunch, because, according to Emily, no-one with any pretensions to be fashionable called it dinner now, even on Sundays. Hester, in her corner by the hearth, was passing the tip of her tongue over her lips; she had always been so fond of mince pies, and these would be the first of the season. Aunt Juley said:

'Mr. Scoles was delightful this morning – a beautiful sermon. I walked in the Gardens.'

Something warned her to say no more, and they waited in silence for the gong; they had just got a gong – Emily had said it was 'the thing'.

It sounded. Dear, dear! What a noise – bom – bom! Timothy would never – Smither must take lessons. At dear James' in Park Lane the butler made it sound almost cosy.

In the doorway of the dining-room, Smither said:

'It's ate it all, Ma'am – it was *that* hungry.'

'Shhh!'

A heavy footstep sounded in the hall; Timothy was coming from his study, square in his frock-coat, his face all brown and red – he had such delicate health. He took his seat with his back to the window, where the light was not too strong.

Timothy, of course, did not go to church – it was too tiring for him – but he always asked the amount of the offertory, and would sometimes add that he didn't know what they wanted all that for, as if Mr. Scoles ever wasted it. Just now he was getting new hassocks, and when they came she had thought perhaps dear Timothy and Hester would come too. Timothy, however, had said:

'Hassocks! They only get in the way and spoil your trousers.'

Aunt Ann, who could not kneel now, had smiled indulgently: 'One should kneel in church, dear.'

They were all seated now with beef before them. and Timothy was saying:

'Mustard! And tell Cook the potatoes aren't browned enough; do you hear, Smither?'

Smither, blushing above him, answered: 'Yes, sir.'

Within Aunt Juley, what with the dog and her mind and the difficulty of assimilating Yorkshire pudding, indigestion had begun.

'I had such a pleasant walk in the Gardens', she said painfully, 'after church.'

'You oughtn't to walk there alone in these days; you don't know what you may be picking up with.'

Aunt Juley took a sip of brown sherry – her heart was beating so! Aunt Hester – she was such a reader – murmured that she had read how Mr. Gladstone walked there sometimes.

'That shows you!' said Timothy.

Aunt Ann believed that Mr. Gladstone had high principles, and they must not judge him.

'Judge him!' said Timothy: 'I'd hang him!'

'That's not quite a nice thing to say on Sunday, dear.'

'Better the day, better the deed', muttered Timothy; and Aunt Juley trembled. He was in one of his moods. And, suddenly, she held her breath. A yapping had impinged on her ears, as if the white dog were taking liberties with Cook. Her eyes sought Smither's face.

'What's that?' said Timothy. 'A dog?'

'There's a dog just round the corner, at No. 9', murmured Aunt Juley; and, at the roundness of Smither's eyes, knew she had prevaricated. What dreadful things happened if one was not quite frank from the beginning! The yapping broke into a sharp yelp, as if Cook had taken a liberty in turn.

'That's not round the corner', said Timothy; 'it's downstairs. What's all this?'

All eyes were turned on Smither, in a dead silence. A sound broke it – the girl had creaked.

'Please, Miss, it's the little dog that followed Madam in.'

'Oh!' said Aunt Juley, in haste; '*that* little dog!'

'What's that?' said Timothy. 'Followed her in?'

'It was so thin!' said Aunt Juley's faint voice.

'Smither,' said Aunt Ann, 'hand me the pulled bread; and tell Cook I want to see her when she's finished her dinner.'

Into Aunt Juley's pouting face rose a flush.

'I take the entire responsibility,' she said. 'The little dog was lost. It was hungry and Cook has given it some scraps.'

'A strange dog,' muttered Timothy, 'bringing in fleas like that!'

'Oh! I don't think,' murmured Aunt Juley, 'it's a well-bred little dog.'

'How do *you* know? You don't know a dog from a door-mat.'

The flush deepened over Aunt Juley's pouts.

'It was a Christian act,' she said, looking Timothy in the eye. 'If you had been to church, you wouldn't talk like that.'

It was perhaps the first time she had openly bearded her delicate brother. The result was complete. Timothy ate his mince pie hurriedly.

'Well, don't let *me* see it,' he muttered.

'Put the wine and walnuts on the table and go down, Smither,' said Aunt Ann, 'and see what Cook is doing about it.'

When she had gone there was silence. It was felt that Juley had forgotten herself.

Aunt Ann put her wineglass to her lips; it contained two thimblefuls of brown sherry – a present from dear Jolyon – he had such a palate! Aunt Hester, who during the excitement had thoughtfully finished a second mince pie, was smiling. Aunt Juley had her eyes fixed on Timothy; she had tasted of defiance and it was sweet.

Smither returned.

'Well, Smither?'

'Cook's washing of it, Miss.'

'What's she doing that for?' said Timothy.

'Because it's dirty,' said Aunt Juley.

'There you are!'

And the voice of Aunt Ann was heard, saying grace. When she had finished, the three sisters rose.

'We'll leave you to your wine, dear. Smither, my shawl, please.'

Upstairs in the drawing-room there was grave silence. Aunt Juley was trying to still her fluttering nerves; Aunt Hester trying to pretend that nothing had happened; Aunt Ann, upright and a little grim, trying to compress the Riot Act with her thin and bloodless lips. She was not thinking of herself, but of the immutable order of things, so seriously compromised.

Aunt Juley repeated, suddenly: 'He followed me, Ann.'

'Without an intro — Without your inviting him?'

'I spoke to him, because he was lost.'

'You should think before you speak. Dogs take advantage.'

Aunt Juley's face mutinied. 'Well, I'm glad,' she said, 'and that's flat. Such a how-de-do!'

Aunt Ann looked pained. A considerable time passed. Aunt Juley began playing solitaire – she played without presence of mind, so that extraordinary things happened on the board. Aunt Ann sat upright, with her eyes closed; and Aunt Hester, after watching them for some minutes to see if they would open, took from under her cushion a library volume, and hiding it behind a firescreen, began to read – it was volume two and she did not yet know 'Lady Audley's secret': of course it *was* a novel, but, as Timothy had said, 'Better the day, better the deed.'

The clock struck three. Aunt Ann opened her eyes, Aunt Hester shut her book. Aunt Juley crumpled the solitaire balls together with a clatter. There was a knock on the door, for not belonging to the upper regions, like Smither, Cook always knocked.

'Come in!'

Still in her pink print frock, Cook entered, and behind her

entered the dog, snowy white, with its coat all brushed and bushy, its manner and its tail now cocky and now deprecating. It *was* a moment! Cook spoke:

'I've brought it up, miss; it's had its dinner, and it's been washed. It's a nice little dear, and taken quite a fancy to me.'

The three Aunts sat silent with their eyes now on the dog, now on the legs of the furniture.

''Twould 'ave done your 'eart good to see it eat, miss. And it answers to the name of Pommy.'

'Fancy!' said Aunt Hester, with an effort. She did so hate things to be awkward.

Aunt Ann leaned forward; her voice rose firm, if rather quavery.

'It doesn't belong to us, Cook; and your master would never permit it. Smither shall go with it to the Police Station.'

As if struck by the words, the dog emerged from Cook's skirt and approached the voice. It stood in a curve and began to oscillate its tail very slightly; its eyes, like bits of jet, gazed up. Aunt Ann looked down at it; her thin veined hands, as if detached from her firmness, moved nervously over her glacé skirt. From within Aunt Juley emotion was emerging in one large pout. Aunt Hester was smiling spasmodically.

'Them Police Stations!' said Cook. 'I'm sure it's not been accustomed. It's not as if it had a collar, miss.'

'Pommy!' said Aunt Juley.

The dog turned at the sound, sniffed her knees, and instantly returned to its contemplation of Aunt Ann, as though it recognised where power was seated.

'It's really rather sweet!' murmured Aunt Hester, and not only the dog looked at Aunt Ann. But at this moment the door was again opened.

'Mr. Swithin Forsyte, miss,' said the voice of Smither.

Aunts Juley and Hester rose to greet their brother; Aunt Ann, privileged by seventy-eight years, remained seated. The family always went to Aunt Ann, not Aunt Ann to the family. There was a general feeling that dear Swithin had come providentially, knowing as he did all about horses.

'You can leave the little dog for the moment, Cook. Mr. Swithin will tell us what to do.'

Swithin, who had taken his time on the stairs which were narrow, made an entry. Tall, with his chest thrown forward, his square face puffy pale, his eyes light and round, the tiny grey imperial below his moustached lips gave to him the allure of a master of ceremonies, and the white dog, retreating to a corner, yapped loudly.

'What's this?' said Swithin. 'A dog?'

So might one entering a more modern drawing-room, have said: 'What's this – a camel?'

Repairing hastily to the corner, Aunt Juley admonished the dog with her finger. It shivered slightly and was silent. Aunt Ann said:

'Give dear Swithin his chair, Hester; we want your advice, Swithin. This little dog followed Juley home this morning – he was lost.'

Swithin seated himself with his knees apart, thus preserving the deportment of his body and the uncreased beauty of his waistcoat. His Wellington boots showed stiff beneath his almost light blue trousers. He said:

'Has Timothy had a fit?'

Dear Swithin – he was so droll!

'Not yet,' said Aunt Hester, who was sometimes almost naughty.

'Well, he will. Here, Juley, don't stand there stuck. Bring the dog out, and let's have a look at it. Dog! Why, it's a bitch!'

This curiously male word, though spoken with distinction, caused a sensation such as would have accompanied a heavy fall of soot. The dog had been assumed by all to be of the politer sex, because of course one didn't notice such things. Aunt Juley, indeed, whom past association with Septimus Small had rendered more susceptible, had conceived her doubts, but she had continued to be on the polite side.

'A bitch,' repeated Swithin; 'you'll have no end of trouble with it.'

'That is what we fear,' said Aunt Ann, 'though I don't think you should call it that in a drawing-room, dear.'

'Stuff and nonsense!' said Swithin. 'Come here, little tyke!'

And he stretched out a ringed hand smelling of dogskin – he had driven himself round in his phaeton.

Encouraged by Aunt Juley, the little dog approached, and sat cowering under the hand. Swithin lifted it by the ruff round its neck.

'Well-bred,' he said, putting it down.

'We can't keep it,' said Aunt Ann, firmly. 'The carpets – we thought – the Police Station.'

'If I were you,' said Swithin, 'I'd put a notice in *The Times*: "Found, white Pomeranian bitch. Apply, The Nook, Bayswater Road." You might get a reward. Let's look at its teeth.'

The little dog, who seemed in a manner fascinated by the smell of Swithin's hand and the stare of his round china-blue eyes, put no obstacle in the way of fingers that raised its upper and depressed its lower lip.

'It's a puppy,' said Swithin. 'Loo, loo, little tyke!'

This terrible incentive caused the dog to behave in a singular manner; depressing its tail so far as was possible, it jumped sideways and scurried round Aunt Hester's chair, then crouched with its chin on the ground, its hind-quarters and tail in the air, looking up at Swithin with eyes black as boot-buttons.

'I shouldn't be surprised,' said Swithin, 'if it was worth money. Loo, loo!'

This time the little dog scurried round the entire room, avoiding the legs of chairs by a series of miracles, then, halting by a marqueterie stand, it stood on its hind legs and began to eat the pampas grass.

'Ring, Hester!' said Aunt Ann. 'Ring for Smither. Juley, stop it!'

Swithin, whose imperial was jutting in a fixed smile, said:

'Where's Timothy? I should like to see it bite his legs.'

Aunt Juley, moved by maternal spasms, bent down and picked the dog up in her arms. She stood, pouting over its sharp nose and soft warm body, like the very figure of daring with the smell of soft soap in its nostrils.

'I will take it downstairs myself,' she said; 'it shan't be teased. Come, Pommy!'

The dog, who had no say whatever in the matter, put out a pink strip of tongue and licked her nose. Aunt Juley had the exquisite sensation of being loved; and, hastily, to conceal her feelings, bore it lolling over her arm away. She bore it upstairs, instead of down, to her room which was at the back of dear Ann's, and stood, surrounded by mahogany, with the dog still in her arms. Every hand was against her and the poor dog, and she squeezed it tighter. It was panting, and every now and then with its slip of a tongue it licked her cheek, as if to assure itself of reality. Since the departure of Septimus Small ten years ago, she had never been properly loved, and now that something was ready to love her, they wanted to take it away. She sat down on her bed, still holding the dog, while below, they would be talking of how to send Pommy to the Police Station or put her into the papers! Then, noticing that white hairs were coming off on to her, she put the dog down. It sidled round the room, sniffing, till it came to the washstand, where it stood looking at her and panting. What *did* it want? Wild thoughts passed through Aunt Juley's mind, till suddenly the dog stood on its hind legs and licked the air. Why, it was thirsty! Disregarding the niceties of existence, Aunt Juley lifted the jug, and set it on the floor. For some minutes there was no sound but lapping. Could it really hold all that? The little dog looked up at her, moved its tail twice, then trotted away to inspect the room more closely. Having inspected everything except Aunt Juley, concerning whom its mind was apparently made up, it lay down under the valance of the dressing-table, with its head and forepaws visible, and uttered a series of short spasmodic barks. Aunt Juley understood them to mean: 'Come and play with me!' And taking her sponge-bag, she dangled it. Seizing it – So unexpected! – the little dog shook it violently. Aunt Juley was at once charmed and horrified. It was evidently feeling quite at home; but her poor bag! Oh! its little teeth *were* sharp and strong! Aunt Juley swelled. It was as if she didn't care what happened to the bag so long as the little dog were having a good time. The bag came to an end; and gathering up the pieces, she thought defiantly: 'Well, it's not as if I ever went to Brighton now!' But she said severely:

'You see what you've done!' And, together, they examined the pieces, while Aunt Juley's heart took a resolution. They might talk as they liked: Finding was keeping; and if Timothy didn't like it, he could lump it! The sensation was terrific. Someone, however, was knocking on the door.

'Oh! Smither,' said Aunt Juley, 'you see what the little dog has done?' And she held up the sponge-bag defiantly.

'Aoh!' said Smither; 'its teeth *are* sharp. Would you go down, ma'am? Mr. and Mrs. James Forsyte are in the drawing-room. Shall I take the little dog now? I daresay it'd like a run.'

'Not to the Police Station, Smither. I found it, and I'm going to keep it.'

'I'm sure, Ma'am. It'll be company for me and Cook, now that Tommy's gone. It's took quite a fancy to us.'

With a pang of jealousy Aunt Juley said: 'I take all the responsibility. Go with Smither, Pommy!'

Caught up in her arms, the little dog lolled its head over the edge of Smither and gazed back sentimentally as it was borne away. And, again, all that was maternal in Aunt Juley swelled, beneath the dark violet of her bosom sprinkled with white hairs.

'Say I am coming down.' And she began plucking off the white hairs.

Outside the drawing-room door she paused; then went in, weak at the knees. Between his Dundreary whiskers James was telling a story. His long legs projected so that she had to go round; his long lips stopped to say:

'How are you, Juley? They tell me you've found a dog,' and resumed the story. It was all about a man who had been bitten and had insisted on being cauterised until he couldn't sit down, and the dog hadn't been mad after all, so that it was all wasted, and that was what came of dogs. He didn't know what use they were except to make a mess.

Emily said: 'Pomeranians are all the rage. They look so amusing in a carriage.'

Aunt Hester murmured that Jolyon had an Italian greyhound at Stanhope Gate.

'That snippetty whippet!' said Swithin – perhaps the first use of the term: 'There's no body in *them*.'

'You're not going to *keep* this dog?' said James. 'You don't know what it might have.'

Very red, Aunt Juley said sharply: 'Fiddle-de-dee, James!'

'Well, you might have an action brought against you. They tell me there's a Home for Lost Dogs. Your proper course is to turn it out.'

'Turn out your grandmother!' snapped Aunt Juley; she was not afraid of James.

'Well, it's not your property. You'll be getting up against the Law.'

'Fiddle the Law!'

This epoch-making remark was received in silence. Nobody knew what had come to Juley.

'Well,' said James, with finality, 'don't say I didn't tell you. What does Timothy say – he'ud have a fit.'

'If he wants to have a fit, he must,' said Aunt Juley. 'I shan't stop him.'

'What are you going to do with the puppies?' said Swithin: 'Ten to one she'll have puppies.'

'You see, Juley,' said Aunt Ann.

Aunt Juley's agitation was such that she took up a fan from the little curio table beside her, and began to wave it before her flushed face.

'You're all against me,' she said: 'Puppies, indeed! A little thing like that!'

Swithin rose. 'Good-bye to you all. I'm going to see Nicholas. Good-bye, Juley. You come for a drive with me some day. I'll take you to the Lost Dogs' Home.' Throwing out his chest, he manoeuvred to the door, and could be heard descending the stairs to the accompaniment of the drawing-room bell.

James said mechanically: 'He's a funny fellow, Swithin!'

It was as much his permanent impression of his twin brother as was Swithin's: 'He's a poor stick, James!'

Emily, who was bored, began talking to Aunt Hester about the new fashion of eating oysters before the soup. Of course it was very foreign, but they said the Prince was doing it; James wouldn't have it; but personally she thought it rather elegant. She should see! James had begun to tell Aunt Ann how Soames would be out of his articles in January – he was a steady chap. He told her at some length. Aunt Juley sat pouting behind her moving fan. She had a longing for dear Jolyon. Partly because he had always been her favourite and her eldest brother, who had never allowed anyone else to bully her; partly because he was the only one who had a dog, and partly because even Ann was a little afraid of him. She sat longing to hear him say: 'You're a parcel of old women; of course Juley can keep what she found.' Because, that was it! The dog had followed her of its own free will. It was not as if it had been a precious stone or a purse – which, of course, would have been different. Sometimes Jolyon did come on Sundays – though generally he took little June to the Zoo; and the moment he came James would be sure to go away, for fear of having his knuckles rapped; and that, she felt sure, would be so nice, since James had been horrid about it all!

'I think,' she said, suddenly, 'I shall go round to Stanhope Gate, and ask dear Jolyon.'

'What do you want to do that for?' said James, taking hold of a whisker. 'He'll send you away with a flea in your ear.'

Whether or no this possibility deterred her, Aunt Juley did not rise, but she ceased fanning herself and sat with the expression on her face which had given rise to the family saying: 'Oh! So-and-so's a regular Juley!'

But James had now exhausted his weekly budget. 'Well, Emily,' he said, 'you'll be wanting to get home. We can't keep the horses any longer.'

The accuracy of this formula had never been put to the proof, for Emily always rose at once with the words:

' Good-bye, dears. Give our love to Timothy.' She had pecked their cheeks and gone out of the room before James could remember what – as he would tell her in the carriage – he had specially gone there to ask them.

When they had departed, Aunt Hester, having looked from one to the other of her sisters, muffled 'Lady Audley's Secret' in her shawl and tiptoed away. She knew what was coming. Aunt Juley took the solitaire board with hands that trembled. The moment had arrived! And she waited, making an occasional move with oozing fingers, and stealing glances at that upright figure in black silk with jet trappings and cameo brooch. On no account did she mean to be the first to speak; and she said, suddenly:

'There you sit, Ann!'

Aunt Ann, countering her glance with those grey eyes of hers that saw quite well at a distance, spoke:

'You heard what Swithin and James said, Juley.'

'I will *not* turn the dog out,' said Aunt Juley. 'I will not, and that's flat.' The blood beat in her temples and she tapped a foot on the floor.

'If it were a really nice little dog, it would not have run away and got lost. Little dogs of that sex are not to be trusted. You ought to know that, at your age, Juley; now that we're alone, I can talk to you plainly. It will have followers, of course.'

Aunt Juley put a finger into her mouth, sucked it, took it out, and said:

'I'm tired of being treated like a little girl.'

Aunt Ann answered calmly:

'I think you should take some calomel – getting into fantods like this! We have never had a dog.'

'I don't want you to have one now,' said Aunt Juley; 'I want it for myself. I – I —' She could not bring herself to express what was in her heart about being loved – it would be – would be gushing!

'It's not right to keep what's not your own,' said Aunt Ann. 'You know that perfectly well.'

'I will put an advertisement in the paper; if the owner comes, I'll give it up. But it followed me of its own accord. And it can live downstairs. Timothy need never see it.'

'It will spoil the carpets,' said Aunt Ann, 'and bark at night; we shall have no peace.'

'I'm sick of peace,' said Aunt Juley, rattling the board. 'I'm sick of peace, and I'm sick of taking care of things till they – till you – till one belongs to them.'

Aunt Ann lifted her hands, spidery and pale.

'You don't know what you're talking about. If one can't take care of one's things, one is not fit to have them.'

'Care – care – I'm sick of care! I want something human – I want this dog. And if I can't have it, I will go away and take it with me; and that's flat.'

It was, perhaps, the wildest thing that had ever been said at Timothy's. Aunt Ann said very quietly:

' You know you can't go away, Juley, you haven't the money; so it's no good talking like that.'

'Jolyon will give me the money; he will never let you bully me.'

An expression of real pain centred itself between Aunt Ann's old eyes.

'I do not think I bully,' she said; 'you forget yourself.'

For a full minute Aunt Juley said nothing, looking to and fro from her twisting fingers to the wrinkled ivory pale face of her eldest sister. Tears of compunction had welled up in her eyes. Dear Ann was very old, and the doctor was always saying —! And quickly she got out her handkerchief.

'I – I'm upset. – I – I didn't mean – dear Ann – I —' the words bubbled out: 'b-b-but I d-do so w-want the little d-d-dog.'

There was silence, broken by her sniffing. Then rose the voice of Aunt Ann, calm, a little tremulous:

'Very well, dear; it will be a sacrifice, but if it makes you happier —'

'Oh!' sobbed Aunt Juley: 'Oh!'

A large tear splashed on the solitaire board, and with the small handkerchief she wiped it off.

'This was a dog that lay, weakly trying to lift a head that would no longer lift; trying to move a tail . . . matted with thorns and burrs, and managing to do nothing very much except to whine in a weak, happy, crying way.'
LASSIE COME-HOME

'At last the time came that he decided to eat the meat from the hand.
He never took his eyes from the god, thrusting his head forward with ears
flattened back and hair involuntarily rising and cresting on his neck.'
WHITE FANG

'She was mainly black with beautiful reddish tan markings, which included a tan waistcoat, tan hoops above her appealing eyes, a tan muzzle, tan paws and undercarriage . . . She met my eyes with an unwavering stare.'
SUKI, THE REJECT

'The little dog bounded joyously up to me before
returning to his post by the bed.'
HERMANN – A HAPPY ENDING

LASSIE COME-HOME

Eric Knight
(British) 1897–1943

SAM Carraclough had spoken the truth early that year when he told his son Joe that it was a long way from Greenall Bridge in Yorkshire to the Duke of Rudling's place in Scotland. And it is just as many miles coming the other way, a matter of four hundred miles.

But that would be for a man, travelling straight by road or by train. For an animal how far would it be – an animal that must circle and quest at obstacles, wander and err, backtrack and sidetrack till it found a way?

A thousand miles it would be – a thousand miles through strange terrain it had never crossed before, with nothing but instinct to tell direction.

Yes, a thousand miles of mountain and dale, of highland and moor, ploughland and path, ravine and river, beck and burn; a thousand miles of tor and brae, of snow and rain and fog and sun; of wire and thistle and thorn and flint and rock to tear the feet – who could expect a dog to win through that?

Yet, if it were almost a miracle, in his heart Joe Carraclough tried to believe in that miracle – that somehow, wonderfully, inexplicably, his dog would be there some day; there, waiting by the school gate. Each day as he came out of school, his eyes would turn to the spot where Lassie had always waited. And each day there was nothing there, and Joe Carraclough would walk home slowly, silently, stolidly as did the people of his country.

Always, when school ended, Joe tried to prepare himself – told

193

himself not to be disappointed, because there could be no dog there. Thus, through the long weeks, Joe began to teach himself not to believe in the impossible. He had hoped against hope so long that hope began to die.

But if hope can die in a human, it does not in an animal. As long as it lives, the hope is there and the faith is there. And so, coming across the schoolyard that day, Joe Carraclough would not believe his eyes. He shook his head and blinked, and rubbed his fists in his eyes, for he thought what he was seeing was a dream. There, walking the last few yards to the school gate was – his dog!

He stood, for the coming of the dog was terrible – her walk was a thing that tore at her breath. Her head and her tail were down almost to the pavement. Each footstep forward seemed a separate effort. It was a crawl rather than a walk. But the steps were made, one by one, and at last the animal dropped in her place by the gate and lay still.

Then Joe roused himself. Even if it were a dream, he must do something. In dreams one must try.

He raced across the yard and fell to his knees, and then, when his hands were touching and feeling fur, he knew it was reality. His dog had come to meet him!

But what a dog was this – no prize collie with fine tricolour coat glowing, with ears lifted gladly over the proud, slim head with its perfect black mask. It was not a dog whose bright eyes were alert, and who jumped up to bark a glad welcome. This was a dog that lay, weakly trying to lift a head that would no longer lift; trying to move a tail that was torn and matted with thorns and burrs, and managing to do nothing very much except to whine in a weak, happy, crying way. For she knew that at last the terrible driving instinct was at peace. She was at the place. She had kept her lifelong rendezvous, and hands were touching her that had not touched her for so long a time.

By the Labour Exchange, Ian Cawper stood with the other out-of-work miners, waiting until it was tea time so that they could all go back to their cottages.

You could have picked out Ian, for he was much the biggest man even among the many big men that Yorkshire grows. In fact, he was reputed to be the biggest and strongest man in all that Riding of Yorkshire. A big man, but gentle and often very slow of thinking and speech.

And so Ian was a few seconds behind the others in realizing that something of urgency was happening in the village. Then he too saw it – a boy struggling, half-running along the main street, his voice lifted in excitement, a great bundle of something in his arms.

The men stirred and moved forward. Then, when the boy was nearer, they heard his cry:

'She's come back! She's come back!'

The men looked at each other and blew out their breath and then stared at the bundle the boy was carrying. It was true. Sam Carraclough's collie had walked back home from Scotland.

'I must get her home, quick!' the boy was saying. He staggered on.

Ian Cawper stepped forward.

'Here,' he said. 'Run on ahead, tell 'em to get ready.'

His great arms cradled the dog – arms that could have carried ten times the weight of this poor, thin animal.

'Oh, hurry, Ian!' the boy cried, dancing in excitement.

'I'm hurrying, lad. Go on ahead.'

So Joe Carraclough raced along the street, turned up the side street, ran down the garden path, and burst into the cottage:

'Mother! Feyther!'

'What is it, lad?'

Joe paused. He could hardly get the words out – the excitement was choking up in his throat, hot and sliding. And then the words were said:

'Lassie! She's come home! Lassie's come home!'

He opened the door, and Ian Cawper, bowing his head to pass under the lintel, carried the dog to the hearth and laid her there.

There were many things that Joe Carraclough was to remember from that evening. He was never to forget the look that passed over his father's face as he first knelt beside the dog that had been his for so many years, and let his hands travel over the emaciated frame. He was to remember how his mother moved about the kitchen, not grumbling or scolding now, but silently and with a sort of terrific intensity, poking the fire quickly, stirring the condensed milk into warm water, kneeling to hold the dog's head and lift open the jowl.

Not a word did his parents speak to him. They seemed to have forgotten him altogether. Instead, they both worked over the dog with a concentration that seemed to put them in a separate world.

Joe watched how his father spooned in the warm liquid, he saw how it drooled out again from the unswallowing dog's jowls and dribbled down on to the rug. He saw his mother warm up a blanket and wrap it round the dog. He saw them try again and again to feed her. He saw his father rise at last.

'It's no use, lass,' he said to his mother.

Between his mother and father many questions and answers passed unspoken except through their eyes.

'Pneumonia,' his father said at last. 'She's not strong enough now . . .'

For a while his parents stood, and then it was his mother who seemed to be somehow wonderfully alive and strong.

'I won't be beat!' she said. 'I just *won't* be beat.'

She pursed her lips, and as if this grimace had settled something, she went to the mantelpiece and took down a vase. She turned it over and shook it. The copper pennies came into her hand. She held them out to her husband, not explaining nor needing to explain what was needed. But he stared at the money.

'Go on, lad,' she said. 'I were saving it for insurance, like.'

'But how'll we . . .'

'Hush,' the woman said.

Then her eyes flickered over her son, and Joe knew that they were aware of him again for the first time in an hour. His father looked at him, at the money in the woman's hand, and at last at the dog. Suddenly he took the money. He put on his cap and hurried out into the night. When he came back he was carrying bundles – eggs and a small bottle of brandy – precious and costly things in that home.

Joe watched as they were beaten together, and again and again his father tried to spoon some into the dog's mouth. Then his mother blew in exasperation. Angrily she snatched the spoon. She cradled the dog's head on her lap, she lifted the jowl, and poured and stroked the throat – stroked it and stroked it, until at last the dog swallowed.

'Aaaah!'

It was his father, breathing a long, triumphant exclamation. And the firelight shone gold on his mother's hair as she crouched there, holding the dog's head – stroking its throat, soothing it with soft, loving sounds.

Joe did not clearly remember about it afterwards, only a faint sensation that he was being carried to bed at some strange hour of darkness.

And in the morning when he rose, his father sat in his chair, but his mother was still on the rug, and the fire was still burning warm. The dog, swathed in blankets, lay quiet.

'Is she – dead?' Joe asked.

His mother smiled weakly.

'Shhh,' she said. 'She's just sleeping. And I suppose I ought to get breakfast – but I'm that played out – if I nobbut had a nice strong cup o' tea . . .'

And that morning, strangely enough, it was his father who got the breakfast, boiling the water, brewing the tea, cutting the bread. It was his mother who sat in the rocking chair, waiting until it was ready.

That evening when Joe came home from school, Lassie still lay where he had left her when he went off to school. He wanted to sit and cradle her, but he knew that ill dogs are best left alone. All evening he sat, watching her, stretched out, with the faint breathing the only sign of life. He didn't want to go to bed.

'Now she'll be all right,' his mother cried. 'Go to bed – she'll be all right.'

'Are you sure she'll get better, Mother?'

'Ye can see for yourself, can't you? She doesn't look any worse, does she?'

'But are you sure she's going to be better?'

The woman sighed.

'Of course – I'm sure – now go to bed and sleep.'

And Joe went to bed, confident in his parents.

That was one day. There were others to remember. There was the day when Joe returned and, as he walked to the hearth, there came from the dog lying there a movement that was meant to be a wag of the tail.

There was another day when Joe's mother sighed with pleasure, for as she prepared the bowl of milk, the dog stirred, lifted herself unsteadily, and waited. And when the bowl was set down, she put down her head and lapped, while her pinched flanks quivered.

And finally there was that day when Joe first realized that – even now – his dog was not to be his own again. So again the cottage rang with cries and protests, and again a woman's voice was lifted, tired and shrilling:

'Is there never to be any more peace and quiet in my home?'

And long after Joe had gone to bed, he heard the voices continuing – his mother's clear and rising and falling; his father's in a steady, re-iterative monotone, never changing, always coming to one sentence:

'But even if he would sell her back, where'd Ah get the brass to buy her – where's the money coming fro'? Ye know we can't get it.'

To Joe Carraclough's father, life was laid out in straight rules. When a man could get work, he worked his best and got the best wage he could. If he raised a dog, he raised the best one he could. If he had a wife and children, he took care of them the best he could.

In this out-of-work collier's mind, there were no devious excep-tions and evasions concerning life and its codes. Like most simple men, he saw all these things clearly. Lying, cheating, stealing – they were wrong, and you couldn't make them right by twisting them round in your mind.

So it was that, when he was faced with any problem, he so often brought it smack up against elemental truths.

'Honest is honest, and there's no two ways about it,' he would say.

He had a habit of putting it like that. 'Truth is truth.' Or, 'Cheating is cheating.'

And the matter of Lassie came up against this simple, direct code of morals. He had sold the dog and taken the money and spent it. Therefore the dog did not belong to him any more, and no matter how you argued you could not change that.

But a man has to live with his family, too. When a woman starts to argue with a man . . . well . . .

That next morning when Joe came down to breakfast, while his mother served the oatmeal with pursed lips, his father coughed and spoke as if he had rehearsed a set speech over in his mind many times that night:

'Joe, lad. We've decided upon it – that is, thy mother and me – that Lassie can stay here till she's all better.

'That's all reight, because I believe true in ma heart that nobody could nurse her better and wi' more care nor we're doing. So that's honest. But when she's better, well . . .

'Now ye have her for a little while yet, so be content. And don't plague us, lad. There's enough things to worry us now wi'out more. So don't plague us no more – and try to be a man about it – and be content.'

With the young, 'for a little while' has two shapes. Seen from one end, it is a great, yawning stretch of time extending into the unlimitable future. From the other, it is a ghastly span of days that has been cruelly whisked away before the realization comes.

Joe Carraclough knew that it was the latter that morning when he went to school and heard a mighty, booming voice. As he turned to look, he saw in an automobile a fearsome old man and a girl with her flaxen hair cascading from under a beret. And the old man, with his ferocious white moustaches looking like an animal's misshapen fangs, was waving an ugly blackthorn stick to the danger of the car, the chauffeur, and the world in general, and shouting at him:

'Hi! Hi, there! Yes, I mean you, m' lad! Damme, Jenkins, will you make this smelly contraption stand still a moment? Whoa, there, Jenkins! Whoa! Why we ever stopped using horses is more than any sane man can understand. Country's going to pot, that's what! Here, m'lad! Come here!'

For a moment Joe thought of running – doing anything to get all these things he feared out of his sight, so that they might, miraculously, be out of his mind, too. But a machine can go faster than a boy, and then, too, Joe had in him the blood of men who might think slowly and stick to old ideas and bear trouble patiently – but who do not run away. So he stood sturdily on the pavement and remembered his manners as his mother had taught him, and said:

'Yes, sir.'

'You're What's-his-name's lad, aren't you?'

Joe's eyes had turned to the girl. She was the one he had seen long ago when he was putting Lassie in the Duke's kennels. Her face was not hearty-red like his own. It was blue-white. On the hand that clutched the edge of the car the veins stood out clear-blue. That hand looked thin. He was thinking that, as his mother would say, she could do with some plumduff.

She was looking at him, too. Something made him draw himself up proudly.

'My father is Sam Carraclough', he said firmly.

'I know, I know,' the old man shouted impatiently. 'I never forget a name. Never! Used to know every last soul in this village. Too many of you growing up now – younger generation. And, by gad, they're all of them not worth one of the old bunch – not the whole kit and caboodle. The modern generation, why . . .'

He halted, for the girl beside him was tugging his sleeve.

'What is it? Eh? Oh, yes. I was just coming to it. Where's your father, m' lad? Is he home?'

'No, sir.'

'Where is he?'

'He's off over Allerby, sir.'

'Allerby, what's he doing there?'

'A mate spoke for him at the pit, I think, and he's gone to see if there's a chance of getting taken on.'

'Oh, yes – yes, of course. When'll he be back?'

'I don't know, sir. I think about tea.'

'Don't mumble! Not till tea. Damme, very inconvenient – very! Well, I'll drop round about five-ish. You tell him to stay home and I want to see him – it's important. Tell him to wait.'

Then the car was gone, and Joe hurried to school. There was never such a long morning as that one. The minutes in the class-room crawled past as the lessons droned on.

Joe had only one desire – to have it become noon. And when at last the leaden moments that were years were gone, he raced home and burst through the door. It was the same cry – for his mother.

'Mother, Mother!'

'Goodness, don't knock the door down. And close it – anyone would think you were brought up in a barn. What's the matter?'

'Mother, he's coming to take Lassie away!'

'Who is?'

'The Duke . . . he's coming . . .'

'The Duke? How in the world does he know that she's . . .'

'I don't know. But he stopped me this morning. He's coming at tea time . . .'

'Coming here? Are ye sure?'

'Yes, he said he'd come at tea. Oh, Mother, please . . .'

'Now, Joe. Don't start! Now I warn ye!'

'Mother, you've got to listen. Please, please!'

'You hear me? I said . . .'

'No, Mother. Please help me. Please!'

The woman looked at her son and heaved a sigh of weariness and exasperation. Then she threw up her hands in despair.

'Eigh, dearie me! Is there never to be any more peace in this house? Never?'

She sank into her chair and looked at the floor. The boy went to her and touched her arm.

'Mother – do something,' the boy pleaded. 'Can't we hide her? He'll be here at five. He told me to tell Father he'd be here at five. Oh Mother . . .'

'Nay, Joe. Thy father won't . . .'

'Won't you beg him? Please, please! Beg Father to . . .'

'Joe!' his mother cried angrily. Then her voice became patient again. 'Now, Joe, it's no use. So stop thy plaguing. It's just that thy father won't lie. That much I'll give him. Come good, come bad, he'll not lie.'

'But just this once, Mother.'

The woman shook her head sadly and sat by the fire, staring into it as if she would find peace there. Her son went to her and touched her bare forearm.

'Please, Mother. Beg him. Just this once. Just one lie wouldn't hurt him. I'll make it up to him, I will. I will truly!'

The words began to race from his mouth quickly.

'I'll make it up to both of you. When I'm growed up, I'll get a job. I'll earn money. I'll buy him things – I'll buy you things, too. I'll buy you both anything you ever want, if you'll only please, please . . .'

And then, for the first time in all his trouble, Joe Carraclough became a child, his sturdiness gone, and the tears choked his voice. His mother could hear his sobs, and she patted his hand, but she would not look at him. From the magic of the fire she seemed to read deep wisdom, and she spoke slowly.

'Tha mustn't, Joe,' she said, her words soft. 'Tha mustn't want like that. Tha must learn never to want anything i' life so hard as tha wants Lassie. It doesn't do.'

It was then that she felt her son's hand trembling with impatience, and his voice rising clear.

'Ye don't understand, Mother. Ye don't understand. It ain't me that wants her. It's her that wants us – so terrible bad. That's what made her come home all that way. She wants us, so terrible bad.'

It was then that Mrs. Carraclough looked at her son at last. She could see his face, contorted, and the tears rolling openly down his cheeks. And yet, in that moment of childishness, it was as if he were suddenly all the more grown up. Mrs. Carraclough felt as if time had jumped, and she were seeing this boy, this son of her own, for the first time in many years.

She stared at him and then she clasped her hands together. Her lips pressed together in a straight line and she got up.

'Joe, come and eat, then. And go back to school and be content. I'll talk to thy father.'

She lifted her head, and her voice sounded firm.

'Yes – I'll talk to him, all right. I'll talk to Mr. Samuel Carraclough. I will indeed!'

At five that afternoon, the Duke of Rudling, fuming and muttering in his bad-tempered way, got out of a car that had stopped by a cottage gate. And behind the gate was a boy, who stood sturdily, his feet apart, as if to bar the way.

'Well, well, m' lad! Did ye tell him?'

'Go away,' the boy said fiercely. 'Go away! Thy tyke's not here.'

For once in his life the Duke of Rudling stepped backward. He stared at the boy in amazement.

'Well, drat my buttons, Priscilla,' he breathed. 'Th' lad's touched. He is – he's touched!'

'Thy tyke's net here. Away wi' thee,' the boy said stoutly. And it seemed as if in his determination he spoke in the broadest dialect he could command.

'What's he saying?' Priscilla asked.

'He's saying my dog isn't here. Drat my buttons, are you going deaf, Priscilla? I'm supposed to be deaf, and I can hear him all right. Now, ma lad, what tyke o' mine's net here?'

The Duke, when he answered, also turned to the broadest tones of Yorkshire dialect, as he always did to the people of the cottages – a habit which many of the members of the Duke's family deplored deeply.

'Coom, coom, ma lad. Speak up! What tyke's net here?'

As he spoke he waved his cane ferociously and advanced. Joe Carraclough stepped back from the fearful old man, but he still barred the path.

'No tyke o' thine,' he cried stoutly.

But the Duke continued to advance. The words raced from Joe's mouth with a torrent of despair.

'Us hasn't got her. She's not here. She couldn't be here. No tyke could ha' done it. No tyke could come all them miles. It's not Lassie – it's – it's just another one that looks like her. It isn't Lassie.'

'Well, bless my heart and soul,' puffed the Duke. 'Bless my heart and soul. Where's thy father, lad?'

Joe shook his head grimly. But behind him the cottage door opened and his mother's voice spoke.

'If it's Sam Carraclough ye're looking for – he's out in the shed, and been shut up there half the afternoon.'

'What's this lad talking about – a dog o' mine being here?'

'Nay, ye're mistaken,' the woman said stoutly.

'I'm mistaken?' roared the Duke.

'Yes. He didn't say a tyke a' thine was here. He said it wasn't here.'

'Drat my buttons,' the Duke sputtered angrily. 'Don't twist my words up.'

Then his eyes narrowed, and he stepped a pace forward.

'Well, if he said a dog of mine *isn't*, perhaps you'll be good enough to tell me just *which* dog of mine it is that isn't here. Now,' he finished triumphantly, 'Come, come! Answer me!'

Joe, watching his mother, saw her swallow and then look about her as if for help. She pressed her lips together. The Duke stood waiting for his answer, peering out angrily from beneath his jutting eyebrows. Then Mrs. Carraclough drew a breath to speak.

But her answer, truth or lie, was never spoken. For they all heard the rattle of a chain being drawn from a door, and then the voice of Sam Carraclough said clearly:

'This, I give ye my word, is th' only tyke us has here. So tell me, does it look like any dog that belongs to thee?'

Joe's mouth was opening for a last cry of protest, but as his eyes fell on the dog by his father, the exclamation died. And he stared in amazement.

There he saw his father, Sam Carraclough, the collie fancier, standing with a dog at his heels the like of which few men had ever seen before, or would wish to see. It was a dog that sat patiently at his left heel, as any well-trained dog should do – just as Lassie used to do. But this dog – it was ridiculous to think of it at the same moment as Lassie.

For where Lassie's skull was aristocratic and slim, this dog's head was clumsy and rough. Where Lassie's ears stood in the grace of twin-lapped symmetry, this dog had one screw ear and the other standing up Alsatian fashion, in a way that would give any collie breeder the cold shivers.

More than that. Where Lassie's coat faded to delicate sable, this curious dog had ugly splashes of black; and where Lassie's apron was a billowing expanse of white, this dog had muddy puddles of off-colour, blue-merle mixture. Lassie had four white paws, and this one had only one white, two dirty-brown, and one almost black. Lassie's tail flowed gracefully behind her, and this dog's tail looked like something added as an afterthought.

And yet, as Joe Carraclough looked at the dog beside his father, he understood. He knew that if a dog coper could treat a dog with cunning so that its bad points came to look like good ones, he could also reverse the process and make all its good ones look like bad ones – especially if that man were his father, one of the most knowing of dog fanciers in all that Riding of Yorkshire.

In that moment, he understood his father's words, too. For in dog-dealing, as in horse-dealing, the spoken word is a binding contract, and once it is given, no real dog-man will attempt to go back on it.

And that was how his father, in his patient, slow way, had tried to escape with honour. He had not lied. He had not denied anything. He had merely asked a question:

'Tell me, does this dog look like any dog that belongs to thee?'

And the Duke had only to say:

'Why, that's not my dog,' and forever after, it would not be his.

So the boy, his mother and his father gazed steadily at the old man, and waited with held breath as he continued to stare at the dog.

But the Duke of Rudling knew many things too – many, many things. And he was not answering. Instead he was walking forward slowly, the great cane now tapping as he leaned on it. His eyes never left the dog for a second. Slowly, as if he were in a dream, he knelt down, and his hand made one gentle movement. It picked up a forepaw and turned it slightly. So he knelt by the collie, looked with eyes that were as knowing about dogs as any man in Yorkshire. And those eyes did not waste themselves upon twisted ears or blotched markings or rough head. Instead, they stared steadily at the underside of the paw, seeing only the five black pads, crossed and recrossed with half-healed scars where thorns had torn and stones had lacerated.

Then the Duke lifted his head, but for a long time he knelt, gazing into space, while they waited. When he did get up, he spoke, not using Yorkshire dialect any more, but speaking as one gentleman might address another.

'Sam Carraclough,' he said. 'This is no dog of mine. 'Pon my soul and honour, she never belonged to me. No! Not for a single second did she ever belong to me!'

Then he turned and walked down the path, thumping his cane and muttering: 'Bless my soul! I wouldn't ha' believed it! Bless my soul! Four hundred miles! I wouldn't ha' believed it.'

It was at the gate that his granddaughter tugged his sleeve.

'What you came for,' she whispered. 'Remember?'

The Duke seemed to come from his dream, and then he suddenly turned into his old self again.

'Don't whisper! What's that? Oh, yes, of course. You don't need to tell me – I hadn't forgotten!'

He turned and made his voice terrible.

'Carraclough! Carraclough! Drat my buttons, where are ye? What're ye hiding for?'

'I'm still here, sir.'

'Oh, yes. Yes. Of course. There you are. You working?'

'Eigh, now – working,' Joe's father said. That was the best he could manage.

'Yes, working – working! A job! A job! Do you have one?' the Duke fumed.

'Well, now – it's this road . . .' began Carraclough.

As he fumbled his words, Mrs. Carraclough came to his rescue, as good housewives will in Yorkshire – and in most other parts of the world.

'My Sam's not exactly working, but he's got three or four things that he's been considering. Sort of investigating, as ye might say. But – he hasn't quite said yes or no to any of them yet.'

'Then he'd better say no, and quickly,' snapped the Duke. 'I need somebody up at my kennels. And I think, Carraclough . . .' His eyes turned to the dog still sitting at the man's heel. '. . . I think you must know – a lot – about dogs. So there. That's settled.'

'Nay, hold on,' Carraclough said. 'Ye see, I wouldn't like to think I got a chap into trouble and then took his job. Ye see, Mr. Hynes couldn't help . . .'

'Hynes!' snorted the Duke. 'Hynes? Utter nincompoop. Had to sack him. Didn't know a dog from a ringtailed filly. Should ha' known no Londoner could ever run a kennel for a Yorkshireman's taste. Now, I want you for the job.'

'Nay, there's still summat,' Mrs. Carraclough protested.

'What now?'

'Well, how much would this position be paying?'

The Duke puffed his lips.

'How much do you want, Carraclough?'

'Seven pounds a week, and worth every penny,' Mrs. Carraclough cut in, before her husband could even get round to drawing a preparatory breath.

But the Duke was a Yorkshireman, too, and that meant he would scorn himself if he missed a chance to be 'practical', as they say, where money is concerned.

'Five,' he roared. 'And not a penny more.'

'Six pounds, ten,' bargained Mrs. Carraclough.

'Six even,' offered the Duke cannily.

'Done,' said Mrs. Carraclough, as quick as a hawk's swoop.

They both glowed, self-righteously pleased with themselves. Mrs. Carraclough would have been willing to settle for three pounds a week in the first place – and as for the Duke, he felt he was getting a man for his kennels who was beyond price.

'Then it's settled,' the Duke said.

'Well, almost,' the woman said. 'I presume, of course . . .' She liked the taste of what she considered a very fine word, so she repeated it. '. . . I presume that means we get the cottage on the estate, too.'

'Ye drive a fierce bargain, ma'am,' said the Duke, scowling. 'But ye get it – on one condition.' He lifted his voice and roared. 'On condition that as long as ye live on my land, you never allow that thick-skulled, screw-lugged, gay-tailed eyesore of an excuse for a collie on my property. Now, what do ye say?'

He waited, rumbling and chuckling happily to himself as Sam Carraclough stooped, perplexed. But it was the boy who answered gladly: 'Oh, no, sir. She'll be down at school waiting for me most o' the time. And, anyway, in a day or so we'll have her fixed up so's ye'd never recognize her.'

'I don't doubt that,' puffed the Duke, as he stumped towards his car. 'I don't doubt ye could do exactly that. Hmm . . . Well, I never . . .'

It was afterwards in the car that the girl edged close to the old man.

'Now don't wriggle,' he protested. 'I can't stand anyone wriggling.'

'Grandfather,' she said. 'You are kind – I mean about their dog.'

The old man coughed and cleared his throat.

'Nonsense,' he growled. 'Nonsense. When you grow up, you'll understand that I'm what people call a hard-hearted Yorkshire realist. For five years I've sworn I'd have that dog. And now I've got her.'

Then he shook his head slowly.

'But I had to buy the man to get her. Ah, well. Perhaps that's not the worst part of the bargain.'

FLUSH: A BIOGRAPHY

Virginia Woolf
(British) 1882–1941

ALL researches have failed to fix with any certainty the exact
year of Flush's birth, let alone the month or the day; but it is
likely that he was born some time early in the year 1842. It is also
probable that he was directly descended from Tray (c. 1816), whose
points, preserved unfortunately only in the untrustworthy medium
of poetry, prove him to have been a red cocker spaniel of merit.
There is every reason to think that Flush was the son of that 'real
old cocking spaniel' for whom Dr. Mitford refused twenty guineas
'on account of his excellence in the field'. It is to poetry, alas, that
we have to trust for our most detailed description of Flush himself
as a young dog. He was of that particular shade of dark brown which
in sunshine flashes 'all over into gold'. His eyes were 'startled eyes
of hazel bland'. His ears were 'tasselled'; his 'slender feet' were
'canopied in fringes' and his tail was broad. Making allowance for
the exigencies of rhyme and the inaccuracies of poetic diction,
there is nothing here but what would meet with the approval of the
Spaniel Club. We cannot doubt that Flush was a pure-bred Cocker
of the red variety marked by all the characteristic excellences of his
kind.

The first months of his life were passed at Three Mile Cross, a
working man's cottage near Reading. Since the Mitfords had fallen
on evil days – Kerenhappock was the only servant – the
chair-covers were made by Miss Mitford herself and of the cheapest
material; the most important article of furniture seems to have been
a large table; the most important room a large greenhouse – it is

unlikely that Flush was surrounded by any of those luxuries, rain-proof kennels, cement walks, a maid or boy attached to his person, that would now be accorded a dog of his rank. But he throve; he enjoyed with all the vivacity of his temperament most of the pleasures and some of the licences natural to his youth and sex. Miss Mitford, it is true, was much confined to the cottage. She had to read aloud to her father hour after hour; then to play cribbage; then, when at last he slumbered, to write and write and write at the table in the greenhouse in the attempt to pay their bills and settle their debts. But at last the longed-for moment would come. She thrust her papers aside, clapped a hat on her head, took her umbrella and set off for a walk across the fields with her dogs. Spaniels are by nature sympathetic; Flush, as his story proves, had an even excessive appreciation of human emotions. The sight of his dear mistress snuffing the fresh air at last, letting it ruffle her white hair and redden the natural freshness of her face, while the lines on her huge brow smoothed themselves out, excited him to gambols whose wildness was half sympathy with her own delight. As she strode through the long grass, so he leapt hither and thither, parting its green curtain. The cool globes of dew or rain broke in showers of iridescent spray about his nose; the earth, here hard, here soft, here hot, here cold, stung, teased and tickled the soft pads of his feet. Then what a variety of smells interwoven in subtlest combination thrilled his nostrils; strong smells of earth, sweet smells of flowers; nameless smells of leaf and bramble; sour smells as they crossed the road; pungent smells as they entered bean-fields. But suddenly down the wind came tearing a smell sharper, stronger, more lacerating than any – a smell that ripped across his brain stirring a thousand instincts, releasing a million memories – the smell of hare, the smell of fox. Off he flashed like a fish drawn in a rush through water further and further. He forgot his mistress; he forgot all human kind. He heard dark men cry 'Span! Span!' He heard whips crack. He raced; he rushed. At last he stopped bewildered; the incantation faded; very slowly, wagging his tail sheepishly, he trotted back across the fields to where Miss Mitford stood shouting 'Flush! Flush! Flush!' and waving her umbrella. And once at least the call was even more imperious; the hunting horn roused deeper instincts, summoned wilder and stronger emotions that transcended memory and obliterated grass, trees, hare, rabbit, fox in one wild shout of ecstasy. Love blazed her torch in his eyes; he heard the hunting horn of Venus. Before he was well out of his puppyhood, Flush was a father.

Such conduct in a man even, in the year 1842, would have called for some excuse from a biographer; in a woman no excuse could have availed; her name must have been blotted in ignominy from the page. But the moral code of dogs, whether better or worse, is certainly different from ours, and there was nothing in Flush's conduct in this respect that requires a veil now, or unfitted him for the society of the purest and the chastest in the land then. There is evidence, that is to say, that the elder brother of Dr. Pusey was anxious to buy him. Deducing from the known character of Dr. Pusey the probable character of his brother, there must have been something serious, solid, promising well for future excellence whatever might be the levity of the present in Flush even as a puppy. But a much more significant testimony to the attractive nature of his gifts is that, even though Mr. Pusey wished to buy him, Miss Mitford refused to sell him. As she was at her wits' end for money, scarcely knew indeed what tragedy to spin, what annual to edit, and was reduced to the repulsive expedient of asking her friends for help, it must have gone hard with her to refuse the sum offered by the elder brother of Dr. Pusey. Twenty pounds had been offered for Flush's father. Miss Mitford might well have asked ten or fifteen for Flush. Ten or fifteen pounds was a princely sum, a magnificent sum to have at her disposal. With ten or fifteen pounds she might have re-covered her chairs, she might have re-stocked her greenhouse, she might have bought herself an entire wardrobe, and 'I have not bought a bonnet, a cloak, a gown, hardly a pair of gloves', she wrote in 1842, 'for four years'.

But to sell Flush was unthinkable. He was of the rare order of objects that cannot be associated with money. Was he not of the still rarer kind that, because they typify what is spiritual, what is beyond price, become a fitting token of the disinterestedness of friendship; may be offered in that spirit to a friend, if one is lucky enough to have one, who is more like a daughter than a friend; to a friend who lies secluded all through the summer months in a back bedroom in Wimpole Street, to a friend who is no other than England's foremost poetess, the brilliant, the doomed, the adored Elizabeth Barrett herself? Such were the thoughts that came more and more frequently to Miss Mitford as she watched Flush rolling and scampering in the sunshine; as she sat by the couch of Miss Barrett in her dark, ivy-shaded London bedroom. Yes; Flush was worthy of Miss Barrett; Miss Barrett was worthy of Flush. The sacrifice was a great one; but the sacrifice must be made. Thus, one day, probably in the early summer of the year 1842, a remarkable couple might have been seen taking their way down Wimpole Street – a very short, stout, shabby, elderly lady, with a bright red face and bright white hair, who led by the chain a very spirited, very inquisitive, very well-bred golden cocker spaniel puppy. They walked almost the whole length of the street until at last they paused at No. 50. Not without trepidation, Miss Mitford rang the bell.

Even now perhaps nobody rings the bell of a house in Wimpole Street without trepidation. It is the most august of London streets, the most impersonal. Indeed, when the world seems tumbling to ruin, and civilisation rocks on its foundations, one has only to go to Wimpole Street; to pace that avenue; to survey those houses; to consider their uniformity; to marvel at the window curtains and their consistency; to admire the brass knockers and their regularity; to observe butchers tendering joints and cooks receiving them; to reckon the incomes of the inhabitants and infer their consequent submission to the laws of God and man – one has only to go to Wimpole Street and drink deep of the peace breathed by authority in order to heave a sigh of thankfulness that, while Corinth has fallen and Messina has tumbled, while crowns have blown down the wind and old Empires have gone up in flames, Wimpole Street has remained unmoved, and, turning from Wimpole Street into Oxford Street, a prayer rises in the heart and bursts from the lips that not a brick of Wimpole Street may be re-pointed, not a curtain washed, not a butcher fail to tender or a cook to receive the sirloin, the haunch, the breast, the ribs of mutton and beef for ever and ever, for as long as Wimpole Street remains, civilisation is secure.

The butlers of Wimpole Street move ponderously even to-day; in the summer of 1842 they were more deliberate still. The laws of livery were then more stringent; the ritual of the green baize apron for cleaning silver; of the striped waistcoat and swallow-tail black coat for opening the hall door, was more closely observed. It is likely then that Miss Mitford and Flush were kept waiting at least three minutes and a half on the door-step. At last, however, the door of number fifty was flung wide; Miss Mitford and Flush were ushered in. Miss Mitford was a frequent visitor; there was nothing to surprise, though something to subdue her, in the sight of the Barrett family mansion. But the effect upon Flush must have been overwhelming in the extreme. Until this moment he had set foot in no house but the working man's cottage at Three Mile Cross. The boards there were bare; the mats were frayed; the chairs were cheap. Here there was nothing bare, nothing frayed, nothing cheap – that Flush could see at a glance. Mr. Barrett, the owner, was a rich merchant; he had a large family of grown-up sons and daughters, and a retinue, proportionately large, of servants. His house was furnished in the fashion of the late 'thirties, with some tincture, no doubt, of that Eastern fantasy which had led him when he built a house in Shropshire to adorn it with the domes and crescents of Moorish architecture. Here in Wimpole Street such extravagance would not be allowed; but we may suppose that the high dark rooms were full of ottomans and carved mahogany; tables were twisted; filigree ornaments stood upon them; daggers and swords hung upon wine-dark walls; curious objects brought from his East Indian property stood in recesses, and thick rich carpets clothed the floors.

But as Flush trotted up behind Miss Mitford, who was behind the butler, he was more astonished by what he smelt than by what he saw. Up the funnel of the staircase came warm whiffs of joints roasting, of fowls basting, of soups simmering – ravishing almost as food itself to nostrils used to the meagre savour of Kerenhappock's penurious fries and hashes. Mixing with the smell of food were further smells

– smells of cedarwood and sandalwood and mahogany; scents of male bodies and female bodies; of men servants and maid servants; of coats and trousers; of crinolines and mantles; of curtains of tapestry, of curtains of plush; of coal dust and fog; of wine and cigars. Each room as he passed it – dining-room, drawing-room, library, bed-room – wafted out its own contribution to the general stew; while, as he set down first one paw and then another, each was caressed and retained by the sensuality of rich pile carpets closing amorously over it. At length they reached a closed door at the back of the house. A gentle tap was given; gently the door was opened.

Miss Barrett's bedroom – for such it was – must by all accounts have been dark. The light, normally obscured by a curtain of green damask, was in summer further dimmed by the ivy, the scarlet runners, the convolvuluses and the nasturtiums which grew in the window-box. At first Flush could distinguish nothing in the pale greenish gloom but five white globes glimmering mysteriously in mid-air. But again it was the smell of the room that overpowered him. Only a scholar who has descended step by step into a mausoleum and there finds himself in a crypt, crusted with fungus, slimy with mould, exuding sour smells of decay and antiquity, while half-obliterated marble busts gleam in mid-air and all is dimly seen by the light of the small swinging lamp which he holds, and dips and turns, glancing now here, now there – only the sensations of such an explorer into the buried vaults of a ruined city can compare with the riot of emotions that flooded Flush's nerves as he stood for the first time in an invalid's bedroom, in Wimpole Street, and smelt eau-de-Cologne.

Very slowly, very dimly, with much sniffing and pawing, Flush by degrees distinguished the outlines of several articles of furniture. That huge object by the window was perhaps a wardrobe. Next to it stood, conceivably, a chest of drawers. In the middle of the room swam up to the surface what seemed to be a table with a ring round it; and then the vague amorphous shapes of armchair and table emerged. But everything was disguised. On top of the wardrobe stood three white busts; the chest of drawers was surmounted by a bookcase; the bookcase was pasted over with crimson merino; the washing-table had a coronal of shelves upon it; on top of the shelves that were on top of the washing-table stood two more busts. Nothing in the room was itself; everything was something else. Even the window-blind was not a simple muslin blind; it was a painted fabric with a design of castles and gateways and groves of trees, and there were several peasants taking a walk. Looking-glasses further distorted these already distorted objects so that there seemed to be ten busts of ten poets instead of five; four tables instead of two. And suddenly there was a more terrifying confusion still. Suddenly Flush saw staring back at him from a hole in the wall another dog with bright eyes flashing, and tongue lolling! He paused amazed. He advanced in awe.

Thus advancing, thus withdrawing, Flush scarcely heard, save as the distant drone of wind among the tree-tops, the murmur and patter of voices talking. He pursued his investigations, cautiously, nervously, as an explorer in a forest softly advances his foot, uncertain whether that shadow is a lion, or that root a cobra. At last, however, he was aware of huge objects in commotion over him; and, unstrung as he was by the experiences of the past hour, he hid himself, trembling, behind a screen. The voices ceased. A door shut. For one instant he paused, bewildered, unstrung. Then with a pounce as of clawed tigers memory fell upon him. He felt himself alone – deserted. He rushed to the door. It was shut. He pawed, he listened. He heard footsteps descending. He knew them for the familiar footsteps of his mistress. They stopped. But no – on they went, down they went. Miss Mitford was slowly, was heavily, was reluctantly descending the stairs. And as she went, as he heard her footsteps fade, panic seized upon him. Door after door shut in his face as Miss Mitford went downstairs; they shut on freedom; on fields; on hares; on grass; on his adored, his venerated mistress – on the dear old woman who had washed him . . . fed him from her own plate when she had none too much to eat herself – on all he had known of happiness and love and human goodness! There! The front door slammed. He was alone. She had deserted him.

Then such a wave of despair and anguish overwhelmed him, the irrevocableness and implacability of fate so smote him, that he lifted up his head and howled aloud. A voice said 'Flush'. He did not hear it. 'Flush', it repeated a second time. He started. He had thought himself alone. He turned. Was there something alive in the room with him? Was there something on the sofa? In the wild hope that this being, whatever it was, might open the door, that he might still rush after Miss Mitford and find her – that this was some game of hide-and-seek such as they used to play in the greenhouse at home – Flush darted to the sofa.

'Oh, Flush!' said Miss Barrett. For the first time she looked him in the face. For the first time Flush looked at the lady lying on the sofa.

Each was surprised. Heavy curls hung down on either side of Miss Barrett's face; large bright eyes shone out; a large mouth smiled. Heavy ears hung down on either side of Flush's face; his eyes, too, were large and bright: his mouth was wide. There was a likeness between them. As they gazed at each other each felt: Here am I – and then each felt: But how different! Hers was the pale worn face of an invalid, cut off from air, light, freedom. His was the warm ruddy face of a young animal; instinct with health and energy. Broken asunder, yet made in the same mould, could it be that each completed what was dormant in the other? She might have been – all that; and he – But no. Between them lay the widest gulf that can separate one being from another. She spoke. He was dumb. She was woman; he was dog. Thus closely united, thus immensely divided, they gazed at each other. Then with one bound Flush sprang on to the sofa and laid himself where he was to lie for ever after – on the rug at Miss Barrett's feet.

THE THIN
RED LEASH

James Thurber
(American) 1894–1961

I T takes courage for a tall thin man to lead a tiny Scotch terrier
pup on a smart red leash in our neighborhood, that region
bounded roughly (and how!) by Hudson and West Streets, where
the Village takes off its Windsor tie and dons its stevedore
corduroys. Here men are guys and all dogs are part bull. Here 'cute'
apartments stand quivering like pioneers on the prairie edge.

The first day that I sallied forth with Black Watch III bounding
tinily at the street end of the thin red leash, a cement finisher, one
of the crowd that finds an esoteric pleasure in standing on the bleak
corner of Hudson and Horatio Streets, sat down on the sidewalk
and guffawed. There were hoots and whistles.

It was apparent that the staunch and plucky Scotch terrier breed
was, to these uninitiated bulldog-lovers, the same as Pekingese. But
Black Watch must have his airing. So I continued to brave such
witticisms as 'Hey, fella, where's the rest of it?' and – this from a
huge steamfitter – 'What d'y say me an' you an' the dog go some-
wheres and have tea?'

Once a dockworker demanded, in a tone indicating he would not
take Black Watch III for an answer, 'What's that thing's name?'

My courage failed me. 'Mike,' I said, giving the leash a
red-blooded jerk and cursing the Scotty. The whole affair was a
challenge to my gumption. I had been scared to call my dog by its
right name.

The gang was on hand in full force the next evening. One of
them snapped enormous calloused fingers at Black Watch and he
bounded away, leash and all, from my grasp.

'Black Watch!' I shouted – if you could call it shouting.

'What did y' call that dog, fella?' demanded a man who, I think, blows through truck exhaust whistles to test them.

'Black Watch,' said I.

'What's that mean?' he asked menacingly.

'It was a Scottish regiment wiped out at Ypres or somewhere,' I said, pronouncing it 'Eeprr.'

'Wiped out where?' he snarled.

'Wiped out at Wipers,' I said.

'That's better,' he said.

I again realized that I had shown the white feather. That night I took a solemn, if not fervent, oath to tell the next heavy-footed lout that flayed my dog to go to hell. The following evening the gang was more numerous than ever. A gigantic chap lunged forward at us. He had the build of a smokestack-wrecker.

'Psst!' he hissed. Black Watch held his ground.

'They're scrappers, these dogs,' I protested amiably.

'What d' they scrap – cockroaches?' asked another man, amid general laughter. I realized that now was the time to die. After all, there are certain slurs that you can't take about your dog – gang or no gang. Just then a monstrous man, evidently a former Hudson Duster who lifts locomotives from track to track when the turn-tables are out of order, lounged out of a doorway.

'Whadda we got here?' he growled.

'Park Avenoo pooch,' sneered one gas-house gangster. The train-lifter eyed Black Watch, who was wagging his tail in a most friendly manner.

'Scotty, ain't it?' asked the train-lifter, producing a sack of scrap tobacco.

'Yeah,' I said, as easily as I could.

'Damn fine dogs, Scotties,' said the train-lifter. 'You gotta good 'un there, when it puts on some age, scout. Hellcats in a fight, too, I mean. Seen one take the tonsils out of a Airedale one day.'

'Yeah?' asked the smokestack-wrecker.

'Yeah,' said the train-lifter.

'Yeah,' said I.

Several huge hands went down to pat a delighted shaggy head. There were no more catcalls or hoots. Black Watch III had been acquitted of Pomeranianism. We're quite good friends now, Black Watch and the gang and I. They call him Blackie. I am grateful to a kind Fate that had given the train-lifter the chance, between carrying locomotives, to see a Scotty in action.

THE SOUL OF CALIBAN

Emma-Lindsay Squier
(American) 1892–1941

FROM French Louie I had this story, which you will accept as true or scout as impossible, according to your liking and knowledge of dogs. For myself, I think it is true, for he was not blessed – or cursed – with imagination.

French Louie is a curious mixture of savagery and simplicity. For many years he lived by trapping in the northern woods. And yet, despite his cruel occupation, he has always loved animals. Many a fox cub he has reared to adulthood when it came to grief in his traps. Many a tear has he shed – I can well believe it – when a dragged and bloody trap told the mute story of an animal's desperate gnawing of a foot or a leg as the price of freedom. One day when he heard a visitor to the menagerie remark that it was a pity that animals had no souls, he flew into a rage, fairly booted the visitor out of the place, and was still sputtering French and English when I dropped in upon him.

'No souls, they say!' he snorted, spreading his hands and puckering his lips in contemptuous mimicry. 'Faugh! They give me the gran' pain! The only animal they ever have, I bet you, he is a canary bird that say "Pretty Poll" all day long!'

'That's a parrot,' I said mildly. But he only snorted.

'No soul, they say! Listen, I tell you somet'ing I bet you nobody believe, by Gar! Or they say, "Oh, dat dog he obey hees instinct." *Bien*, all I say ees, who know what ees instinct and what ees soul? And I bet you many a man he ain't got the soul that that dog got instinct – no, by Gar!'

It was in the sheep country of Alberta that Louie knew the dog, Caliban. Leon Suprenon was his owner, and Louie used to visit the sheep man at his ranch, far removed from civilization.

'Leon he was one fine educated man, by Gar,' he told me. 'Books – with pictures – he had many of them in hees 'ouse. Dat dog, Caliban, he name' heem from a pleh by Shakespeare – you have heard of heem?'

'Yes,' I said, unsmiling.

'You know a pleh with a dog name Caliban in eet?'

'Not a dog,' I answered, 'but a poor imprisoned monster, ugly, deformed, and very wicked, yet somehow very pitiful.'

French Louie nodded vigorously.

'*C'est la même chose*,' he assured me. 'Dat dog, Caliban – oh, *mon Dieu*, he was ugly! Hees lip she always lifted up like zis – in a snar-rl – all the time dat lip! And hees eyes – leetle, mean-looking eyes, wid a frown between dem always, and teeth dat would snep together – *clop*! No tramps ever came near the place of Leon Suprenon. Dey know dat dog, Caliban; he was not a beast to be trifle' with.'

'What kind of a dog was he?' I asked of Louie the Frenchman.

He shrugged his shoulders, spread out his hands and shook his head. No kind, and every kind, was what I gathered from his description – a big, shaggy dog, as large as a sheepdog, and much more stockily built. His hair had no silky smoothness to it. Rather it was like the rough, matted fur of a wolf – and Louie maintained that that Caliban had wolf blood in him. There was a strain of bulldog, too, that made his legs short and bowed a bit. His under-jaw came out pugnaciously – always with that lifted lip which was no fault of his, but which gave his face a perpetually savage expression.

Ugly he must have been; yet useful, too. As a guard against tramps and the lawless characters who are to be found in any part of the country where civilization is at a distance, he was invaluable. As a sheepdog, too, he had not his equal in Alberta. Perhaps it is too much to say that he could count the sheep his master owned. But it is true that he would watch them, passing into the big corrals, his sharp, shaggy ears pointed, his small, close-set eyes never wavering in their intense regard, his whole body taut with concentration. And if any lingered or did not come, Caliban would need no word of command to stir him to action. Like an arrow he would dart out, snapping at the lagging heels, turning in a scatter-brained ewe, or dashing off across the fields to find a sheep which he knew had strayed or had fallen into the river.

A dog of strange, tumultuous jealousies, and incomprehensible tenderness. So rough was he, when herding the sheep, that Leon Suprenon was always shouting: 'Caliban, you devil! Stop biting that sheep or I'll beat your ugly brains out!'

Caliban would stop short, regard his master with a long, disdainful stare, and then look back at the sheep, as if to say: 'Those silly things! What difference does it make whether I bite their heels or not?'

And yet – that was the dog that, after seeing the sheep into the corral one winter afternoon when a blizzard was threatening to blow down from the north, did not come into the house to dream and twitch under the kitchen stove as was his custom. When darkness fell Leon noticed the dog's absence at first with unconcern, and then with growing uneasiness. The rising wind flung itself viciously upon doors and windows, the white snow whirled up against the panes with sharp, sibilant flurries. Leon went to the door and called. The blizzard drove his voice back in his throat; the wind hurled him against the portals, and drove an icy blast of snow into the hall.

Leon Suprenon was not the man to be daunted by a storm. He remembered that after the gates were shut, Caliban had stood steadily gazing away towards the dim fields, where the menacing curtain of oncoming wind and snow was blotting out the contours of stream and distant forest.

So he took a lantern and fought his way out into the terrible night, out towards the sheep corrals, and then out towards the invisible fields beyond the stream. A mile he went – perhaps more – fighting his way against the fury of the storm. It was out by the cluster of pine-trees that marks the east line of the ranch that he met Caliban, coming home.

The dim light of the lantern threw a weak golden circle against the driving white mistiness of the snow. And into the nebulous ring of light came Caliban, grim, staggering, a grotesque monster looming out of the white darkness, his mouth strangely misshapen by something he was carrying – *a lamb*, newly born. Beside him, struggling weakly yet valiantly against the driving snow, came the mother sheep, which had given birth to her baby in the midst of the dreadful blizzard. Caliban was coming slowly, adapting his pace to hers, stopping when she would stop, yet with unmistakable signs that he expected her to struggle forward with him. And the lamb – the weak, bleating little thing that swung from his teeth as lightly as if it had been a puff of thistledown.

Now the dog Caliban never begged for caresses. He was not the sort of dog to leap and bark and wag his tail when the master came home. Between him and Leon Suprenon there was an understanding – a man's understanding of mutual respect and restraint. A word of commendation sufficed him, or sometimes a pat on the head. But never, as long as Leon had owned the dog, could he recall a time when Caliban had ever sought to ingratiate himself by being friendly and playful, as the other dogs would do.

Nevertheless, Caliban had his jealousies, fierce, deep and primitive. He killed a dog that Leon petted casually; he took it by the throat and crushed it with his great teeth, then flung the quivering body down and stared at it with those baleful, close-set eyes. There was blood on the perpetual snarl of his lifted lip.

Then fearlessly he awaited his punishment. Leon beat him cruelly. But Caliban never flinched or whimpered, just stood there hunching himself up and shutting his eyes, licking his lips a bit as the blows hurt him more and more. When it was over, he shook himself, stretched, then pricked up his ears and looked Leon in the face, as if to say: 'Well, that's over. Now have you any orders.' If he had whimpered once – but he did not. Leon swore furiously, and had the dead dog buried in the meadow. He did not caress the other dogs after that. They were valuable to him – but Caliban was priceless. And Leon knew that the only way of breaking his stubborn spirit would be to kill him.

Caliban had one abiding hatred: cats. Whereas the other dogs chased them joyously, or ignored them as inferior creatures, Caliban loathed them, chased them savagely, killed them mercilessly. He had a short, brutal way of doing it; if he caught a luckless cat – and he would run like a yearling buck, that dog Caliban – he would give it one shake, like the crack of a whip, and then toss the cat into the air. It usually died with a broken neck and a broken back. And by the law of the survival of the fittest, the cats that escaped from Caliban's savage sallies were wise in their generation and kept out of his way.

But there was one small cat, not yet out of kittenhood, that had either come recently to the ranch, or else by an accident had not crossed Caliban's path – a gentle cat, all grey, with a white paw which she was always licking as if proud of it.

One day she sat sunning herself on the porch before the house. Caliban came by that way, and saw her.

With the savage, deep-throated growl that all the other cats had learned to fear as the most deadly thing of life, he leaped at her, caught her, flung her up into the air.

Perhaps it was supreme ignorance of danger that saved her from death. For the gentle little cat had not tried to run from the on-coming whirlwind of teeth and gleaming eyes. She lay where Caliban had flung her, dazed, inert, staring at the terrible dog, with round, uncomprehending eyes. He saw that he had not killed her. He came nearer, ready to shake her with the peculiarly deadly twist that he knew so well. Still she did not move. She could not. She only mewed, a very small, pitiful mew, and her stunned body twitched a little.

Caliban hesitated, sniffed at her, turned away. After all, he seemed to tell himself, you could not kill a weak, helpless thing like that – a thing that could not run.

Leon Suprenon came out and found the little cat. He took her up very gently, and she tried to purr as he stroked her quivering, hurt body.

'Caliban,' Leon said sternly, 'that was not a sportsmanlike thing to do. I am ashamed of you!'

And to his great surprise, Caliban, the insolent, the ever-snarling, put his tail between his legs and slunk down the porch steps. He too was ashamed.

But Caliban, that ugly, misshapen dog with the perpetual snarl on his lifted lip, could make amends. And to the best of his ability he did. The gentle little cat did not die, but never did she fully recover the use of her limbs. She had a slow, halting way of walking, and running was an impossibility. She would have been an easy prey for the joyous, roistering dogs that chased cats, not from enmity, but because it was the proper thing to do. But Caliban stood between her and eager, sniffing dogs like a savage, sinister warrior. Too well did the other ranch dogs know the menace of those close-set eyes, the ugly, undershot jaw, and the snarl that showed the glitter of deadly, clamping teeth. They learned – through experience – that the little grey cat was not to be molested.

Not only did Caliban become the little grey cat's protector; he became her friend. She would sit on the fence and watch for the sheepdogs to come up to the house after the day's work was done. When the other dogs filed past her, she paid no attention, realizing perfectly that they dared not harm her. And when Caliban came, close at the heels of Leon Suprenon, she would yawn and stretch, purr loudly, and drop squarely and lightly on the big dog's back. He would carry her gravely into the kitchen, lie down while she got slowly off his back, and would lie under the stove, with the little cat purring and rubbing about his face. It was not in him to show affection. But he permitted her carefully to wash his face and ears, tug at burrs that matted his heavy coat, and to sleep between his forefeet.

Once another cat, emboldened by the grey cat's immunity from danger, went to sleep between Caliban's great paws. When he awoke and found the intruder peacefully purring against his chest, he gave one terrific growl, sprang to his feet, seized the strange cat and shook it. Savagely he flung it across the room. It was dead before ever it struck the floor.

Now it was at this time that Leon Suprenon married Amelie Morin, from Dubuiqui, and brought her to the ranch that was bounded by dark forests and deep, turbulent rivers. She chafed a little under the isolation of the place, and shivered when at night the wolves howled far back on the distant slopes. But she loved Leon Suprenon, and in time became reconciled to the loneliness of the ranch – still more reconciled when a baby was born to her, and was strong and healthy and beautiful.

Caliban had accepted the girl, Amelie, stoically, without apparent resentment. It was as if he knew that sooner or later his master would bring home a woman to share the lonely ranch-house. But the baby – that was a different thing. He had not bargained on the small intruder who became at once the lord and tyrant of the household. When Leon took up the tiny baby in his arms, Caliban growled, and his eyes became a baleful red.

When Leon put the baby in its crib, and spoke to it foolishly, fondly, as all fathers do, Caliban came and stood beside him, looking down at the red-faced crinkly-eyed baby, and again the dog growled, deep in its throat.

One day when Leon caressed the child, Caliban sprang, trying to tear the infant out of his arms. Leon kicked the dog furiously aside, and beat him with a leather whip.

'Caliban, you devil!' he panted between the blows. 'If you ever touch that baby, I'll kill you!'

And, as if the dog understood, he hunched himself and shut his eyes, licking his lips as the heavy lash fell again and again. Then he shook himself, stared at his master with sombre, unwavering eyes, and went out of the house without once looking back.

For a whole week he did not return. One of the ranchmen reported that he had seen Caliban in the forest, that the dog had mated with a female wolf.

Leon Suprenon said that it was not true, and that Caliban would come back. But Amelie cried out:

'No, no! That dog, he is a monster! Never again would I feel that my baby was safe!'

'You misjudge him,' Leon said soothingly, 'he is a little jealous of the baby, it is true, but he will overcome that in time. An ugly-looking dog, I grant you, but he is very gentle, nevertheless.'

'*Gentle* – that beast!' The girl shut her eyes and shuddered.

Caliban did come back. He appeared at the kitchen door one day when Leon was out looking after the sheep – sullen, defiant, his glittering, close-set eyes seeming to question whether or not he would be welcomed. The perpetual snarl on his lifted lip and the misshapen ugliness of his powerful body made him ever more repellent to the girl Amelie, who snatched up her baby from where he was playing on the floor, ran with him to the bedroom, and closed and bolted the door. But a royal welcome he received from the little grey cat, that dragged herself towards him with purring sounds of joy. She mewed delightfully, rubbed against his bowed legs, and tried to lick his face. Caliban, for the first and last time, bent his ugly head, and licked the little grey cat, briefly and furtively.

The dog had learned his lesson as to the status of the baby. And whether or not his heart was seared with that savage, primitive jealousy which he had shown at first so plainly, no hint of it now appeared. At first he ignored the child, even when it crawled towards him as he lay under the kitchen stove. Later he would watch the round-faced baby with rigid, attentive eyes – eyes in which there were blue-green wolf gleams behind the honest brown. Sometimes he would sniff at the child questioningly, as if trying to ascertain for himself what charm such a helpless crawling little animal could possibly have for the man who was his master and his idol.

Little by little Amelie's distrust lessened, and she was willing that the baby should lie in his crib on the sunny porch, when Caliban was stretched out on the steps with the little grey cat sleeping between his paws.

Then one day, after a morning of housework within doors, she came out to take the baby – and he was gone. The crib was empty, the little blankets were rumpled into confusion. The dog Caliban still lay sleeping upon the porch, and the little grey cat purred drowsily against his furry chest.

Amelie screamed, and the men came running up from the sheep pens and barns, snatching up sticks of wood, or fumbling with guns. Leon came running with a face the colour of chalk; and Amelie clung to him, screaming, sobbing, wild with hysterical fear. She was certain that some wild animal had snatched her baby out of his crib and devoured him.

'Nonsense!' said Leon Suprenon positively. 'No wild animal could have come near the house with Caliban on guard.'

After an hour of frantic searching, they found the child. Back of the ranch house where the garbage was dumped and burned, there they found the baby, playing happily with an old tin can, dirty and bedraggled, yet quite unhurt and unharmed.

In the first moment of acute relief, no one thought to question how the child had come so far. But afterwards —

Leon stood in deep thought, staring down at Caliban, who returned his look steadily, unflinchingly, as was his wont. For the first time a doubt of the dog's integrity came into his mind. He knew Caliban's great strength, knew that the dog could have carried the baby as easily as he had carried the newborn lamb. And the garbage pile – there was a grim humour in that which pointed to Caliban's line of reasoning. Undesirable things were thrown out there; things put upon the garbage pile were never brought back into the house; therefore, if the baby were put out there, with the rest of the rubbish . . .

'Caliban, you devil!' said Leon Suprenon between clenched teeth. Yet he could not beat the dog. The evidence was only circumstantial.

Had the thing happened to anyone else's child, he would have laughed heartily at the story. But to him it was not so funny. Anything might have happened to the child. The dog might have dropped it; or stray wolves might have come down out of the woods. The baby might have cut its hands terribly on broken glass or rusty tin cans.

'Caliban,' said Leon Suprenon sternly, 'you have spoiled my belief in you. I will never be able to trust you again.'

The great ugly dog stared at him with those glittering, close-set eyes, then turned away abruptly and lay down. It was as if he accepted the defeat of his plans, the humiliation, the loss of his master's trust, with stoical resignation. It was almost as if he had shrugged his shoulders.

Now there came the winter-time – a lean, terrible winter, when the wolves howled about the ranch, sometimes becoming so bold as to come close to the barns, and corrals, and the house.

The spring was late, and even when the snow began to melt, and the first warm breezes to come up from the south, still the howling of the wolf-pack was heard on distant hills, and still tracks were found in the crusted snow about the barn and the sheep corrals.

One day in the spring an urgent message came to Amelie Suprenon, begging her to come to a neighbouring ranch where a woman lay in childbirth.

She could only go on horseback – and the need for her help was imminent. She saddled her horse herself, for the men were out on the ranges. Then she hesitated as to leaving or taking the baby. But Leon had said he would return at noon, and the sun was then almost at the zenith. She scribbled a note for him, put the baby in the bedroom in the little pen which Leon had made for it, and shut the door.

Then she mounted her horse and rode hard and fast to the woman who was in need of her.

Leon Suprenon did not get the note. A hint of spring sickness had come upon some of the sheep, and he worked all through the morning and late into the afternoon with sheep dip and sprays. When he was about to return to the ranch-house, one of the men told him that he had seen Amelie riding by, at noon, in the direction of the Pourers' ranch. Leon frowned a bit. He did not like to have Amelie ride alone, especially on the forest roads. He flung himself upon his horse, shouted to his men to go on with their work, and took a short cut across the fields to ride home with Amelie.

He met her just as she came out of the door, tired, but smiling.

'Such a sweet little baby boy!' she called to Leon as he rode nearer. Then her face suddenly clouded.

'The baby – our baby —' she said uncertainly. 'You did not leave him alone?'

Leon stared back at her, his forehead wrinkled.

'The baby?' he repeated. 'Why, surely, Amelie, he is with you?'

For an instant she did not reply. A slow fear was dawning in her heart that stretched her eyes wide and made them hard and glassy.

'No – no,' she almost whispered. 'I left a note – I thought you would come at noon. The baby then – he is there alone – perhaps with – *Caliban* —' Her voice died away, as if she were afraid of the name she had spoken.

Leon tried to laugh, to make light of her fears. But his lips were a bit stiff, and he breathed as he helped her into the saddle.

'Come, come, Amelie, you worry too much. The little one will be quite well – you shall see – only very hungry perhaps and exercising his small lungs terrifically. As for Caliban—'

Amelie slashed at her horse's flank with the whip. Her face was dead-white.

'Where was that dog – that terrible beast, when you came away?' she gasped as they galloped down the snowy road.

'I don't know,' Leon jerked out grimly, as if thinking aloud. 'I can't remember seeing him – yes, yes, he stood looking away towards the ranch-house; I remember now that he barked once – then trotted away. I thought he was rounding up a sheep. I did not call him back. One of the men laughed and said that he was going to meet the lady —'

'*Wolf!*' the girl finished hoarsely. 'Oh, *grand Dieu*, guard my baby! He is in danger, I tell you, Leon; I feel it, I know it! That beast – that horrible beast who mates with bloodthirsty wolves – you would not believe it, Leon, but I tell you it is true – true! Oh, my baby, my little baby!'

She lashed her horse with frenzied, hysterical hands, and the startled animal reared and plunged forward. Fast, faster, the slender hoofs pounded through the snowy slush of the road, and Leon's horse followed, breathing hard and straining at the bit.

They did not speak again, the husband and wife, but rode, rode as if for the saving of a life.

It was Amelie who dismounted first, when at the end of that wild ride her horse came to a stop, panting and trembling. She dashed the unlocked door wide open, and an instant later a wild scream sent the blood ebbing from Leon's face and made his hands numb clods of flesh as they fumbled for the gun in his belt.

The scene he saw as he stumbled through the hallway turned him sick with a deadly nausea of horror and despair.

Amelie lay fainting in the open doorway of the bedroom. Beyond, an empty cradle, an open window, with muddy tracks on the window-sill, told a dreadful story. But the thing that made him cry out, savagely, hoarsely, was the dog – Caliban. The snarling, misshapen beast stood in the doorway, staring at him with red, malevolent eyes – *and there was blood on the heavy jowls and the thick matted hair of the chest.*

'You – you devil!' Leon screamed like a madman – and fired.

The dog still stood there, just an instant. The small, close-set eyes blinked slightly, the ugly head jerked back once – and he fell in a silent, twitching heap.

'Oh, God! Oh, God!' Leon was sobbing, hardly knowing what he said or did. And then – he heard a baby crying.

Stunned, incredulous, almost believing himself in a tortured dream, the man went slowly forward. The baby lay behind the door, lay where it had been dragged to safety. It was crying with fright and hunger, beating the air vaguely with its pink little hands and over by the dresser, in a pool of blood – lay a dead wolf.

'There is a grave on the ranch of Leon Suprenon,' said French Louie solemnly, in the language of his people, 'where the dog, Caliban, lies buried. And above it is a tombstone of marble – yes, the whitest of marble – with this inscription:

Here lies Caliban, a dog. He died as he lived, misjudged, maligned, yet unafraid. In life he never failed in duty, and in death he was faithful to his trust.

'And dat is why,' said Louie, the Frenchman, lapsing into the argot of his daily life, 'dat I get so mad inside of me when people say animals dey have no souls. Did not the dog, Caliban, have a soul? Oh, *mon Dieu!* I know dis: when he died dat day, and hees spirit went out of hees big, ogly body and rose up to the skies, the good Saint who guards the gates up dere he look out, and say: "Why, Caliban, ees dat you? Come in, *mon brave*. I did not know you. How beautiful you have grown!"'

MR. GEROLMAN LOSES HIS DOG

from *The Rise and Fall of the Mustache*

Robert J. Burdette
(American) 1844–1914

M R. Gerolman stood on the front porch of his comfortable
home on West Hill one morning looking out at the drizzling
rain in anything but a comfortable frame of mind. He looked up and
down the yard, and then he raised his umbrella and went to the gate
and looked up and down the street. Then he whistled in a very
shrill manner three or four times, and listened as though he was
expecting a response. If he was, he was disappointed, for there was
no response save the pattering of the rain on his umbrella, and he
frowned heavily as he returned to the porch, from which sheltered
post of observation he gloomily surveyed the dispiriting weather.

'Dag gone the dag gone brute,' he muttered savagely, 'if ever I
keep another dog again, I hope it will eat me up.'

And then he whistled again. And again there was no response. It
was evident that Mr. Gerolman had lost his dog, a beautiful ashes of
roses hound with seal brown spots and soft satin-finish ears. He was
a valuable dog, and this was the third time he had been lost, and
Mr. Gerolman was rapidly losing his temper as completely as he had
lost his dog. He lifted his voice and called aloud:

'H'yuh–h–h Ponto! h'yuh Ponto! h'yuhp onto! h'yup onto, h'yup
onto, h'yuponto, h'yuponto! h'yup, h'yup, h'yup!'

As he ceased calling, and looked anxiously about for some
indications of a dog, the front door opened and a woman's face,

shaded with a tinge of womanly anxiety and fastened to Mrs. Gerolman's head, looked out.

'The children call him Hector,' a low sweet voice said for the wistful, pretty face; but the bereaved master of the absent dog was in no humor to be charmed by a beautiful face and a flute-like voice.

'By George,' he said, striding out into the rain and purposely leaving his umbrella on the porch to make his wife feel bad, 'it's no wonder the dog gets lost, when he has so dod binged many names that he don't know himself. By Jacks, when I give eleven dollars for a dog, I want the privilege of naming him, and the next person about this house that tries to fasten an old pagan, Indian, blasphemous name on a dog of mine, will hear from me about it; now that's all.'

And then he inflated his lungs and yelled like a scalp hunter.

'Here, Hector! here, Hector! here rector, hyur, rector, hyur rec, h'yurrec, k'yurrec k'yurrec, k'yurrec! Godfrey's cordial, where's that dog gone to? H'yuponto, h'yupont! h'yuh, h'yuh, h'yuh! I hope he's poisoned – h'yurrector! By George, I do; h'yuh Ponto, good dog, Ponty, Ponty, Ponty, h'yuh Pont! I'd give fifty dollars if some one had strychnined the nasty, worthless, lop-eared cur; hyurrec, k'yurrec! By granny, I'll kill him when he comes home, if I don't I hope to die; h'yuh Ponto, h'yuh Ponto, *h'yuh* Hec!!'

And as he turned back to the porch the door again opened and the tremulous voice sweetly asked:

'Can't you find him?'

'Naw!!!, roared the exasperated dog-hunter, and the door closed precipitately and was opened no more during the session.

'Here, Ponto!' roared Mr. Gerolman, from his position on the porch, 'Here, Hector!' And then he whistled until his head swam and his throat was so dry you could light a match in it. 'Here, Ponto! Blast the dog. I suppose he's twenty-five miles from here. Hector! What are you lookin' at, you gimlet-eyed old Bedlamite?' he savagely growled, apostrophizing a sweet-faced old lady with silky white hair, who had just looked out of her window to see where the fire was, or who was being murdered. 'Here, Ponto! here Ponto! Good doggie, nice old Pontie, nice old Heckie dog –

Oh-h-h,' he snarled, dancing up and down on the porch in an ecstasy of rage and impatience, 'I'd like to tramp the ribs out of the long-legged worthless old garbage eater; *here, Ponto, here!'*

To his amazement he heard a canine yawn, a long-drawn, weary kind of a whine, as of a dog who was bored to death with the dismal weather; then there was a scraping sound, and the dog, creeping out from under the porch, from under his very feet, looked vacantly around as though he wasn't quite sure but what he had heard some one calling him, and then catching sight of his master, sat down and thumped on the ground with his tail, smiled pleasantly, and asked as plainly as ever dog asked in the world,

'Were you wanting me?'

Mr. Gerolman, for one brief instant, gasped for breath. Then he pulled his hat down tight on his head, snatched up his umbrella with a convulsive grasp and yelled 'Come 'ere!' in such a terrific roar that the white-haired old lady across the way fell back in a fit, and the dog, surmising that all was not well, briefly remarked that he had an engagement to meet somebody about fifty-eight feet under the house, and shot under the porch like a shooting dog-star. Mr. Gerolman made a dash to intercept him, but stumbled over a flower stand and plunged through a honey-suckle trellis, off the porch, and down into a raging volcano of moss-rose bush, straw, black dirt, shattered umbrella ribs, and a ubiquitous hat, while far under the house, deep in the cavernous darkness, came the mocking laugh of an ashes of roses dog with seal brown spots, accompanied by the taunting remark as nearly as Mr. Gerolman could understand the dog,

'Who hit him? Which way did he go?'

FLURRY AT THE SHEEP DOG TRIAL

from *Sam Small Flies Again*

Eric Knight
(British) 1897–1943

THE wind came clear over the great flat part of the moor near Soderby. The gusts eddied, tearing away wisps of smell – the smell of men packed in knots, of sheep, of trampled heath grass. The size of the flatland made the noises small – the sharp barks of dogs, the voices of men speaking in deep dialect.

The men of the different sections stood in separate knots. Those from Polkingthorpe were ranged about Sam, their eyes on him trustingly, half fearfully, as if they were a little awed by what they had done, and the size of the bets they had made from village loyalty.

'Now, Sam,' Gaffer Sitherthwick mumbled slowly, 'tha's sure she can do it? For Ah've put up one pound again' two pound ten that she's the winner.'

'Now hold up, Gaffer,' Capper Wambley wavered. 'Tha must remember she's never been really trained as a shepherd; but what Ah say is, the way Sam's trained her this past week she'll do owt he tells her best she can. And best ye can do is best, as any man'll agree.'

'Thankee, Capper,' Sam acknowledged. 'Now, lads, if ye don't mind, Ah'd like to give her sort of secret instructions – and calm her down.'

He led Flurry away from the knot of men, though she looked as though she needed no calming down. She was sedate and confident in her gait. At a distance, he knelt beside her and pretended to be brushing her coat.

'Now tha sees how it is, Flurry,' he said. 'There's t'four pens at each corner. In each is a sheep. Tha has to go to each one, take t'sheep out, and then put all four into t'middle pen. . . . Now thee watch this one – this is t'Lancashire entry, and she was champion last year. And she's no slouch.'

They watched the black sheep dog from Lancashire, sailing across the field at a gallop, neatly collecting the sheep.

'See how t'shepherd holds his crook like to make a door for t'middle pen, Flurry? Now that's all Ah can do to help. Ah can point or signal, but Ah can nobbut make a sort of angle to help wi' t'sheep at t'middle pen.'

There was a burst of applause, which meant that the Lancashire dog had set the record time for the trial.

'Come on, then, Miss Smartie,' Sam said. 'It'll be us.'

Sam heard his name being announced. He walked with Flurry to the ring. He knelt beside her.

'Now remember – no biting sheep or tha'll lose points.'

She gave him a look that should have withered him.

'Go,' said the judge.

Away Flurry sailed, her belly almost flat to the ground. She went from pen to pen, chivvying the sheep into a compact knot. She brought them to the center pen, driving at them adeptly so that before they could stand, sheep-wise and stubborn, and wonder where they were going, they were safe in the center pen. Then she sat at the gate, her tongue lolling out, and a burst of applause said she had made good time.

Sam hurried over to his mate. He rushed at Capper Wambley, who owned, without doubt, the finest watch in the village.

'How about it, Capper?'

The old man cleared his throat importantly and stared at his watch.

'Well. T'road Ah make it – wi' exact computations – is that there ain't a split-second difference between thee and Lancashire. But mind ye – that's unofficial, o' course.'

So the chums rocked in impatience as the last tests were run off, and then they stood in the common hush as the judge took off his hat and advanced.

'First place,' he announced, 'is a tie between Joe Pettigill's Black Tad and Sam Small's Flurry, as far as time is concerned. But the judges unanimously award first place, on the basis o' calmer conduct in handling t'sheep, to Pettigill's Black Tad fro' Lancashire.'

Of course, Sam and his friends were quite put out about it, and Gaffer Sitherthwick almost had apoplexy as he thought of his lost pound. . . . Thus it might have been a black day in the history of Polkingthorpe Brig had not Pettigill decided to gloat a bit. He walked over past the chums and said triumphantly, 'Why don't ye all coom over to Lancashire and learn reight how to handle a tyke?'

This was, of course, too, too much for any Yorkshireman to bear. So Sam came right back at him. 'Oh, aye?' he said.

It wasn't a very good answer, but it was all he could think of at the moment.

'Oh, aye,' echoed Pettigill. . . .

'Ah admit tha's got a fine bitch there, Pettigill, but ma tyke ain't used to sheep. But if it came, now, to a test o' real intelligence – well, here's five pounds even fro' me and ma mates says we'll win at any contest tha says.'

'Then thy good money goes after thy bad,' the Lancashire lad said.

So it was arranged that an extra test would be held, with each man picking his own test to show the intelligence of his dog. Mr. Watcliffe, a well-to-do sheep dealer who was one of the judges, agreed to make the decision as to which dog was best.

The moor rang with excited chatter as the news spread, and everyone scurried around to lay bets. The Polkingthorpe men all got side bets down – except the Gaffer. He declined, morosely, to bet any more. So the contest got under way. Pettigill and Sam drew straws to see which dog should show off first.

Pettigill got the short straw and had to start. 'Now, lass,' he said to his dog, 'over there Ah've put a stick, a stone, ma cap, and a handkerchief. Will some sporting gentleman call out which one Ah should bid her bring first?'

'T'stick!' a voice called.

'Tad. Fotch me yon stick,' Pettigill ordered.

Away raced the dog and brought it. One by one, as requested, the champion brought back the correct articles, dropping them at its owner's feet. The men burst into applause as it ended. Then up stepped Sam. He knelt beside Flurry and spoke so all could hear.

'Lying i' front o' Joe Pettigill,' he announced, 'is four articles. When Ah say "Go!" ma tyke'll first take t'cap, go to the far sheep pen, and drop it inside there. Next she'll take t'stick, and drop it at the feet o' t'biggest lad on this moor. Third she'll take t'stone and drop it at t'feet o' t'second-best dog trainer on this moor. Finally, she'll take t'handkerchief—' and here Sam beamed floridly – 'and drop it afore t'handsomest and knowingest man around these parts. Now ista ready?'

Sam looked at Flurry, who jumped to her feet and leaned forward as if held by an invisible leash. The crowd almost moaned in a sort of excitement, for they had never heard of a dog that could understand such a complicated set of commands.

'Go!' said Sam.

Away sailed Flurry, veering past Joe Pettigill's feet and snatching up the cap on the dead gallop without stopping. Going in the water-smooth racing stride of a collie, she went out to the far pen, dropped the cap, and streaked back. She snatched the stick and loped toward the crowd. The men parted to let her through. She quested about, until she saw Ian Cawper. She dropped it at his feet and the men moaned astonishment.

Back she went for the stone. She picked it up, and then stood, as if at a loss. The men drew in their breath.

But Flurry merely looked up at Joe Pettigill, walked forward one step and dropped the stone again.

The men roared in approval.

'That means Pettigill's second-best dog trainer,' they said. 'But now for Sam!'

Flurry now had the handkerchief. She was walking to Sam, who stood, waiting triumphantly. Flurry came nearer to his feet, and then began to circle round him.

'She's forgot,' the men breathed. 'She don't know what to do wi' it.'

Sam looked down, with a sort of agony in his eyes, for Flurry was trotting away from him – going away with the handkerchief in a hesitating sort of way. She was looking about her. She was walking to the center.

And then everyone saw what it was.

Flurry was going up to Mr. Watcliffe, the judge. She dropped the handkerchief at his feet, walked back to Sam, and sat properly at heel.

This time there was no cheering, for in that entire crowd it seemed as if a ghost had passed and lightly touched the back of every man's head, touching low down toward the neck where the short hairs grow, a touch that left a tingling sensation.

All one could hear was the voice of Mr. Watcliffe. 'Why, bless my soul,' he was saying. 'Bless my very body and soul. She's almost human. Bless my soul.'

Then he seemed to waken to his responsibility.

'Ah judge that the test has been won by Sam Small's tyke. If he will step forward, Ah'll give him the wager money.'

This broke the spell. Sam went forward to collect, and the Polkingthorpe men went round with a roar to garner in the side bets they had made in the crowd. Everyone was in pocket except Gaffer Sitherthwick, which was also something to make that day a memorable one in Polkingthorpe's history. Seldom, if ever, did the Gaffer come out on the wrong side of money matters.

Together the chums all started home. Joe Pettigill stopped them and spoke like a true sport.

'That's a champion tyke tha has there, lad,' he said.

'Thankee,' said Sam with the customary modesty. 'We nobbut won by luck.'

'But how about ma cap up there?' the Lancashireman asked.

'Nay, Ah nobbut said she'd tak' it,' Sam pointed out. 'It'll cost thee another five pound to have her bring it back.'

Pettigill frowned, then grinned in appreciation.

'Here, Tad,' he said. 'Go up and get ma cap.' And away sailed his own fine dog.

Away, too, went Sam, with all the men slapping him on the back, applauding his wit, skill, acumen, and perspicacity. They streamed over the moor toward Polkingthorpe Brig to tell the story of their mighty triumph.

THE PICK
OF THE PUPPIES

from *Jock of the Bushveldt*

Sir Percy Fitzpatrick
(South African) 1862–1931

THERE were six puppies, and as the waggons were empty we
fixed up a roomy nest in one of them for Jess and her family.
There was no trouble with Jess; nobody interfered with her, and she
interfered with nobody. The boys kept clear of her; but we used to
take a look at her and the puppies as we walked along with the
waggons; so by degrees she got to know that we would not harm
them, and she no longer wanted to eat us alive if we went near and
talked to her.

Five of the puppies were fat strong yellow little chaps with dark
muzzles – just like their father, as Ted said; and their father was an
imported dog, and was always spoken of as the best dog of the breed
that had ever been in the country. I never saw him, so I do not
really know what he was like – perhaps he was not a yellow dog at
all; but, whatever he was, he had at that time a great reputation
because he was 'imported,' and there were not half a dozen
imported dogs in the whole of the Transvaal then. Many people
used to ask what breed the puppies were – I suppose it was because
poor cross faithful old Jess was not much to look at, and because no
one had a very high opinion of yellow dogs in general, and nobody
seemed to remember any famous yellow bull-terriers. They used to
smile in a queer way when they asked the question, as if they were
going to get off a joke; but when we answered, 'Just like their father –
Buchanan's *imported* dog,' the smile disappeared, and they would

241

give a whistle of surprise and say 'By Jove!' and immediately begin to examine the five yellow puppies, remark upon their ears and noses and legs, and praise them up until we were all as proud as if they had belonged to us.

Jess looked after her puppies and knew nothing about the remarks that were made, so they did not worry her, but I often looked at the faithful old thing with her dark brindled face, cross-looking eyes and always-moving ears, and thought it jolly hard lines that nobody had a good word for her; it seemed rough on her that every one should be glad there was only one puppy at all like the mother – the sixth one, a poor miserable little rat of a thing about half the size of the others. He was not yellow like them, nor dark brindled like Jess, but a sort of dirty pale half-and-half colour with some dark faint wavy lines all over him, as if he had tried to be brindled and failed; and he had a dark sharp wizened little muzzle that looked shrivelled up with age.

Most of the fellows said it would be a good thing to drown the odd one because he spoilt the litter and made them look as though they were not really thoroughbred, and because he was such a miserable little rat that he was not worth saving anyhow; but in the end he was allowed to live. I believe no one fancied the job of taking one of Jess's puppies away from her; moreover, as any dog was better than none, I had offered to take him rather than let him be drowned. Ted had old friends to whom he had already promised the pick of the puppies, so when I came along it was too late, and all he could promise me was that if there should be one over I might have it.

As they grew older and were able to crawl about they were taken off the waggons when we outspanned and put on the ground. Jess got to understand this at once, and she used to watch us quite quietly as we took them in our hands to put them down or lift them back again. When they were two or three weeks old a man came to the waggons who talked a great deal about dogs, and appeared to know what had to be done. He said that the puppies' tails ought to be docked, and that a bull-terrier would be no class at all with a long tail, but you should on no account clip his ears. I thought he was speaking of fox-terriers, and that with bull-terriers the position was the other way round, at that time; but as he said it was 'the thing' in England, and nobody contradicted him, I shut up. We found out afterwards that he had made a mistake; but it was too late then, and Jess's puppies started life as bull-terriers up to date, with long ears and short tails.

I felt sure from the beginning that all the yellow puppies would be claimed and that I should have to take the odd one, or none at all; so I began to look upon him as mine already, and to take an interest in him and look after him. A long time ago somebody wrote that 'the sense of possession turns sand into gold,' and it is one of the truest things ever said. Until it seemed that this queer-looking odd puppy was going to be mine I used to think and say very much what the others did – but with this difference, that I always felt sorry for him, and sorry for Jess too, because he was like her and not like the father. I used to think that perhaps if he were given a chance he might grow up like poor old Jess herself, ugly, cross and unpopular, but brave and faithful. I felt sorry for him, too, because he was small and weak, and the other five big puppies used to push him away from his food and trample on him; and when they were old enough to play they used to pull him about by his ears and pack on to him – three or four to one – and bully him horribly. Many a time I rescued him, and many a time gave him a little preserved milk and water with bread soaked in it when the others had shouldered him out and eaten everything.

After a little while, when my chance of getting one of the good puppies seemed hopeless and I got used to the idea that I would have to take the odd one, I began to notice little things about him that no one else noticed, and got to be quite fond of the little beggar – in a kind of way. Perhaps I was turning my sand into gold, and my geese into swans; perhaps I grew fond of him simply because, finding him lonely and with no one else to depend on, I befriended him; and perhaps it was because he was always cheerful and plucky and it seemed as if there might be some good stuff in him after all. Those were the things I used to think of sometimes when feeding the little outcast. The other puppies would tumble him over and take his food from him; they would bump into him when he was stooping over the dish of milk and porridge, and his head was so big and his legs so weak that he would tip up and go heels over head into the dish. We were always picking him out of the food and scraping it off him: half the time he was wet and sticky, and the other half covered with porridge and sand baked hard by the sun.

One day just after the waggons had started, as I took a final look round the outspan place to see if anything had been forgotten, I found the little chap – who was only about four inches high – struggling to walk through the long grass. He was not big enough or strong enough to push his way – even the stems of the down-trodden grass tripped him – and he stumbled and floundered at every step, but he got up again each time with his little tail standing straight up, his head erect, and his ears cocked. He looked such a ridiculous sight that his little tragedy of 'lost in the veld' was forgotten – one could only laugh.

What he thought he was doing, goodness only knows; he looked as proud and important as if he owned the whole world and knew that every one in it was watching him. The poor little chap could not see a yard in that grass; and in any case he was not old enough to see much, or understand anything, for his eyes still had that bluish blind look that all very young puppies have, but he was marching along as full of confidence as a general at the head of his army. How he fell out of the waggon no one knew; perhaps the big puppies tumbled him out, or he may have tried to follow Jess, or have climbed over the tail-board to see what was the other side, for he was always going off exploring by himself. His little world was small, it may be – only the bedplank of the waggon and the few square yards of the ground on which they were dumped at the outspans – but he took it as seriously as any explorer who ever tackled a continent.

The others were a bit more softened towards the odd puppy when I caught up to the waggons and told them of his valiant struggle to follow; and the man who had docked the puppies' tails allowed, 'I believe the rat's got pluck, whatever else is the matter with him, for he was the only one that didn't howl when I snipped them. The little cuss just gave a grunt and turned round as if he wanted to eat me. I think he'd 'a' been terrible angry if he hadn't been so s'prised. Pity he's such an awful-looking mongrel.'

But no one else said a good word for him: he was really beneath notice, and if ever they had to speak about him they called him 'The Rat.' There is no doubt about it he was extremely ugly, and instead of improving as he grew older, he became worse; yet, I could not help liking him and looking after him, sometimes feeling sorry for him, sometimes being tremendously amused, and sometimes – wonderful to relate – really admiring him. He was extraordinarily silent; while the others barked at nothing, howled when lonely, and yelled when frightened or hurt, the odd puppy did none of these things; in fact, he began to show many of Jess's peculiarities; he hardly ever barked, and when he did it was not a wild excited string of barks but little suppressed muffled noises, half bark and half growl, and just one or two at a time; and he did not appear to be afraid of anything, so one could not tell what he would do if he was.

One day we had an amusing instance of his nerve: one of the oxen, sniffing about the outspan, caught sight of him all alone, and filled with curiosity came up to examine him, as a hulking silly old tame ox will do. It moved towards him slowly and heavily with its ears spread wide and its head down, giving great big sniffs at this new object, trying to make out what it was. 'The Rat' stood quite still with his stumpy tail cocked up and his head a little on one side, and when the huge ox's nose was about a foot from him he gave one of those funny abrupt little barks. It was as if the object had suddenly 'gone off' like a cracker, and the ox nearly tumbled over with fright; but even when the great mountain of a thing gave a clumsy plunge round and trotted off, 'The Rat' was not the least frightened; he was startled, and his tail and ears flickered for a second, but stiffened up again instantly, and with another of those little barks he took a couple of steps forward and cocked his head on the other side. That was his way.

He was not a bit like the other puppies; if any one fired off a gun or cracked one of the big whips the whole five would yell at the top of their voices and, wherever they were, would start running, scrambling and floundering as fast as they could towards the waggon without once looking back to see what they were running away from. The odd puppy would drop his bone with a start or would jump round; his ears and tail would flicker up and down for a second; then he would slowly bristle up all over, and with his head cocked first on one side and then on the other, stare hard with his half-blind bluish puppy eyes in the direction of the noise; but he never ran away.

And so, little by little, I got to like him in spite of his awful ugliness. And it really was awful! The other puppies grew big all over, but the odd one at that time seemed to grow only in one part – his tummy! The poor little chap was born small and weak; he had always been bullied and crowded out by the others, and the truth is he was half starved. The natural consequence of this was that as soon as he could walk about and pick up things for himself he made up for lost time, and filled up his middle piece to an alarming size before the other parts of his body had time to grow; at that time he looked more like a big tock-tockie beetle than a dog.

Besides the balloon-like tummy he had stick-out bandy-legs, very like a beetle's too, and a neck so thin that it made the head look enormous, and you wondered how the neck ever held it up. But what made him so supremely ridiculous was that he evidently did not know he was ugly; he walked about as if he was always thinking of his dignity, and he had that puffed-out and stuck-up air of importance that you only see in small people and bantam cocks who are always trying to appear an inch taller than they really are.

When the puppies were about a month old, and could feed on porridge or bread soaked in soup or gravy, they got to be too much for Jess, and she used to leave them for hours at a time and hide in the grass so as to have a little peace and sleep. Puppies are always hungry, so they soon began to hunt about for themselves, and would find scraps of meat and porridge or old bones; and if they could not get anything else, would try to eat the raw-hide nekstrops and reims. Then the fights began. As soon as one puppy saw another busy on anything, he would walk over towards him and, if strong enough, fight him for it. All day long it was nothing but wrangle, snarl, bark and yelp. Sometimes four or five would be at it in one scrum; because as soon as one heard a row going on he would trot up hoping to steal the bone while the others were busy fighting.

It was then that I noticed other things about the odd puppy: no matter how many packed on to him, or how they bit or pulled him, he never once let out a yelp; with four or five on top of him you would see him on his back, snapping right and left with bare white teeth, gripping and worrying them when he got a good hold of anything, and all the time growling and snarling with a fierceness that was really comical. It sounded as a lion fight might sound in a toy phonograph.

Before many days passed, it was clear that some of the other puppies were inclined to leave 'The Rat' alone, and that only two of them – the two biggest – seemed anxious to fight him and could take his bones away. The reason soon became apparent: instead of wasting his breath in making a noise, or wasting strength in trying to tumble the others over, 'The Rat' simply bit hard and hung on; noses, ears, lips, cheeks, feet and even tails – all came handy to him; anything he could get hold of and hang on to was good enough, and the result generally was that in about half a minute the other puppy would leave everything and clear off yelling, and probably holding up one paw or hanging its head on one side to ease a chewed ear.

When either of the big puppies tackled the little fellow the fight lasted much longer. Even if he were tumbled over at once – as generally happened – and the other one stood over him barking and growling, that did not end the fight: as soon as the other chap got off him he would struggle up and begin again; he would not give in. The other puppies seemed to think there was some sort of rule like the 'count out' in boxing, or that once you were tumbled over you ought to give up the bone; but the odd puppy apparently did not care about rules; as far as I could see, he had just one rule: 'Stick to it,' so it was not very long before even the two big fellows gave up interfering with him. The bites from his little white teeth – sharp as needles – which punctured noses and feet and tore ears, were most unpleasant. But apart from that, they found there was nothing to be gained by fighting him: they might roll him over time after time, but he came back again and worried them so persistently that it was quite impossible to enjoy the bone – they had to keep on fighting for it.

At first I drew attention to these things, but there was no encouragement from the others; they merely laughed at the attempt to make the best of a bad job. Sometimes owners of other puppies were nettled by having their beauties compared with 'The Rat,' or were annoyed because he had the cheek to fight for his own and beat them. Once, when I had described how well he had stood up to Billy's pup, Robbie caught up 'The Rat,' and placing him on the table, said: 'Hats off to the Duke of Wellington on the field of Waterloo.' That seemed to me the poorest sort of joke to send five grown men into fits of laughter. He stood there on the table with his head on one side, one ear standing up, and his stumpy tail twiggling – an absurd picture of friendliness, pride and confidence; yet he was so ugly and ridiculous that my heart sank, and I whisked him away. They made fun of him, and he did not mind; but it was making fun of me too, and I could not help knowing why; it was only necessary to put the puppies together to see the reason.

After that I stopped talking about him, and made the most of the good points he showed, and tried to discover more. It was the only consolation for having to take the leavings of the litter.

Then there came a day when something happened which might easily have turned out very differently, and there would have been no stories and no Jock to tell about; and the best dog in the world would never have been my friend and companion. The puppies had been behaving very badly, and had stolen several nekstrops and chewed up parts of one or two big whips; the drivers were grumbling about all the damage done and the extra work it gave them; and Ted, exasperated by the worry of it all, announced that the puppies were quite old enough to be taken away, and that those who had picked puppies must take them at once and look after them, or let some one else have them. When I heard him say that my heart gave a little thump from excitement, for I knew the day had come when the great question would be settled once and for all. Here was a glorious and unexpected chance; perhaps one of the others would

not or could not take his, and I might get one of the good ones. . . .
Of course the two big ones would be snapped up: that was certain;
for, even if the men who had picked them could not take them,
others who had been promised puppies before me would exchange
those they had already chosen for the better ones. Still, there were
other chances; and I thought of very little else all day long,
wondering if any of the good ones would be left; and if so, which?

In the afternoon Ted came up to where we were all lying in the
shade and startled us with the momentous announcement:

'Billy Griffiths can't take his pup!'

Every man of us sat up. Billy's pup was the first pick, the
champion of the litter, the biggest and strongest of the lot. Several
of the others said at once that they would exchange theirs for this
one; but Ted smiled and shook his head.

'No,' he said, 'you had a good pick in the beginning.' Then he
turned to me, and added: 'You've only had leavings.' Some one said
'The Rat,' and there was a shout of laughter, but Ted went on; 'You
can have Billy's pup.'

It seemed too good to be true; not even in my wildest imaginings
had I fancied myself getting the pick of the lot. I hardly waited to
thank Ted before going off to look at my champion. I had seen and
admired him times out of number, but it seemed as if he must look
different now that he belonged to me. He was a fine big fellow, well
built and strong, and looked as if he could beat all the rest put
together. His legs were straight; his neck sturdy; his muzzle dark and
shapely; his ears equal and well carried; and in the sunlight his
yellow coat looked quite bright, with occasional glints of gold in it.
He was indeed a handsome fellow.

As I put him back again with the others the odd puppy, who
had stood up and sniffed at me when I came, licked my hand and
twiddled his tail with the friendliest and most independent air, as if
he knew me quite well and was glad to see me, and I patted the poor
little chap as he waddled up. I had forgotten him in the excitement
of getting Billy's pup; but the sight of him made me think of his
funny ways, his pluck and independence, and of how he had not a
friend in the world except Jess and me; and I felt downright sorry for

him. I picked him up and talked to him; and when his wizened little face was close to mine, he opened his mouth as if laughing, and shooting out his red tongue dabbed me right on the tip of my nose in pure friendliness. The poor little fellow looked more ludicrous than ever: he had been feeding again and was as tight as a drum; his skin was so tight one could not help thinking that if he walked over a mimosa thorn and got a scratch on the tummy he would burst like a toy balloon.

I put him back with the other puppies and returned to the tree where Ted and the rest were sitting. As I came up there was a shout of laughter, and – turning round to see what had provoked it – I found 'The Rat' at my heels. He had followed me and was trotting and stumbling along, tripping every yard or so, but getting up again with head erect, ears cocked and his stumpy tail twiddling away just as pleased and proud as if he thought he had really started in life and was doing what only a 'really and truly' grown-up dog is supposed to do – that is, follow his master wherever he goes.

All the old chaff and jokes were fired off at me again, and I had no peace for quite a time. They all had something to say: 'He won't swap you off!' 'I'll back "The Rat"!' 'He is going to take care of you!' 'He is afraid you'll get lost!' and so on; and they were still chaffing about it when I grabbed 'The Rat' and took him back again.

Billy's failure to take his puppy was so entirely unexpected and so important that the subject kept cropping up all the evening. It was very amusing then to see how each of those who had wanted to get him succeeded in finding good reasons for thinking that his own puppy was really better than Billy's. However they differed in their estimates of each other's dogs, they all agreed that the best judge in the world could not be certain of picking out the best dog in a good litter until the puppies were several months old; and they all gave instances in which the best looking puppy had turned out the worst dog, and others in which the one that no one would look at had grown up to be the champion. Goodness knows how long this would have gone on if Robbie had not mischievously suggested that 'perhaps "The Rat" was going to beat the whole lot.' There was such a chorus of guffaws at this that no one told any more stories.

The poor little friendless Rat! It was unfortunate, but the truth is that he was uglier than before; and yet I could not help liking him. I fell asleep that night thinking of the two puppies – the best and the worst in the litter. No sooner had I gone over all the splendid points in Billy's pup and made up my mind that he was certainly the finest I had ever seen, than the friendly wizened little face, the half-cocked ears and head on one side, the cocky little stump of a tail, and the comical dignified plucky look of the odd puppy would all come back to me. The thought of how he had licked my hand and twiddled his tail at me, and how he dabbed me on the nose, and then the manful way in which he had struggled after me through the grass, all made my heart go soft towards him, and I fell asleep not knowing what to do.

When I woke up in the morning, my first thought was of the odd puppy – how he looked to me as his only friend, and what he would feel like if, after looking on me as really belonging to him and as the one person that he was going to take care of all his life, he knew he was to be left behind or given away to any one who would take him. It would never have entered his head that he required some one to look after him; from the way he had followed me the night before it was clear he was looking after me; and the other fellows thought the same thing. His whole manner had plainly said: 'Never mind old man! Don't you worry: I am here.'

We used to make our first trek at about three o'clock in the morning, so as to be outspanned by sunrise; and walking along during that morning trek I recalled all the stories that the others had told of miserable puppies having grown into wonderful dogs, and of great men who had been very ordinary children; and at breakfast I took the plunge.

'Ted,' I said, bracing myself for the laughter, 'if you don't mind, I'll stick to "The Rat".'

If I had fired off a gun under their noses they would have been much less startled. Robbie made a grab for his plate as it slipped from his knees.

'*Don't* do that sort of thing!' he protested indignantly. 'My nerves won't stand it!'

The others stopped eating and drinking, held their beakers of steaming coffee well out of the way to get a better look at me, and when they saw it was seriously meant there was a chorus of:

'Well, I'm hanged.'

I took him in hand at once – for now he was really mine – and brought him over for his saucer of soaked bread and milk to where we sat at breakfast. Beside me there was a rough camp table – a luxury sometimes indulged in while camping or trekking with empty waggons – on which we put our tinned-milk, treacle and such things to keep them out of reach of the ants, grasshoppers, Hottentot-gods, beetles and dust. I put the puppy and his saucer in a safe place under the table out of the way of stray feet, and sank the saucer into the sand so that when he trod in it he would not spill the food; for puppies are quite stupid as they are greedy, and seem to think that they can eat faster by getting further into the dish. He appeared to be more ravenous than usual, and we were all amused by the way the little fellow craned his thin neck out further and further until he tipped up behind and his nose bumping into the saucer seesawed him back again. He finished it all and looked round briskly at me, licking his lips and twiddling his stumpy tail.

Well, I meant to make a dog of him, so I gave him another lot. He was just like a little child – he thought he was very hungry still and could eat any amount more; but it was not possible. The lapping became slower and more laboured, with pauses every now and then to get breath or lick his lips and look about him, until at last he was fairly beaten: he could only look at it, blink and lick his chops; and, knowing that he would keep on trying, I took the saucer away. He was too full to object or to run after it; he was too full to move. He stood where he was, with his legs well spread and his little body blown out like a balloon, and finished licking the drops and crumbs off his face without moving a foot.

There was something so extraordinarily funny in the appearance and attitude of the puppy that we watched to see what he would do next. He had been standing very close to the leg of the table, but not quite touching it, when he finished feeding; and even after he had done washing his face and cleaning up generally, he stood there stock still for several minutes, as though it was altogether too much trouble to move. One little bandy hind leg stuck out behind the table leg, and the bulge of his little tummy stuck out in front of it; so that when at last he decided to make a move the very first little lurch brought his hip up against the table-leg. In an instant the puppy's appearance changed completely: the hair on his back and shoulders bristled; his head went up erect; one ear stood up straight and the other at half cock; and his stumpy tail quivered with rage. He evidently thought that one of the other puppies had come up behind to interfere with him. He was too proud to turn round and appear to be nervous: with head erect he glared hard straight in front of him, and, with all the little breath that he had left after his big feed, he growled ferociously in comical little gasps. He stood like that, not moving an inch, with the front foot still ready to take that step forward; and then, as nothing more happened, the hair on his back gradually went flat again; the fierceness died out of his face; and the growling stopped.

After a minute's pause, he again very slowly and carefully began to step forward; of course exactly the same thing happened again, except that this time he shook all over with rage, and the growling was fiercer and more choky. One could not imagine anything so small being in so great a rage. He took longer to cool down, too, and much longer before he made the third attempt to start. But the third time it was all over in a second. He seemed to think that this was more than any dog could stand, and that he must put a stop to it. The instant his hip touched the leg, he whipped round with a ferocious snarl – his little white teeth bared and gleaming – and bumped his nose against the table-leg.

I cannot say whether it was because of the shout of laughter from us, or because he really understood what had happened, that he looked so foolish, but he just gave one crestfallen look at me and with a feeble wag of his tail waddled off as fast as he could.

Then Ted nodded over at me, and said: 'I believe you have got the champion after all!'

And I was too proud to speak.

THE
LOVE-MASTER

from *White Fang*

Jack London
(American) 1876–1916

As White Fang watched Weedon Scott approach, he bristled and snarled to advertise that he would not submit to punishment. Twenty-four hours had passed since he had slashed open the hand that was now bandaged and held up by a sling to keep the blood out of it. In the past White Fang had experienced delayed punishments, and he apprehended that such a one was about to befall him. How could it be otherwise? He had committed what was to him sacrilege – sunk his fangs into the holy flesh of a god, and of a white-skinned superior god at that. In the nature of things, and of intercourse with gods, something terrible awaited him.

The god sat down several feet away. White Fang could see nothing dangerous in that. When the gods administered punishment they stood on their legs. Besides, this god had no club, no whip, no firearm. And furthermore, he himself was free. No chain nor stick bound him. He could escape into safety while the god was scrambling to his feet. In the meantime he would wait and see.

The god remained quiet, made no movement; and White Fang's snarl slowly dwindled to a growl that ebbed down in his throat and ceased. Then the god spoke, and at the first sound of his voice the hair rose on White Fang's neck and the growl rushed up in his throat. But the god made no hostile movement, and went on calmly talking. For a time White Fang growled in unison with him, a correspondence of rhythm being established between growl and voice. But the god talked on interminably. He talked to White Fang as White Fang had never been talked to before. He talked softly and soothingly, with a gentleness that somehow, somewhere, touched White Fang. In spite of himself and all the pricking warnings of his instinct, White Fang began to have confidence in this god. He had a feeling of security that was belied by all his experience with men.

After a long time the god got up and went into the cabin. White Fang scanned him apprehensively when he came out. He had neither whip nor club nor weapon. Nor was his uninjured hand behind his back hiding something. He sat down as before, in the same spot, several feet away. He held out a small piece of meat. White Fang pricked his ears and investigated it suspiciously, managing to look at the same time both at the meat and the god, alert for any overt act, his body tense and ready to spring away at the first sign of hostility.

Still the punishment delayed. The god merely held near to his nose a piece of meat. And about the meat there seemed nothing wrong. Still White Fang suspected; and though the meat was proffered to him with short inviting thrusts of the hand, he refused to touch it. The gods were all-wise, and there was no telling what masterful treachery lurked behind that apparently harmless piece of meat. In past experience, especially in dealing with squaws, meat and punishment had often been disastrously related.

In the end, the god tossed the meat on the snow at White Fang's feet. He smelled the meat carefully, but he did not look at it. While he smelled it he kept his eyes on the god. Nothing happened. He took the meat into his mouth and swallowed it. Still nothing happened. The god was actually offering him another piece of meat. Again he refused to take it from the hand, and again it was tossed to him. This was repeated a number of times. But there came a time when the god refused to toss it. He kept it in his hand and steadfastly proffered it.

The meat was good meat, and White Fang was hungry. Bit by bit, infinitely cautious, he approached the hand. At last the time came that he decided to eat the meat from the hand. He never took his eyes from the god, thrusting his head forward with ears flattened back and hair involuntarily rising and cresting on his neck. Also a low growl rumbled in his throat as warning that he was not to be trifled with. He ate the meat, and nothing happened. Piece by piece he ate all the meat, and nothing happened. Still the punishment delayed.

He licked his chops and waited. The god went on talking. In his voice was kindness – something of which White Fang had no experience whatever. And within him it aroused feelings which he had likewise never experienced before. He was aware of a certain strange satisfaction, as though some need were being gratified, as though some void in his being were being filled. Then again came the prod of his instinct and the warning of past experience. The gods were ever crafty, and they had unguessed ways of attaining their ends.

Ah, he had thought so! There it came now, the god's hand, cunning to hurt, thrusting out at him, descending upon his head. But the god went on talking. His voice was soft and soothing. In spite of the menacing hand the voice inspired confidence. And in spite of the assuring voice the hand inspired distrust. White Fang was torn by conflicting feelings, impulses. It seemed he would fly to pieces, so terrible was the control he was exerting, holding together by an unwonted indecision the counter-forces that struggled within him for mastery.

He compromised. He snarled and bristled and flattened his ears. But he neither snapped nor sprang away. The hand descended. Nearer and nearer it came. It touched the ends of his upstanding hair. He shrank down under it. It followed down after him, pressing more closely against him. Shrinking, almost shivering, he still managed to hold himself together. It was a torment, this hand that touched him and violated his instinct. He could not forget in a day all the evil that had been wrought him at the hands of men. But it was the will of the god, and he strove to submit.

The hand lifted and descended again in a patting, caressing movement. This continued, but every time the hand lifted the hair

*'Turi was sitting in a meadow, surveying the landscape.
He was four months old and a Finnish Spitz, pricked of ear,
curled of tail and the colour of a fox.'*
Turi – Son of Repo

'There was a sharp bend about half way down and here Jock
invariably sailed over the wall . . . zooming over the grey stones . . .'
JOCK: TOP DOG

'It takes courage for a tall thin man to lead a tiny Scotch terrier pup
on a smart red leash in our neighborhood . . .'
THE THIN RED LEASH

'But he permitted her carefully to wash his face and ears, tug at burrs
that matted his heavy coat, and to sleep between his forefeet.'
THE SOUL OF CALIBAN

lifted under it. And every time the hand descended the ears flattened down and a cavernous growl surged in his throat. White Fang growled and growled with insistent warning. By this means he announced that he was prepared to retaliate for any hurt he might receive. There was no telling when the god's ulterior motive might be disclosed. At any moment that soft, confidence-inspiring voice might break forth in a roar of wrath, that gentle and caressing hand transform itself into a vice-like grip to hold him helpless and administer punishment.

But the god talked on softly, and ever the hand rose and fell with non-hostile pats. White Fang experienced dual feelings. It was distasteful to his instinct. It restrained him, opposed the will of him toward personal liberty. And yet it was not physically painful. On the contrary, it was even pleasant, in a physical way. The patting movement slowly and carefully changed to a rubbing of the ears about their bases, and the physical pleasure even increased a little. Yet he continued to fear, and he stood on guard, expectant of unguessed evil, alternately suffering and enjoying as one feeling or the other came uppermost and swayed him.

'Well, I'll be gosh-swoggled!'

So spoke Matt, coming out of the cabin, his sleeves rolled up, a pan of dirty dish-water in his hands, arrested in the act of emptying the pan by the sight of Weedon Scott patting White Fang.

At the instant his voice broke the silence White Fang leaped back, snarling savagely at him.

Matt regarded his employer with grieved disapproval.

'If you don't mind my expressin' my feelin's, Mr Scott, I'll make free to say you're seventeen kinds of a damn fool, an' all of 'em different, an' then some.'

Weedon Scott smiled with a superior air, gained his feet, and walked over to White Fang. He talked soothingly to him, but not for long, then slowly put out his hand, rested it on White Fang's head, and resumed the interrupted patting. White Fang endured it, keeping his eyes fixed suspiciously, not upon the man that petted him, but upon the man that stood in the doorway.

'You may be a number one tip-top minin' expert, all right, all right,' the dog-musher delivered himself oracularly, 'but you missed the chance of your life when you was a boy an' didn't run off an' join a circus.'

White Fang snarled at the sound of his voice, but this time did not leap away from under the hand that was caressing his head and the back of his neck with long, soothing strokes.

It was the beginning of the end for White Fang – the ending of the old life and the reign of hate. A new and incomprehensively fairer life was dawning. It required much thinking and endless patience on the part of Weedon Scott to accomplish this. And on the part of White Fang it required nothing less than a revolution. He had to ignore the urges and promptings of instinct and reason, defy experience, give the lie to life itself.

Life, as he had known it, not only had had no place in it for much that he now did, but all the currents had gone counter to those to which he now abandoned himself. In short, when all things were considered, he had to achieve an orientation far vaster than the one he had achieved at the time he came voluntarily in from the Wild and accepted Grey Beaver as his lord. At that time he was a mere puppy, soft from the making, without form, ready for the thumb of circumstance to begin its work upon him. But now it was different. The thumb of circumstance had done its work only too well. By it he had been formed and hardened into the Fighting Wolf, fierce and implacable, unloving and unlovable. To accomplish the change was like a reflux of being, and this when the plasticity of youth was no longer his; when the fibre of him had become tough and knotty; when the warp and the woof of him had made of him an adamantine texture, harsh and unyielding; when the face of his spirit had become iron and all his instincts and axioms had crystallized into set rules, cautions, dislikes, and desires.

Yet again, in this new orientation, it was the thumb of circumstance that pressed and prodded him, softening that which had become hard and remoulding it into fairer form. Weedon Scott was in truth this thumb. He had gone to the roots of White Fang's nature, and with kindness touched to life potencies that had languished and well-nigh perished. One such potency was *love*. It took the place of *like*, which latter had been the highest feeling that thrilled him in his intercourse with the gods.

But this love did not come in a day. It began with *like*, and out of it slowly developed. White Fang did not run away, though he was allowed to remain loose, because he liked this new god. This was certainly better than the life he had lived in the cage of Beauty Smith, and it was necessary that he should have some god. The lordship of man was a need of his nature. The seal of his dependence on man had been set upon him in that early day when he turned his back on the Wild and crawled to Grey Beaver's feet to receive the expected beating. This seal had been stamped upon him again, and ineradicably, on his second return from the Wild, when the long famine was over and there was fish once more in the village of Grey Beaver.

And so, because he needed a god and because he preferred Weedon Scott to Beauty Smith, White Fang remained. In acknowledgment of fealty, he proceeded to take upon himself the guardianship of his master's property. He prowled about the cabin while the sled-dogs slept, and the first night-visitor to the cabin fought him off with a club until Weedon Scott came to the rescue. But White Fang soon learned to differentiate between thieves and honest men, to appraise the true value of step and carriage. The man who travelled, loud-stepping, the direct line to the cabin door, he let alone, though he watched him vigilantly until the door opened and he received the endorsement of the master. But the man who went softly, by circuitous ways, peering with caution, seeking after secrecy – that was the man who received no suspension of judgment from White Fang, and who went away abruptly, hurriedly, and without dignity.

Weedon Scott had set himself the task of redeeming White Fang – or rather, of redeeming mankind from the wrong it had done White Fang. It was a matter of principle and conscience. He felt that the ill done White Fang was a debt incurred by man, and that it must be paid. So he went out of his way to be especially kind to the Fighting Wolf. Each day he made it a point to caress and pet White Fang, and to do it at length.

At first suspicious and hostile, White Fang grew to like this petting. But there was one thing that he never outgrew – his growling. Growl he would, from the moment the petting began till it ended. But it was a growl with a new note in it. A stranger could not hear this note, and to such a stranger the growling of White Fang was an exhibition of primordial savagery, nerve-racking and blood-curdling. But White Fang's throat had become harsh-fibred from the making of ferocious sounds through the many years since his first little rasp of anger in the lair of his cubhood, and he could not soften the sounds of that throat now to express the gentleness he felt. Nevertheless, Weedon Scott's ear and sympathy were fine enough to catch the new note all but drowned in the fierceness – the note that was the faintest hint of a croon of content and that none but he could hear.

As the days went by, the evolution of *like* into *love* was accelerated. White Fang himself began to grow aware of it, though in his consciousness he knew not what love was. It manifested itself to him as a void in his being – a hungry, aching, yearning void that clamoured to be filled. It was a pain and an unrest, and it received easement only by the touch of the new god's presence. At such times love was a joy to him – a wild, keen-thrilling satisfaction. But when away from his god the pain and the unrest returned; the void in him sprang up and pressed against him with its emptiness, and the hunger gnawed and gnawed unceasingly.

White Fang was in the process of finding himself. In spite of the maturity of his years and of the savage rigidity of the mould that had formed him, his nature was undergoing an expansion. There was a burgeoning within him of strange feelings and unwonted impulses. His old code of conduct was changing. In the past he had liked comfort and surcease from pain, disliked discomfort and pain, and he had adjusted his actions accordingly. But now it was different.

Because of this new feeling within him he ofttimes elected discomfort and pain for the sake of his god. Thus, in the early morning, instead of roaming and foraging or lying in a sheltered nook, he would wait for hours on the cheerless cabin-stoop for a sight of the god's face. At night, when the god returned home, White Fang would leave the warm sleeping-place he had burrowed in the snow in order to receive the friendly snap of fingers and the word of greeting. Meat, even meat itself, he would forgo to be with his god, to receive a caress from him, or to accompany him down into the town.

Like had been replaced by *love*. And love was the plummet dropped down into the deeps of him where like had never gone. And responsive out of his deeps had come the new thing – love. That which was given unto him did he return. This was a god indeed, a love-god, a warm and radiant god, in whose light White Fang's nature expanded as a flower expands under the sun.

But White Fang was not demonstrative. He was too old, too firmly moulded, to become adept at expressing himself in new ways. He was too self-possessed, too strongly poised in his own isolation. Too long had he cultivated reticence, aloofness, and moroseness. He had never barked in his life, and he could not now learn to bark a welcome when his god approached. He was never in the way, never extravagant nor foolish in the expression of his love. He never ran to meet his god. He waited at a distance; but he always waited, was always there. His love partook of the nature of worship – dumb, inarticulate, a silent adoration. Only by the steady regard of his eyes did he express his love, and by the unceasing following with his eyes of his god's every movement. Also, at times, when his god looked at him and spoke to him, he betrayed an awkward self-consciousness, caused by the struggle of his love to express itself and his physical inability to express it.

He learned to adjust himself in many ways to his new mode of life. It was borne in upon him that he must let his master's dogs alone. Yet his dominant nature asserted itself, and he had first to thrash them into an acknowledgment of his superiority and leadership. This accomplished, he had little trouble with them. They gave trail to him when he came and went or walked among them, and when he asserted his will they obeyed.

In the same way, he came to tolerate Matt – as a possession of his master. His master rarely fed him. Matt did that – it was his business; yet White Fang divined that it was his master's food he ate, and that it was his master who thus fed him vicariously. Matt it was who tried to put him into the harness and make him haul sled with the other dogs. But Matt failed. It was not until Weedon Scott put the harness on White Fang and worked him that he understood. He took it as his master's will that Matt should drive him and work him, just as he drove and worked his master's other dogs.

Different from the Mackenzie toboggans were the Klondike sleds with runners under them. And different was the method of driving the dogs. There was no fan formation of the team. The dogs worked in single file, one behind another, hauling on double traces. And here, in the Klondike, the leader was indeed the leader. The wisest as well as strongest dog was the leader, and the team obeyed him and feared him. That White Fang should quickly gain this post was inevitable. He could not be satisfied with less, as Matt learned after much inconvenience and trouble. White Fang picked out the post for himself, and Matt backed his judgment with strong language after the experiment had been tried. But though he worked in the sled in the day, White Fang did not forego the guarding of his master's property in the night. Thus he was on duty all the time, ever vigilant and faithful, the most valuable of all the dogs.

'Makin' free to spit out what's in me,' Matt said one day, 'I beg to state that you was a wise guy all right when you paid the price you did for that dog. You clean swindled Beauty Smith on top of pushin' his face in with your fist.'

A recrudescence of anger glinted in Weedon Scott's grey eyes, and he muttered savagely: 'The beast!'

In the late spring a great trouble came to White Fang. Without warning, the love-master disappeared. There had been warning, but White Fang was unversed in such things, and did not understand the packing of a grip. He remembered afterwards that this packing had preceded the master's disappearance; but at the time he suspected nothing. That night he waited for the master to return. At midnight the chill wind that blew drove him to shelter at the rear of the cabin. There he drowsed, only half asleep, his ears keyed for the first sound of the familiar step. But, at two in the morning, his anxiety drove him out to the cold front stoop, where he crouched and waited.

But no master came. In the morning the door opened and Matt stepped outside. White Fang gazed at him wistfully. There was no common speech by which he might learn what he wanted to know. The days came and went, but never the master. White Fang, who had never known sickness in his life, became sick. He became very sick – so sick that Matt was finally compelled to bring him inside the cabin. Also, in writing to his employer, Matt devoted a post-script to White Fang.

Weedon Scott, reading the letter down in Circle City, came upon the following:

'That damn wolf won't work. Won't eat. Ain't got no spunk left. All the dogs is licking him. Wants to know what has become of you, and I don't know how to tell him. Mebbe he is going to die.'

It was as Matt had said. White Fang had ceased eating, lost heart, and allowed every dog of the team to thrash him. In the cabin he lay on the floor near the stove, without interest in food, in Matt, nor in life. Matt might talk gently to him or swear at him, it was all the same; he never did more than turn his dull eyes upon the man, then drop his head back to its customary position on his fore-paws.

And then, one night, Matt, reading to himself with moving lips and mumbled sounds, was startled by a low whine from White Fang. He had got upon his feet, his ears cocked toward the door, and he was listening intently. A moment later Matt heard a footstep. The door opened, and Weedon Scott stepped in. The two men shook hands. Then Scott looked around the room.

'Where's the wolf?' he asked.

Then he discovered him, standing where he had been lying, near to the stove. He had not rushed forward after the manner of other dogs. He stood, watching and waiting.

'Holy smoke!' Matt exclaimed. 'Look at 'm wag his tail!'

Weedon Scott strode half across the room toward him, at the same time calling him. White Fang came to him, not with a great bound, yet quickly. He was awkward from self-consciousness, but as he drew near his eyes took on a strange expression. Something, an incommunicable vastness of feeling, rose up into his eyes as a light and shone forth.

'He never looked at me that way all the time you was gone,' Matt commented.

Weedon Scott did not hear. He was squatting down on his heels, face to face with White Fang, and petting him – rubbing at the roots of the ears, making long caressing strokes down the neck to the shoulders, tapping the spine gently with the balls of his fingers. And White Fang was growling responsively, the crooning note of the growl more pronounced than ever.

But that was not all. What of his joy, the great love in him, ever surging and struggling to express itself, succeeding in finding a new mode of expression? He suddenly thrust his head forward and nudged his way in between the master's arm and body. And here, confined, hidden from view all except his ears, no longer growling, he continued to nudge and snuggle.

The two men looked at each other. Scott's eyes were shining.

'Gosh!' said Matt in an awe-stricken voice.

A moment later, when he had recovered himself, he said: 'I always insisted that wolf was a dog. Look at 'm!'

With the return of the love-master, White Fang's recovery was, rapid. Two nights and a day he spent in the cabin. Then he sallied forth. The sled-dogs had forgotten his prowess. They remembered only the latest, which was his weakness and sickness. At the sight of him as he came out of the cabin, they sprang upon him.

'Talk about your rough-houses,' Matt murmured gleefully, standing in the doorway and looking on. 'Give 'm hell, you wolf! Give 'm hell! – an' then some!'

White Fang did not need the encouragement. The return of the love-master was enough. Life was flowing through him again, splendid and indomitable. He fought from sheer joy, finding in it an expression of much that he felt and that otherwise was without speech. There could be but one ending. The team dispersed in ignominious defeat, and it was not until after dark that the dogs came sneaking back, one by one, by meekness and humility signifying their fealty to White Fang.

Having learned to snuggle, White Fang was guilty of it often. It was the final word. He could not go beyond it. The one thing of which he had always been particularly jealous was his head. He had always disliked to have it touched. It was the Wild in him, the fear of hurt and of the trap, that had given rise to the panicky impulses to avoid contacts. It was the mandate of his instinct that that head must be free. And now, with the love-master, his snuggling was the deliberate act of putting himself into a position of hopeless helplessness. It was an expression of perfect confidence, of absolute self-surrender, as though he said, 'I put myself into thy hands. Work thou thy will with me.'

One night, not long after the return, Scott and Matt sat at a game of cribbage preliminary to going to bed. 'Fifteen-two, fifteen-four an' a pair makes six,' Matt was pegging up, when there was an outcry and sound of snarling without. They looked at each other as they started to rise to their feet.

'The wolf's nailed somebody,' Matt said.

A wild scream of fear and anguish hastened them.

'Bring a light!' Scott shouted, as he sprang outside.

Matt followed with the lamp, and by its light they saw a man lying on his back in the snow. His arms were folded, one above the other, across his face and throat. Thus he was trying to shield himself from White Fang's teeth. And there was need for it. White Fang was in a rage, wickedly making his attack on the most vulnerable spot. From shoulder to wrist of the crossed arms, the coat sleeve, blue flannel shirt, and undershirt were ripped in rags, while the arms themselves were terribly slashed and streaming blood.

All this the two men saw in the first instant. The next instant Weedon Scott had White Fang by the throat and was dragging him clear. White Fang struggled and snarled, but made no attempt to bite, while he quickly quieted down at a sharp word from the master.

Matt helped the man to his feet. As he arose he lowered his crossed arms, exposing the bestial face of Beauty Smith. The dog-musher let go of him precipitately, with action similar to that of a man who has picked up live fire. Beauty Smith blinked in the lamp-light and looked about him. He caught sight of White Fang, and terror rushed into his face.

At the same moment Matt noticed two objects lying in the snow. He held the lamp close to them, indicating them with his toe for his employer's benefit – a steel dog-chain and a stout club.

Weedon Scott saw and nodded. Not a word was spoken. The dog-musher laid his hand on Beauty Smith's shoulder, and faced him to the right about. No word needed to be spoken. Beauty Smith started.

In the meantime the love-master was patting White Fang and talking to him.

'Tried to steal you, eh? And you wouldn't have it! Well, well, he made a mistake, didn't he?'

'Must 'a' thought he had hold of seventeen devils,' the dog-musher sniggered.

White Fang, still wrought up and bristling, growled and growled, the hair slowly lying down, the crooning note remote and dim, but growing in his throat.

MOSES

Walter D. Edmonds
(American) 1903–98

I T was a long climb. The scent was cold, too; so faint that when he found it behind the barn he could hardly trust himself. He had just come back from Filmer's with a piece of meat, and he had sat down behind the barn and cracked it down; and a minute later he found that scent reaching off, faint as it was, right from the end of his nose as he lay.

He had had the devil of a time working it out at first, but up here it was simple enough except for the faintness of it. There didn't appear to be any way to stray off this path; there wasn't any brush, there wasn't any water. Only he had to make sure of it, when even for him it nearly faded out, with so many other stronger tracks overlaying it. His tail drooped, and he stumbled a couple of times, driving his nose into the dust. He looked gaunt when he reached the spot where the man had lain down to sleep.

The scent lay heavier there. He shuffled round over it, sifting the dust with an audible clapping of his nostrils to work out the pattern the man had made. It was hard to do, for the dust didn't take scent decently. It wasn't like any dust he had ever come across, either, being glittery, like mica, and slivery in his nose. But he could tell after a minute how the man had lain, on his back, with his hands under his head, and probably his hat over his eyes to shield them from the glare, which was pretty dazzling bright up this high, with no trees handy.

His tail began to cut air. He felt better, and all of a sudden he lifted up his freckled nose and let out a couple of short yowps and then a good chest-swelled belling. Then he struck out up the steep going once more. His front legs may have elbowed a little, but his hind legs were full of spring, and his tail kept swinging.

That was how the old man by the town entrance saw him, way down below.

The old man had his chair in the shadow of the wall with a black-and-yellow parasol tied to the back of it as an extra insurance against the sun. He was reading the 'Arrivals' in the newspaper, the only column that ever interested him; but he looked up sharply when he heard the two yowps and the deep chest notes that, from where he sat, had a mysterious floating quality. It was a little disturbing; but when he saw a dog was the cause he reached out with his foot and shoved the gate hard, so that it swung shut and latched with a sound like a gong. Only one dog had ever come here, and that sound had been enough to discourage him; he had hung round for a while, though, just on the edge, and made the old man nervous. He said to himself that he wasn't going to watch this one, anyway, and folded the paper in halves the way the subway commuter had showed him and went on with the 'Arrivals.'

After a while, though, he heard the dog's panting coming close and the muffled padding of his feet on the marble gate stone. He shook the paper a little, licked his thumb, and turned over half a sheet and read on through the 'Arrivals' into the report of the Committee on Admissions. But then, because he was a curious old man, and kindhearted, noticing that the panting had stopped– and because he had never been quite up to keeping his resolves, except once – he looked out of the gate again.

The dog was sitting on the edge of the gate stone, upright, with his front feet close under him. He was a rusty-muzzled, blue-tick foxhound, with brown ears, and eyes outlined in black like an Egyptian's. He had his nose inside the bars and was working it at the old man.

'Go away,' said the old man. 'Go home.'

At the sound of his voice the hound wrinkled his nose soberly and his tail whipped a couple of times on the gate stone, raising a little star dust.

'Go home,' repeated the old man, remembering the dog that had hung around before.

He rattled the paper at him, but it didn't do any good. The dog just looked solemnly pleased at the attention, and a little hopeful, and allowed himself to pant a bit.

This one's going to be worse than the other, the old man thought, groaning to himself as he got up. He didn't know much about dogs anyway. Back in Galilee there hadn't been dogs that looked like this one – just pariahs and shepherds and the occasional Persian greyhound of a rich man's son.

He slapped his paper along the bars; it made the dog suck in his tongue and move back obligingly. Peter unhooked his shepherd's staff from the middle crossbar, to use in case the dog tried to slip in past him, and let himself out. He could tell by the feeling of his bare ankles that there was a wind making up in the outer heavens and he wanted to get rid of the poor creature before it began really blowing round the walls. The dog backed off from him and sat down almost on the edge, still friendly, but wary of the shepherd's staff.

Why can't the poor dumb animal read? thought Peter, turning to look at the sign he had hung on the gatepost.

The sign read:

TAKE NOTICE
NO
DOGS
SORCERERS
WHOREMONGERS
MURDERERS
IDOLATERS
LIARS
WILL BE
ADMITTED

When he put it up, he had thought it might save him a lot of trouble; but it certainly wasn't going to help in the case of this dog.

He expected he would have to ask the Committee on Admissions to take the matter up; and he started to feel annoyed with them for not having got this animal on the list themselves. It was going to mean a lot of correspondence and probably the Committee would send a memorandum to the Central Office suggesting his retirement again, and Peter liked his place at the gate. It was quiet there, and it was pleasant for an old man to look through the bars and down the path, to reassure the frightened people, and, when there was nothing else to do, to hear the winds of outer heaven blowing by.

'Go away. Go home. Depart,' he said, waving his staff; but the dog only backed down on to the path and lay on his wishbone with his nose between his paws.

Peter went inside and sat down and tried to figure the business out. There were two things he could do. He could notify the Committee of the dog's arrival, or he could give the information to the editor. The Committee would sit up and take notice for once if they found the editor had got ahead of them. It would please the editor, for there were few scoops in Heaven. And then, as luck would have it, the editor himself came down to the gate.

The editor wasn't Horace Greeley or anybody like that, with a reputation in the newspaper world. He had been editor of a little country weekly that nobody in New York, or London, or Paris had ever heard of. But he was good and bursting with ideas all the time. He was now.

'Say, Saint Peter,' he said, 'I've just had a swell idea about the "Arrivals" column. Instead of printing all the "Arrivals" on one side and then the "Expected Guests" on the other, why not just have one column and put the names of the successful candidates in uppercase type? See?' He shoved a wet impression under Peter's nose and rubbed the back of his head nervously with his ink-stained hand. 'Simple, neat, dignified.'

Peter looked at the galley and saw how simple it would be for him, too. He wouldn't have to read the names in lowercase at all. It would make him feel a lot better not to know. Just check the uppercase names as they came to the gate.

He looked up at the flushed face of the editor and his white beard parted over his smile. He liked young, enthusiastic men, remembering how hard, once, they had been to find.

'It looks fine to me, Don,' he said. 'But the Committee won't like losing all that space in the paper, will they?'

'Probably not,' the editor said ruefully. 'But I thought you could pull a few wires with the Central Office for me.'

Peter sighed.

'I'll try,' he said. 'But people don't pay attention to an old man, much, Don. Especially one who's been in service.'

The editor flushed and muttered something about bums.

Peter said gently, 'It doesn't bother me, Don. I'm not ashamed of the service I was in.' He looked down to his sandals. He wondered whether there was any of the dust of that Roman road left on them after so long a time. Every man has his one great moment. He'd had two. He was glad he hadn't let the second one go. 'I'll see what I can do, Don.'

It was a still corner, by the gate; and, with both of them silently staring off up the avenue under the green trees to where the butterflies were fluttering in the shrubbery of the public gardens, the dog decided to take a chance and sneak up again.

He moved one foot at a time, the way he had learned to do behind the counter in the Hawkinsville store, when he went prospecting toward the candy counter. These men didn't hear him any more than the checker players in the store did, and he had time to sniff over the gatepost thoroughly. It puzzled him; and as the men didn't take any notice, he gumshoed over to the other post and went over that, too.

It was queer. He couldn't smell dog on either of them and they were the best-looking posts he had ever come across. It worried him some. His tail drooped and he came back to the gate stone and the very faint scent on it, leading beyond the gate, that he had been following so long. He sat down again and put his nose through the bars, and after a minute he whined.

It was a small sound, but Peter heard it.

'That dog,' he said.

The editor whirled round, saying, 'What dog?' and saw him.

'I was going to let you know about him, only I forgot,' said Peter.

'He came up a while ago, and I can't get rid of him. I don't know how he got here. The Committee didn't give me any warning and there's nothing about him in the paper.'

'He wasn't on the bulletin,' said the editor. 'Must have been a slip-up somewhere.'

'I don't think so,' said Peter. 'Dogs don't often come here. Only one other since I've been here, as a matter of fact. What kind of a dog is he anyway? I never saw anything like him.' He sounded troubled and put out, and the editor grinned, knowing he didn't mean it.

'I never was much of a dog man,' he said. 'But that's a likely-looking foxhound. He must have followed somebody's scent up here. Hi, boy!' he said. 'What's your name? Bob? Spot? Duke?'

The hound lowered his head a little, wrinkled his nose, and wagged his tail across the stone.

'Say,' said the editor. 'Why don't I put an ad in the "Lost and Found?" I've never had anything to put there before. But you better bring him in and keep him here till the owner claims him.'

'I can't do that,' said Peter. 'It's against the Law.'

'No dogs. Say, I always thought it was funny there were no dogs here. What happens to them?'

'They get removed,' said Peter. 'They just go.'

'That don't seem right,' the young editor said. He ruffled his back hair with his hand. 'Say, Saint,' he asked, 'who made this law anyway?'

'It's in Revelation. John wasn't a dog man, as you call it. Back in Galilee we didn't think much of dogs, you see. They were mostly pariahs.'

'I see,' said the editor. His blue eyes sparkled. 'But say! Why can't I put it in the news? And write an editorial? By golly, I haven't had anything to raise a cause on since I got here.'

Peter shook his head dubiously.

'It's risky,' he said.

'It's a free country,' exclaimed the editor. 'At least nobody's told me different. Now probably there's nothing would mean so much to the owner of that dog as finding him up here. You get a genuine dog man and this business of passing the love of women is just hooey to him.'

'Hooey?' Peter asked quietly.

'It just means he likes dogs better than anything. And this is a good dog, I tell you. He's cold-tracked this fellow, whoever he is, Lord knows how. Besides, he's only one dog, and look at the way the rabbits have been getting into the manna in the public garden. I'm not a dog man, as I said before, but believe me, Saint, it's a pretty thing on a frosty morning to hear a good hound hightailing a fox across the hills.'

'We don't have frost here, Don.'

'Well,' said the editor, 'frost or no frost, I'm going to do it. I'll have to work quick to get it in before the forms close. See you later.'

'Wait,' said Peter. 'What's the weather report say?'

The editor gave a short laugh.

'What do you think? Fair, moderate winds, little change in temperature. Those twerps up in the bureau don't even bother to read the barometer anymore. They just play pinochle all day, and the boy runs that report off on the mimeograph machine.'

'I think there's a wind making up in the outer heavens,' Peter said. 'When we get a real one, it just about blows the gate stone away. That poor animal wouldn't last a minute.'

The editor whistled. 'We'll have to work fast.' Then suddenly his eyes blazed. 'All my life I wanted to get out an extra. I never had a chance, running a weekly. Now, by holy, I will.'

He went off up the Avenue on the dead run. Even Peter, watching him go, felt excited.

'Nice dog,' he said to the hound; and the hound, at the deep gentle voice, gulped in his tongue and twitched his haunches. The whipping of his tail on the gate stone made a companionable sound for the old man. His beard folded on his chest and he nodded a little.

He was dozing quietly when the hound barked.

It was a deep, vibrant note that anyone who knew dogs would have expected the minute he saw the spring of those ribs; it was mellow, like honey in the throat. Peter woke up tingling with the sound of it and turned to see the hound swaying the whole hind half of himself with his tail.

Then a high loud voice shouted, 'Mose, by Jeepers! What the hell you doing here, you poor dumb fool?'

Peter turned to see a stocky, short-legged man who stuck out more than was ordinary, both in front and behind. He had on a gray flannel shirt, and blue denim pants, and a pair of lumberman's rubber packs on his feet, with the tops laced only to the ankle. There was a hole in the front of his felt hat where the block had worn through. He wasn't, on the whole, what you might expect to see walking on that Avenue. But Peter had seen queer people come to Heaven and he said mildly, 'Do you know this dog?'

'Sure,' said the stout man. 'I hunted with him round Hawkinsville for the last seven years. It's old Mose. Real smart dog. He'd hunt for anybody.'

'Mose?' said Peter. 'For Moses, I suppose.'

'Maybe. He could track anything through hell and high water.'

'Moses went through some pretty high water,' said Peter. 'What's your name?'

'Freem Brock. What's yours?'

Peter did not trouble to answer, for he was looking at the hound; and he was thinking he had seen some people come to Heaven's gate and look pleased, and some come and look shy, and some frightened, and some a little shamefaced, and some satisfied, and some sad (maybe with memories they couldn't leave on earth), and some jubilant, and a whole quartet still singing 'Adeline' just the way they were when the hotel fell on their necks in the earthquake. But in all his career at the gate he had never seen anyone express such pure, unstifled joy as this rawboned hound.

'Was he your dog?' he asked Freeman Brock.

'Naw,' said Freem. 'He belonged to Pat Haskell.' He leaned his shoulder against the gatepost and crossed one foot over the other. 'Stop that yawping,' he said to Mose, and Mose lay down, wagging. 'Maybe you ain't never been in Hawkinsville,' he said to Peter. 'It's a real pretty village right over the Black River. Pat kept store there and he let anybody take Mose that wanted to. Pretty often I did. He liked coming with me because I let him run foxes. I'm kind of a fox hunter,' he said, blowing out his breath. 'Oh, I like rabbit hunting all right, but there's no money in it. . . . Say,' he broke off, 'you didn't tell me what your name was.'

'Peter,' said the old man.

'Well, Pete, two years ago was Mose's best season. Seventy-seven fox was shot ahead of him. I shot thirty-seven of them myself. Five crosses and two blacks in the lot. Yes, sir. I heard those black foxes had got away from the fur farm and I took Mose right over there. I made three hundred and fifty dollars out of them hides.'

'He was a good dog, then?' asked Peter.

'Best foxhound in seven counties,' said Freem Brock. He kicked the gate with his heel in front of Mose's nose and Mose let his ears droop. 'He was a fool to hunt. I don't see no fox signs up here. Plenty rabbits in the Park. But there ain't nobody with a gun. I wish I'd brought my old Ithaca along.'

'You can't kill things here,' said Peter.

'That's funny. Why not?'

'They're already dead.'

'Well, I know that. But it beats me how I got here. I never did nothing to get sent to this sort of place. Hell, I killed them farm foxes and I poached up the railroad in the preserve. But I never done anything bad.'

'No,' said St. Peter. 'We know that.'

'I got drunk, maybe. But there's other people done the same before me.'

'Yes, Freem.'

'Well, what the devil did I get sent here for, Pete?'

'Do you remember when the little girl was sick and the town doctor wouldn't come out at night on a town case, and you went over to town and made him come?'

'Said I'd knock his teeth out,' said Freem, brightening.

'Yes. He came. And the girl was taken care of,' said Peter.

'Aw,' Freem said, 'I didn't know what I was doing. I was just mad. Well, maybe I'd had a drink, but it was a cold night, see? I didn't knock his teeth out. He left them in the glass.' He looked at the old man. 'Jeepers,' he said. 'And they sent me here for that?'

Peter looked puzzled.

'Wasn't it a good reason?' he asked. 'It's not such a bad place.'

'Not so bad as I thought it was going to be. But people don't want to talk to me. I tried to talk to an old timber-beast named Boone down the road. But he asked me if I ever shot an Indian, and when I said no he went along. You're the only feller I've seen that was willing to talk to me,' he said, turning to the old man. 'I don't seem to miss likker up here, but there's nowhere I can get to buy some tobacco.'

Peter said, 'You don't have to buy things in Heaven.'

'Heaven?' said Freeman Brock. 'Say, is that what this is?' He looked frightened all at once. 'That's what the matter is. I don't belong here. I ain't the kind to come here. There must have been a mistake somewhere.' He took hold of Peter's arm. 'Listen,' he said urgently. 'Do you know how to work that gate?'

'I do,' said Peter. 'But I can't let you out.'

'I got to get out.'

Peter's voice grew gentler.

'You'll like it here after a while, Freem.'

'You'll let me out.'

'You couldn't go anywhere outside,' Peter said.

Freem looked through the bars at the outer heavens and watched a couple of stars like water lilies floating by below. He said slowly, 'We'd go someplace.'

Peter said, 'You mean you'd go out there with that dog?'

Freem flushed.

'I and Mose have had some good times,' he said.

At the sound of his name, Mose's nose lifted.

Peter looked down at the ground. With the end of his shepherd's staff he thoughtfully made a cross and then another overlapping it and put an X in the upper left-hand corner. Freem looked down to see what he was doing.

'You couldn't let Mose in, could you, Pete?'

Peter sighed and rubbed out the pattern with his sandal.

'I'm sorry,' he said. 'The Committee don't allow dogs.'

'What'll happen to the poor brute, Pete?'

Peter shook his head.

'If you ask me,' Freem said loudly, 'I think this is a hell of a place.'

'What's that you said?'

Peter glanced up.

'Hello, Don,' he said. 'Meet Freem Brock. This is the editor of the paper,' he said to Freem. 'His name's Don.'

'Hello,' said Freem.

'What was that you said about Heaven being a hell of a place?' asked the editor.

Freem drew a long breath. He took a look at old Mose lying outside the gate with his big nose resting squashed up and sideways against the bottom crossbar; he looked at the outer heavens, and he looked at the editor.

'Listen,' he said. 'That hound followed me up here. Pete says he can't let him in. He says I can't go out to where Mose is. I only been in jail twice,' he said, 'but I liked it better than this.'

The editor said, 'You'd go out there?'

'Give me the chance.'

'What a story!' said the editor. 'I've got my extra on the Avenue now. The cherubs will be coming this way soon. It's all about the hound, but this stuff is the genuine goods. Guest prefers to leave Heaven. Affection for old hunting dog prime factor in his decision. It's human interest. I tell you it'll shake the Committee. By holy, I'll have an editorial in my next edition calling for a celestial referendum.'

'Wait,' said Peter. 'What's the weather report?'

'What do you think? Fair, moderate winds, little change in temperature. But the Central Office is making up a hurricane for the South Pacific and it's due to go by pretty soon. We got to hurry, Saint.'

He pounded away up the Avenue, leaving a little trail of stardust in his wake.

Freem Brock turned on Saint Peter.

'He called you something,' he said.

Peter nodded.

'Saint.'

'I remember about you now. Say, you're a big shot here. Why can't you let Mose in?'

Peter shook his head.

'I'm no big shot, Freem. If I was, maybe —'

His voice was drowned out by a shrieking up the Avenue.

'Extry! Extry! Special Edition. Read all about it. Dog outside Heaven's Gate. Dog outside . . .'

A couple of cherubs were coming down the thoroughfare, using their wings to make time. When he saw them, Freem Brock started. His shoulders began to itch self-consciously and he put a hand inside his shirt.

'My gracious,' he said.

Peter, watching him, nodded.

'Everybody gets them. You'll get used to them after a while. They're handy, too, on a hot day.'

'For the love of Pete,' said Freem.

'Read all about it! Dog outside Heaven's Gate. Lost Dog waiting outside . . .'

'He ain't lost!' cried Freem. 'He never got lost in his life.'

'"Committee at fault,"' read Peter. 'Thomas Aquinas isn't going to like that,' he said.

'It don't prove nothing,' said Freem.

'Mister, please,' said a feminine voice. 'The editor sent me down. Would you answer some questions?'

'Naw,' said Freem, turning to look at a young woman with red hair and a gold pencil in her hand. 'Well, what do you want to know, lady?'

The young woman had melting brown eyes. She looked at the hound. 'Isn't he cute?' she asked. 'What's his name?'

'Mose,' said Freem. 'He's a cute hound all right.'

'Best in seven counties,' said Peter.

'May I quote you on that, Saint?'

'Yes,' said Peter. 'You can say I think the dog ought to be let in.' His face was pink over his white beard. 'You can say a hurricane is going to pass, and that before I see that animal blown off by it I'll go out there myself – I and my friend Freem. Some say I'm a has-been, but I've got some standing with the public yet.'

The girl with red hair was writing furiously with a little gold glitter of her pencil. 'Oh,' she said.

'Say I'm going out too,' said Freem. 'I and Pete.'

'Oh,' she said. 'What's your name?'

'Freeman Brock, Route Five, Boonville, New York, U.S.A.'

'Thanks,' she said breathlessly.

'How much longer before we got that hurricane coming?' asked Freem.

'I don't know,' said the old man anxiously. 'I hope Don can work fast.'

'Extry! Owner found. Saint Peter goes outside with hound, Moses. Committee bluff called. Read all about it.'

'How does Don manage it so fast?' said Peter. 'It's like a miracle.'

'It's science,' said Freem. 'Hey!' he yelled at a cherub.

They took the wet sheet, unheeding of the gold ink that stuck to their fingers.

'They've got your picture here, Pete.'

'Have they?' Peter asked. He sounded pleased. 'Let's see.'

It showed Peter standing at the gate.

'It ain't bad,' said Freem. He was impressed. 'You really mean it?' he asked. Peter nodded.

'By cripus,' Freem said slowly, 'you're a pal.'

Saint Peter was silent for a moment. In all the time he had minded Heaven's Gate, no man had ever called him a pal before.

Outside the gate, old Mose got up on his haunches. He was a weather-wise dog, and now he turned his nose outward. The first puff of wind came like a slap in the face, pulling his ears back, and then it passed. He glanced over his shoulder and saw Freem and the old man staring at each other. Neither of them had noticed him at all. He pressed himself against the bars and lifted his nose and howled.

At his howl both men turned.

There was a clear gray point way off along the reach of the wall, and the whine in the sky took up where Mose's howl had ended.

Peter drew in his breath.

'Come on, Freem,' he said, and opened the gate.

Freeman Brock hesitated. He was scared now. He could see that a real wind was coming, and the landing outside looked almighty small to him. But he was still mad, and he couldn't let an old man like Peter call his bluff.

'All right,' he said. 'Here goes.'

He stepped out, and Mose jumped up on him, and licked his face.

'Get down, darn you,' he said. 'I never could break him of that trick,' he explained shamefacedly to Peter. Peter smiled, closing the gate behind him with a firm hand. Its gonglike note echoed through Heaven just as the third edition burst upon the Avenue.

Freeman Brock was frightened. He glanced back through the bars, and Heaven looked good to him. Up the Avenue a crowd was gathering. A couple of lanky, brown-faced men were in front. They started toward the gate.

Then the wind took hold of him and he grasped the bars and looked outward. He could see the hurricane coming like an express train running through infinity. It had a noise like an express train. He understood suddenly just how the victim of a crossing accident must feel.

He glanced at Peter.

The old saint was standing composedly, leaning on his staff with one hand, while with the other he drew Mose close between his legs. His white robe fluttered tight against his shanks and his beard bent sidewise like the hound's ears. He had faced lack of faith, in others; what was worse, he had faced it in himself; and a hurricane, after all, was not so much. He turned to smile at Freem. 'Don't be afraid,' he said.

'Okay,' said Freem, but he couldn't let go the gate.

Old Mose, shivering almost hard enough to rattle, reached up and licked Peter's hand.

One of the brown-faced men said, 'That's a likely-looking hound. He the one I read about in the paper?'

'Yep,' said Freem. He had to holler now.

Daniel Boone said, 'Let us timber-beasts come out with you, Saint, will you?'

Peter smiled. He opened the gate with a wave of his hand, and ten or a dozen timber-beasts – Carson, Bridger, Nat Foster – all crowded through, and started shaking hands with him and Freeman Brock. With them was a thin, mild-eyed man.

'My name's Francis,' he said to Freem when his turn came. 'From Assisi.'

'He's all right,' Daniel Boone explained. 'He wasn't much of a shot, but he knows critters. We better get holt of each other, boys.'

It seemed queer to Freem. Here he was going to get blown to eternity and he didn't even know where it was, but all of a sudden he felt better than he ever had in his life. Then he felt a squirming round his legs and there was Mose, sitting on his feet, the way he would on his snowshoes in cold weather when they stopped for a sandwich on earth. He reached down and took hold of Mose's ears.

Let her blow to blazes, he thought.

She blew.

The hurricane was on them. The nose of it went by, sweeping the wall silver. There was no more time for talk. No voices could live outside Heaven's Gate. If a man had said a word, the next man to hear it would have been some poor heathen aborigine on an island in the Pacific Ocean, and he wouldn't have known what it meant.

The men on the gate stone were crammed against the bars. The wind dragged them bodily to the left, and for a minute it looked as if Jim Bridger were going, but they caught him back. There were a lot of the stoutest hands that ever swung an ax in that bunch holding onto Heaven's Gate, and they weren't letting go for any hurricane – not yet.

But Freem Brock could see it couldn't last that way. He didn't care, though. He was in good company, and that was what counted the most. He wasn't a praying man, but he felt his heart swell with gratitude, and he took hold hard of the collar of Mose and felt the license riveted on. A queer thing to think of, a New York State dog license up there. He managed to look down at it, and he saw that it had turned to gold, with the collar gold under it. The wind tore at him as he saw it. The heart of the hurricane was on him now like a million devils' fingers.

Well, Mose, he thought.

And then in the blur of his thoughts a dazzling bright light came down and he felt the gate at his back opening and he and Peter and Francis and Daniel and the boys were all drawn back into the peace of Heaven, and a quiet voice belonging to a quiet man said, 'Let the dog come in.'

'Jesus,' said Freem Brock, fighting for breath, and the quiet man smiled, shook hands with him, and then went over and placed his arm around Peter's shoulders.

They were sitting together, Freem and Peter, by the gate, reading the paper in the morning warmth, and Peter was having an easy time with the editor's new type arrangement. 'Gridley,' he was reading the uppercase names, 'Griscome, Godolphin, Habblestick, Hafey, Hanlon, Hartwell, Haskell . . .'

'Haskell,' said Freem. 'Not Pat?'

'Yes,' said Peter. 'Late of Hawkinsville.'

'Not in big type?'

'Yes.'

'Well, I'll be . . . Well, that twerp. Think of that. Old Pat.'

Peter smiled.

'By holy,' said Freem. 'Ain't he going to be amazed when he finds Mose up here?'

'How's Mose doing?'

'He's all right now,' said Freem. 'He's been chasing the rabbits. I guess he's up there now. The dew's good.'

'He didn't look so well, I thought,' Peter said.

'Well, that was at first,' said Freem. 'You see, the rabbits just kept going up in the trees and he couldn't get a real run on any of them. There, he's got one started now.'

Peter glanced up from the paper.

Old Mose was doing a slow bark, kind of low, working out the scent from the start. He picked up pace for a while, and then he seemed to strike a regular knot. His barks were deep and patient.

And then, all of a sudden, his voice broke out – that deep, ringing, honey-throated baying that Freem used to listen to in the late afternoon on the sand hills over the Black River. It went away through the public gardens and out beyond the city, the notes running together and fading and swelling and fading out.

'He's pushing him pretty fast,' said Freem. 'He's going to get pretty good on these rabbits.'

The baying swelled again; it came back, ringing like bells. People in the gardens stopped to look up and smile. The sound of it gave Peter a warm tingling feeling.

Freem yawned.

'Might as well wait here till Pat Haskell comes in,' he said.

It was pleasant by the gate, under the black-and-yellow parasol. It made a shade like a flower on the hot stardust. They didn't have to talk, beyond just, now and then, dropping a word between them as they sat.

After a while they heard a dog panting and saw old Mose tracking down the street. He came over to their corner and lay down at their feet, lolling a long tongue. He looked good, a little fat, but lazy and contented. After a minute, though, he got up to shift himself around, and paused as he sat down, and raised a hind leg, and scratched himself behind his wings.

ACKNOWLEDGMENTS

All possible care has been taken to make full acknowledgment in every case where material is still in copyright. If errors have occurred, they will be corrected in subsequent editions if notification is sent to the publisher. Grateful acknowledgment is made for permission to reprint the following:

'April Day' by Mazo de la Roche was first published in *The Sacred Bullock and Other Stories*, Toronto, Macmillan, 1939. © 1939, Mazo de la Roche. We wish to thank the Estate of Mazo de la Roche for its kind permission to reproduce 'April Day' in this collection.

'Dog at Timothy's' from *On Forsyte Change* by John Galsworthy. Reprinted by permission of The Society of Authors as the Literary Representative of the Estate of John Galsworthy.

'Flurry at the Sheep Dog Trial' from *Sam Small Flies Again* and an extract from *Lassie Come-Home* by Eric Knight. Reprinted by permission of Betty Knight Myers, Winifred Knight Mewborn and Jennie Knight Moore.

Excerpt from *Flush: A Biography* by Virginia Woolf, copyright 1933 by Harcourt Brace & Company and renewed 1961 by Leonard Woolf, reprinted by permission of the publisher and The Society of Authors as the Literary Representative of the Estate of Virginia Woolf.

'Garm: A Hostage' from *Actions and Reactions* by Rudyard Kipling. Reprinted by permission of A.P. Watt Ltd. on behalf of The National Trust.

'Moses' by Walter D. Edmonds. Reprinted by permission of Harold Ober Associates Incorporated. Copyright 1938, 1965 by Walter D. Edmonds.

'Jock: Top Dog' and 'Hermann – A Happy Ending'. Copyright © 1995 by The James Herriot Partnership. From *James Herriot's Favorite Dog Stories* by James Herriot. Reprinted by permission of St. Martin's Press, Incorporated (US) and Michael Joseph Ltd. (UK).

Acknowledgments

'Lost Dog' by Penelope Lively, from *A House Inside Out* by Penelope Lively. Copyright © 1987 by Penelope Lively, text. Used by permission of Dutton, a division of Penguin Putnam Inc. and Penguin Books Ltd. (UK).

'Rex' by D.H. Lawrence, from *Phoenix II: Uncollected Papers of D.H. Lawrence* by D.H. Lawrence, edited by Roberts and Moore. Copyright © 1959, 1963, 1968 by the Estate of Frieda Lawrence Ravagli. Used by permission of Viking Penguin, a division of Penguin Books USA Inc. (US) and Laurence Pollinger Limited and the Estate of Frieda Lawrence Ravagli (UK).

'Snapshot of a Dog' by James Thurber. Copyright © 1935 by James Thurber. Copyright © renewed 1963 by Helen Thurber and Rosemary A. Thurber. 'The Thin Red Leash' by James Thurber. Copyright © 1955 by James Thurber. Copyright © renewed 1983 by Helen Thurber and Rosemary A. Thurber. Reprinted by arrangement with Rosemary A. Thurber and the Barbara Hogenson Agency.

'Suki, The Reject' by Diana Pullein-Thompson. Copyright © Diana Pullein-Thompson, 1998.

THE END